The
CORNER BOOTH CHRONICLES

BALLANTINE BOOKS ■ NEW YORK

The
CORNER BOOTH CHRONICLES

A Novel

Mimi Thebo

A Ballantine Books Trade Paperback Original

Copyright © 2009 by Mimi Thebo
Reading group guide copyright © 2009 by Random House, Inc.

Published in the United States by Ballantine Books,
an imprint of The Random House Publishing Group,
a division of Random House, Inc., New York.

BALLANTINE and colophon are registered
trademarks of Random House, Inc.
RANDOM HOUSE READER'S CIRCLE & Design is a
registered trademark of Random House, Inc.

ISBN 978-0-345-49220-3

Printed in the United States of America

www.randomhousereaderscircle.com

1 2 3 4 5 6 7 8 9

Book design by Dana Leigh Blanchette

For Andy and Olivia

The
CORNER BOOTH CHRONICLES

In the middle of oil, wheat, and cattle, the small town of Eudora twinkles in the night. Once, there had been a constellation of such towns sprinkled between the great city in the east and the county seat in the west. But one by one, the other stars had flickered and died. Now, great swathes of corporate-farmed land are as dark and devoid of life as the vastness of space.

Let's pretend we are God, or the farming insurance satellite crew, and keep watching from above.

As dawn appears in a line across the unbroken horizon, the prairie (or what is left of it) begins to come to life. Hawks and buzzards circle below, looking for any nocturnal rodents so tardy in returning to their nest as to make a suitable avian breakfast. Deer emerge from tree cover near creek beds and around the lake to browse. The farmers are already up; cows wait by the milking area, thermoses are tucked into warming tractors.

Two joggers, out near the state park, suddenly diverge, the smaller, lighter jogger pulling briskly away from the larger, darker one, who stops for a moment and watches the lighter one run away. The lighter one seems to have something wrong with its eyes. The arms keep dropping out of their rhythmic drumming of air to wipe them.

Too late, the larger, darker jogger gives chase, but by now, the smaller, lighter one has a considerable lead. It puts on yet another sprint going under the bridge and past the sign, and still shows no symptoms of flagging as it hurtles past the high school.

At the only corner in town with a traffic light, the lighter jogger, revealed by the increasing daylight to be female, tears off to the left.

Behind her, with some urgency, the light blinks amber, urging everyone in this marginal community to proceed with caution. But, since it had been doing so all of her life, Janey Lane did not heed the warning.

Others, however, did. When Mark Ramirez walked stiffly past the bakery, his face set in forbidding lines of anger, nobody said anything for a while. All three of the people present at that early hour *noticed,* of course. They noticed that his girlfriend, Janey, was not with him; they noticed that he was not running with his usual loose and easy stride; they noticed that his open, friendly face was closed for business. But they thought before they said anything.

Margery Lupin had just finished the morning baking and was sliding in a tray of maple-iced long johns. She straightened her back while she watched Mark walk by.

She was getting too old for this, she decided, for the five-hundred-and-twenty-first time that week. And indeed, she had retired over two years previously, sold the bakery and taken off. But then the new owner had been hurt and the family had asked her to come back and help out. And here she was, two years later, still lifting trays and cleaning out the Hobart bowls.

Margery sighed. "He looks how I feel," she said.

Ben Nichols, sheriff's deputy, shook his head. "It's terrible," he said, "what women do to men. That boy was happy as anything last night at the bowling awards."

Odie Marsh, Ben's senior in law enforcement, sniffed. "It's probably his fault. Janey's a peach."

Ben was just about to argue that Mark might be equally blameless when the UPS man arrived.

It was a small package requiring Margery's signature. Ben, who had just started to put on a few spare pounds around his middle, noticed with disgust that the very fit young man doing the delivery did not even glance at the assorted donuts, buñeolos, empanadas, and croissants before trotting back out to his shiny brown van.

The package was home-wrapped, with brown paper and string. Margery, who knew Eudora well, took the precaution of removing herself to the far end of the bakery before opening it.

At last, Odie could bear it no longer. "What is it?" he called.

Margery came slowly around the counter, reading the back of a book. "It's Margaret's latest novel," she said. Her oldest daughter was an author. Eudora generally felt that this was not Margery's fault. The other kids had turned out just fine.

"Let's have a look," Odie said. He took the book from her hand and squinted at the title. "What does it say?" he asked, holding it at arm's length and squinting at it again.

"*The Vortex,*" Margery said, and then, "Odie, when are you going to get your eyes checked?"

There was diabetes in Odie's family and lately things had gone a little fuzzy, both close up and in the near distance. Odie was afraid to discover he had also succumbed to the disease and so refused to visit the ophthalmologist.

He said, "There is nothing wrong with my eyes," in a raised and slightly hysterical voice, and Ben snatched the book from his hand.

Ben, who knew all about Odie's fear of diabetes, but who also lived with his own abject fear of Odie's impaired driving (for, as the senior partner, Odie was reluctant to let Ben behind the wheel), said, "Well then, why did you back the car into a tree day before yesterday? And nearly got us killed when you hung that U-ey on Highway Ten in the fog and didn't see the silver Bronco?"

At this point, coffee, book, and Margery herself all forgotten, the two officers went out to the car to continue their dispute in private, or what they thought of as private, shouting in a car during the business opening hour on Eudora's main street. Of course, the first order of the day for most business owners in town, after turning on the lights and setting staff to work, was finding a reason to go next door and discover if the tantalizing fragments they had overheard (something about a tree? something about a book?) could be explained by other listeners further down the street.

Margery kept reading *The Vortex* by Margaret Lupin. It was set in 1969. Charles Warrington, a young undercover narcotics detective calling himself Trick, was working in a small university town in the Midwest, and had infiltrated a group of hippies. The leader of the hippie household, Tiger, and his girlfriend, Jules, had just given the detective a great deal of LSD to make him talk.

It was interesting. Margery remembered the era well, and the details were just right. Strange, because Margaret had been little at the time, though a noticing child. Trick was a big, rawboned blond with slightly watery blue eyes. He seemed a bit familiar.

So did that Jules girl.

Janey Lane was walking to work when Ben and Odie came barreling past, shouting at each other in the squad car. Something about a book and Margery Lupin. It didn't seem enough to get two grown men so exercised, but Janey had recently learned that serious arguments could begin over the most trivial of things.

She shook her head and continued on her way to the Wellness Center, where she was the administrative linchpin.

You would never know, looking at Janey Lane, the passions that stirred beneath her crisp checked blouse. Any other woman who had run five miles and hurriedly showered and changed and who, during that five-mile run, had sustained a major difference of opinion with her boyfriend, would look hot, bothered, and somewhat disheveled.

But Janey was (outwardly, anyway) cool and collected. Her honey brown hair, which she scorned to highlight, swung demurely from its ponytail. Her crisp shirt was tucked into a formfitting navy skirt. Beneath it, bare, tanned legs ended in serviceable sandals with a modest heel, which clicked as she walked. Over her arm was a canvas bag with her needs for the day. Tortoiseshell sunglasses protected her eyes.

Hector Rodriguez, the handsome young mayor of Eudora, caught up with her on the corner. "What's that all about?" he asked, nodding toward the disappearing squad car.

Janey pulled off her sunglasses to converse, revealing large brown eyes. "Something about a book and Margery Lupin," she said. "They seemed pretty upset." She smiled. "I've got to run," she said, before crossing the street.

Hector watched her as she walked. Those eyes, he thought. Ay, Mama! Janey has really grown into them. He remembered, just two years ago, when she'd seemed a scrawny little bug-eyed thing. But now . . . he couldn't help but observe the movement of Janey's bottom under the close-fitting skirt as she continued walking briskly toward work. . . . She wasn't no size zero anymore.

Mark Ramirez is a lucky boy, he thought to himself. But of course, he was himself an extremely fortunate man in the girlfriend department. And Kelly would probably not appreciate him standing to watch Janey Lane's bottom.

So, like any true Eudoran, Hector went to find out what else he could learn about Odie and Ben's argument from Pattie Walker.

In the end, four or five local businesspeople with no pressing morning engagements walked down to the bakery together.

Sure enough, they found Margery Lupin sitting down at a dirty table and reading in public. Now if you are from another kind of place, with another kind of work ethic, this may not mean anything to you. But Margery Lupin, who had intoned the mantra, "Time to lean, time to clean," to hundreds of young bakery assistants, had never been known to visibly rest during working hours in all her forty-four years of retail baking.

Something, the assembled thought, was seriously wrong.

They watched her for a few moments outside the window without discussion. Then, with a kind of communal feel for what was appropriate in this kind of situation, they sent in the most gentle and ladylike of their party to help with a completely unforeseen crisis of mental illness in the former rock of sanity known as Margery Lupin. They sent in Pattie Walker.

It shows the eminence in the community to which Pattie Walker had risen that she would be automatically selected in such a situation. No one even had to say anything. They just kind of nudged her forward with their eyes and she opened the door.

Margery showed Pattie Walker the book and said something to Pattie, who spoke herself, waving in the direction of the various local business owners still congregating on the sidewalk. Then Margery started to laugh, laugh really hard, and Pattie laughed too, bending over and wrapping her arms around herself, the way she did when she was truly tickled. Finally the remainder of the business owners, some two or three (the rest having at this point felt foolish and hurried away), came inside the bakery.

"It's Margaret's latest," Margery explained, showing them the cover. She opened it and said, "Look."

On the dedication page it read, "To my mother, Margery Lupin, who has always been my inspiration."

There was a collective sigh of satisfaction. Eudorans feel they are, as a people, a little bit superior to anyone anywhere else and this dedication validated that elemental fact in a gratifyingly public way.

Then they looked at the cover again. *The Vortex.* Kind of a fancy name. It showed a typical Midwestern town—Victorian houses with gingerbread trim and white picket fences; a few ranch-style homes on the edges, with nicely landscaped front yards. A tornado loomed in the distance, and closer up, you could see that in every one of those yards was an unusual looking plant, kind of like sweet corn, but with five pointed palmate leaves. Suddenly they all knew what it was, and just as suddenly, they all decided not to be the one to say the word *marijuana*.

The investigatory party broke up and reported back along their various routes to their businesses. By ten A.M. the whole of the town was in possession of the facts.

" . . . and every single house had pot growing in the garden." Pattie Walker was still breathless from running to her appointment.

"You'd better sit down, Pattie," Janey Lane said. "Or else when you climb those stairs your blood pressure is going to read crazy."

The waiting room was almost empty. A child with a persistent cough and his mother stacked blocks in the corner, and two elderly medication reviews examined a *National Geographic* in seats strategically located near the donut box, but business was a little slow that morning. Janey went to the water cooler and poured Pattie a cup. "Here," she said.

Pattie thanked her and then, as Janey sat down and opened the sleek laptop on which she managed the affairs of the practice, said, "I saw Mark this morning. He seemed kind of upset."

Janey didn't look up from the screen, but her big brown eyes grew noticeably moister. "Well," she said. "We're all upset." Her tone did not encourage further discussion.

"He's a good boy," Pattie said.

"Yes, he is," Janey agreed. "But I'd like him to be a good man."

She snapped the laptop shut with a definitive click. "Lottie can see you now," she said, and stood up to take the cup.

Pattie reported both this conversation and the news about the book to Lottie Emery, the herbal practitioner and midwife. Lottie said little.

All Pattie got was, "Your blood pressure still seems a little volatile. You're going to have to take it easy when the hot weather hits." Then Lottie washed her hands at the stylish glass sink.

A moment passed, an uncomfortable, silent moment. Then Lottie dried her hands and asked, "Is Phil going with you to the scan?"

"He'd better," Pattie said. "I told him about fifty times. If it's another boy, I swear I'm going to scream." The three Walker boys had raised the bar in the town for sheer naughtiness, against some formidable opposition. Pattie was not alone in hoping this one was a girl.

"You probably won't be able to tell this early. How did Phil take the news?"

Pattie had hopped down to put her clothes to rights. "I'm not sure, really," she said. "He's gotten kind of quiet."

Lottie looked thoughtful as she moisturized.

"Don't you think anything about this book?" Pattie asked.

Lottie produced one of her infuriatingly calm smiles. "It sounds interesting, like all of Margaret's books. Did you read *New Amsterdam*?"

"You know very well I didn't," Pattie had said. "I've never read any of her writing. But I'll tell you what: I'm going to read this one."

And so, the whole thing began.

Pattie was not alone.

The UPS truck had previously disgorged items from Amazon .com to various households in Eudora. In fact, when Dr. Jim Emery was new in town and before his curious and alarming courtship of Lottie Emery, then Lottie Dougal, the UPS truck had been an almost daily visitor to what was then the luxurious apartment on Main Street and which now formed the alternative medicine section of the doctor's practice. But now the UPS truck made an extended stay in the locale.

With admirable precision and enviable briskness and attention to efficiency, the UPS man, in his crisp brown uniform, knocked at a good 60 percent of the doors in Eudora the following week. By the end of the orgy of book-buying, Eudorans felt bad that they didn't know the young man's name, and the youngest of Janey's sisters had developed a crush.

Janey Lane and Mark Ramirez had been going steady for two years. They had not been high school sweethearts. Indeed, it would have been impossible for them to meet in high school, although they had both attended Eudora High at the same time. During their high school years, Mark had been invisible.

The entire Latino community had been invisible. That they were there, and that they had, say, jobs and houses, was undeniable. But the Anglo community had managed to ignore them anyway. It really wasn't until Maria and Bill Lopez opened Mayan Memories restaurant and the quarry went through all its problems that the paler populace had begun to notice they were not alone.

Shortly after Mark had popped into visibility, he had done some noticing, too. Indeed, it was during a town meeting about the quarry crisis that he and Janey Lane had clicked.

Clicked was the perfect word for it, Mark mused. This morning he was supposed to be selecting and ordering Christmas stock for Dougal Stationery Supplies and had indeed set aside the morning to do so. But as he sat at his tiny desk in the storeroom, listening to the distant tinkle of the doorbell and the murmur of Martina Bumgartner's retail proficiency, his mind wandered back to the early days of his courtship.

Two years ago, he had been carrying a wounded heart.

Until he was eighteen, in common with almost all the young

men of his acquaintance, Mark had been running after Kylie Requena. The fact that she was barely sixteen had seemed immaterial. Kylie obviously was perfectly capable of handling the amorous advances of older boys. After expending an enormous amount of energy and currency, Mark had gotten absolutely nowhere with her and then had been unceremoniously rejected.

With Janey, the whole experience had been so different, so painless. He had noticed her and she had noticed him. He had kissed her and she had kissed him. He had promised to be true to her and she had promised to be true to him. He took care of her and she took care of him. For two years now, it had been bliss.

Where it had gone wrong still eluded him. They were happy. They were working toward getting engaged and, someday, married. Of course, he would like them to be financially secure before beginning such a large undertaking, but they were saving and that would come. He could not, personally, envisage a time when he wanted to be a father, but he also could not imagine dying without children surrounding the bed. There was time. They were young.

Of course, he had noticed that Janey had been a little tense recently. But, what with the expanding doctor's practice, and her own family concerns, she had worries of her own, he was sure. She had embraced joining the National Guard with him last year, to save a bit more money for their future, but he knew it had been a bit of a challenge for her, carrying that big pack and doing all that running. Still, she had coped with it well and seemed to enjoy the early mornings they spent together, pounding out toward the state park on the Millennium Walkway. They had wonderful talks together, before the world woke up, just the two of them.

In fact, just that morning, during their run, they had been chatting about when they would get engaged. They very amicably agreed to wait until Mark could save up and buy the ring in cash, rather than go into debt for it. One of the major points on which they clicked was fiscal responsibility and it was almost a pleasure to be prudent and careful together. Mark had seldom felt so content with the world, as he had at that moment, listening to the birds call and running down the road with the woman he knew was his helpmeet for life.

And yet, only a mile down the road, when discussing something as safe and as ordinary as which new car Mark should buy, Janey suddenly flashed into anger, shouting that he didn't love her and that she didn't want to wait forever to have a home of her own.

It was, Mark felt, inexplicable. He had no idea how he had lost the security and love in which he had been reveling. It was as if he'd stepped into an alternative reality.

And right after that she had burst into a sprint, completely at the wrong time according to their training regime, and left him in the dust.

Mark sighed and looked back at the stack of Christmas catalogues. He tried to concentrate on the pop-up snowman offerings of two rival providers. It was your closures, with pop-ups, where the quality mattered. You had to have pop-ups that securely fastened or you had unhappy customers.

Stationery was understandable.

Women were baffling.

Artie Walker, the town's librarian, had already read *The Vortex* cover to cover, but he wouldn't tell anybody how it ended. He was besieged in his booth at Gross Home Cooking, where he breakfasted on Wednesday mornings. This week, as during most weeks, his older brother, Phil, had managed to arrange his schedule in order to do a little brotherly bonding over two short stacks of pancakes.

Now, one reason Artie wouldn't reveal any more about *The Vortex* was Phil's unusual interest in the novel. Phil was dyslexic before folks knew what that was, and even though he could read just fine now, he'd never willingly cracked the spine of a book. Newspapers, yes. Magazines, sure. But never a book. Artie thought that if he and Pattie Walker could just keep up their campaign of drip-feeding him information about this book, they might drive him to pick it up himself.

The proprietor, Zadie Gross, fought her way through with the decaf pot. "Let the poor boy alone," she growled.

"How far you got, Zadie?" Phil asked her.

Zadie confessed she'd only finished the first chapter. "Same as me," Park Davis, the pharmacist, said mournfully.

"Same as Pattie," Phil echoed, equally mournfully.

"I'm not even done with the first chapter." Oscar Burgos was coming off a double shift at the quarry, where he was the security manager. "I think we got coyotes. Something keeps coming under the fence and it's big enough to set off all the alarms. I read that bit about his fiancée four times. I had to keep jumping into the golf cart." He dipped a fried potato in the yolk of his egg.

"I feel for that Yolanda," Becky Lane interjected from the grill. "She seems like a nice girl and it's a shame the way Warrington treats her, sleeping with that hippie girl Jules behind her back. He has no intention of going through with that wedding. He should just let her go."

There was general agreement on this point. "That's gotta be Lawrence, don't you think?" Park Davis asked. "You went to college in Lawrence, didn't you, Artie? Do you reckon that's Lawrence?"

Artie considered whether or not to answer, deliberately adjusting the angle of the handle of his coffee cup. Then he looked up and grinned. "Yes," he said. "I can definitely tell you that's Lawrence."

Phil looked at Park with respect. "That's more than I got out of him," he said. "And I'm buying the pancakes."

"Lawrence, huh? No wonder the language is so bad," Zadie said.

There was a murmur of agreement. In good weather, university kids often came to town, and it had been extensively noted that even the girls had potty mouths.

Zadie rested the pot on the table. She said, "I got a funny feeling about this Warrington fella," she said. "I feel like I know him."

"That's because he's a hound," Becky Lane said, delivering Artie's and Phil's pancakes to the table. "And he reminds you of every hound you ever met."

Momentarily Becky's ex-husband, Barney Lane, was recalled by all assembled.

Jim Evans, who had been nursing a cup of coffee for an unusually long time, called out from the round corner booth where the farmers always sat. "Say, didn't the oldest Lupin girl go to college with Chuck in Lawrence? I seem to recall when he came here the first time, she brought him."

Phil, Park, Becky, and Artie were too young to remember Chuck's arrival. Vaguely, they could recall a time when Chuck's Beer and Bowl was not Chuck's Beer and Bowl but something else to do with bowling, but it was not a distinct memory. As far as they were concerned, big, rawboned Chuck had been born behind that bar, dispensing shoes and pitchers with his slightly watery blue eyes.

Oscar said, "I only remember when the sign went up." Back then, the Mexican American population of Eudora had been small and had taken little interest in the affairs of the town.

That left Zadie and Jim.

Zadie looked at Jim, and Jim looked at Zadie. "Yes, the oldest Lupin girl did bring Chuck to Eudora," she said. "And she dropped out of college just about the same time."

Becky said, "Do you both really think that's Chuck in that book? Do you think Margaret Lupin would write about real people?"

Becky turned to Artie. "Would she do that?"

Artie paused in mid-syrup. "She's known for it. From what I

read, she pretty much had to leave New York after *New Amsterdam* was published."

Zadie absently felt the side of the cooling decaf pot. "Well, I never," she said. "Jim, what do you think?"

"I don't know nothing about it. I ain't read a single word. Mary won't have it in the house, says it's not Christian."

"She's got a point," Park said. "Stacey and I keep it upstairs. We don't want the kids reading it."

Silence fell for a moment on the impromptu literary society. Nothing moved but Phil's and Artie's forks. News, after all, comes and goes, but you can only eat pancakes when they're hot.

"What," asked Artie indistinctly, "is Margaret's older sister's name?"

"Janine," Zadie answered. "They called her Janine Elspeth. I always thought that was kind of cruel."

"Huh," said Becky Lane. "Warrington's first name in the book is Charles, which is kind of close to Chuck. And the pusher's girlfriend's name is Jules, which starts with *J*, like Janine."

Eyes met, flashing around the diner like semaphore signals. And then suddenly everybody got interested in either the contents of their plates or their work.

Nothing more was said about Chuck or the oldest Lupin girl. This was, they all seemed to decide communally, getting uncomfortably close to gossip. But in the privacy of their own homes that night, they conveyed Jim and Zadie's suspicions to their nearest and dearest. Phil told Pattie. Park Davis told Stacey. Artie Walker told his wife, Rosemary. Oscar Burgos mentioned it to his sister, Maria Lopez. Becky Lane told her daughters. And many telephone calls were made, quite a few long distance.

The evening before, the citizens of Eudora had been universally certain that the most desirable thing to do with one's leisure time was read *The Vortex* by Margaret Lupin. But that evening, it was torn between reading more and going down to Chuck's Beer and Bowl.

May is a blessed time in Eudora. It falls in one of the two brief periods of the year when you can turn off the heat and still not need the air conditioner. Any tornadoes have usually come and gone. The children are still in school and the college kids are busy with finals. There are no major religious festivals or civic occasions and citizens are left to plant their gardens and maybe water a bit. There is as yet no need for vigorous hoeing.

If *The Vortex* had been published in August, when everyone is frantic with canning and preserving, or during the Maple Leaf Festival, or around Christmas, it might well have gone unnoticed and the events in this chronicle would never have occurred. But in May, there is nothing much to distract even the hardest working of Eudora's hard-working population.

Hector Rodriguez, the mayor and the president of the bank, was reading *The Vortex*. Doctor and Lottie Emery were taking turns reading it aloud to each other in bed. Mark Ramirez, who suddenly had a lot of time on his hands, was reading *The Vortex*. Clement McAllister, the retired banker, who hadn't read a book since Louis L'Amour died, was reading *The Vortex*, and though Phil Walker wasn't reading it, he asked Pattie so many questions about it and followed the plot so closely he might as well have been. In the Lane family home, there were two copies and a wall chart showing who could read which one when.

In fact, the only person who was not in some way following *The Vortex* was Chuck Warren. Chuck was completely unaware of the publication of Margaret's latest novel and the way it had gripped the imagination of the town. He noted that business was down on Monday night and unusually busy on Tuesday night, but didn't really wonder why. These things happened. The adult league was over for the year, the championship having been won, for the second time in a row, by the Mayan Memories Restaurant contingent, and the junior league had not yet begun.

Bowling, like softball, formed a large part of the reason children in Eudora lived long enough to become teenagers as their mothers coped with the long summer break from school. Chuck and his cash register were pleased to do their part to ensure the survival of another generation.

When the hot weather hit, and it would hit soon, he'd get busy in the evenings with people wanting to socialize in the a.c. of the bar. He'd had a good winter. He could wait.

There was always work to do in the bowling trade. There were shoes to be cleaned and polished, balls to be examined, lanes to be dusted, equipment of all sorts to be fixed. He could always clean the cheese pump on the nachos machine if he got bored.

No, Chuck was not desperate for customers. And so, on Wednesday night, when the unexpected crowds descended and he had to change the keg, he was not elated, but felt a little puzzled. Especially since, rather unusually, the crowd at the bar seemed to want him to participate in their conversations.

"Hey, Chuck, what do you think of Lawrence? Didn't you grow up around there?"

"You tell us, Chuck, was there a lot of pot-smoking in Lawrence when you were there?"

And then an interesting one. "What did Janine Lupin look like when you first met her?"

Chuck had answered the first two questions rather shortly, but this last one made him smile. The interlocutor, Phil Walker, continued, "I mean, did she have blue hair or anything like her sister did when she went off to college?"

"No," Chuck said, still smiling. "No, when I met her she had long brown hair. She was still pretty skinny, too. She got kinda big after the babies."

"Oh yeah," Phil said, "I remember. She was a bit of a hippie, wasn't she? Stopped shaving her legs."

"And her armpits," Chuck said. "First girl I ever knew that didn't."

The bar had gone absolutely silent during this exchange, but as soon as it was apparent Chuck was not going to say more, the entire complement of customers downed their mugs of beer, said goodnight, and went home.

Chuck was left with forty-eight dollars in the cash register he hadn't expected, two dollars in tips, and twenty-one mugs to go into the dishwasher. Other than that, the place was as silent as it ever got, what with the jukebox and the game machines blaring their solicitations.

He went to the front door and looked out across the parking lot, at the empty spaces in front of the movie house and the complete lack of traffic heading out to Food Barn.

"Huh," he said. "Funny."

And then he went back inside and began to disassemble the nacho machine.

Janey Lane was just finishing the fourth chapter when her mother appeared at her bedroom door.

Becky didn't beat around the bush. "Another night in?" she asked, coming to sit on the bed. Janey had to move her legs quickly.

"Yes," she said. She rested the book over her breasts like armor, tucking her head so that the dust jacket scraped her chin.

"What's up with you and Mark?"

Janey shrugged. "Nothing," she said. "It's just not going anywhere. I think maybe I should move on."

Becky nodded slowly. "I figured you might be thinking something like that."

Janey looked at her mother.

Becky Lane was still a handsome woman. She was a bit meatier than her daughters, and some hard years showed on her face, but her kind eyes made up for it all. She turned them on her daughter now. "You haven't had the best role models as far as relationships go," she said.

Janey let the book rise up over her mouth and looked down its spine.

Becky sighed. "One thing I can tell you," she said. "Moving on isn't all it's cracked up to be. And Mark's a good boy."

Janey sat up and shut the book. "Everyone tells me he's a good *boy*. But I need him to grow up, Mama," she said. She bit her lips and her big brown eyes filled with tears. "I don't know if he's gonna."

Becky pulled her daughter close and spoke into her hair. "I don't, either," she said. "But don't you reckon you should give him the chance?"

Janey sniffed and pulled away. "I can't keep waiting like this. It's . . . ."—she took a deep, shuddering breath—"it's embarrassing."

Becky nodded, trying not to smile. "Tell him," she said. "You gotta tell him. You gotta say it, right out." Janey collapsed back against her mother's body. The bulk of it was reassuringly solid and made her feel small and protected.

But Becky took her daughter by her shoulders and pushed her upright again, giving her a kiss on her forehead, instead. Janey was not small anymore, and had to solve her problems by herself.

"Say it," Becky said again. "It's the only way you're going to find out."

And Janey Lane nodded her lovely head.

"Who do we know that graduated in, say, sixty-eight, sixty-nine?" Phil interrupted Pattie's reading.

"Shut up," she said. "Warrington's trying to convince Tiger to hire him as a double agent for the dope runners."

"Was there more sex?"

"Just a kiss. A good one, though."

There was a moment of silence while Pattie turned the page. Phil rolled over on his side and closed his eyes. But then he opened them again and rolled back onto his back. "We gotta know *somebody*," he said.

"Okay," Pattie said, putting *The Vortex* down on her lap. "Why is it so important that we know somebody who graduated in sixty-eight or -nine?"

"Because they'd have the sixty-eight or sixty-nine high school yearbook." Phil said this in an overtly smug way that indicated to his wife of some years' standing he felt he was being extremely intelligent.

But he could see from her expression that she hadn't followed his line of reasoning, so he continued, "And we could see what Janine Lupin looked like back then and see if it looks like Jules in the book."

"I'm not sure about all this," Pattie said. "I thought authors just made stuff up."

"Artie says Margaret Lupin always uses people she knows in her books. He says she just about got run out of New York City on a rail."

A short cry came from down the hall in Ben's room (the four-year-old had always been a poor sleeper) and both parents tensed. But it was only a dream and he quieted back down on his own.

"Well," Pattie continued in a whisper, "that'd make them, what, fifty-four, fifty-five? I don't know anybody just that age."

"What about Oscar Burgos?" Phil hissed.

"No. Oscar and Maria didn't get here until we were in the eighth grade. Back in the sixties the quarry was still pretty much white." Pattie picked *The Vortex* up again.

"Who would know?" Phil asked.

Pattie ignored him, so he poked her in the ribs. "What?" she said. "Look, you want to know what happens as much as I do. Why don't you let me read the damn book?"

"Who would know? About who was fifty-five?"

"I don't know. Somebody older. Zadie or Margery or . . . no, better not ask Margery . . . you know. Older." She settled back down.

The Lane residence is three blocks away from the Walker house. As Janey passed the Walkers', she glanced up at the dim bedroom lights. She did not assume that Pattie was sitting up reading *The Vortex*. . . . In her softened and hopeful heart, she saw the light as a sign. Surely if Phil Walker, who rumor had it had been the wildest, most untamable young man in several counties, could still make love to his wife on a work night, then it was possible that Mark Ramirez could be brought to see the errors of his ways. Mark, too, could learn to change as a result of true love.

Janey had not made a great deal of effort toward her personal appearance. It was late and she didn't want to have to wake him up, so she didn't dawdle. She had just brushed her hair into another ponytail and grabbed some sweats. She strode through the dim night streets to the small house Lottie and Pattie's father had built and which Mark now rented.

It was a small shotgun shack, a one bedroom affair without a corridor or a second story and it sat a bit back from the road. At one time, Lottie had used it as a consultancy for her herbal practice and nearly everybody in town had, at some point or another, sat on the back porch until called and then traipsed through the bedroom, past the bathroom and the kitchen, to sit in the living room and ask for medical advice. Back then it had been brightly lit some nights until past eleven. But now, at only ten o'clock, only one light shone.

It was the living room light, she noted with relief. Janey stood outside the fence and rehearsed her speech once more. "I love you, Mark," she said to the hydrangea bush, "and I always will. But I need you, too. I need to make a life with you. And I want that life to start now."

One of the Harper aunties was walking their horrible old pug, but Janey, intent on her rehearsal, hadn't heard the telltale wheezing. "You go for it, girl," the auntie said, giggling, as Pug continued his asthmatic waddle. "It sounds good to me."

Flustered, Janey fumbled with the gate and pushed it shut behind her.

It took Mark a moment to answer the door and when he did, he seemed uncomfortable. "Janey!" he exclaimed, in a somewhat theatrical and false tone.

But Janey already felt so uncomfortable that she barely noticed. She gulped and while only halfway through the door, began her speech. "I love you, Mark, and I want to make a life with you." She walked forward as she spoke. "But—"

Once inside the room, she stopped speaking.

Kylie Requena was sitting on Mark's sofa, her shoes off and her feet tucked under her perfectly formed bottom. Glasses of wine and a bowl of chips sat on the coffee table. Kylie smiled at Janey, revealing brilliant white teeth.

Janey raised her hands, as if to ward off the vision. "Oh," she gasped, immediately turning. "Oh," she said again, running out the door.

"Janey," Mark called after her, as she fumbled with the tricky gate again. "Don't go. It's not like that."

But Janey barely heard him. She only noticed one thing as she forced her suddenly leaden legs to run again—Mark Ramirez didn't follow her. Mark Ramirez stayed in his little white house with Kylie Requena.

The Eudora Empire Cinema was unwontedly quiet of late, which surprised no one who knew its owner, Jim Flory. Jim had been, most of the last two decades, more comfortable as the town drunkard than as a business owner, and the schedule at the movie house had always been erratic. However, in the past two years he had been sober and for the last eighteen months he had been building his business back up with a verve and vitality that had warmed the hearts of Eudorans.

Eudorans, however, are well inured to backsliding, having had plenty of experience observing how difficult it is to effect long-lasting change. So after Flory's initial burst of enthusiasm during which he simply could not keep away from his place of business when his industry began to slack a bit; shock was not listed as foremost in the reaction of the townspeople.

Curiosity, however, was. For Jim Flory was not, it appeared, drinking. He remained nattily dressed, even sporting some very trendy casual wear. In fact, if anything, his appearance showed preternatural care, and it was noticed that after purchasing both facial masques and moisturizer from Maple Leaf Pharmacy he had not bestowed them as gifts on any of his female friends. In fact, an empty masque jar had been prominent in his recycling.

He had also been spending a great deal of time away from town. At first he had explained to acquaintances (who obligingly repeated the news to their own intimate circle, thus broadcasting it to the town at large) that he had set up a group of independent cinema owners in the city and had been attending meetings, and this was largely believed. But then as the meetings seemed to be taking place over the weekend, when movie houses are usually quite busy, this explanation had begun to be doubted. As Flory's disinterest in his own movie house coincided perfectly with his putative growth in interest of this group, it seemed unlikely that his absences could be attributed to fraternal cinematic zeal.

By now, showings of films had began to become irregular, and advertisements of the schedule were often not ready in time to be inserted in the county paper. Worse still, sometimes he did manage to insert the advertisements and then ignored them. Customers who had traveled from the city or the county seat on the basis of this information just to see Flory's handwritten sign, SORRY, SOMETHING CAME UP, were not amused.

Eudorans, who as a people rejoice in reversing the flow of income from the town to the city by any means short of actual armed robbery, found this to be an appalling dereliction of duty. Add the fact that the popcorn was sometimes a day old and soon it was agreed that Jim Flory had lost the plot once again, and in a spectacular way.

But he was not drunk. Nor did he appear to be indulging in any of the other drugs available in the city.

His eyes and skin were as clear as a child's (pharmacist Park Davis had to reorder Jim's favorite face masque twice due to popular demand after his wholesome skin tone was discerned), and he neither trembled nor staggered. His new lightweight cotton sweaters never smelled of smoke, only his favorite Aramis cologne. He did not shrink from greeting his fellow townspeople—in fact, he was unusually chatty and happy.

For a while, Eudora wondered.

And then one weekend, a weekend for which Flory had prepared his advertisement in time and had caught up on all his cleaning in the cinema (including completely overhauling the popcorn machine and scrubbing that disgraceful glass), an unknown Audi with a light blue metallic finish was spotted in the driveway of the big Flory house. The next morning, it was still there and the driver accompanied Jim to breakfast at Gross Home Cooking.

His name was Bob. He was a man of medium height and build, mostly bald but with a ring of curling salt-and-pepper hair around the perimeter of his head. He wore ordinary clothes, boots and jeans and a dark navy sweater of no obvious brand, and his smile was neither unfriendly nor too ready. There was, indeed, no reason to believe he was anything other than a regular guy, except for the fact that his Audi had been parked all night at the Flory place and that Jim was fairly incandescent with joy and pride.

Now, it must be said that overt homosexuality is not encouraged in Eudora. Many Eudorans had read their Leviticus, and censored such activity. Many of the more migratory elements of Eudoran society, those strange birds who hatch there but fly away once fledged, fly because of their own homosexuality and the Leviticus-reading segment of the community. But as long as you don't rub the townsfolk's noses right in it, tolerance is generally accorded. Nothing is normally said, at least not to one's face.

However, Bob's appearance at Gross Home Cooking was felt to be pushing the envelope of community tolerance.

It wasn't that they touched. They didn't even whisper, but addressed any remark to each other in a normal tone. And these were commonplace utterances to do with passing the syrup, whether or not Bob wanted the Tabasco (he did), and which segments of the newspaper to swap (neither read the sports section). And still, the atmosphere in the place grew tenser with each moment, and as much as they ordered, praised, and tipped, Zadie Gross was pleased to see them go.

Eudora was fond of Jim Flory. If it had been another man, the discussions that took place extensively the following week would have been short. Universal condemnation does not require discussion, only a meaningful exchange of glances.

But even the Leviticus-readers (none of whom, it must be said, read their Leviticus so extensively as to restrict their portions of Alaskan king crab claws at the annual Baptist Surf-n-Turf barbecue) hesitated to utterly condemn Jim Flory. The oldest of them tended to blame it all on Jim's grandmother. Lydia was married to Jim Flory's paternal grandfather in a whirlwind romance. She had been a resident of Charleston, Virginia, and if you really wanted to get to the root of the problem, it was in her parents, who had spoiled her rotten. A more headstrong, greedy, selfish woman you were unlikely to meet. And when Flory's grandfather died in the Battle of the Somme, she proceeded to raise the monster that was Flory's father without any masculine guidance.

He had been wild and brutish. No one had expected the pale little girl Flory's grandmother had picked out for her son to marry to last five minutes. But she outlived him, though sad and strange all her life, which was hardly surprising. She was married before she could tell time and bruised after the first honeymoon week. Jim Flory—growing up kind and decent, caring for his mother and brother, beginning to take on the maintenance of the home from the time he was about eleven—his strength of character seemed like a miracle to those who knew his background.

And since those who knew his background were among the majority of the Leviticus-reading population, there was much discussion about how folks felt regarding the Audi with the metallic light blue finish and the person it had brought to town.

Bob was long gone, having only stayed one night. However, the industry the visit had inspired in Jim Flory himself did not abate. The entire time the town was weighing his character in the balance, he had been talking to Lottie and the doctor, reading *The Vortex*, and planning a counter-culture season for the Eudora Empire Cinema. It is doubtful if he even noticed that folks stopped talking when he walked by.

Eudora had been discussing Jim Flory all his life.

It is outside the scope and interest of this chronicle to enter into the philosophical, ethical, and theological debates that raged during that week. However, it is important, given the events that followed, and the pivotal role that this relationship would play, to at least mention this other stone thrown into the water, which ended up having such consequential ripples.

▪ ▪ ▪

Since Chuck Warren had arrived in Eudora, he had been pretty much a loner. Oh, he never lacked for company, should he desire any. . . . He'd always had a fridge full of beer and something to smoke, plus the attractions of his bass boat, jet ski, and superwide TV with premium cable. But he'd never really fit in. He ended up getting friendly with groups of people, at first slightly younger than himself, and then increasingly younger, who shared his tastes. But they would eventually marry or move, and the circle would become diminished until, once again, it was only Chuck left to sit up late smoking dope and watching porn on the Dutch channel.

Women tended to drift away. At first they found him exotic and fun, and then they found him a little inflexible, and then they found him boring and irritating beyond belief. He seemed to have little or no capacity for personal change. He had arrived in Eudora a typically lecherous and party-seeking twenty-one-year-old boy, and now he was exactly the same, but thirty-four years older. When the group before last of young, pleasure-seeking people attempted to adopt him into their circle (and this had included Phil Walker), he gave it a miss. He was just too old to go through it all again. The desertion had started to seem personal.

He only took one cooler to the lake now.

At times, he wondered out loud what it was all for. With his small capacity for change, he had small sense of progression. Childless, he had no sense of life's cycles. The inevitability of death still seemed to come as a shock to him, whenever it was mentioned, and he had no religion to soften the blow. For some years he saw the world as a source of entertainment. As one of his ex-wives said (when she was still a wife but soon-to-become ex), it was the thought that the universe might continue without him as its audience that struck him as catastrophic.

When his shoulder twinged with bursitis, as it did a week after Bob's visit, Chuck would often discourse about the shadow of mortality. Lately, since Chuck had been listened to more closely, folks had begun to wonder whether it was the certainty of death that was bothering him, or the certainties of his monotonous life.

He was polishing a glass when Jim Flory walked in.

"I've got a little proposition for you," Flory said. "And before you get your hopes up, let me remind you that you aren't my type."

This was a long-running joke. Chuck smiled and asked Jim to shoot.

Jim shot. He said, "What with everybody reading *The Vortex,* it seems like a good time to do a counter-culture season."

He thought he would start with *Easy Rider,* he said; then go on to *Help* and *Yellow Submarine,* then Nicolas Roeg's *Performance,* perhaps finishing off with either *Naked Lunch* or *Fear and Loathing in Las Vegas,* though he was leaning toward the latter on account of the box office draw of Mr. Johnny Depp. It was well known that all the women of the Branch line (which included Lottie Emery, Pattie Walker, and some three dozen cousins) and the entire Lane family would pay to watch Johnny Depp sit on a chair for two hours.

Chuck, though not a big movie fan, was moderately enthusiastic about these plans. Jim had tapped directly into his own personal aesthetic—several of the films Jim had named were his favorites. But he didn't see what he could do.

"Well," Jim said, "since so many of the movies are set in the seventies, I thought you might like to do a promotion . . . you know, something like bring your tickets for a discount on your Large Draft/Nacho Combo. And you might put up posters in here."

At this point, Chuck said, he just couldn't work out the connection. He put down the glass he was polishing and leaned on the avocado Formica bar. "Why in here?" he asked.

And Jim Flory, never being one to shy from a discussion of style, said, "Well, because you've kept this place like a museum, Chuck. It's perfect."

"What are you talking about, Flory? It's not a museum, it's a bowling alley."

"Well, it's a museum, too. I mean, look at those beer lights! You've got the Hamm's bear one with the waterfall. I used to think that was gorgeous when I was about ten. And the jukebox with the disco lighting, not to mention the music on it—"

"What's wrong with the music?" Chuck was stung.

"Nothing, if you like Van Halen."

"Everybody likes Van Halen. And I've got some more modern stuff on there."

Flory said, "Oh, yes?" He went over and began flipping through the cardboard menu, set behind glass.

"Yeah, I got Blondie and stuff." Chuck had grown defensive.

"Chuck," Jim said, laughing. "Blondie stopped their major recording twenty years ago." He flipped. "And you've only got one single."

"I got Oasis."

"Ten years ago."

Chuck looked around the bar and out into the hall. It was as if, he said later, a film had fallen from his eyes. The orange and brown Naugahyde bar stools and booths. The smoked-glass shades for the fluorescent strip lighting. The pinball machine. The yellow-, green-, and brown-striped bowling shoes. The beer signs. The Afro-haired graphics for the ladies' and men's room doors. The very avocado counter against which he was leaning.

He snatched his hands back.

He was stuck in the seventies. And had been, now, for thirty years.

Pattie Walker was reading *The Vortex*. The pusher, Tiger, had decided to start a marijuana farming operation. Warrington told his commanding officer and there had been a strange meeting, at which it became clear to Warrington that the police officers in charge of narcotics were planning to steal and market the marijuana crop. Now, Warrington wasn't sure who the good guys were, especially since the horticulturalist in charge of the crop was a hot little hippie chick named Doreen.

"What's happening now?" Phil Walker interrupted.

Pattie Walker had, at this point, had enough. It was, she later told her sister Lottie, a long day. Now, if you are a man, or a woman without children at home, you might not understand about long days such as Pattie had recently undergone. But if you are a mother with children at home, and a large home at that, who goes out to work and does her own cooking and cleaning, and keeps on doing it when she is in the early stages of pregnancy, you will start to understand the depths of weariness from which Pattie Walker spoke.

"Phil, would you just shut up and let me read the damn book? If you're so interested, why don't you get a copy and read it yourself?"

Stung, her husband said, "You know it'd take me a hundred years to read a book like that."

It's important to realize that Pattie was not just suffering from fatigue. When you have a home and a business and children . . . when you *have it all* as the phrase goes, you also have a volatile collection of things that can go wrong, especially when your house is ninety-two years old and your longtime employee left two years ago and the new girl isn't working out so good and your children are the Walker boys.

Add pregnancy to that cocktail of emotional triggers and you might, like Lottie, be able to understand why Pattie replied, "Oh, bullshit. You read *Sports Illustrated* quick enough. You're just lazy."

Phil, to whom this epithet had been applied regularly at school, in a time when teachers did not readily recognize dyslexia, was now more than stung. He was hurt. He said, "Pattie, that's not fair."

But Pattie didn't hear him, or didn't choose to hear him. He lay there for a moment and looked at the clock: ten-twenty. And then he got out of bed.

Pattie hadn't deigned to notice Phil being hurt, but she sure deigned when he started to get dressed.

"Where are you going at this time of night?"

"I'm going for a beer," Phil said. "If I'm not too lazy to get there. Heck, I'm so damned lazy I'll probably just lay down about halfway there on the sidewalk for a nap." And, since his apparel did not take long to either select or don, he was then able to slam out the bedroom door, noting with satisfaction as he left the house that he'd woken up Ben.

He guessed Pattie wasn't going to get much reading done, after all.

It had been a slow night at Chuck's Beer and Bowl and Chuck was looking forward, after the bombshell of Jim Flory's visit, to quietly getting out of his head and allowing some sleep to provide perspective when Phil Walker walked in with his hair going in twelve different directions and asked for a draw.

The young couple who had been sitting in the corner holding hands and talking over a Coke got up and left, as if Phil had suddenly made the bar uninhabitable.

And he *had* brought a kind of atmosphere with him. Chuck got the mug out of the freezer and poured the Coors. Coors! he thought. He could remember when Coors had seemed rather exotic, when it was a prized beer brand. Today there were all kinds of beer you could order through the state retailers but he was still stuck pouring Coors. His lack of attention made the spill inevitable. The beer overflowed, cascading around the lip of the mug, missing the drip tray and spattering all over the floor.

Chuck cursed, put the mug on the drip tray, and bent down with a dishcloth to try and contain the spill before it was a mop job. At this he was successful, but when he tried to come to an upright position, he banged the drip tray with the back of his head, which made the mug shoot up in the air, arc (discharging its contents on both Chuck and the floor), and then land about half an inch up from Chuck's left temple.

Beer, glass, and Chuck hit the floor in quick succession.

Later Phil said that his exclamation of "Oh shit!" had been, to his shame, mainly about the loss of his large draft. But when Chuck did not appear over the edge of the Formica counter, Phil leaned over to see what was going on and said, "Oh, shit!" again, in a more humanitarian tone.

The heavy mug had not broken, but Chuck was lying in a sticky pool of beer. Phil was relieved that when he gently shook Chuck and called his name, Chuck's eyes blinked open and his feet began to scramble at the vinyl tiles. Phil helped him up and took him around the bar to sit on a stool and lean against the counter. He found a clean dishtowel and put some ice inside for Chuck to hold against the side of his head. And then he went into the utility closet between the bathrooms and got out the mop and the bucket.

"Are you okay?" he asked, as he filled the latter with hot water and dish soap.

Chuck nodded wearily. He said, "Every damn thing has gone wrong today."

"I know just how you feel."

Phil Walker began mopping the bar floor. It is good, when one is angry and out of sorts, to have something physical to do. He mopped with unwonted vigor.

And that was when Jim Evans walked in.

This event was just as surprising to Phil and Chuck as if Elvis himself had entered the building.

Consider the facts:

First, Jim was a man of regular habits and it was getting on for eleven P.M. on a weekday.

Second, he was a farmer on the far side of seventy who had been up and about since sparrows fart.

And finally, his wife, Mary, was a formidable Baptist, one of the sisterhood who regularly signed petitions to have Chuck's beer license revoked and the town made dry.

There was absolutely no explanation that sprung to either Chuck's or Phil's mind why Jim Evans should be at this hour in the den of iniquity that was Chuck's Beer and Bowl.

Phil and Chuck stared at Jim. Jim stared at Phil Walker, who made a good living as a telephone engineer and had no reason to be mopping the floor of the bowling alley bar, and at Chuck Warren, who was holding an ice pack to the side of his head.

"What the heck's going on here?" he asked.

Some women, when pregnant, get more emotional. Some actually get less, feeling detached from their surroundings as if the job they were doing with their bodies is so important that other considerations are mundane. Pattie Walker vacillated between the two. She had quite callously hurt her husband's feelings, but now was overwhelmed with a suffocating sense of guilt.

It had been, as noted, a very long day. Carla Bustamonte, the new girl at the Fabric Shack, had taken a great deal of the day off with her sideline in the wedding dress business. That she could pursue this sideline was an agreed-upon element of Carla's employment, but it was an element that Pattie deeply regretted. The wedding dress business was growing, and much as poor Carla (who was working herself ragged) tried, she wasn't pulling her full weight at the Shack. And that left Pattie to pick up the slack.

Then there were the kids. Ben had settled back down quickly enough after Phil's outburst, and Pattie had checked on the other two. They looked like such angels when they slept in their Spider-man jammies. It was hard to believe that just that day they'd been given three weeks of detention for hiding in the girls' bathroom during lunch. They had evidently been peeking and eavesdropping on the private concerns of the young ladies of Eudora Primary, and had nearly sent little Marcie Hudpucker into hysterics when they burst out, shouting, "Boo!" They need the strong guidance of their father, Pattie thought, and what have I done? Sent him off into the night, unloved.

The Walker house was an immense Victorian, with all the inconveniences and charm it could hold between four walls. On the bedroom floor, the inconveniences were mainly to do with the plumbing and the charm was largely contained in a window seat beneath a round oriel window on the first-floor landing. Pattie shivered in her tank top, even though she had on warm pink sweatpants. She pulled her velour-covered knees close to her chest and sat for a moment, staring at the sidewalk where Phil would have walked, if he were walking back. She waited there for what seemed a very long time.

Although there was an emergency ward at the hospital in town, it was not unusual for the doctor's home phone to ring in the night, or for it to end up being for Lottie. So neither one of them resented Pattie calling and asking for some help.

Phil had brewed a pot of coffee to Chuck's instructions and Jim Evans had enjoyed chuckling at the whole story. Chuck's shirt was starting to dry out, and it looked like he was going to have a shiner but didn't show signs of a concussion. He and Phil were drinking beer. The cash register had not been involved in any of the beverage servings.

We owe this account, once again, to the doctor, who put together quite a bit from what Phil had said and what Chuck and Jim Evans let slip during the Grand Opening celebrations and the subsequent trip to the hospital. So this is, therefore, a reconstruction, not an eyewitness account. Nonetheless, it is felt to be fairly accurate. The details of the discussion that are contentious or controversial have been omitted from the chronicle. If the reader feels they know more than is here displayed, they are free to embellish the account as they see fit.

A silence fell. Not an uncomfortable silence, but a masculine one, where things were phrased in minds and discarded, things all three of them knew would have to be said at some point in the evening, but perhaps not right then.

Then they all spoke at once.

Jim asked Chuck how the fish were biting.

Chuck asked Jim what brought him out so late.

Phil said he didn't usually see Jim in Chuck's.

Another silence fell. Chuck and Phil, with a mutual assumption that the majority ruled, waited for an explanation from Jim.

Jim sat with his hands curled around his coffee cup and his shoulders slightly hunched. His gimme cap rode low against the fluorescent lights and the enquiring stares of his fellow men; his face sunk in both thought and shadow.

Phil and Chuck were content to wait, sipping their beer.

At last Jim sighed. He said, "I ain't been sleeping so good lately. Got a lot on my mind. Tonight, I just couldn't stand it, so I got in my truck and drove around a bit, trying to get sleepy. I saw the light and . . . I been meaning to talk to Chuck, here."

"Me?" Chuck said, surprised. "What's on your mind?"

Jim smiled grimly. "That's the sixty-four-thousand-dollar question," he said. He drank some coffee and grimaced. "Boy, you make some bad coffee, son," he said to Phil Walker.

"Sorry, Jim." Phil grinned. "Pattie bought me one of those machines where you make it with foil packets. She says I still manage to ruin it."

"What's the sixty-four-thousand-dollar question?" Chuck asked.

Again, Jim grimaced. "Well, it's more like three hundred and seventy-three thousand, last I looked," he said.

"Dollars?" Chuck asked. "Money?"

"Uh-huh." Jim nodded, seemingly smaller inside his battered Carhartt jacket. "I don't think I gotta tell you boys to keep your mouths shut."

"That's a lot of money," Phil said.

"That's farming for you," Jim replied. "You do the best you can, but you still got to deal with the luck. These last five years, I would have been better off taking my production loan and going to Vegas." He took another swallow and shuddered. "I ain't been able to bring myself to do nothing this spring, nothing at all. Every time I get an idea, I just keep thinking about all the things that can go wrong. I'm paralyzed."

Phil and Chuck had been staring, openmouthed. Much later, Phil said he'd been unable to take in much of Jim's speech. Jim Evans was a standard in the farming community. Even if you knew nothing about the science and practice of farming, and it is doubtful that either Phil or Chuck did, you knew a good farmer when you saw one.

A good farmer was industrious and clever with the use of materials. He did not rush out to replace, he knew how to mend. A good farmer had good fence, maintained his barns, remained busy in bad weather. A good farmer networked, banded together with his fellows to get things done, researched his market, did not reach for the quick buck but thought ahead.

It was well known throughout the entire community that Jim had done all of those things.

Hell, Phil thought, just last week he had overheard one of the other old guys in the corner asking Jim for advice. And the rest of them had listened intently to what Jim had to say. Jim *had* to be a good farmer for that to happen.

"Clement called me in last week," Jim said. "Them sum' bitches want to foreclose. Clement talked them into another harvest, but he doesn't know I didn't put in the winter wheat." He rubbed his face.

"Dude." Chuck's tone made it clear he was aghast. "That's terrible," he said.

"Terrible," Phil echoed.

Again, the three men retreated into their private thoughts. The poker machine tinkled invitingly. The jukebox sent diamonds of color over the shiny brown linoleum. Above them, the beer signs hummed and buzzed.

And then Chuck asked, "Can I do anything?"

Jim looked at him for a long moment. "Well, that kinda depends," he said. "Are you the guy in that book?"

"What book?" Chuck asked.

And Phil started to explain.

Jim Flory had been beaten up plenty of times before. His father was of course the first of his assailants, and then he'd been fairly regularly set upon during his school years. And this was not the first time he'd been jumped coming out of a nightclub.

It happened, he thought, as he reeled from the first punch to his head and attempted to keep his arms free of the hands grabbing them. In the world of men, this seemed to be acceptable behavior for a significant minority of the population.

He thought about this aspect of male society as they dragged him off to a dark corner of the adjacent parking lot. Part of him was concerned with begging and promising money, but he knew, even then, that talking was futile, and so it did not hold his complete attention. He also knew that he was about to get hurt, and having noted the pointed cowboy-style boots on the feet of his assailants, that this pain would be significant.

Rather than think about what was happening, Jim Flory chose instead to use some room in his mind to consider philosophically the gender bias of violent aggression. It was, he thought, as the subsequent punches sent him to the ground, all about mob mentality. Even little boys tended to run in packs, and unlike little girls, did not find their places within these packs on the basis of eloquence or beauty. The playground was a place of running and shoving and shouting—of Indian burns and slap hand—of punches thrown and threats to kick ass.

But here, Jim lost his train of thought. He could no longer push what was happening out of his mind.

He had automatically gone into a curl, assuming the fetal position on the broken asphalt in the corner of the parking lot. The fetal position, he knew from long experience, had its benefits and its shortcomings. His face, throat, and chest were protected, but his kidneys, spine, skull, and hands were not. Now it was all a matter of how skilled the group was at this game. They didn't really have much longer. It was a busy city street and soon someone would notice. In the minute or so left, a really competent queer-basher could do considerable damage, while your amateur would only give a few half-hearted kicks.

There were five of them. One seemed to be keeping a lookout and three were of the amateur persuasion, who occasionally got lucky with a blow to a vulnerable spot, but had no true calling for this kind of work.

But one of them knew his business. And he was concentrating now, after a thorough kidney bashing that made Jim retch bile, and a well-placed blow to the skull that caused him to nearly lose consciousness, on probing for Jim's testes with the toe of his boot. The inevitable shout of an intervening passerby and the scurrying away of his assailants did not come as fast as Jim would have liked, though the ambulance arrived with commendable speed.

It is always difficult to talk when your mouth is bloody and you have just lost teeth, but Jim was able to give his name and address and mention where his car was parked. And then, before he had time to embarrass himself by crying, he closed his eyes on the sight of his rescuers and the bustling paramedics and allowed himself to pass out.

■ ■ ■

Pattie Walker came into Chuck's Beer and Bowl just before midnight, Chuck's usual closing hour. For a moment, after she came around the partition into the bar, she just stood and stared.

Chuck and Phil were sitting together in a booth with the farmer, Jim Evans. They were talking in low voices, and Evans was writing on the back of an envelope. As she got over the shock and moved closer, she could see that there was a small diagram and a list of numbers. The farmer had been figuring.

Figuring is an essential part of earnest conversation in farming circles. Two sharp young agri-business graduates would probably meet for a latte and open up their Excel spreadsheets, but the old guys, they just grabbed whatever paper was handy and a pencil and started scribbling equations. If a less practically minded citizen mentioned building anything—say, a boat dock, or a bookshelf—one of these old guys would be unable to resist costing it out on the back of a feedbill. Zadie Gross regularly cleared away elaborately estimated schemes for abandoned enterprises of this nature from the round table in the corner of Gross Home Cooking.

Any child of the area knew that figuring meant some sort of business. Pattie immediately grew suspicious. She grew even more suspicious when, upon seeing her, Jim carefully folded the envelope and buttoned it into the shirt pocket where he kept his wallet.

Chuck was the first to greet her.

"Hey, Pats," he said. "You come to see if Phil fell off the edge?"

She didn't smile. "Something like that," she said.

Phil flushed. One's wife coming to roust one during a session with one's male companions could lead to being termed "whipped." He gave Pattie a hard stare. "You didn't need to do that, honey," he said. "Chuck here just had a little accident. It's all over now."

"Is that right?" Pattie said, in a voice colder than the ice bin.

"Should have seen it," Jim said. "Beer all over the place and Chuck with a lump on his head as big as a hen's egg."

"Sorry to hear that," Pattie said. Her voice held no appreciable addition of warmth.

Now, what we have here is a marital deadlock. Pattie had come to apologize. She was thinking about Phil and had assumed Phil would be thinking about her, about their relationship and the argument they'd just had.

But clearly, Phil was not. Phil was busy doing something that, to an experienced wife and mother like Pattie, smelled like mischief. She had woken up the doctor and Lottie, and Lottie had come over in the middle of the night to sit with the boys just so Pattie could come to the bar and comfort Phil. But Phil didn't need comforting.

Pattie found this galling.

On Phil's side of things, it was even worse. Not only had Pattie driven him out of the house with her ungrateful and demeaning comments, but now she'd chased him as if he were the family dog who had strayed. She might as well have brought a collar and a leash with her.

The tension was palpable.

"Well," Jim Evans said, "I gotta make an early start. I sure appreciate it, boys." He stood up and settled his gimme cap more firmly on his head. "See you tomorrow, Chuck," he said, and then he nodded to Pattie before giving her a wide berth on his way to the door.

Phil stood up slower. "I'll see you, Chuck," he said. "Watch that drip tray, now."

Chuck grinned. "It throws a mean punch," he said.

Pattie waited until Phil walked past her and then spun on her heel and followed without a word of farewell.

Chuck, an experienced contender in marital encounters of this kind, whistled a long, low note and resumed his closing routine with a heart made lighter by contentment with his single status.

Phil and Pattie began the five-minute walk home, which would take them the better part of an hour.

Topics covered included:

1. Pattie's ungrateful nature.
2. Phil's selfishness and touchiness.
3. The effects of pregnancy and exhaustion on one's temperament.
4. A cogent refutation of the theory that one's essential temperament is changed by such things as hormones.
5. A discussion about the gender-based workload in the parenting business.
6. The disadvantages of single parenting, allied with a rather pessimistic view of the future of the textile business.
7. An ethical monologue about male responsibility in several aspects of parenting, starting with conception.
8. A provocative theory that all pregnancies are attempts by the female to enslave the male.
9. A short, but compelling advertisement for the comfort of the spare room and its fitness for Phil's needs.

They entered the house in silence and Phil went directly up the stairs, not pausing at the second floor where the family bedrooms all were, but continuing up to the third floor of the study and the spare room. Pattie found Lottie so soundly asleep on the sofa that she didn't have the heart to wake her. She just moved a pillow so that her sister wouldn't wake up with a crick in her neck, and covered her with one of the new chenille throws.

She then checked on the kids, picking up some dirty clothes she had somehow missed on her last two patrols and putting them into the laundry chute. Pattie had applied makeup and worn a bra for her trip down to Chuck's. She carefully removed both, using a special wipe to take off her mascara. She put on her moisturizer. She folded up the lacy bra and put it back with her best underwear, tracing the little bow with one finger before shutting the drawer. And then she threw herself onto her lonely bed and sobbed her heart out.

∎ ∎ ∎

Mark Ramirez, who couldn't sleep, had finally decided to make Janey talk to him. He still thought she was being totally unreasonable. He had sent twenty text messages during the day and had tried to phone her at work and at home with no success. He had no idea what had started this inexplicable descent into misunderstanding, but he was tired of being patient and was going to get to the bottom of it.

Maria Lopez had listened to the whole story during his lunch break at Mayan Memories. "You're in big trouble," she had said, refusing to elaborate. "You better buy a dozen roses and put on some knee pads."

Mark had shrugged. "I haven't done anything wrong," he'd said. "She's got to be reasonable, that's all."

But Linda Bustamonte, the restaurant's assistant, had interjected, "What do you want? Do you want her to be reasonable? Or do you want her to be in love? Nobody gets both at the same time."

The next bite of tortilla stuck so hard in his throat he'd had to wash it down with water to keep from choking.

So here he was, walking down Janey's street. He was three blocks away when he heard a woman crying, crying so hard you'd think her eyes would fall right out.

At the sound, Mark froze in his tracks. What would he do, if he ever heard Janey cry like that? Even worse, what if he ever actually *made* her cry that hard himself, because of something he had done? Of course, he would never do anything to hurt her on purpose. But he often got things wrong without even trying.

If he ever hurt her that bad, he would just have to die. He would never be able to forgive himself. He would never be able to get the sound of her tears out of his mind.

He took one, two more steps. He could see the Lane house, see that the light in her room was still on.

Mark Ramirez knew that he would die for Janey Lane. If a bear or a mountain lion came after them, he would push her out of the way and let the wild beast tear his flesh, just to keep her safe. If she ever needed it, he would give her his heart, tear it right out of his body himself and hand it to the doctor.

He had courage enough to do any of those things. All of them, even. But he couldn't go to the Lane house that night, because Mark Ramirez didn't have the courage to hear Janey Lane cry.

He stood for a long moment, looking at the light, wanting to see her and yet fearing to hurt her. Finally Mark Ramirez walked away, taking another way home, so he wouldn't have to hear the sobbing woman again.

There is a reason why your Walker boys, always wild to a fault, tend to marry fairly early. It's as if Nature herself understands the uxorious ballast their buoyant spirits require.

If Phil had woken up in his own bed, with Pattie's bottom pressing into the small of his back, he might have started the day thinking, "Whoa, doggies! We were way out of line last night. I'd better talk to Chuck and Jim before this goes any further."

But Phil woke up in the cold and narrow bed of the spare room and thought no such thing. Burning with the zeal of a man who will not conform to anyone's expectations, he was determined to go his own way.

Dr. James Emery had settled well into the Eudoran way of life, after an unpromising start. This spring, he was going a bit overboard with the home improvements, and it was making him tired and tetchy, but Eudorans had no problem with tired and tetchy physicians after sixty-five years of former doctor P. J. O'Connell. They were also used to new husbands going overboard with power tools and paint.

The old Spencer place was looking good. He and Lottie had moved in once it was drywalled and the kitchen and bathroom had been done. They'd been finishing the rest bit by bit, living in one room at first and then gradually expanding. He was working on the spare room now. You could see the light behind the blinds and the silhouette of someone wallpapering.

Since everyone in town knew that the doctor had been wallpapering, they cut him some additional slack for his tetchiness. It was a difficult task to manage after a day's work, and the doctor's natural after-dinner activity was sitting slumped in a chair watching movies. The fact that he was attempting the wallpapering at all made the older population of the town (who formed the bulk of his regular practice) feel a warmth of pride in his efforts.

For this activity was truly Eudoran. Don and Albert Simpson were often called upon to do construction work, but they did not generally paint. Hiring someone else to paint or paper your walls would be as wasteful as neglecting to grow your own vegetables. Only the elderly and infirm asked others to raise their zucchinis or gloss their trim, and even most of them managed to bully a family member into doing it for free.

It had been interesting to watch the doctor's progress. Lottie had helped him do the dining room first. It was a rich winey red, which had seemed a mistake when one saw it going on through the open windows of last summer, but then as one peeked in over winter, with the pale pine furniture and the logs glowing in the wood stove, it had looked just right.

Indeed, the deep leaf green of the living room and the gold of the family room and breakfast nook, though unusual, were universally approved. When the décor moved upstairs, everyone was surprised by the blowsy floral chosen for the master bedroom wallpaper, huge pink and red roses. It seemed a strange choice after all those jewel tones downstairs, and was thoroughly discussed all February, until the curtains went up.

There had been a shade in the second bedroom, but as Lane Nichols had seen the doctor buying three rolls of blue ticking stripe in the True Value Hardware at the county seat, that was no great mystery, if not a universally approved choice.

However, nobody had the faintest idea of what the doctor was putting up on the walls of the spare bedroom. The only thing that was obvious to any dog or power walker who happened to glance up as they passed the old Spencer place was that the paper had a pattern of some description and that this pattern made the strips more difficult to match than the blowsy roses in the main bedroom or the striped ticking of the second bedroom. Sometimes you could hear the cursing right down the block.

"Janey!" the doctor shouted now.

Janey Lane picked up the telephone and pushed a button. "There's no need to shout, Doc," she said. "Just push the yellow button."

"Sorry!" the doctor shouted. "I keep forgetting."

"Just hold down the yellow button," Janey said into the telephone. "You don't even have to pick up the phone." She nodded to Nancy McAllister and told her to go in. Everyone else in the office smiled at each other.

"He'll get the hang of it, Janey," Hal Davis (uncle of Park Davis, and the former town pharmacist) said. "No flies on him."

Janey, who seemed to have some kind of a cold, smiled and sniffed.

Janey Lane was known for her composure and her competence. It was, therefore, a shock to everyone in the waiting room when Janey began to stammer on the phone. "Uh, uh, uh, oh!" she said. "I'll get him . . . oh, no, he's with a patient . . . oh, but he'll want to . . . and I presume you'll need Mr. Flory's medical records?"

And then she realized what she had done. The entire waiting room was transfixed.

It was all over town in an hour. Something had happened to Jim Flory.

Janey took her break on the sofa in Lottie's consulting room.

"I'm so sorry," she said, twisting her handkerchief into a rope. "It just slipped out."

Lottie, smiling, sat down and put her arm around Janey's shoulders. "Janey, that's the first mistake you've made in about two years," she chided. "Don't you think you should cut yourself some slack?"

Janey sighed, glancing up at her employer's beautiful face. "I—" she began, but then just repeated, "I'm sorry," as if she had thought better of saying what she'd been about to say.

Lottie smiled again, hugging Janey tightly. "You think Doc and I don't know about relationship problems?" she asked, in that same chiding tone. "You think we don't understand?"

Now it was Janey's turn to smile, a tremulous expression that vanished as soon as it appeared. "Can you make me a spell, Lottie?" she asked.

Lottie's eyes narrowed and her mouth tightened. "What do you need a spell for?"

"I'd like to be as beautiful as Kylie Requena, for starters."

Lottie nodded and stood up. She went to the little kitchen off her room. Janey followed her, watching her put things into the juicer—some potato, some apple, some cucumber and mint. Lottie whirred them through the liquidizer. "Lie down," she said.

Gulping, Janey went to the treatment table and did as she was told. She suddenly felt very cold.

"Close your eyes," Lottie said.

Something cool and moist was first put on her right eye and then another on her left. Then a hot, damp washcloth arrived over them both. Janey could hear Lottie humming something behind her. "Open your mouth, and stick out your tongue," Lottie said.

Janey started to comply and then asked, "What is it?"

Lottie laughed. "Oh, come on, Janey," she said.

Trembling, Janey stuck out her tongue. Something dropped onto it. "Licorice?" she asked.

"And a bit of angelica and feverfew." Lottie held her hand.

"Are you taking my pulse?"

"No, I'm just holding your hand."

Lottie continued humming and Janey began to relax. Whatever it was Lottie had put on her eyes felt wonderful.

Almost too soon, Lottie took off the washcloth and the cotton pads and helped Janey sit up. "I nearly fell asleep," Janey said.

"You'll sleep well tonight," Lottie promised. She went and got a mirror. "Are you ready?" she asked.

Janey gulped again. Now she was more frightened than she had been throughout the entire process. If Lottie had really used witch-craft to change her face, Becky was going to kill her.

Lottie smoothed one strand of hair from Janey's forehead and then stood behind her, so that she could see Janey's reflection as well. Slowly she raised the mirror.

"But I look just the same!" Janey said.

"Of course you do," Lottie replied. "You're every bit as beautiful as Kylie Requena. And you have better feet."

"But what was all that?" Janey pointed to the treatment table.

"Your eyes were red. I thought maybe you weren't looking at yourself properly. So, I put a pack on them. And I gave you some herbs that help clear your mind. Now you can see straight and think straight, too."

Lottie leaned her own head next to Janey's. "Look at those gor-geous eyes," she said. "I've never seen eyes prettier than yours. And you've got a nice, straight nose and a lovely complexion. You've got nice little lips, too, and they're always pink. Can you see all those things, now?"

And the funny thing was, Janey could.

The worst part about fighting with a longtime partner isn't that you miss the romantic side of life. Romance is, in fact, in long-time partnerships, something usually relegated to the "to be done when we get a minute" list and perfectly happily married couples who have been blessed by a family often miss the romantic side of life for years altogether. No, the worst part is that one's wife or husband has also become one's best friend. You've got nobody to talk to.

Pattie was dying to see what Phil thought could have happened to Jim Flory. But Phil didn't even come home for dinner. She had to cook, do the dishes, and bathe three boys, all by herself. While she was in the kitchen, her beloved offspring decided to take all the sofa and chair cushions and build a fort, using Pattie's newly bought and quite expensive chenille throws as roofing material. They'd found missiles in the fruit bowl that she, as a good mother, had left invitingly on the coffee table. The coffee table itself had been used as a barricade, in conjunction with the living room door.

While she was upstairs, scrubbing them clean and corralling them into pajamas and beds (with the usual combination of bribery and brute force) and even when she was reading the rather blood-thirsty pirate adventure they all enjoyed, part of her mind was calculating how long it was going to take her to clean up that unholy mess and wondering if Phil came home if he'd do it.

She needn't have wondered. When she came down, exhausted and half-soaked by her efforts, Phil still wasn't home. She moved the furniture, put the chenille throws in the washer on delicate, scrubbed squished banana out of the carpet, found the exploded throw pillow, and vacuumed up the feathers. And she was busy with the furniture polish and the scratch removing kit on the coffee table when she heard the back door open. Thirty seconds later, she heard footsteps going upstairs.

She waited while she rubbed in the polish with firm circular movements as recommended on the package, but the footsteps didn't come back down. She had homemade burritos sitting in the oven and some nicely seasoned rice ready to warm again in the steamer and a side salad plastic-wrapped in the refrigerator.

But the footsteps didn't come back down.

She moved on to step three of the scratch removal process. But still, no footsteps. Every second that ticked by hurt her.

Maybe he was with the boys. Maybe they'd been up to some devilment upstairs and he'd had to deal with it. She heard the shower go on. Maybe that's all that was keeping him, maybe he was dirty and in a minute he'd come downstairs and they'd talk about it and she'd say she was sorry and so would he.

But the footsteps didn't come back downstairs, even long after the shower went off. They'd been married more than ten years and had dated two before that. Pattie knew how long it took Phil to comb his hair and select the perfect T-shirt and boxer shorts combo for the evening. It was not that long.

The last step was to "admire her healed furniture." Pattie neglected this step, even though the coffee table had recovered remarkably well. She tidied away the polishing kit under the sink and then looked at the oven. Should she turn it off? Should she leave it on?

Pattie went upstairs, listening for clues all the way. It seemed unnaturally silent. Phil wasn't a consciously noisy man, but a man who lived his life mainly out of doors was always a bit noisier than a man who did not. Phil didn't seem aware of how a drawer could be shut quietly, or how to get out of bed without swinging his legs and landing with both feet in a sort of jump. And there was nothing, nothing of this in what Pattie heard. She looked in their bedroom and then continued up to the third floor.

The guest room light was on. Pattie hesitated and then knocked at it softly. She heard Phil jump up from the bed and then he opened the door a fraction, wedging his body in the crack. "Yes?" he asked coldly.

Pattie felt her mouth go dry. "I, um," she said. "I, um, left you some dinner downstairs. . . . Do you want me to . . ."

"I already ate," Phil said. His eyes would not meet hers and he seemed to be holding something behind his back.

Pattie grinned weakly. She said, "It sure was hard looking after those three on my own and making dinner, too, tonight. They just about wrecked the living room."

Phil's eyes grew hard and cold and met hers without flinching. "Well, I guess that's what it's like without me to help," he said.

Every night, Pattie thought. He's going to make me go through this every night. Just to prove some kind of point.

"Yeah," she said. "I guess so." She tried hard not to cry, and just managed it. She took a deep breath. "So you won't be wanting any dinner."

"No," Phil said.

Pattie turned to walk to the stairs. But then she turned back. "They're your kids, too, you know," she said. "You have a responsibility."

"Fine," he said. "I'll do tomorrow night." And he shut the door.

Pattie walked down to their bedroom, which seemed abnormally tidy. Phil's work clothes weren't on the floor. His drawers weren't open. She went to his dresser and opened it.

It was empty.

News, or what is considered "real" news in Eudora, does not generally come from public sources. There is no newspaper in the town, and though the weekly in the county seat covers Eudora's game scores and weddings, it seldom interests itself in any other affairs. The nearest radio station is in the city, forty-five miles away, and the television stations are there, too. As for the national press and media, after a brief and heady period during the quarry take-over, Eudora ceased to exist in the national consciousness.

Faced with such persistent and endemic neglect, the town took a pragmatic attitude. The rest of the world ignored Eudora and so

Eudora largely ignored the rest of the world. It took something big happening outside the city boundaries to really register and even then, interest faded quickly. There was always just so much else going on.

In fact, during the space of this chronicle, Eudora is at war. While Jim Flory recovers from the surgery on his ruptured spleen, while Phil Walker is residing in the spare room and Mark Ramirez pines for Janey Lane, while Chuck undergoes his midlife crisis and Jim Evans is deep into his desperate plot, Eudora is at war.

If you look closely, you can see flags still adorning many houses and businesses and faded yellow ribbons around the waists of some of the trees. The county paper had published free posters saying WE SUPPORT OUR TROOPS and some people still had theirs in a window, though they had fared poorly in last summer's sun and now read WSOT in large pink letters on a uniformly brown background.

Anyone gullible enough to have believed Merve and Stan's warning, at the county seat True Value Hardware store, to seal their doors and windows against chemical missiles had long since come to their senses and removed what they now knew to be rather overpriced duct tape and plastic sheeting. The old guys in the round booth at the diner had finally stopped laughing about it, though they had made Merve and Stan's customers feel stupid for a good eighteen months after the sale had been rung up.

For though Eudora knew itself to be at war, it hadn't felt any immediate effect. They were some eleven hundred miles from the nearest border. Their immigrant population was, actually, about half of the total population, which formed a community of that comfortable size that can notice a strange face instantly. There had been, when war was first declared, a sense of heightened alertness. But even then, the unlikelihood of an invasion or infiltration beginning in Eudora had been apparent even to the most uneducated and fervent of the townspeople.

In the last two years, much had changed in Eudora. Maria

Lopez, proprietor of Mayan Memories, had often thought about this as she fed little William. Even now, though he had taken feeding into his own hands (and onto the floor, walls, and ceiling), she often considered it as she watched him in what was still his fitful baby sleep.

When she was growing up in Eudora, she had been invisible. They all had. The entire Mexican American community traded mainly at back doors and parked in the alleys of Main Street. They had their own medical adviser and although they went to the same schools, there had never been a brown face on the cheerleading squad, nominated for Homecoming Queen, or quarterbacking the Cyclones.

But all that had changed, and changed so quickly and thoroughly that Maria herself could hardly believe it. Now they had a Latino mayor, the people of the town owned the quarry, and three of the businesses downtown were either owned or managed by Mexican immigrants. Young William, thought Maria, could go anywhere, become anything. He'd never know the concept of having limitations imposed on his dreams. He'd never have anyone look right through him.

The rocker in William's room was comfortable. Maria often sat there for a while when she got home from work. She only worked five days a week now, and never worked a full day. She'd drop William off at Candy Cane Day Care about ten, work through lunch and oversee prep for dinner, while she pored over the books and receipts at a table, occasionally making a phone call. Then she'd greet and take the orders of most of the guests herself. But she was home by nine. Home, showered, and ready to sit and look at William sleep, before she maybe watched a little television or caught up on the ironing, or read a little more of *The Vortex*.

Of course, even while she was stocking napkins or calling the produce people to ask them how they could call the slime they'd sent the previous week "cilantro," she was still thinking about

William, about what he was doing right then. He was waking up from his nap, he was having his snack, he was doing his dance moves, he was being read a story, then playing with blocks while he waited for Daddy. Then Bill was there, and William's little eyes would light up and he would clap his hands. And then Bill would lift him up, and remember William's bag and fleece and take it all to the truck and strap William in. Now William was watching television on the big bed, while Bill had his shower. Then William was playing with Daddy (and you never had any idea what they would think of doing: sometimes Maria wondered which one was supposed to be the adult). And now William was having his dinner. And now, just as she might be chatting to a table from the city or carrying out a tray of main courses, William had fallen asleep.

Of course, it hurt a little. Every moment she wasn't with him hurt a little. But she wasn't going to be able to be with him all his life. And he was happy. And he was going to be a lot happier in the future because Mama was a smart woman with her own healthy business.

Bill seemed to understand it all. They never even had to talk it out. He never minded that she sat up there in the rocker, sometimes for hours, just watching William toss and turn and mutter. Watching his little fingers make fists and then relax. Watching his face get all scrunched up and then smooth out again. Sometimes she woke up in the chair at three or four in the morning and had to creep into her own bed.

But tonight she was writing an email.

Maria didn't mind writing. Bill would rather chew his arm off than write a letter and for the entirety of their marriage she had signed every birthday card to his mother and every Christmas card to his workmates. But Maria didn't mind. She rather liked writing letters and messages. She just relaxed and thought about what was happening in her life and let the words flow.

This email was, however, different. Kylie Requena's brother,

Bruce, had been in Tigrit, a town northwest of Baghdad, for nearly two years. At first, he had been excited and he had always had something to say about his training on the trucks, about the people he was meeting, about the landscape and all the kinds of lizards he'd found. But now, in his emails, he didn't say much, he just kept asking for news from home. Maria thought she'd become pretty good at keeping him up on the gossip. He said her letters nearly made up for the meatloaf.

Just as she got settled in the chair and switched on the computer, the phone rang. It was Pattie.

"You doing anything?" Pattie asked.

Maria hesitated before answering. "Um . . . why?"

Now it was Pattie's turn to hesitate. "Oh . . . well . . . Phil's on child care duty and I was just wondering if I could come over for a minute."

Maria could tell there was something wrong, but then, Pattie often had something wrong. She had that kind of complicated life when things went wrong all the time. It was probably Carla. Things weren't going so well at the Fabric Shack with Carla. She looked at her computer and at the clock. She was going to have to choose. "Well—" she started to say.

"Oh, if it's a hassle, forget it," Pattie said brightly. "I know how busy you are. I'll catch you later."

For a moment, while the computer blipped and whirred into life and connectivity, Maria wondered if she'd done the right thing. But then she was writing to that poor boy, and she knew she'd got her priorities right.

In the Ben Nichols household, meatloaf was something to celebrate. In fact, Molly Nichols made the best meatloaf in town, even better than Zadie Gross at Gross Home Cooking. And so, when Molly planned to make meatloaf, she picked a night and invited the whole family over. Ben's dad, Henry, drove in from the lake and Lane and Denise Nichols brought over their two rugrats, Lane arriving a little late because some of his high-school-aged help had let him down at the garage.

Ben and Lane had not been particularly close as brothers. Ben and Lane were much the same ages as Artie and Phil, respectively, but had never had their close relationship. Ben had always envied Artie and Phil their companionship and easy banter. Lane had seemed remote and defensive to Ben all through their very separate childhoods and well into their equally separate adulthoods.

But something about his occupation had drawn him out. Since Lane took over the ownership of the gas station, and spoke to everyone in town once a week or so, he'd opened up. And since Ben had married Molly and had Tommy, Lane had seemed warmer, more interested in his brother. It was as if by becoming a husband and a father, Ben had somehow closed the two-year gap between them.

Although he'd never admit it, Ben looked forward to seeing Lane at things like this. They'd get into a little corner and hang out and talk. And sure enough, when Lane finally arrived and got his plate, he came and sat down by Ben. But he hardly said a word. Ben kept bringing up conversational topics and Lane kept letting them drop. Ben was just about to take offense when he noticed Lane's bottom lip. Lane had a bad childhood habit of chewing on his bottom lip, to which he only resorted in times of great anxiety. And there it was, a whole red raw strip on one corner.

"What's the matter?" Ben asked. "What's going on? Is it Denise? One of the kids?"

Lane didn't attempt to deny that he was worried, but he shook his head. "No," he said, "it's nothing like that."

But he didn't say anything else.

Ben didn't like this. This asking questions business was a little humiliating. He resolved not to say more about it. If Lane wanted to tell him, that was Lane's decision. Ben wasn't going to frisk around his ankles like a puppy, begging for his confidences.

He lasted about thirty seconds. "Is it the business?" he asked.

Lane took a big gulp of iced tea and then made a face. He hated artificial sweetener, and Molly never remembered. "None of these kids are as good as Bruce. Bruce never made me wait on him. He always showed up on time. Even one day when he had the flu and was shaking and shivering, he showed up for his shift, by God."

Ben's brow furrowed. "Are you talking about Bruce Requena? You *miss* Bruce Requena?"

Lane nodded. "Best damn worker I ever had."

"But I thought he was a pest, always hanging around, using the tools on his banger, and—"

"Hell, they all do that," Lane interrupted. "They all think they're just about ready to crew at Nascar. No. Bruce was a good kid. *Is* a good kid. Man, now, of course."

Ben thought for a moment. "Didn't he enlist?"

Lane stood up so fast he nearly knocked over his tea. "I don't want to talk about it," he said. He walked away, chewing his bottom lip furiously.

Pattie Walker didn't do all the laundry in the basket. She did her clothes and the boys' stuff, but she left Phil's. She thought about it for a long time, but in the end, she left them.

It was strange, having Phil in charge of dinner while she skulked upstairs. She came out to kiss the boys goodnight, once they had been forcibly settled in their beds, and then went down the stairs as Phil went up. He'd brought home some of those deli pizzas from Food Barn for dinner, but not enough for her. There was one slice left of his favorite "MeatyHottie" and no pineapple and ham at all. She'd have to cook for herself; well, make a salad, anyway.

She wouldn't have even done that, except for the baby. Her tastebuds seemed to have stopped working. Even her favorite lime and chili salad dressing recipe had no zing. It just burned her tongue a bit on the edge without any lime coming through at all.

Pattie was miserable, so unhappy she thought she might die from misery. She had loved Phil Walker all the way through grade school and high school, loved him in a doomed, fatalistic way. She never thought she would stand a chance with someone so glamorous and good. But she had, and she'd played her cards right and she'd landed him.

And he'd loved her, too. He'd loved Pattie Dougal from a strange and broken home, even though she wasn't as beautiful as her sister or very smart or even a very good cook. He'd loved her anyway. And now, with just one tiny word, she'd made him not love her anymore.

The children and the house seemed to mock her. These were the things she thought had protected her from this misery, this inevitable moment of despair. But now she knew, as she had known from the moment she watched Phil Walker skin the cat on the Eudora Grade School jungle gym (long since removed for safety reasons), that she was not good enough for Phil. A broken heart had been inevitable. Because she hadn't turned away then, she was aching now. She'd known it then, known it would happen. But she had been unable to stop looking at him, so vital in his striped T-shirt, so clean and big and bright. Phil Walker was just too wonderful for Pattie Dougal.

Since that day, this pain had been biding its time. She'd known it would get her in the end. And now it had.

She couldn't bear to touch his clothes, to smell him on them. She might completely break down. And besides, what good was it, to do these little things? Clean? Do laundry? Bake sugar cookies and ice them with summer scenes for the end-of-year bake sale?

Nobody noticed. It didn't make anyone love you. It didn't make you safe. It didn't make you as clean and big and bright as Phil Walker. It didn't make you wonderful, if you were just ordinary.

Pattie's back hurt and her mouth was dry. She was tired. If she could, she would have just run away. Maybe if she wasn't pregnant, she would have just emptied the bank accounts and gone to . . . where do people go? Mexico or India or someplace. The boys would be all right with Phil. They'd probably be happier without her, the way she was these days.

She could just cry and cry wherever she went. She could be all by herself and far away from him and just sit on a beach and cry into the sea.

But how could she run away from her family when she was carrying one of them inside her?

Pattie Walker had to drag herself up the stairs and into bed. She had to force herself to brush her teeth and wash her face. She didn't moisturize. She didn't even read a chapter. She just shut her eyes and welcomed oblivion.

"Well it just about made me sick. I mean, really physically sick," Zadie Gross said. She was presiding over the early breakfast service with Becky Lane while Manuel Bustamonte manned the grill. She had a pot of regular in one hand and a pot of decaf in the other.

The literary society was back in session, discussing, of course, *The Vortex* by Margaret Lupin.

"When those policemen started imagining what they were going to do to the girls on the marijuana farm. They were so horrible! And saying that they'd get away with it, because who would believe a hippie chick. . . ." Zadie shivered. "It just made me feel sick."

"It's horrible," Nancy McAllister said. She was having breakfast with Clement and Hector Rodriguez. Clement was talking business with Hector before the bank opened, because Hector was taking a few big meetings today about the quarry pension fund while Clement and Nancy drove into the city for an appointment at the big hospital. "Horrible," she repeated. "What that pusher character did to Jules, making her"—the next two words were uttered in a low tone—"have sex"—and then at her usual volume—"with that cocaine dealer while he watched." Nancy shuddered. "And if that's really"—again, she lowered her voice—"Janine Lupin . . ."

Zadie leaned closer. "I know," she said. And meaningful glances were exchanged.

That was the main topic of discussion in the diner that morning. If the Jules character was really Janine Lupin, how *could* Margaret Lupin have written about her being degraded in that way in a book? What kind of sister would do that? What kind of an aunt would do that to her nieces and nephews?

From five o'clock all the way through to seven, there was hardly another topic of conversation. Zadie lost track of the number of times people asked her, in a casual, roundabout sort of way, if she'd talked to Margery Lupin about it. Finally she'd announced, loud enough to be heard over the clatter of forks and cups, "Any of you guys want to ask Margery Lupin about that book, the bakery's open, you just go on down." Whereupon her customers grew extremely interested in the contents of their plates.

"Exactly," Zadie said. "I don't want to ask her, either."

At eight o'clock Janey Lane came through the door, clutching a piece of paper. Something about her face made conversation stop. Becky Lane slowly put the last short stack in her hand in front of the customer and said, "Honey, what's the matter?"

Janey's bottom lip wobbled. "Mommy? I gotta go to Iraq."

There had been a certain coolness between Pattie Walker and Becky Lane ever since Becky Lane had left Pattie's employ. In fact, there had been a bit of a coolness long before that, when Mr. Dougal had died and Pattie had asked Lottie to come home and run the stationery store instead of running it herself and having Becky manage the Fabric Shack. But lately, there were signs of a thaw.

The fact was, they missed each other. Becky and Zadie got along really well, of course, but Zadie didn't enter into Becky's parental concerns. And from Pattie's point of view, the longer she worked with Carla Bustamonte, the more she appreciated Becky

Lane. They had weathered many crises in each other's company, both personal and professional.

And so perhaps it was natural that soon after Janey Lane pulled herself together and went to work and Becky began to fall apart, that Becky should find herself drawn to the Fabric Shack's back room.

Pattie hadn't heard a knock at the back door for many months, but when she opened it and found Becky there, shaking and crying, she drew her inside, sat her down, and flipped the coffee pot on in a smooth series of economic movements. Carla was (for once) there, but there were no customers; for the time being, anyway.

Pattie put her arm around Becky and Becky poured out the whole story: " . . . and they've said they're going to wait, but I don't think they have and you know Mark is real Catholic in the contraception department, so I'm worried about *that* and I know she is. But Mark says they need to save up a deposit on the house. I sure can't help them and the insurance money Mark got when his folks died is pretty much all used up just from keeping him in food and clothes through high school. They're both making good money, but they've got to do everything right, you know, they have to have a nice ring to get engaged and they have to have a house big enough for a family to get married, and I kind of see their point. You maybe could have a baby in that house your daddy built, but once it was walking, you'd be going crazy. So it seemed like a real good idea when her and Mark signed up with the National Guard, because all that money went right into their savings account." She broke off for a minute to see if Pattie was following her. Pattie nodded.

"So that's what they did and they both thought it was fun because, you know, they're both fit and they liked the running and all that being active. And Janey even thought it was fun learning how to . . . to . . . shoot a rifle—" Here Becky abruptly stopped speaking and just sobbed.

Carla came into the room. "Do you think we can get more of that red-flowered rayon?" she asked in a business-like tone. "Martina wants four yards of it for a dress and there's only three left on the roll."

When Pattie looked up there were tears in her eyes. "Yes," she said hoarsely and then said, "Yes," again, less hoarsely. "But it will take a week. Tell her not to buy the three now and start the dress because another batch might not match perfectly."

Carla was now peering over the cupboards and shelves to identify the sobbing visitor. "Okay," she said. She left reluctantly.

"Is Mark going, too?" Pattie asked.

Becky shook her head. "No. There's two bunches of them, and they put them each in one of the bunches. Mark and Janey used to laugh about it . . . " She winced at the memory. "They used to . . . you know . . . fight each other in exercises and games and stuff." She sighed, a horrible, shuddering sound, and blew her nose again. "They're only taking Janey's bunch." She sighed again. "I'm going to kill him."

"Oh, Becky, I'm so sorry." Pattie cast about for something to say, something positive. Not two years earlier she had put one of the troop support signs in her window. But now, the idea of saying something uplifting and patriotic seemed crass and stupid. "Is there any way she can get out of it?"

Becky shook her head. "I don't think so," she said sadly.

Pattie poured the coffee and put the low-fat cream and a spoonful of sweetener in Becky's. "Here," she said.

"Thanks." Becky dabbed at her eyes. "I must look a mess," she said.

"You look fine."

"You know, I came here on autopilot."

"I'm glad you did." The two women looked at each other for a moment and Pattie put her arm around Becky's shoulders again and gave her a squeeze. With her free hand, she wiped her own eyes. "I hope I haven't been nasty to you, Becky. I just miss you here so much. . . ."

"It's okay," Becky said. "But I couldn't stay. I've got a share in the diner."

Pattie nodded her glossy head, a gesture that she supplemented with "I know," and a sniff. "I should have offered you a share here. I don't know what I was thinking."

Becky took a deep breath. "That's so good to hear. Thank you," she said.

Carla came back into the store room. "You guys okay back here? You need anything?" Carla was a true Eudoran and was, of course, dying of curiosity.

Pattie looked at Becky, and Becky indicated that she could go ahead. "Janey Lane's been called up. She's the first soldier in Eudora to go to Iraq."

Carla said, "I'm sorry to hear about Janey. That's too bad. But she's not the first soldier to go to Iraq. Bruce Requena's been in Tigrit for over a year, now."

Jim Evans was acting strangely. When he didn't sow his winter wheat, people out at the Coop thought he was getting old and thinking about selling. But then, no notice of sale had appeared. He turned four good wheatfields into pasture and ran a few scrawny steers on it even though he'd been completely arable for thirty years. He missed the milo season and didn't participate in oats, barley, or soybeans, either. Then he bought some seedcorn but no pesticides or herbicides. He was using a nonchemical fertilizer.

Well, folks thought, he's going organic. Some of the old boys did, just like the young men who talked about niche markets and maximizing potential by concentrating on quality. Some of the old guys just said it was the right way to farm and they remembered how to do it and if it tripled the price for half the yield, they could live with that.

But when one of these young thrusters, Lance Bumgartner, asked Jim which grant he'd applied for and if he was going on the three- or the six-year plan, Jim just looked at him and asked what in the Sam Heck he was talking about.

So no one knew what was going on at the Evans place. And after a while, this grew intolerable.

Jim and Mary Evans mixed. She was, of course, a staunch member of the Baptist Church, and had presided over many a committee meeting. In her sunset years, she declined office, but still produced pies, fried chicken, or ice cream as needed. She was a formidable quilter, even now, and met with her fellow crafts-women at the Arts Center with great frequency (maintaining, on the vexed subject of hand versus machine piecing and quilting, a need-based medical perspective based on the quilter's arthritic condition). And then she was a volunteer for several civic events, and had retained the post of organizer/fundraiser for the famous Maple Leaf Festival Breakfast on the Prairie (which, with the propane stoves and the tents, the transport and hygiene issues, and the thousands of paper plates, was a nightmare burden no other woman contemplated shouldering).

Jim himself, while less organized in his social life, was still to be seen frequently in town. He was a charter member of the brother-hood that arrived midmorning at the diner, having already done what would seem like a full day's work to most of the townspeople, and have a cup of coffee. He did most of the day-to-day shopping for Mary while he was there. He got around. He kept up with things.

But they didn't visit much. It was partly because their only child had died young. And it was partly because Mary's family was still back in Virginia and hardly knew she existed, now that her last sib-ling had passed on. Then, too, Jim's brother had not made it through World War Two, and Jim's father had faded soon after. Mrs. Evans had hung on another twenty years, but the rest of the Evanses kind of evaporated with old Mr. Evans's death. It had been like a stone thrown in a flock of crows. They had all whirled away in separate directions.

There had been a reason why Mary did so much for the church. There wasn't anybody or anything else for her to do things for.

And because they didn't visit much, people didn't visit them. In fact, if Jim and Mary had been a trifle more integrated into that give and take, that lending and borrowing that often characterizes social intercourse in farming communities, Jim might never have taken his crazy chance. But Jim had been one of your self-sufficient types. He kept his tools hung up on a pegboard with a magic marker outline drawn around each implement.

It is a discouraging thing to borrow, say, a ball-peen hammer in such circumstances. The naked outline of the hammer Jim had put in your hands would be filled only with a manila luggage tag bearing your own name and the date. It all looked a bit forensic and somehow the sense of sharing was absent. Even though the hammer was going home in your truck, you knew that it would bother you until you brought it back.

So, though things at the Evanses' place clearly required investigation, nobody wanted to be the one to investigate. Until Jim bought an extraordinary amount of irrigation tubing and Phil Walker and Chuck Warren began their unprecedented visits.

Every other afternoon, like clockwork, Phil and Chuck drove too fast down the gravel in Phil's truck, straight to the Evanses' place. They were smiling and had the air off and their arms sticking out. The last time they drove by, they were singing along to the car radio. John Denver's "Thank God I'm a Country Boy." You could hear it for miles—and many folks did.

The Barfords (George, Dorothy, and their son Blaine and his wife, Candy) had gathered on the front porch to watch the grandkids do some Irish dancing when this exhibition flashed by. Dorothy screwed up her mouth and shook her head before voicing the concerns of all.

"That's different," she said.

"No, *Mark*," Becky Lane said, heavily accenting his name with sarcasm, "they won't take you instead."

Mark Ramirez sank down on the high stool behind the cash register at the stationery store. Becky, still in her uniform, was pleased to see the blood drain from his face. "I thought it was safe," he said. "They'd already served in Afghanistan. I didn't think there was any way they'd get called out again."

He looked at Becky, his eyes wide and his forehead creased. "You've got to believe me, Mama Lane," he said. "I wouldn't lie to you. I would never do anything to hurt Janey."

Becky began to cry again. "Well, why are you tomcatting around with Kylie Requena? Why are you buying a car instead of an engagement ring?"

"What?" Mark looked at Becky as if she were insane. "It's a company car! I'm not spending any of the ring money. And Kylie and I have been friends for a long time. She wanted to talk to me about her brother."

"Just buy Janey the damn ring, Mark. Set a date. That's all she wants." Becky dashed away more tears with the back of her hand. Mark pulled off some of the roll of tissue they used to clean the glass counter and handed it to her wordlessly. "It's all such a mess," she said.

Mark came around the counter and put his arms around Becky. "I'm sorry," he said. "I'll fix it somehow. It'll be all right."

Becky leaned her head on his arm. This was not the way she had expected the interview to go. "I don't want to lose you, either," she said, giggling as she sniffed again.

"Nobody," Mark said heroically, "is going to lose anybody."

▪ ▪ ▪

So it had been with the best of intentions that Mark had called at the Lane family residence that Friday night. Linda Lane, Janey's older sister, answered the door. "She's in her room," Linda said. "She's expecting you." Linda's tone of voice made it clear that she personally considered this expectation a vain one.

Mark had not brought a dozen red roses. He'd brought half a dozen yellow ones, mixed in with black-eyed Susans, some greenery and some baby's breath. The lady out at Food Barn had been really helpful. Linda sniffed when she saw them. "Pretty," she said coldly.

"Where's Mama Lane?" Mark asked, uncomfortable with Linda's quelling demeanor.

"We talked her into laying down," Linda said. "She couldn't stop crying."

Mark had changed into his weekend wear, but knowing Becky Lane was crying made him feel as if he was still wearing a collar and tie and that they were a size too small. "I'll . . ." he said, and his voice felt choked. "I'll just go to see Janey."

Later, Linda confided to her colleagues at the bank that she had never had any great hopes for this conversation. Later, Mark confided to his friends at Mayan Memories that it was no wonder Linda Lane remained single.

He knocked briefly at Janey's door before opening it. When most people's eyes look sad, they look red and they get dark circles underneath. Janey's just had a moist luminescence that made them glow. Mark said later that when he looked at her that night, he suddenly felt humble. Her eyes had such purity. If they were the windows of her soul, then Janey clearly had a great soul. Before her, he felt small and unworthy.

"I, uh," he began. "I was, uh, thinking that we could maybe take a walk and go see the softball?"

Janey, who'd had enough of sitting in her room by now, nodded and pulled on her shoes before he'd even finished his sentence. On their way out, Janey asked Linda if she wouldn't mind putting the flowers in some water. Grimly Linda assented.

It was a nice evening, still light, of course, and a bit breezy. They walked a block or so in silence. Mark reached for Janey's hand and she let him take it, even welcoming his touch with a slight squeeze of her own.

He stopped and faced her. A strand of her hair had caught on her lips and he coaxed it back from her face. He looked down at their feet, standing together on a square of pavement, and thought that's what it was really like, it was like they were on some kind of a raft together in the middle of an unforgiving sea. He thought that if he had to step off that raft, he would be lost.

He said, "I was so sorry to hear about—"

But she stopped him. "It's not your fault," she said.

He nodded. "I called the unit," he said. "I asked if I could go in your place, but—"

A flash of irritation passed over her face and she exhaled her exasperation. "Now, why did you do that, Mark? You've just made us both look like idiots."

"Because it's all my fault," he said simply. "And because if anything happens to you, I . . . I don't know what I'd do."

Janey took a deep breath. "You know, I'm getting a bit tired of reassuring other people. I kind of hoped you'd reassure me, instead."

Mark didn't really listen to this. He heard it, and recalled it later, but he didn't pay any attention to it at the time. When he did report it later, to Maria Lopez, telling her what he said next, she hit him on the side of his head with a folded dishtowel.

"You are everything to me, Janey. I love you with all my heart." It was a bit early in the evening for this, but Mark felt the time had come and he was a flexible man. He knelt down on the pavement square and fumbled in the pocket of his Dockers.

("You didn't?" Maria gasped when she heard. "You're *loco completamente*.")

"Marry me, Janey," he said. "Marry me before you have to go."

Janey Lane narrowed her beautiful eyes and considered him for a moment. Suddenly she seemed nearly as cold as her older sister. "Let me get this straight," she said, and Mark already knew that it was unlikely his efforts were to be crowned with success. At this point, flowers received and proposal uttered, Janey was meant to be nestling in his arms. Not folding hers and looking down on him as if he were an interesting bug on a pin.

"Let me get this straight," she said. "You feel guilty about me getting called up. So now you think we can afford to get married after all."

Though he knew it was the wrong thing to do, Mark nevertheless proffered the little black velvet box. When he opened it, the world grew so quiet that the little hinge creaked.

Janey nodded, swallowing and pursing her lips. "Nice," she said. "So we went into the National Guard to save up money. And we waited to get married until we did. And you didn't want to buy an engagement ring or even announce our engagement until you had saved up for a party and the ring and it had to be a nice, big ring. Three months' salary." Mark noticed that Janey's voice was rising in both pitch and volume.

"And now you've been caught canoodling with Kylie and I've been called up and you feel so guilty that you've finally discovered a use for your Visa card." She swallowed again and her eyes filled with tears.

Mark reached for her hand, attempting to wrestle the ring onto her finger. He felt at the time—he explained later to Linda's and Maria's moans of despair—that if he could only get her to accept the ring, everything else would sort itself out.

Janey took the ring away from him and threw it into the road.

Maria said that if he had ignored it and had thrown down the box, too, and just kissed her, right then and there, he could have saved the day. But of course, he ran out to get the ring before someone ran over it.

And when he turned around, Janey Lane was gone. The square of pavement she'd been standing on was empty. He couldn't even be sure which one it had been. Now the whole world was only the unforgiving sea.

Jim Flory came home in an ambulance on Sunday. Bob's Audi followed.

This had been expected. Jim's car had arrived on Saturday, driven by a nameless visitor wearing a Ralph Lauren polo shirt and crisp walking shorts. Bob's Audi had followed then, too. Groceries had been unloaded from the trunk, along with bags from pharmacies and department stores. It was noted by Artie Walker (the sunshade on May's stroller happened to need a bit of adjustment at that crucial moment, as Artie returned from taking the two-year-old for their customary Saturday morning breakfast) that Bob opened the Flory place with a key on his own fob, not the key with the green plastic frog's head that was ordinarily granted to Jim's visitors.

Windows were opened. A vacuum cleaner hummed. The man in the natty shorts and deck shoes did the windows, using the ladder for the second story but not the third floor. There, he climbed out of the windows.

They evidently stopped for lunch, and midafternoon a delivery vehicle had brought a hospital bed and some other equipment. Shortly thereafter, passersby could hear the sound of someone drilling inside competing with the sound of Bob pushing the lawnmower outside. Not long after this, Bob and the unknown natty visitor (still remarkably natty considering he'd helped with the yardwork as well as the housework) hopped back into the Audi and sped away.

It was an impressive preparation for what was, in fact, a low-key return. Late on Sunday afternoon, Jim Flory arrived, looking bent and pale. One leg was in a walking cast, but the big silver crutch seemed to hurt him—after a few steps, the ambulance staff took it away and half carried him through the door.

Now, usually, in such circumstances, Eudora knows what to do. Casseroles and pies are baked. Salads are mixed, put in large bowls with plastic wrap over the top and carefully transported. Cards and flowers are brought to the door in profusion. No one needs to teach Eudora anything about rallying around.

But there was hesitation in the way they rallied this time.

Lottie Emery and the doctor brought a dish of lemon chicken and couscous. Maria Lopez ran over with some caldo. Pattie Walker brought a big tray of her soft oatmeal cookies and Phil Walker brought a potato salad on the same day, but at different times. But then it kind of petered out.

The problem was, of course, Bob. If Jim had been able to look after himself, well, he wouldn't have been able to move for all the Jell-O molds and green bean casseroles. But when you knew that you'd have to talk to Bob . . . well . . . you might not be sure what you could say to the guy. The second day, all that was delivered to the Flory place was an extra meatloaf Zadie made and sent over with Manuel Bustamonte (who complained bitterly at first but then was received so graciously with a glass of iced tea and a soft oatmeal cookie that he volunteered to go again in a couple of days with a tuna noodle casserole).

On the third day, Bob walked the length of downtown. First he went all the way down to Maple Leaf Pharmacy, and Park Davis filled orders for painkillers, dressings, and antibiotics, while Bob collected a basket of Jim Flory's favorite face creams, mud packs, and exfoliators. Not that the pharmacist would ever have told, but Mark Ramirez was behind Bob in line and told Maria Lopez at lunch.

Bob stepped into Mayan Memories and thanked Maria for the caldo, collecting a take-out menu on the trip. These exertions must have made him hungry, because he then stopped at the bakery, had a cherry bear claw and a latte and read *USA Today*. Odie Marsh, upon hearing this, said he was surprised at the cherry bear claw and had figured Bob would have preferred a cream-filled long john. This was considered to be a terribly crude remark, but it was so repeated that by dinnertime the whole community had heard the joke and had commented on how crude and unnecessary it had been.

Bob made an appointment with Janey Lane for Doc Emery to visit Jim, got three novels from the library (mysteries), and withdrew two hundred dollars from Jim's account.

He was quite an ordinary-looking man. Tall, a little chubby, balding and graying. Handsome, but not flashily so. He was soft-spoken and polite. He had made his purchases selectively and with due care to economy and value. Eudora would have ordinarily liked someone like Bob. It was unfortunate he just happened to be impossible to befriend.

Carla Bustamonte was a treasure. She knew fabric and could sew like a dream. She was, therefore, well qualified to give customers advice and the front window mannequins had never been so well dressed. Every pattern she made up sold out within days.

Eudorans are crafty. They like to make their own decorations. And they are frugal. Even teenaged girls in Eudora were more likely to spend ten or twelve dollars on fabric and a zipper and construct their own scandalously short skirt than buy one ready-made. And then you had the county seat customers, who had lost their fabric store during the Wal-Mart years, and who now had to drive all the way to Eudora to get just the right thing for their weddings, proms, and summer dresses.

And so, while the Fabric Shack was never going to be a big money spinner, it made enough to support the manager and assistant in relative comfort, especially when the assistant was allowed to live rent-free in the small apartment above the shop, as was Carla Bustamonte.

Seamstresses are always in some demand, especially from working women, and Carla was both more and less than a mere seamstress. She was a dress designer, had a degree in it, and had worked in New York City and everything. Her wedding dresses were exquisite and unusual and had been popular among the Mexican American community for four or five years. When Lottie Emery wore one (an ivory blush satin affair that looked as though it had belonged to a 1930s movie star) to St. Anthony of Padua for her wedding to the doctor, the rest of Eudora also became aware of Carla's talents.

So, the upstairs of the Fabric Shack was nearly as full of fabric and sewing as the downstairs, and Carla frequently worked half the night on one of her creations. At times, she was so behind, she begged Pattie for a day off. At times she did not beg and worked until she was ill. And so had *more* days off.

There's always a catch with treasure.

Now, if things had not gone so wrong between Pattie and Phil, things might have continued in this way at the Shack for years. But on the day of Pattie's second ultrasound, Pattie was feeling nervous enough, what with not knowing if Phil was going to show and everything. So when Carla called down the stairs and asked if Pattie would mind if she kept working upstairs for a couple more hours, Pattie simply lost it.

She had not lost it with Phil. She had not lost it with Maria, who should, she felt, have been more in touch and realized all was not well with her best friend. She had not lost it with Lottie or with the various people who had come into the shop and quoted Leviticus and St. Paul after she had visited the Flory place with soft oatmeal cookies. But she sure lost it with Carla.

Carla, halfway down the stairs, was aghast. It was, she said later to her cousin Linda Bustamonte and to Maria Lopez, like she was trying to talk to an alien who had taken over Pattie's body. Pattie was red in the face, shouting and screaming and accusing Carla of trying to kill her, and Carla was just standing there with one foot on one step and the other on the other step and her pincushion wristband still on, just kind of frozen.

But when Pattie started to cry and sat right down in the middle of the aisle, Carla said she felt like she just had to go and help her. Carla practically carried Pattie into the back room and ran to put the BACK IN FIVE MINUTES sign on the door before going back to her employer.

Pattie was at that stage of losing one's temper when one is bitterly ashamed. Carla sat patiently, passing Kleenex, until Pattie started to tell Carla things Carla hadn't known.

Carla didn't know Pattie was pregnant. Once she heard this, she immediately forgave Pattie and discounted all of Pattie's previous invective. Carla didn't know Phil was sleeping in the spare room. Carla hadn't known it was the day of Pattie's ultrasound. Pattie had told her it was a teeth-cleaning appointment.

A mere five minutes earlier, Carla could only think about how quickly she could pack her things. But now she found herself apologizing to Pattie, which made Pattie cry harder and tell her not to be so nice, she didn't deserve it.

We are not certain whose idea it was to merge the two businesses. Accounts from Pattie and Carla do not make it clear. But at this point, as frequently happens in the company of ladies when the air is cleared, old grievances were aired by each party, in explanation of past behaviors and resentments. Pattie was upset that she didn't get to do any sewing. Carla was ticked off not to get more of a discount, when she was not only an employee but Pattie's best customer. They were both mad that they had not managed the workloads in their respective businesses better, as often Carla's high seasons were Pattie's low seasons, and vice versa.

It was not long into this conversation, however, that they both confessed that they hated the name Fabric Shack and that a lot of their craft supplies could more easily fit into the stationery store's inventory. Pattie mentioned that she owned part interest in a printing company in the county seat, if Carla wanted to do some leaflets. Carla confessed she'd begun to expand her wedding dress business to the Latino community in the city and that leaflets might be quite handy.

Pattie went to her sonogram in a thoughtful frame of mind, leaving a promise to help Carla with some beadwork upon her return. And the store was opened again.

When worried or upset, Janey Lane threw herself into her work. When her mother, Becky, had found that lump last year that turned out to be a cyst, Janey had created the cross-referencing patient record system that worked with the practice search engine, using keywords and phrases. When her sister, Linda, had indulged in a brief affair with a married man in the county seat, Janey had attacked Lottie's haphazard storage system for twigs, branches, and leaves, adapting industrial restaurant fittings to hang some things and using some lab equipment to allow storage with air flow of others. Now all of Lottie's supplies were neatly separated and labeled.

But this new problem was a difficult one. Janey was worried about the doctor, who was increasingly irritable, especially in the mornings.

Doc had never been what you call a morning person, but usually a cappuccino or four would set him right, especially if Lottie wasn't downstairs and he could hook a couple of donuts from the box in the waiting room. But now his first cappuccino habitually went cold and icky on the corner of his desk and he actually waved away donuts, even a cheese Danish. He said he felt queasy.

In spite of this, he seemed to be putting on weight. The other day, when Janey went in to shine his plants with a banana peel, he was stretching out his back (he was doing a lot of this, too) and she could clearly see a pot belly beginning to strain the buttons of his Oxford shirt. Later, she'd noticed that the worn brown belt that held up his chinos had been moved out a notch. You could see where the old one had been, and it was a good inch from where it was now.

His irritability and sense of fragility made it difficult to discuss and plan for Janey's upcoming absence. At the same time, it made it even more imperative that they discuss it and plan for it as soon as possible. Dr. Emery was clearly in no state to deal with any administrative blips.

Janey tried to talk to Lottie about this. She chose a time when Lottie had a window, took a pad and pencil, and (after letting the doctor know he had to come out and get the next two patients) went up the stairs to the alternative medicine area.

Lottie was in the preparation room, squatting on her heels, plucking the heads off dried flowers heaped on the floor. "Hop up on the counter," she said. "I thought I'd just get this done while we talk."

Janey obligingly hopped. "It's about the doctor," she began. "He's kind of . . . on edge . . . and I'm a little worried about how he'll cope when I have to leave."

"Uh-huh," Lottie said, nodding. "I'm wondering how we're both going to cope." She stood up for a moment and stretched her back. Janey couldn't help but notice that Lottie, too, seemed to be less angular than usual. A tummy, which Janey had never before seen Lottie possess, pushed against the front of Lottie's long print dress.

What could be happening? she wondered. Lottie, like all her

grandmother Branch's kin, were notoriously healthy eaters. Janey had a brief and ridiculous mental image of the doctor and Lottie sacked out on the sofa, eating potato chips. A giggle escaped her.

"No, I'm serious," Lottie said. "You're the linchpin of this practice, Janey. I don't think we can actually replace you. We'll just have to get some agency person to come in to do the reception work and try and take on your admin stuff ourselves."

At this point, the hair actually stood up on the back of Janey's neck. Neither the doctor nor his herbalist wife were gifted in this way. The mess that would face Janey when she got back from Iraq would be so overwhelmingly chaotic that, as Janey sat on the counter imagining it, she seriously considered the alternative of dying for freedom. It seemed, just for a moment, more attractive than trying to sort out a year of the Emerys' self-administration.

"Oh no," she said weakly.

Lottie grimaced. "I know," she said. "But what else can we do? Nobody else is going to understand such a complex practice. Just the reception part of your job is going to be hard for most people."

Janey nodded. Sometimes it was tough to decide which patients should see whom for what. There were economic and cultural issues to take into account, as well as the personality of the patient and the nature of their complaint. Sometimes a bronchial cough went to the doctor and sometimes to Lottie. It depended on whether the patient had any pre-existing respiratory problems, had to pay for medication, could be trusted to breathe steam, etcetera. She pitied the agency employee.

"And, of course, it comes at a bad time for us," Lottie said, squatting down again. No Lane woman could bear to watch anyone doing a big job on their own. Janey jumped down from the counter and squatted on her heels, too, beginning to pick heads off flowers and put them in the big paper bag.

"Why?" she finally asked. "Why is it such a bad time?"

Lottie looked over at Janey for a moment, hesitating. And then she smiled her wonderful, naughty smile. "I'll tell you later," she said. "I promise."

And Janey had to be content with that.

Hector Rodriguez was a glamorous figure. He was the official escort of what can only be described as a starlet. Kelly Brookes, after an exciting year as Miss USA, during which Hector was frequently called upon to spend part of his Friday afternoons on airplanes, jetting off to various events and promotions, had landed small but quite visible parts in three movies. Hector, Eudora's handsome Latino mayor, was a part of Kelly's image. He went to premieres. He did some publicity. He went to parties and stood with his arm around Kelly's slender waist, waving and smiling while a hundred flashbulbs popped.

The first six months had been fun. It was a bit expensive, driving to the airport all the time, and he'd had to invest in two tuxedos, one to wear and one for the dry cleaners out at Food Barn, but he could afford it now that he was the president and managing director of the bank. He owned a small house (which had once belonged to Margery Lupin) with a small mortgage. His car was four years old. He worked hard the four and a half other days of the week, so that he could take off on his exotic weekend jaunts. Nothing suffered.

The next year was not as exciting, but it was still enjoyable. It was nice to be on first-name terms with two movie stars and one senator. It was great for the town and his family to see him occasionally on television.

But now it was the third year, and he was getting sick of it. Many in his new social circle had the most appalling manners. Even Kelly, who was from the city, was frequently disgusted. The parties had stopped being fun and started to seem a waste. He kept finding himself thinking about the air miles for award party guests, the price and recyclability of the centerpieces, the food on untouched plates, the dresses worn only once, the shoes, the bags. He found himself absently calculating during glitzy charity functions, trying to see if the charity had actually made a profit from the event. He had tired of the Malibu beach houses, furnished extravagantly for a few days' occupancy a year.

"Can we stay home this weekend?" he had started to ask Kelly.

And "I can come home on Thursday," she would say on the phone, though in truth she didn't have a home, but lived out of suitcases like a gypsy. He would work all of Friday afternoon and she would arrive at the city airport and rent a car. She'd let herself into his house and inspect the fridge. Sometimes she'd already have dinner made when he got home. Sometimes she'd be asleep, fully clothed, on the sofa, her suitcase still in the trunk of the car.

The Friday after Janey Lane announced she was being mobilized, Hector came home to find Kelly asleep in the bathtub. That she hadn't planned to endanger her life in this way was clear. There *was* a razor on the side of the tub, but there was also a hair masque, some apricot kernel facial cleanser, and a half-read novel. There were still bubbles in the water, but it had gone cold. Hector called her name and shook her. She woke up but struggled to sit up. He stripped off his suit jacket, pulled the plug, spread a big bath towel onto the floor, and lifted her out. Then he ran to the bed and pushed back the covers and, after patting her dry, carried her into it.

He kicked off his shoes and crawled in himself, holding her cold body until she started to shiver and cry, when he decided she was warm enough to leave for a second so he could call an ambulance.

But, "D-d-d-d-on't," Kelly begged. "P-p-p-ublic-c-c-city."

So he called the doctor's home number instead.

Dr. Emery and his wife, Lottie, arrived together not ten minutes later. The doctor started his examination and Lottie asked the questions, having sent Hector to fill the two hot water bottles she'd brought with her and to wrap them up in tea towels. She rubbed some cream that smelled of ginger on Kelly's famous chest and put one of the hot water bottles on top of it.

The doctor talked about core temperature and reaction time.

Lottie rubbed the cream onto the soles of Kelly's feet and asked her about her sleep patterns. She had Hector make some hot chocolate.

Kelly was still having the occasional violent shiver when they were ready with diagnoses and advice.

"Hypothermia," the doctor said. "If your head had slipped under the water, you might have been too far gone to know which way was up. You're lucky you didn't die."

Kelly made a small, weak sound and Hector took her hand.

"You can't keep going like this, Kelly," Lottie said. "You need a stable base, and to get into some kind of routine. I suspect your diet is as chaotic as your sleep, and eventually this will compromise your immune system and give you some long-lasting problems."

"You're all right now," the doctor said. "Your core temperature is back to normal, your pupils are equal and reactive, and none of your extremities show any sign of damage. If you're not too sleepy, you might want to get up and move around a little bit, go for a walk. It's still warm outside. It might do you a world of good."

"Eat something spicy," said Lottie. "In fact, if you walked down to Mayan Memories and had dinner there, you could do both."

"Thank you," Kelly said.

The doctor snapped his bag shut as Lottie rolled up her bundle. "No problem," the doctor said. "But don't hesitate to call an ambulance in a medical emergency. This one we could handle. If we hadn't been able to handle it, though, the delay could have really cost you."

It didn't take long for Kelly to brush her hair into a ponytail and put on a pair of jeans and a trendy T-shirt. She still shivered, so she also wore a thick cotton sweater of Hector's, and a pair of his argyle socks with her Dr. Scholl's sandals. The late spring sunshine had left the sidewalk radiating heat. Kelly patted her hands on the brick front of the bank as they went past. Father Tim Gaskin, who was driving past on his way to bingo night in an adjoining parish, thought it was a sweet gesture.

Hector did not think it was a sweet gesture. He was at that stage in a loved one's near-death experience when one is as mad as a wet hen. "What were you thinking?" he asked crossly. "You must have noticed you were dozing off. Why didn't you get out of the tub?"

They were in front of the fabric store at this point and Kelly came to a halt at the tone in his voice. "What did you say?" she asked.

Now, a man who has been married for quite some time will know, when this question is asked, one does not repeat one's previous comment word for word. One quickly rephrases it into something unexceptionable. But Hector was new to the relationship game. And so he simply raised his voice and repeated it word for word.

Carla Bustamante, who was just out of sight behind a bit of backdrop, working on the window display, heard it perfectly.

"I was *exhausted*, Hector," Kelly said. "That's why. Didn't you hear what Lottie said? Do you think it's easy, trying to get established in the film industry? I had a five o'clock call for retakes on Thursday. We didn't finish until ten that night. Then there was a charity thing I'd promised to do yesterday morning and it started at eight. And then, instead of going home and sleeping, I got on a damn plane to come and see *you*."

"Well, it's not exactly easy for me, either, Kel. I work crazy hours all through the week just so I can be at your beck and call. I know the name of the man who drives the shuttle bus at airport parking. I know how many kids he's got. I know he's going on vacation in two weeks. He'll probably send me a postcard, I know him so well.

I've spent over four hundred dollars already this year just on parking there. Really, he should have sent me a Christmas card, too."

They resumed walking at this point, and so the rest of the argument is lost. But we do know that when they arrived at Mayan Memories, they were both red in the face and panting, as if they'd run the whole way.

They were at one of the central tables. The entire Lane family was dining at the other, but due to Becky Lane's preoccupation with Janey's military future, she hardly registered what happened between Kelly and Hector.

We are reliant, therefore, upon the testimony of Linda Bustamonte, as the Requenas in their booth closest to the kitchen were too far away to hear and the rest of the restaurant was occupied by strangers.

Linda says that the one thing you've got to understand is that Kelly and Hector always look perfect. You never see them slobbing around in sweats or anything and they never have spinach stuck in their teeth or greasy hair. They always look just like they're gonna be in a magazine and Linda thinks that's because they so often are, that they always feel they've got to be ready.

But that night, Hector was wearing a casual shirt over his undershirt and it seemed like the undershirt was wet, because the casual shirt had a wet mark on the back that got bigger for a while until it got smaller. Also, he wasn't wearing any socks with his loafers and his belt on his jeans was black and more like something you would wear with a suit. Anyone else, she said, would have looked nice like that, but for Hector, it was a mess.

And then there was Kelly, who often wore no makeup but who hadn't looked just like this before, like she was really not wearing *anything,* no tinted moisturizer or eye cream or . . . nothing . . . and her hair wasn't brushed really good in her ponytail and she was dressed like she'd done it in the dark.

And they were usually smiling and holding hands. But tonight, they'd begun to hiss at each other over their menus before she even got there with the ice water. Once she *had* got there, they broke off to order, but not until she heard Hector say that Kelly didn't have any responsibilities and Kelly reply, "Ha!"

Usually when Linda or Maria brought salsa and chips for Hector, Kelly made a point of pushing them away to his side of the table. But this time it was different. She dove right in and crammed half a handful into her mouth, right after hissing something about "not having a mommy and a daddy to look after me." As far as Linda could tell, for a long while after this comment, Hector said nothing, but sat with his arms crossed, fuming, while Kelly shoveled in carbohydrates.

Clement and Nancy McAllister arrived just then, to join the most recently arrived party of strangers, Clement smiling around the room and apologizing to his guests for being late. Clement waved jovially at Hector and Kelly, bustled over, and slid two beers on the table before patting Hector on the back, winking at Kelly, and rejoining his friends.

Locked in what appeared to be a staring contest, Hector and Kelly both raised their beers to their lips and drank a good half of them before slamming them back down on the table. Neither blinked.

Hector and Kelly had seemed to order on autopilot. When their food arrived (cheese enchiladas for Hector; the seafood salad for Kelly, dressing on the side), they stared at the plates in disgust. Linda said their faces looked like she'd put doggie doo in front of them.

Maria was taking the new table's order and, as Linda prepared baskets of chips, she had leisure to watch Hector taste his food and push it away in disgust. Then she saw Kelly glance down at her salad and compare it to the rich sauce and melting cheese on Hector's rejected enchiladas and draw the latter toward her, beginning some brisk action with her fork. After the first taste, Kelly began talking with her mouth full, and when the fork wasn't needed to convey serious amounts of enchilada to her perfectly shaped lips, she was jabbing it in Hector's direction as he clearly received a dressing down of mammoth proportions.

When she paused for breath, he looked at his beer, drained the bottle, and wiped his mouth with the back of his hand. Then, still unsmiling, he said something to her.

The fork clattered down to the table from Kelly's hand, and Linda hastily grabbed the water pitcher as an excuse to get closer.

She was in time to hear the end of Kelly's sentence.

" . . . you say?"

Slowly Linda reached for Priss Lane's water glass, her ears straining.

"I said," Hector said, "I think we should . . . "

But the rest was drowned out by Priss's scream. Linda had poured ice water down the back of her dress.

Well, by the time the apologies and mopping up was over, Hector and Kelly had paid and gone. Maria was so busy that she had only noticed the couple looked tired, and hadn't made any efforts whatsoever to hear their conversation as she presented the bill and collected the money and tip.

But Linda noticed that Hector closed the door with one hand, because he was using the other to hold one of Kelly's, and that her beer was still half full and the enchiladas had not been finished. She thought this was a good sign.

Carla Bustamonte had just finished the display window. It was her finest effort ever and marked the first step in the new direction of the Fabric Shack.

She had used Velcro stickies to pin up a large, translucent representation of a stained glass window to the black background. Pale pink artificial roses were heaped on the display floor. Small golden cherubim were suspended from the display ceiling by fishing line. And, in the center, was the dress.

It was one of the most beautiful dresses Carla had ever made, and, in the kind of irony that so often happens in this world, it had been made for a woman patently unfit to wear it. So unfit had she been, that when she was discovered by her groom entertaining several of his friends in a highly indecorous position on his new pool table while he was meant to be on a business trip, she did not bother to call Carla and tell her that the dress would not, after all, be needed. Carla had made it at a huge loss.

It did not seem like a loss now. The clear white would be trying to any bride without the whitest of teeth, but it glowed in the display lights. The high collar arched down deliciously, delicately, past the jaw, the neck and the collarbone to cut away to a low-cut bodice. That it *was* low was undeniable, but it did not look cheap, not with the tight, long sleeves, not with the severe, square neckline . . . though it was so low you could really call it a bustline . . . not with the high, stiff collar. The skirt swept smartly back to form a short train, leaving a slim silhouette in the front. The bodice arched down over the tummy and up over the hips. It would make an elephant look graceful. It would make a graceful woman look like an angel.

Just before she shut off the light, Carla opened the side panel slightly to adjust one of the rose branches and saw Kelly staring open-mouthed at the dress. Hector did not seem to see it at all. He only looked at Kelly.

You might think a couple could conduct a long-term silent quarrel under their own roof in relative secrecy. After all, even in Eudora, no one monitors bedroom activity. No one click counts the number of kisses exchanged, or endearments whispered.

But nonetheless, people began to notice that there was a coolness in the Walker household that had not been there before.

First of all, Pattie and Phil had stopped leaving the house together. You might see one or the other of them, but you never saw them both. Pattie went to the diocese's focus group on vocations, but Phil stayed at home. Phil went to a concert in the county hall with Chuck on Sunday night, but Pattie didn't go.

And then there was the food. Every other day or so, Phil would get take-out from Mayan Memories or some pizza from Food Barn or do some barbecuing. It was Maria Lopez who first realized that he never got enough for Pattie. He got the boys' favorite chimichangas and got his own pollo mole, but he didn't get Pattie's special avocado chicken quesadilla. And Pattie was never out in the backyard when he barbecued. And they'd stopped having Sunday dinners after church. Indeed, after church the house seemed quiet and abandoned, or at least as quiet as a house containing the Walker boys could be.

Flowers drooped in the yard, their beds invaded by grass and dandelions. Pattie'd always done the planting and weeding and Phil the watering. But now nobody seemed to be doing anything, and the lawn was shaggy.

Anybody who noticed such things, by which we mean nearly the whole of Eudora's population, could tell that something had gone adrift in the Walkers' marriage.

Charlotte "Lottie" Emery (Lottie Dougal, that was) had always been slightly aloof from the give-and-take of news in Eudora. She had been one of those odd birds Eudorans sometimes hatched, the ones that fly away once fledged, never to return. But Lottie then had, inexplicably, returned, even after living somewhere international. And married the doctor, after a long and extremely worrying courtship. But though her marriage and her occupation as an herbal practitioner put her in the center of Eudoran life, she remained just that slight bit aloof. Indeed, the doctor himself, incomer that he was, was far more inclined to trade in news than his native Eudoran wife.

So it was unprecedented for Lottie to come, as she did, to see

Maria Lopez in the middle of the afternoon. She asked for a cup of tea and if Maria had a moment.

Maria did not. Maria was knee-deep in proving to her butchers that she had already paid a large invoice. She had bank statements and check stubs littered all over the table and was itching to give the jumped-up little twerp in their accounts department a piece of her mind on the telephone.

Still, she motioned for Lottie to slide into the booth, which Lottie did. Gabe Burgos brought over a cup of tea and Maria signed that there would be no need to ring up a bill.

Lottie took a long time to deal with her tea bag and spoon and honey. She stirred for a long time, too, all the while concentrating on her cup. Finally she looked up. She said, "Sorry," and then she said, "I don't know how to say this, but . . . "

Maria took pity. "Something is the matter with Phil and Pattie," she said.

Lottie collapsed in relief. "Yes!" she exclaimed. And then she leaned forward and in a low voice said, "It's been three weeks since she's let me come in the door. Do you know anything?"

Well, the floodgates of confidence were opened and a veritable storm of evidence was exchanged, including the diocesan meeting, barbecues, Sunday dinners, take-out, evasive answers on the phone, and Pattie's and Phil's general demeanor. Maria told Lottie about Pattie losing it with Carla. Linda Bustamonte, who was putatively filling salt shakers nearby, then chipped in, telling them both about the every-other-afternoon country drives Phil was taking with Chuck out to the Evans place. She had heard about it from Zadie Gross, who had come to borrow some white pepper for the diner, and had heard it straight from the farmers' table.

Lottie shook her head. "Normally," she said, "I'd just ask her what was going on, but when I do, she just seems so . . . "

"She called me once and wanted to come over," Maria said. "But I was writing Bruce and I said I was busy . . . and now it's not

like talking to her at all. She's all closed off. She's more like y—"
Maria broke off in confusion.

"Me." Lottie nodded. An uncomfortable silence descended that
was, in a way, more normal than the conversation that preceded it
had been.

Lottie pushed a lock of hair that had fallen into her eyes behind
one ear. "Yeah, well. I have my reasons why I'm not really . . . "

Friendly? Maria and Linda supplied mentally. Approachable?
Neighborly?

Lottie chose to leave it blank. She knew they knew what she
meant.

"But you know, Pattie," Lottie continued, "she's never been that
way."

"I can't believe I said that." Maria rolled her eyes. "But you
know, you're right, people got reasons for clamming up. . . . Usually
it's because they've been hurt real bad." They sat for a moment
again and then she said, "Do you think something has hurt Pattie
real bad?"

The three women exchanged glances. Both of them knew it
wasn't something. It was some*one*. Phil Walker.

The old Flory place was right on the western edge of the main
street and occupied most of the block on which it stood. The bank
was on the next corner and then the movie house. Across from this,
on the other side of the wide street lined with maple trees, was the
diner, Gross Home Cooking.

If you were in a hurry, you could probably walk it in under two
minutes. It took Jim Flory nearly twenty.

He was using one of those new kinds of crutches with the metal
collar for your arm and hobbling along about an inch at a time. It
was Monday morning about ten o'clock and the diner was full of
local businesspeople, farmers on their first break and some passing
trade using the old highway to the county seat. Conversation fal-

tered as they all watched Jim's unsteady progress. It took him about five minutes to cross the street, and he almost got mowed down by the trash truck that was being hurriedly driven so the boys could have their own usual break at the diner. There was a collective gasp as they swerved just in time.

Every man Jack (and woman Jill) who was watching positively itched to go out and carry Jim Flory into the diner. And this would have happened, without a doubt, if it had not been for Bob's observable attitude. Bob was looking around and whistling. He was not holding Jim's free arm. He did not jump at the trash truck, but actually elbowed Jim and laughed heartily. He had his hands in his pockets and responded to the things Jim was saying with compressed lips and wry smiles.

"Heartless," Becky said, pausing on a round of decaf refills. "He's not helping him a bit. Poor Jim looks fit to crawl in a minute."

Zadie, who had the regular pot, came to the window and observed for herself. "I don't know," she said. "Jim can be kind of whiny."

There was general discussion on these two points. Stacey Harper (working from home that day, instead of going into the city art gallery where her expertise was compensated with a ridiculously large salary) and Park Davis took opposite sides, Park being more inclined toward Becky's point of view and Stacey (who, despite her career, was a hands-on mother) taking Zadie's. Her clinching argument was "You've got to be firm sometimes when someone's sick. Otherwise they linger."

"You mean 'malinger,'" Park said. "Pretending to be sick when you're not."

"No, I mean 'linger,'" Stacey snapped. "Don't get well when they should. Take their time over it. Make a song and dance about it."

"Well, if somebody's really ill—" and this interesting discussion, which was being closely followed by many present, would have degenerated into an argument about the last time the flu virus invaded the Harper–Davis household and Park's subsequent three-week collapse, if Jim and Bob had not at that moment arrived on the sidewalk.

Bob waved Jim inside and stood in front of the two newspaper machines as if he were doing a detailed cost comparison.

Jim struggled with the door (and here Lane Nichols just had to jump up and open it for him), but once inside found his way to the counter and sank gingerly onto a stool.

There were large green patches on his face where bruises had faded and it was still misshapen with swelling. His hands also seemed a bit off kilter, as if the fingers had been newly installed from one of those kits that has instructions without words. His Old Navy sweatshirt bulged with bandages and even his good leg had a swollen knee clearly visible beneath the hem of his pull-on shorts. Part of his head had been shaved—when he bent to look at the menu, you could see stitches underneath the stubble.

Eudora had frequently seen Jim Flory look bad, but he'd never looked really terrible before. He hunched over his menu and his body curled protectively as if he were still trying, even now, to avoid a punch.

And now it was obvious why Bob was forcing Jim Flory to get out and about by himself. Jim looked like a whipped dog, cowardly and cringing. It was the old "get back up on the horse that threw you" philosophy that was driving Bob's treatment of Jim Flory. He'd probably been working on Jim for days, just to get him to leave the house.

No one knew what to say. You do not slap a man in that state on his back and ask him, "How's it hanging?" You do not call from across the room, "But you should have seen the other guy, eh, Jim?" Even Becky and Zadie hesitated, unsure of how to greet such a specter of a person.

But, finally, just as Bob came in with both papers, Zadie up-turned Jim's coffee cup and asked, "Decaf or regular, Jim?"

And Jim looked up and said, "Regular, please." Conversation resumed.

Lane Nichols rose to pay. As he passed he said, "Good to see you out and about, Jim."

Jim mumbled, "Thanks."

And then something happened. Bob had looked up from his paper and Lane Nichols met Bob's eye. And then Lane nodded, a man-to-man kind of nod, an "I consider you a peer" kind of nod. Bob, though a little surprised, nodded back, a kind of "I am aware of the honor you have just done me" kind of nod, though with one of his wry smiles on the end.

And that was it, really. That was the end of Bob's impossibility.

George and Blaine Barford got up from the farmers' table to pay and get toothpicks and George backtracked to say to Bob, "Sad business," in an undertone, while shaking his head.

Bob replied, "Yes," shaking his head back.

Then to Jim, in the loud, false heartiness such men reserve for the infirm, George said, "And you watch out for banana skins, huh?" At which Jim attemped to smile.

After this stab at conviviality, Jim excused himself to go to the men's room. Bob did not offer to help him.

Park Davis immediately came and seated himself on Jim's stool. Without preamble, he asked Bob, "Is it true that there were five or six of them?"

Bob nodded.

Park shook his head, this time in disgust. Zadie floated up behind the counter and refilled cups. "I can't understand what started it," she said. "Jim's got lovely manners."

The place grew noticeably quiet. It was apparent that several of the men present could understand what had started it, given Jim's sexual proclivities. Stacey came and stood with her hand on Park's shoulder, pushing down hard, the way women do when they do not want their menfolk to speak.

"Queer bashers," Bob said. "It could have been anybody who left the bar."

"So he didn't . . . ," Park said.

Bob shook his head. This time the headshake meant no, Jim hadn't made inappropriate advances to his assailants. The atmosphere inside the diner perceptively lightened.

"Not that . . . ," Stacey said.

But Park disagreed, saying, "Well . . . "

By which everyone knew that though Stacey might not think it is ever permissible to inflict such a beating on anyone, Park felt that there were times it might be justified and was relieved that Jim's had not been one of those times.

"It's just awful," Becky Lane said, and then, "Those hash browns are gonna burn."

Zadie Gross scooted back to the grill.

Although Clement McAllister had left his payment and carefully calculated tip on the table, he, too, came over to the group near the cash register. "In any case," he said to Park, "five or six against one isn't reasonable. Man to man might be another story."

Though Bob rolled his eyes, assent was murmured and heads were nodded. It was clear the entire diner agreed with this ethical position.

"Have you got everything you need?" Park asked, as if now at pains to counterindicate any previous lack of support for Jim Flory. "If you need me to order anything, just give me a ring. If I don't have it in stock, I can usually get it the next day."

Bob sighed. "That's really nice," he said, "but I think we're good for right now."

"Nancy's going out to Food Barn tomorrow," Clement said. "Here's our phone number. She'd be glad to pick up anything and drop it by."

"Thanks," Bob said, and then he sighed. "I might do that. He's still a bit too wobbly for a supermarket and I hate to leave him that long."

"When Betty Requena had her accident," explained Mark Ramirez (who had spent a good half hour explaining himself to Becky and was now waiting while she heated up a cinnamon roll and got him a cup of coffee to go—she had refused to serve him earlier), "they worked out a schedule so that Don could have some time to himself."

"Yeah," Becky said. "Lots of people did an hour here or there."

"Well," Bob said, patting his stomach. "I wouldn't mind doing some laps in the pool. All this good food is making my twelve-pack a whole case."

Jim came out of the bathroom to find a cluster of people chatting to Bob. They made way for him to sit down.

"Well," Stacey said, "you guys know where we are, if you need anything." She said, "I can do an hour or two tomorrow night, if you want to go swimming. The high school pool is open till ten."

"Thanks," Bob said again, as Zadie slid two breakfasts and a bottle of Tabasco in front of them. The crowd dispersed.

"Aren't you just Mister Congeniality," Jim murmured, but not too low for Zadie to hear.

"They're nice people," Bob said, his voice redolent of tried patience. "They really seem to care."

"Just give me the TV section." But when Bob proffered it, Jim snatched it out of Bob's hand. "Swimming," he said scornfully, as he shook it open and laid it beside his plate.

Becky Lane whispered to Zadie Gross, "I see what you mean about the whiny."

Zadie gave her a meaningful look. "That Bob is a saint," she said.

Pattie Walker's day care crisis came later that same day. Candy Cane Day Care catered mainly to the six and unders, but also provided after-school and school-break activities for older children, usually ex–Candy Caners or older brothers and sisters of current Candy Caners. These were run as an additional service for little profit and were a great source of gratitude on behalf of the parents so honored.

Of course, the older ones could get a bit lively, but when you have known someone from the teething stage, you tend to be tolerant of their little peccadilloes and naughtiness. Given this, it has to be said that even the tolerant, nurturing staff of Candy Cane Day Care could be pushed too far.

We still do not know how the Walker boys discovered that a serviceable explosive could be devised from flour. Perhaps Phil left them unattended on the Internet. Perhaps they had found a recipe on their frequent trips to the library, where their mother hid in the stacks reading relationship books with planets in the title, which she hastily shelved whenever anyone walked by.

The bike shed rose into the air about twenty feet before it shot in all directions, and before the tricycles and scooters that caused so much damage to the sand pit, ball pool, and swing set came raining down. There was no need to investigate the identity of the perpetrators. The Walker boys stood in self-congratulatory poses by the playground and when approached by staff, asked if the staff had seen it, and hadn't it been awesome? They were only too ready to claim responsibility.

Right after the volunteer firemen and the sheriff's department had been notified, Pattie Walker picked up the phone at the Fabric Shack and was asked to remove *all* of her children immediately.

Pattie was an experienced mother. She took a deep breath (something Lorna Davis, the manager of the Candy Cane Day Care Center, should have done before calling) and asked if everyone was all right. Then she asked if the boys were somewhere safe. Then she said she'd be there in a minute.

This last was a lie. Instead of her initial reaction, which was to run around in circles looking for her car keys, she tried something different. She called Phil on his cell phone and told him she was up to her eyeballs, and could he please go get the kids from Candy Cane as there was something wrong. Nobody was hurt, but something had happened.

"What?" Phil asked. "What's happened?"

Boys will be boys, eh? Pattie thought grimly to herself. Let him deal with it for a change. "Can you get there?" she asked.

"Well, I guess I can get back to this tomorrow. I'll have to let Larry know what's going on but . . . "

"Good," Pattie said. "You get there, then and I'll . . . ooooh," she lied. "Oooooh. You're breaking up. Your cell. I can hardly hear you."

And she put the phone back down. She picked it up immediately and pushed the speed dial for Phil's cell phone again, but then clicked it off and slowly, slowly, eased it back onto the charger stand. "No," she said to herself. "*Let* him. Let *him.*"

About an hour and a half later, Phil Walker shoved eleven-year-old Patrick and nine-year-old Daniel through the back door of the Fabric Shack. He was carrying Ben, who was wrapped around him monkey style, crying his eyes out.

Pattie couldn't help herself. She immediately reached out for Ben, who buried his face in his mother's neck and inarticulately sobbed out his woes.

Phil's hair was standing on end, evidence that he'd been running his hands through it in exasperation. He did this again. "We're going to have to pay for the damage," he said. "I asked about their insurance and if we could just pay the deductible, but evidently it doesn't cover *terrorism.*" He pushed the older boys further toward their mother, as if he couldn't bear to have them in his proximity.

"They *might* take Ben back in the fall," he said. "*If* we can convince them that he's not going to follow in his brothers' footsteps."

"I'm a *good* boy!" Ben cried, clearly overcome with the injustice of it all.

But Phil wasn't done imparting news. "Right now I have to take these two down to the county courthouse to be formally charged. They're going to have to go to a hearing and everything."

Pattie sat Ben down on a stack of worsteds and gave him a Kleenex. "If you do that," she said, "I'll make dinner. We'll give them an early bath and have a talk about what we'll do."

Phil considered for a long moment. Then, "Okay," he said.

When, moments after Phil had taken Ben back in his arms and pushed the older boys back out again, there was a knock at the back door, Pattie flung it open, sure he was backing out of their meeting. When it was somebody else, it took a moment for her to register the identity of the person who had knocked, because all she could see was their not-Philness. And then it took her a little longer again, because the tall woman had her hair swathed in a scarf. Large dark glasses hid half her face.

The stranger looked around the alley nervously and then said, "Mrs. Walker, it's me, Kelly. Can I come in and talk to you about"— and here her voice dropped in both tone and volume—"that wedding dress?"

Jeb Olensen had been growing and dealing marijuana for over thirty years, only ten blocks away from the county courthouse. It was a considerable achievement. Many of his erstwhile colleagues had visited the prison system or had run afoul of larger drug-dealing organizations with more rigid power structures and ruthless management styles. But for three decades, Jeb had been growing weed in his attic, drying it, cleaning it, weighing it, and packaging it up and selling it for a small but steady profit, using a woodworking setup in an outbuilding to explain both his electricity use and his income. He actually wasn't that bad at the woodworking, either. He just hated it.

For all of that time, Chuck Warren had been one of his major customers and a close friend. Where once Chuck would sit at Jeb's and chat about music or sport, now they often talked about 401(k)s and stocks, but they had a real relationship, based on mutual respect and firm boundaries.

This much we know. Jeb was shortly to get out of the business, and afterward would talk about his past fairly freely. We are not certain that Chuck consulted Jeb on whatever he and Phil were doing at the Evanses' place, but we are not stupid and have a pretty darned good idea.

One thing we do know: Around this time, Jeb discussed with Chuck the potency of the newer strains of marijuana, which he, Jeb, refused to grow and which his newer customers demanded. Jeb showed Chuck articles about the links between these strains of marijuana and various mental illnesses and spoke at length about THC levels and toxicity. By which you can see that Jeb was already at this point contemplating his retirement.

And Chuck, on whom it had been recently and forcibly impressed that he was tragically behind the times, listened to Jeb in a way he might not have listened two months before.

That evening, Phil and Pattie had a crucial encounter. But the way things turned out, Chuck's encounter with Jeb that same evening may have had an even more lasting effect on the Walker marriage.

At this time of year in Eudora, backyards are busy places. Seeds have been planted and seedlings are being thinned and moved in the earth. There is watering and hoeing to do aplenty and the more vigorous and frost-resistant plants are already requiring support. People with greenhouses are either smugly beginning to pick tomatoes or fighting desperate battles with insect populations. Lawns are reaching the apex of their mowing cycle, with some men positively looking forward to the annual July drought. Children have just reached that stage of summer where the days stretch on endlessly, they've begun to come to terms with boredom, and they've developed an obsession with a random toy or project, investing long hours in something that will soon become meaningless but is currently the center of all life.

And so, we must confess, the town's enthusiastic encounter with contemporary literature here faltered. It was not that *The Vortex* wasn't a good book. It was not that they didn't want to find out how it ended. But the citizens of Eudora had now discovered how Chuck Warren got to town and acquired the money to buy the bowling alley. The fine print didn't really interest them.

Also, after a day's work and an evening of hoeing, watering, inspecting for pests, and lengthily discussing twine preferences with one's loved ones, the idea of reading about those horrible people in that book just didn't appeal. As Maria Lopez said, "Everybody in the thing is just so nasty." The language was bad enough, but the way people acted was shocking. At first it had been fascinating and then titillating, but finally it had become . . . sickening. That things like that really did happen, and there were truly people like those characters, was an undeniable truth. But one of the main reasons for living in Eudora, for putting up with the inconveniences of a small rural community, was to avoid those kinds of human beings. Spending night after night with them, especially with that Tiger person and those horrible policemen, was at first distasteful and then intolerable.

"I just can't look at it anymore," Zadie Gross said. "I got a Georgette Heyer out of the library instead." And though it is drummed in early to Eudorans that one should finish what one started, nobody in town could blame her. Even Artie Walker had been understanding, and he was a vigorous champion of contemporary fiction in general and Margaret Lupin in particular.

Artie and the other real readers in town went on and followed the twists and turns of Trick's and Jules's cross and double cross. They gasped at the danger and were relieved when the two ended up faithful to their friendship, if not in any kind of love.

But everybody else, once they figured out how it was going to end, read a little bit of the last two pages and put it down on the nightstand for good.

Except for Chuck Warren. One night, when Oscar Burgos was walking the long way home from the quarry, he peered in the open door of the bowling alley and saw Chuck seated in the yellow light of the beer signs, drinking coffee and turning pages, way after midnight. He was galloping through it. Chuck might have been the last one to start the book, but he was certainly one of the first to finish.

It seemed no coincidence that Chuck, who had appeared so content for years, would at this point grow savagely restless. He cleaned everything with a nervous energy he had previously not possessed, until the bowling alley shone like a jewel. He painted his living room and changed all the furniture. He had his boat raised out of the water, cleaned the hull, and detailed the deck and cabin. He began to talk about trading in his truck for something different, maybe a sports car.

Of course, Eudora noticed these things. Much of the town felt for him and ached to help. But there was nothing you could do for someone like him, someone who, in so many ways, lived apart from his fellows. You could only watch and wait.

Phil and Pattie's talk did not go well.

Later, Pattie confided that there had seemed to be a seamless downward progression in the discussion. They started out speaking reasonably about who would look after the boys the following day and in a heartbeat were laying blame on each other for Daniel and Patrick's minuscule sense of social responsibility. Pattie said that during this conversation, she understood the concept of Satan for the first time; she could account for no other way that the talk would take such rapid and sudden turns into places neither Pattie nor Phil wished to go. In no time, without any direction or control from either party, the main topic shifted from child care altogether and became a debate over who earned more.

Now, in this post-feminist world, we are supposed to be above such considerations. But in real life, a man does not like to think of being dependent on his wife's income. He might not mind the income at all, but the thinking about it will still rankle. In the Davis–Harper family, for instance, Stacey often made more for what seemed to Park to be three-day weeks than the pharmacy cleared after salaries and overheads for a six-day opening. This rankled Park until Stacey decided to take over the day-to-day family accounting, after which it didn't bother Park at all as long as nobody mentioned it.

Three separate dog walkers reported raised voices and then downright shouting coming from the Walker place. Neighbors were able to corroborate, and also observed Phil standing on the sidewalk with what seemed to be a hastily packed duffle bag (there were things hanging out of the zipper) saying, "I'm going, I'm going," in a taunting, sing-song voice.

While Pattie was seen at the door, clutching what appeared to be bank statements, saying, "It's all here in black and white, all here in black and white."

Then Phil slammed open the door to his truck and got in, shouting over his shoulder, "Fine. You don't need me. I'm outta here." He took his time shutting the door, and revved the engine unnecessarily, but Pattie ran to the sidewalk only after the truck had gone, sinking down onto the road where it had been and weeping bitterly.

One of the neighbors called Lottie. Lottie despised Vivien Merton for many reasons and another one would be for the honeyed way Vivien poured the sad news into the telephone.

It took just about every ounce of Christian spirit Lottie had to thank her. She drove over with the doctor and they picked Pattie up off the asphalt and half-carried her into the Walker house, shutting the door firmly and drawing the curtains.

Phil went over to Chuck's and moved into the spare room.

Everybody in town knew all about it by the time Margery Lupin opened the bakery the next morning.

Now, you might think that June is a busy time in the wedding dress business, but actually, it's rather slack. You always get your whirlwinds, but Carla did not deal in ready-made. So, once the last-minute fittings were done, for both the brides who ate and the brides who forgot to eat when they got nervous, Carla was able to take her pincushion off her wrist with a sense of a good job done well.

When Lottie called her about taking over at the Shack for the rest of the week, Carla said yes.

So that wasn't, the doctor said, the real problem. He was discussing the situation with Janey Lane over two large cappuccinos that morning. They had scheduled in some time to talk about Janey's imminent departure and administrative routines, which she had annotated with Post-it notes in a large file. But the news had overwhelmed this agenda.

"The real problem," the doctor said, "is who we're going to find to babysit."

For Carla could not run the Shack single-handed for long. It was a two-woman job, especially now that they were sharing the dressmaking side of things, and Pattie, finding fulfillment in her career where she was not finding it in either motherhood or marriage, was not about to let go of the Shack at such an exciting point in its development. She had also admitted that she was at her wit's end about the boys and quite out of ideas and energy to deal with them.

"Those boys need discipline," Janey said. "A really firm hand."

"That's what Artie always says," the doctor remarked. Artie and Rosemary Walker were bringing up angelic little May along firm lines and had always felt Phil and Pattie's parenting to be slack. But since Patrick and Daniel's little brother Ben was pretty angelic himself, Phil and Pattie always argued it was a case of nature and not nurture. Almost everyone in town took a side in this long-running debate, and almost everyone enjoyed airing their opinions on the subject. But the doctor and Janey agreed that now was not the time to exchange their own personal views and subsided into private thought while they drank some coffee.

An idea then came to Janey. She turned it one way and another, but it seemed to be a good one, with long-reaching possibilities. She asked, "You know my sister, Priss?"

The doctor's eyes lit up. "Do you think she'd come work for the practice?" he asked eagerly.

"No way," Janey said bluntly. "She's only seventeen and a worse gossip than Zadie Gross. Bad at math, too. And anyway, she's still got a year of high school."

The doctor sighed and mournfully spooned a bit of foam into his mouth.

"No, I thought about Priss for Pattie. Priss is a fantastic babysitter. Been doing it since she was eleven. She'd love sitting days; she keeps whining that the only way she can make enough money to go out is by working the same nights she wants to go out."

The doctor nodded, and then said, "And if Candy Cane takes Ben back . . . "

"That's right, she could do afternoons all year, pick the boys up from school and Ben up from Candy Cane. And she can cook and do a little housework."

"Of course, Phil and Pattie have managed all right until now," the doctor said.

But Janey and the doctor made eye contact. Both knew that Phil might not be coming back.

■ ■ ■

There was a steady stream of women arriving at the Walker house that night. Lottie came by, of course, and Maria was there, but also Becky Lane came by with Janey and Priss. Two bottles of chardonnay were opened, but Pattie and Lottie contented themselves with chamomile tea, and young Priscilla had apple juice. Priss's child care help was offered and accepted. Casseroles were put into the freezer. Tears were shed.

It was late, nearly ten o'clock, and it had started to rain. The women sat around the table, silent.

So much had been said that the companionable silence was welcome. There comes a moment in such a gathering of women, when each participant is content just to enjoy the feeling of sisterhood, when the company itself is enough reason to stay sitting and not to, say, jump up and put the leftover crackers and cookies in Tupperware and wash the mugs and glasses. Men tend to begin their conversations in this mellow mood of appreciating the grace of fellowship. Women usually only get there after a long, hard journey.

Lottie sounded regretful when she cleared her throat. Everyone looked at her in the yellow glow provided by the dimmer switch. She leaned forward, opened her mouth, and said . . . nothing, shutting it again.

Priss and Becky were puzzled, but Pattie, Janey, and Maria were used to Lottie's awkward discursive style and waited and, sure enough, she tried again.

"I've been meaning to tell Pattie something," she said. "Janey, too. Well, everybody, really."

Now Becky couldn't resist an interrogatory lift of the eyebrows. Priss, on her best behavior, stifled a sigh.

Lottie tucked one brazenly streaked lock behind her ear and smiled rather shyly into her cup. "I didn't want to say anything, because we've had disappointments before. But it's been nearly six months now and ⸱ . . . " She looked up at Pattie. "I think we're due about two weeks apart."

Pattie's face collapsed, just folded down into itself. Sobbing, she held out her arms and Lottie came over and held her. "That's . . . that's wonderful," Pattie said. "I've been feeling so *alone* with this baby. That's so . . . " She sniffed and squeezed Lottie tight.

Lottie, somewhat embarrassed by this display of emotion, pulled back a little and patted Pattie's back, smiling.

Pattie's eyes narrowed. "Hey," she said. "You haven't gained a damn pound. Look at you!"

"Oh, I have," Lottie smiled, holding her loose dress closer to her waist. You could just see a smooth bump.

"Hell, I'm bigger than that and I'm not pregnant," Becky said. "That's just disgusting! Hand me another cookie."

"Me too," Maria said, also taking another cookie. "It's depressing."

"I wondered what was going on," Janey said, and then thought for a moment. "But what about the doctor? He's gaining more weight than you are!"

When Lottie confided Jim's phantom pregnancy symptoms you could hear the laughter all the way to the Merton household.

"I don't know what's going on over at the Walker house," Vivien Merton sniffed. "Sounds like a bunch of hens cackling."

Paul Merton put down his book and listened. "Sounds like a good time," he said. "Poor lady deserves one, don't you think?"

A man, you see, cannot abandon his wife and children in a place like Eudora without censure. Phil Walker, with his cheeky grin and his charming manner, had been, since he could toddle, a favorite of all the ladies in town. Men, too, had liked him for his style and verve and his essential kindness. He had been adorable and then cute and then handsome. He made neither enough money to inspire envy nor too little for respect. He could dance like a dream and cook like an angel. He was a popular guy.

The popular walk in a cloud of glamour in a small town. When they enter a room, people look up. When they go down the street, they are greeted. When they enter a place of business, eyes light up and frequently they get their hands shaken.

Phil had never noticed this before. He thought of Eudora as a nice, friendly place where people lived in an atmosphere of cordiality. He had noticed that at times, this cordiality was withdrawn from certain people, but saw that as an aberration.

Now Phil himself was the aberration.

He went into Gross Home Cooking on Wednesday morning only to have Zadie say curtly, "Artie couldn't make it." Why Artie had told Zadie and not Phil himself, who lived with his cell phone strapped permanently to his hip, was a mystery to Phil. But he accepted this with his usual easy tolerance and approached the businessmen's table to ask if he could join them.

Clement McAllister took a long drink of coffee and then looked Phil right in the eye. Phil had never noticed before how mean the semi-retired banker could look when he wasn't grinning. Clement said, "I'm afraid we're waiting for someone."

The diner got suddenly quiet.

Park Davis, the pharmacist; Lane Nichols, the gas station owner; and Spector Williams, the barber, all looked up from the booth. Phil said later the only time he'd seen such cold faces before was on a string of large-mouth bass.

Phil Walker nearly reeled into a booth of his own.

He sat there for a considerable time. Becky Lane ignored him, walking right by him with the coffee pot five or six times while Phil held his cup up in the air. Finally he said, "Oh, come on, Becky."

To which Becky replied, "It's Mrs. Lane to you, Mr. Walker," though she filled his coffee cup.

And then Phil said, "I'll have my usual."

And Becky said, "We're out of pancakes."

And Phil said, "No, you're not. I can see some on the grill."

And Zadie called over, "We've just run out, just right now."

So Phil called back, "Can't you make some more?"

And Zadie put down her spatula and came over, saying, "You know, Mr. Walker, I just don't feel like it."

Phil stood up with his throat trying to work around a lump and thrust his hand in his pocket for his money clip. "Don't worry, Mr. Walker," Zadie said. "Coffee's on the house."

Phil stumbled out the door fully understanding that he was now officially outcast.

Although it is not unknown for Eudorans to put two and two together and make five, a community with such well-honed powers of observation often gets things more or less right. In other words, they often make four.

And so, at around this time, when copies of *The Vortex* had been undisturbed on nightstands for long enough to need dusting, and Phil Walker was revealed as a heartless dastard, there came a communal realization. This chronicle will not attempt to either prove or disprove this realization. It will simply explain it and leave it up to you to decide. But the chronicle would be very surprised if this realization were wrong.

Now, there are three pieces of news that are essential to re-create this communal realization. The first is that something weird is going on at the Evans place and it seems to involve agriculture and such unlikely co-conspirators as Phil Walker and Chuck Warren. The second is that Chuck Warren had come to Eudora to hide from both the police and organized crime and had bought the bowling alley with proceeds from marijuana growing and trading. The third is that Phil Walker is not the good guy everyone had always assumed him to be.

Now, you hold those three pieces of information in your mind for just a second while you imagine picking up and dusting a book called *The Vortex* with pictures of pot plants growing all over it. And I'll bet you start adding things up, too.

This communal realization is not being chatted about. In fact, it is never spoken out loud. Looks are exchanged and eyebrows raised, and half sentences occasionally allude, but nobody spells it right out.

And that is because of Mary Evans.

Mary Evans is a Baptist to the bone and a better, kinder woman you would never want to meet. You only have to taste her home-made ice cream to know that this is a woman on the fast track to heaven.

Nobody wanted Mary Evans to lose her home, her car, and her savings and bank account. Nobody wanted her husband to go to jail.

And that is surely what would happen if the communal realization were spoken and got to the ears of the sheriff's department. The law is very clear. It's all very well for people like Jeb to praise citizens growing their own marijuana, arguing that the only way to vanquish organized crime is to take away the income it gets from dealing the plant. Jeb can make growing dope sound like the most moral activity in the world. But the federal government takes quite another view, and takes that view very seriously indeed.

So the communal realization remained unspoken. But as Chuck and Phil, every other afternoon, jumped in Phil's truck and sped out of town, tongues were clucked and eyes were rolled. And when Jim Evans came to town, he was treated with such gentleness and pity that he later said it was like he was dying of cancer and everybody knew it but him.

At this time, people also tried to pity Pattie Walker. But it was difficult.

First of all, Priss Lane had whipped the Walker boys into shape in no time. The very first day Pattie came home from the Fabric Shack, worn out and grieving, she noticed that the lawn was mowed and the flower beds were weeded before she even got to the front door. Inside, the living room was spotless and the dining room table was set.

And sitting at the dining room table were three unidentifiable children. They were sitting still. They were clean. They had on buttoned shirts and their hair was brushed.

"Welcome home, Mommy," Ben said.

Pattie started to cry. They all jumped up and hugged her. "This is amazing," she said. Priss appeared around the side of the kitchen door, holding something steaming in oven gloves.

"Okay, boys, don't forget," she said.

They scooted back to the table and sat down. Pattie moved toward her chair in a daze.

"Daniel," Patrick hissed, and Daniel jumped up and ran around to pull out his mother's chair.

Pattie met Priss's eye and Priss winked. "Thank you, honey," Pattie said.

Priss disappeared and came back with a platter and a bowl. Patrick whispered to his mother, "Fried chicken, mashed potatoes, green beans, and gravy."

Pattie said, "Wow."

"And biscuits," Ben said. "You forgot the biscuits." He turned to his mother. "I did the rolling."

"Well, I did the cutting," Patrick said. "*And* the mixing."

Pattie, with difficulty, restrained her jaw from dropping open. "Did you help cook, too?" she asked Patrick.

"No," he said. "I was finishing the yard work. I took three loads of grass cuttings down to the dump in the little red wagon."

"What about ball practice?"

Her eldest shrugged. "I fit it in. Priss says if you hustle you can fit most things in."

"Yeah," Ben said. "Priss says if you don't learn to hustle you get fat and boring."

"I *like* hustling," Patrick confided. "I didn't think I would. It's a lot better than doing stupid activities at Candy Cane or just sitting around watching cartoons."

Priss put some butter on the table and then took off her apron. "Well, I'll see you tomorrow," she said.

"Aren't you going to stay and eat with us?" Pattie asked.

"Oh no. Mom's expecting me. See you!" As Priss bounced toward the door, Pattie didn't think she'd ever seen a girl so pretty.

"I," Patrick said, with considerable pretension, "am now going to say grace."

And Pattie fervently made the sign of the cross and prayed intense thanks.

But it was not only her home situation that was improved. Even the furor surrounding Phil Walker's departure from the marital home and the communal realization of what was happening at the Evans place did not wholly eclipse the significance of a wedding dress not made from a McCall's or Butterick pattern appearing in the window of the Fabric Shack and the new levels of cordiality that existed between the two co-workers within.

And when the new sign appeared, it was obvious why.

The doctor and Lottie Emery tended to go to bed early. At first, this had been due to their overwhelming and all-consuming passion. But these days, it was because they were both exhausted.

"How was Phil?" Lottie asked, yawning.

"Stupid," the doctor said. "He's having a midlife crisis. It's classic, but he can't see it. I tried to talk to him, but right now, it's as bad as talking to Chuck."

"What is he doing?" Lottie asked. "He's always been so busy. I can't imagine him just hanging out at the bowling alley."

The doctor sat down on the rug and started his sit-ups. He

talked in rhythm. "He's got this . . . old yearbook," he said. "Lord knows . . . where he got hold of it. He keeps it . . . hidden from Chuck."

Lottie lay on her side, watching him. "What's he doing with an old yearbook?" she asked.

"Research . . . evidently." The doctor kept going—past twenty, past thirty as Lottie watched. "I saw a picture . . . of Janine Lupin . . . and she did look just like . . . how I picture Jules."

"No!" Lottie giggled and then sobered. She said, "I just thought about telling Pattie, but she'll ask me how I know." She lay on her back and looked at the white ceiling. Its fresh plaster had taken seventeen coats of paint. Every time she looked at it, her arms ached with the memory. "It makes me sad," she said.

"I'll tell you what will make you sad," the doctor said, finishing and flopping down next to her, breathless. "Except for Janine, every single one of those kids is dead."

"What kids?"

"The graduating class of sixty-nine. There were only eighteen of them. Four boys got a farm deferment, but the rest went to Vietnam."

"They didn't all die in Vietnam," Lottie said, aghast. They both sat up.

"Phil's been figuring it all out. May Evans died with three boys and another girl when they drove off the bridge later that summer," the doctor counted off on his elegant fingers. "That took care of two soldiers and a farmer."

"That still leaves three farmers and eleven soldiers," Lottie said.

"One of the farmers got run over by his own tractor," the doctor said, "and one soldier died in basic training . . . sounded like heatstroke to me."

"Two farmers and ten soldiers."

"Four of the boys died on the same mission. They were on a helicopter crew," the doctor said.

"That leaves the two farmers and six soldiers."

"Two of the soldiers were POWs who never came back, and one went MIA. There were rumors he stayed in Cambodia with a girl he met there, but the family's never found him."

"He was a Bumgartner," Lottie said. "I heard about him." She counted again. "Okay, that means two farmers and three soldiers."

"One of the soldiers was sent to Germany and got in a knife fight. Fatal hemorrhage."

"Hell," Lottie said. "Now we're down to two soldiers and two farmers."

"Okay," the doctor said. "Here's where it gets weird. One of the farmers had formed a relationship with one soldier's girlfriend. Soldier came home, found them together, killed the farmer and then himself."

"Oh yeah," Lottie said. "That was Tom Pollard and Ernie Svarski." She thought for a second. "The Pollards moved to California after that."

"Leaving one soldier and one farmer," the doctor said. "The soldier died of what sounds like cancer caused by extensive exposure to dioxin. The farmer got depressed and drank himself to death before he was forty." He sighed. "Spoils of war, eh?"

"It's not all Vietnam-related, Jim," Lottie argued.

"Look at it this way," the doctor said. "If the soldiers hadn't just been to basic training, they might not have been so careless with their lives the night they drove off the bridge. If the soldiers hadn't been to war, they might not have shot people and gotten into knife fights. If all his friends hadn't been dead, the farmer might not have slipped into chronic alcohol abuse."

"It's a lot of ifs," Lottie said. "It's not like you to play fast and loose with the evidence."

"Well," the doctor conceded, "maybe I'm just thinking about Janey."

▪ ▪ ▪

When a man turns forty, he's likely to look as much backward as forward. And Phil Walker, during his time in his own spare room, had been doing a lot of this. In a way, he had regressed, gone back to that blissful time when Pattie Dougal was one of many young women with whom he could dally and life was one large search for a good time.

Then, he had spent time with Chuck, drinking beer and smoking dope and watching strange movies. And during the weeks in his own spare room, he also spent time with Chuck, and it was enjoyable. Chuck did not tell you to stop biting your nails. Chuck did not mention that the grass was looking a bit long. Chuck did not, in the middle of a sporting event, suddenly remember that a vital episode of a hospital drama was on another channel.

This enjoyment didn't exactly stop when Phil moved in, but it changed. Chuck remained consistent. He still didn't do any of those irritating things, but he also didn't, it seemed, change his towels or stock his refrigerator with food or have much sympathy for a broken heart. "Been there," was all Chuck would say whenever Phil broached the subject of his fight with Pattie. It was unsatisfactory. And the milieu of the bowling alley and bachelor house, which had been so attractive and comfortable when Phil was visiting from his own home, suddenly became tawdry and depressing.

He'd had a few visitors. The doctor had come by. Jim Emery had a beer and said that he wasn't going to take sides, and had seemed quite interested in the old yearbook Artie had found at the library. But then the doctor had talked about pregnancy and the emotional and physical symptoms women endure almost nonstop. In the end, Phil was glad to see him go.

"Is he always that boring?" Chuck asked from his new tan suede recliner, a bag of Doritos open on his lap and a beer in the beverage holder. He was watching a baseball game.

It then struck Phil that Chuck was sitting the same way he'd sat the night before and the night before that. A week or so earlier, he'd had lime instead of cheese Doritos. And *Chuck* thought *Jim* was boring.

Phil wanted to see the boys, but didn't want to call Pattie to arrange it. He'd picked up the phone a couple of times but the thought of hearing her voice made him either mad or sad and he couldn't bear it either way. After a while, he'd stopped trying to dial.

The whole talking thing was difficult right now. So many people weren't talking to him that his occasional forays into town (like to buy some athlete's foot spray at the pharmacy . . . his athlete's foot always got bad when he was stressed) were uncomfortable and silent. He himself had been silent through much of the doctor's visit, finding it difficult to bridge the gap between how much the doctor knew about what Pattie was going through and how little the doctor knew about what he, Phil, was going through.

So it was with a palpable sense of relief when the doorbell rang one night after Phil had put together a rudimentary meal in Chuck's underequipped kitchen to find Father Gaskin on the doorstep.

They sat in the kitchen and shared Phil's chicken stir-fry. The conversation started off talking about star anise and ended up with an intense discussion of trust in relationships. Father Gaskin asked what would make Phil Walker return to the marital home. Phil said he wanted an apology and a bit of respect.

Now, see, here is where your Catholic priest is at a disadvantage to, say, his Lutheran brother. Because Father Gaskin, with all the best intentions in the world, then drove around to the Walker place. Pattie was lying on the sofa with her swollen ankles elevated above her heart and had merely shouted "Come in" at whoever had rung the doorbell and "In here" when she heard hesitant footsteps in the hall. She began to struggle to her feet and to offer refreshment when she saw who it was, but Father Gaskin refused all this and then initiated a discussion that revolved around what Pattie Walker should do to get Phil Walker to return to the marital home.

Pattie tried to interrupt this discourse a number of times to talk about her side of the story but Father Gaskin, in his zeal, seemed not to realize that another side existed. He waxed lyrical during a short homily on the wedding vows, linking his hands across his stomach in a benign but complacent gesture. He appeared to be completely confident that he was well on his way to healing this unseemly rift in his parish.

A married clergyman would not have done this. And a married clergyman, if he had, would not have been surprised if the recipient of these counsels raised up off the sofa and started to shout.

But Father Gaskin was surprised, very surprised, and immediately retreated, thinking that if Phil Walker had to put up with this kind of behavior, it was nearly understandable that he'd taken refuge with Chuck Warren.

His last view of Pattie was of her red face. She was hot and disheveled, standing on the front porch and shrieking after him that she wanted an apology and some respect, too, and had he ever thought of that?

It was very disappointing.

The next day, Pattie went to pick up some lunch at Mayan Memories, and the Ladies' Altar Society was at the long table. Usually the Altar Society, while knowing that Pattie was a busy businesswoman unable to join wholeheartedly with their concerns, would have some task for her to do or ask her advice on some matter of finance or taste. Just friendly, inclusive gestures, meant to indicate that they knew she would, when retired, be a leading light in the organization and that they, currently, valued her as such. So, Nancy McAllister might say, "Pattie, do you think you could donate some unbleached muslin for the Ascension backdrop?" or, "Pattie, if we did a bring-and-buy supper, do you think the families would come?"

In fact, it was not unusual for Pattie to pull up a chair and have some iced tea and join in a planning session for a few minutes.

But today wasn't like that. When Pattie approached the door, the high-pitched and decorous chatter of some twenty Catholic ladies was audible on the sidewalk. When she opened the door and closed it behind her, you could have heard a pin drop.

There is a kind of smile ladies give in uncomfortable social situations such as this, a kind of quick grimacing with plenty of teeth and averted eyes. You imagine twenty of those and you'll begin to get an idea of how Pattie felt. She could hear her footsteps. She said, "Oh, hello, everyone. I didn't know you were meeting here today!" in a jolly tone as forced and false as their answering smiles. Twenty women said, "Yes," and little else in the same gay tone.

As Pattie passed the table and reached the counter, the conversation behind her resumed in a low undertone.

She really didn't have to guess what they'd been talking about.

Maria said later that Pattie's face was as white as a piece of paper. Maria had asked if Pattie wanted some of her special chicken and avocado quesadillas and Pattie nodded. Maria had said that it wasn't busy and that she could bring them over when they were ready and Pattie had looked so grateful that even Maria wanted to cry. Then Pattie turned around and walked quickly out of the restaurant.

Janey Lane was taking some time off to go for her final physical. The doctor wasn't happy about it. "Why don't they just send me the forms and let me do it?" he grumbled. "I don't see why you should go all the way to the base for something that would take me about five minutes."

"I think they do us all together," she said.

There was a pause, during which Lottie joined them in the kitchen. "Did I leave my rosemary honey in here?" she asked. "I ran out of tea honey a few weeks ago and I think I used the rosemary-infused stuff." She began opening cupboard doors and peering at their contents. Clutched in one hand, she had a small bag that rattled with stones. She poked at various jars with the other.

"Janey's got to go to the base for her physical tomorrow," the doctor said. "I don't know who's going to do the phones."

Lottie's back stiffened, but she said casually, "I don't have anybody scheduled yet in the afternoon. I can do them."

"You know, guys, I'm due to ship out on Monday. I don't think I can work all week. I've got to pack and be at the base on Saturday morning."

"I just can't believe it," the doctor said. "I just can't believe they're going to make you go to Iraq. I just can't." He leaned against the counter, covering his mouth with one of his fine, white hands, as though by not allowing any more words about it to escape, he could make the whole situation go away.

Janey lost her temper. "Well, you'd better believe it," she said emphatically. "I don't know what you two are going to do. You haven't hired a receptionist, you haven't even called the agency. And neither one of you will even *look* at my notes."

The doctor and Lottie looked at the floor.

Janey sighed in exasperation.

Doc Emery allowed one sentence to emerge before once again pressing his lips closed with his hand. "I just don't want to think about it."

Lottie said, "I keep thinking it won't happen, that something will make it go away." Her eyes filled with tears and she quickly turned and opened a cupboard. "Here it is."

The doctor reached out and took Lottie's arm as she went for the honey. "Lottie, can't you do a spell?" he said. "You've got to know something that will work."

Lottie froze at the word *spell*.

She asked, "Jim? Do you really want me to try and magic away Janey's mobilization orders?"

Janey said that here she actually stamped her foot. "You aren't even listening to me!" she cried.

Lottie, holding the bag in one hand and the rosemary honey in another, turned from the cupboard. She took a deep breath and then waved her hands around Janey in a figure eight. "One, two, three, four, Janey Lane won't go to war."

Janey covered her eyes and shook her head. "Would you please . . . ," she tried.

But Lottie kept chanting. And then the doctor joined in, "One, two, three, four, Janey Lane won't go to war."

Janey said she couldn't help it. She started to giggle. And then all three of them were laughing like fools.

"You're so *silly!*" she scolded her employers. "Nobody else will ever come work for you two if you two don't straighten up."

Both amused and exasperated, she later recounted the whole story to both her family and that of the friend who was loaning her a travel hair straightener. At the time, she'd only calmed down when Lottie had shared her honey tea.

Becky Lane was all right, as long as she kept herself busy. As Becky was very good at keeping herself busy, she was more or less okay those days leading toward Janey's inevitable departure. But there were times when her self-control deserted her.

She was sitting with Linda that night, having a beer and some microwave popcorn. Janey was off borrowing the travel hair straightener and Priss was on a date.

When the news came on and they rather casually announced that a car bomb in Tigrit had killed two American soldiers and injured one, Becky broke down and cried like a baby.

▪ ▪ ▪

Kylie Requena had been a wild and flighty young lady. Gorgeous, like all the Requena women in their youth (they were also superb cooks and by middle age this took its inevitable toll), she had played fast and loose with several hearts. She had also spent all her *quinceañera* money on shoes and clothes, and generally behaved in such a way as to cause concern.

But between sixteen and eighteen, Kylie changed. First of all, she had helped to care for her Auntie Betty during her slow and incomplete head injury recovery. And then she'd been keeping in daily touch with her brother, who had gone to war, filling him in on everything that had happened in Eudora and hearing, in Bruce's short and poorly spelled and punctuated replies, all about what Bruce thought of hometown events.

Because of these changes, Kylie had begun to think of others more than herself, had begun attending Mass of her own volition, not just when her mother felt up to the task of dragging her out of bed and forcing her to cover her chest and thighs. Part of this was a somewhat cynical posture to do with being soulful and unattainable for the benefit of the students of Eudora High (where everyone was so impressed by her new demeanor that she was the runner-up for Homecoming Queen). But part of it was due to a very real change of heart and direction.

Her grades had also improved dramatically. So dramatically, indeed, that she was encouraged to go for the SATs and the results had astonished everyone except her uncle Don, who had developed the unshakable conviction that Kylie had hung the moon.

Now, there are two universities in the state, but Kylie had no money to go to either and a lively fear, instilled by her parents, of getting too much into debt with student loans. But she had enrolled in the local community college and secured work as an assistant at the hospital (this role combined elements of porter, cleaner, and nurse's aide). She was planning a career in nursing.

Mark Ramirez had long felt for Kylie Requena the kind of warm regard a man who has chosen his life partner can have for the girl who had once broken his heart. He felt, indeed, that he owed Kylie a favor for the favor she had done him (if she had not set him free, he would not have been available for the much more suitable Janey Lane), and so he was interested in her welfare and her future.

Kylie herself seemed to see Mark as an extension of her family. The Requena women always matured rapidly, so though her brother, Bruce, was two years older, since puberty she had felt him to be her little brother. Her father, Jesus, and her uncle, Don, were capable men, but they were older and busy and weighed down with responsibility. Her older male cousins lived in the city and were not available as often as she would have liked. So, while Jesus kept her yellow 1972 VW Bug running, and Don had helped her pick it out, it was Mark who had discussed (in a long-running forum that had eventually made Janey Lane grind her teeth in her sleep) which kind of car she should buy.

If Linda Lane had been cold to Mark Ramirez, it was nothing compared to the icy reception she granted Kylie Requena.

Two years before, Kylie would have lost her temper and flounced away. But the new Kylie could see more in Linda Lane than Linda knew. More, perhaps, than Linda wanted anyone to see.

The Lane family had two living rooms. The one by the kitchen, where the TV was, had a sofa and a recliner that were more or less in constant use. But the one by the front door, which had a loveseat and two hard chairs, was reserved for formal conversations. This is where Linda left Kylie.

Janey Lane was not, as Kylie feared, red-eyed or disheveled. Wearing a clean white tank top and some olive green sweats with the word ARMY printed across the bottom, she still managed to look elegant. Kylie, in her bejeweled jeans and floral chiffon blouse, felt as if she had been caught trying too hard.

"Look," Kylie began, but Janey interrupted.

"Sorry, but would you like some iced tea?"

Kylie smiled. This was going to go well, she thought. "That'd be nice," she said.

Janey got up and left the room. A clock hung above a white wooden mantelpiece, which was above an electric fireplace. The clock ticked very loudly. And it seemed to tick for a long time.

At last Janey reappeared, a small cardigan now over her shoulders, carrying a tray. "Do you like sugar?" she asked.

Kylie, afraid to be left alone any longer, lied. "I like it however you made it," she said. "I'm flexible."

At last the tea was poured and coasters were found for the piecrust tables that sat on either side of the hard chairs. Janey settled herself opposite Kylie.

"Janey," Kylie began, "I got to tell you. There's nothing going on between me and Mark."

Janey nodded slowly. She said, "Well, that's too bad, Kylie. I hate to think of him alone."

Inwardly, Kylie sucked her teeth and winced, thinking, Mark, you are in real bad trouble. Outwardly, she smiled sadly. "I'm sorry to hear you feel that way," she said. "He's a good guy, and I think he really loves you."

Janey smiled tightly. "Well, a couple of years ago he thought he really loved you. So maybe he'll find somebody else." She took a big drink of tea. "Can I help you with anything else?"

The key ring for Kylie's car had a small Hello Kitty with a revolving head. In moments of stress, she found it soothing to spin the head around on the neck until it looked like a possessed Linda Blair in *The Exorcist*. She did this now.

She asked, "Is it true you're going to Tigrit?"

Janey shrugged. "That's the scuttlebutt," she said. "I don't know for sure if it's true or not, but the people who told me haven't been wrong yet."

Again, the Hello Kitty got the *Exorcist* workout. Kylie said, "You know Bruce is there. . . . Could you try to look for him?"

"Sure," Janey said. She thought for a moment. "It must have been pretty hard for you to come here and ask."

Kylie writhed a little in the hard chair. "I'm worried about him," she said. "I've got a bad feeling."

"What kind of bad feeling?"

Kylie resolutely put her car keys on the floor. "I don't know, Janey," she said. "He doesn't ever talk about it out there, not really. I mean, at first he used to tell me all about the trucks he was fixing and everything he was learning. And then he kept talking about wanting to be a driver and how if he got a certain license he could be a trucker when he got home and travel around and make really good money. And the day they told him he got to learn how to be a driver, he was so excited."

She broke off and licked her shapely lips. "But now that he *is* a driver . . . he don't talk about it all, not at all. He talks about what's happening here. He can't believe Hector's going out with a movie star. He's really upset about you and Mark. But nothing about what's happening *there*." Again she reached for her keys and gave the Hello Kitty's head a spin. "It's a bad feeling," she said.

Janey swallowed. "I'll find him," she promised. "I don't know what I'll be able to do . . . "

Kylie shrugged, a gesture that meant, clearly, you can only do your best.

Janey nodded, slowly but repeatedly, a gesture that meant she had taken on this task as a priority. She asked, "Can you text me your email address? Mark has my number."

Kylie nodded and stood, smiling her thanks, a weak, wavering thing very unlike the hundred-watters that had so entranced the spectators when she twirled her baton. She said, "If there's anything I can do . . . "

Janey bit her bottom lip. Her doelike eyes grew moist again.

"Just . . . look after Mark," she said. "It doesn't really matter who he loves or who he doesn't love. Just make sure he's okay."

Kylie looked up at the ceiling and blinked. She said, "If you make me get mascara in my eyes, I'll never be able to drive."

And they both laughed, sniffing.

Janey walked Kylie to the door, but didn't watch her get into her car. There was only so much a woman could take. Watching a gorgeous Latina with waist-length shining curls, an astonishing figure, and a lovely face would be enough for any woman to bear. Watching her when you have just discovered her great capacity to love would be even more difficult. Add that she'd also just agreed to watch your boyfriend while you went to war and you, too, might want to shut the door on the sight of Kylie's shapely legs folding into her Bug.

"What did *she* want?" Linda asked, coming to collect the pitcher of iced tea.

"She wanted to tell me that there's nothing going on between her and Mark. And she wanted me to find her brother when I get to base in Iraq." Janey leaned against the door as if she was too tired to walk back into the house.

"Oh, is that all?" Linda said. "Does she want you to do her ironing, too?"

"She's a nice girl," Janey said, closing her eyes.

"She looks like a hooker. How much eye makeup can one girl use? There's going to be a shortage."

"She looks great, and we both know it," Janey said, twisting up one corner of her mouth. "That's the problem with Kylie, isn't it?"

Linda sighed. "Yeah, that and she's younger than we are."

Janey opened her eyes and laughed, arching her back. She went into the room and got the two glasses and the tray. As she and Linda walked down the hall she said, "She looks great, she's just eighteen, she's a nice girl. . . . What's not to hate?"

Suddenly serious, Linda turned to face her sister, causing Janey to stop quickly. One of the tea glasses nearly slid to the floor. "Don't let him go," she said. "Don't leave with it like this. If you love him, fight for him."

Janey said, "Oh, Linda, of course I love him. But he's got to love me, too."

The engagement of Kelly Brookes and Hector Rodriguez made all the celebrity magazines. Her agency had thrown a big party in association with a whitening toothpaste. A Hollywood production company had thrown another. A well-known jeweler with a flagship store on Rodeo Drive had been pleased to provide their choice of rings and was thus reaping the benefits of an astonishing amount of free advertising. Kelly, in a royal blue Grecian-style chiffon creation (also provided free of charge), and Hector, in one of his well-fitting dinner jackets, looked wonderful in their picture in *People* magazine. Hector's easy smile was blinding on *Entertainment Tonight*.

But the news wasn't quite as well received in Eudora.

The first signs of strain came from Hector's parents. Mr. and Mrs. Rodriguez were hard-working, first-generation immigrants who spoke fluent Spanish and avoided speaking English whenever possible. He had always done overtime and she had always had an eye for a bargain and so, through frugal living, they had managed to put money away and were comfortable, knowing their retirement was secure.

Hector had worried them. He was their youngest, and they had thought they knew what to expect. But Hector never conformed to their expectations. He had seemed preternaturally still and contemplative as a child, even as a toddler. His rages and tantrums had been violent, but he had been the kind of child who is happy to watch an anthill for hours. He was also unusually clean. This, coupled with his rather slow approach to puberty, had worried his father, but not as much as Hector's freakish academic ability, especially in math.

When Hector had been selected for his job at the bank, his parents knew a moment of relief. They waited for him to move out, to find a girl, perhaps, and a house. But he had done none of those things, instead working very long hours and studying for a degree in economics and then an MBA, driving into the city sometimes three nights a week.

When he had offered to pay a percentage of the cost of adding on to the house, when they had been thinking around the problem of the new roof, and when he had shown them how to extend their mortgage at a favorable rate, they had come to terms with his permanent residency in the family home. His new quarters were not entirely separate, but were comfortable enough for anyone to envision a man remaining in them for a considerable time. He had developed regular and modest habits. He was a little odd, but his oddness no longer alarmed them.

But then he had bloomed late, and had shot forth such brilliant flowers it had nearly made them afraid. He had become the senior vice president of the bank. He had almost single-handedly saved the quarry. He, their son, had run for mayor. He had won and also won the heart of the soon-to-be Miss USA. He had bought Margery Lupin's house and remodeled it, throwing open great spaces of interior, pulling up carpet in favor of ceramic tiles, and doing interesting things with windows.

And now, now he was getting married to a Hollywood actress. A star, really. It was disconcerting to be at the grocery store on a Monday and see a face staring out at you from a magazine cover that had been sitting around your Sunday lunch table just twenty hours previously. It was worrisome to flick on *Entertainment Tonight* for the new Mel Gibson film trailer only to see your son and his girlfriend smiling and waving at you from a red carpet, a million flashbulbs popping. And then you would know that in a week or so, she would be scrubbing the black marks on the casserole pan that you can't ever get clean and taking the peelings out to the composter like a normal person.

The only way the Rodriguezes could handle this disturbing phenomenon was to treat the mayor just like the rest of their children. He, too, got a flannel shirt and soap-on-a-rope for Christmas. His girlfriend got some hand-crafted placemats. Rena knew full well that Kelly lived out of two suitcases and some boxes and did not, actually, even have a table or time to cook her own meals. That was not the point. The point was that girlfriends got hand-crafted placemats. The point was that girlfriends helped with doing the dishes, so you could spend time in the kitchen and get to know each other.

The Rodriguezes managed their son's unnatural success by ignoring it and treating him just like his brothers and cousins. And so, with a beer in his hand that he seldom drank, Hector would be asked to come and give his opinion on what was wrong with the riding lawn mower. He would walk down the street where the male half of the family had gathered to inspect his uncle's new snow blower. He would be asked to bring work clothes and help fix somebody's fence.

It didn't matter that he was inept at all these activities, or that he was manifestly uninterested. It mattered that he was there, filling the outline for his generation, who were now fathers of children themselves and taking on such projects as seeing what was wrong with the roof on Diego's shed. Hector would stand at the edges of such gatherings, bending to look at things when required, giving an opinion (almost always useless) when asked, and being with the male part of his family, all the rest of whom could never conceal their impatience, once a meal was done, to get outdoors or into a garage or shed and mess around with something dirty.

Since this entire background was understood in Eudora, it was also understood why Mr. Rodriguez had booked the church hall for a Saturday night in order to throw an engagement party for Hector and Kelly Brookes. It did not matter that United Artists and Pearl Drops toothpaste had done the same thing. He had booked a banda group. He had asked Mrs. Rodriguez (who had her misgivings about this event) to attend to the decorations and the food, while he arranged for the delivery of kegs and talked among his peers of beer bottles.

This is how things were done, and so Mr. Rodriguez would do it.

One of the last institutions in Eudora to integrate was the men's softball league. There were two teams for quite some time, a Friday team in the Friday league and a Saturday team in the Saturday league. The Saturday league was, largely, a suburban and city league, more or less good-natured and unencumbered by great ambitions and rivalries. The Friday league was the serious league, playing other small rural communities. Fights occurred over umpire calls. Men wept. People took time off work to attend far-flung games. Weddings were arranged around the game schedule.

Now, it just so happened that in the bad old days, when the quarry was owned by a series of uninterested multinational corporations, the quarry workers were too tired to play on Fridays. And so they played on Saturday nights and the Saturday night team rapidly became much browner than the Friday night team. For a long time, it was understood that if you were American without a hyphen, you played on Friday nights, but if you were American hyphenated with "Mexican," you played on Saturdays.

For some years, this had been tiring for Father Gaskin. Only a man in holy orders could umpire in the Friday night league. It was not a written rule, but one of great common sense. Who else could keep the peace? Who else would be above the invidious partisanship that dominated the entire league? In fact, the league was rather an ecumenical exercise, as in one hamlet the Methodist minister obliged but in the next a Southern Baptist Reverend Brother donned the mask and the pads.

With the sense of ethics we look for in our religious leaders, Father Gaskin felt he could not umpire for the Friday night league and then not also do so for the Saturday night league. And so, for some years, the segregation of the softball teams continued. This was unsatisfactory for many parties. First of all, the Latino players could hear the screams and roars of the Friday night league from their backyards, and to be excluded from such passionate expressions of baseball-like endeavors was, especially for the Yucatecan contingent, unbearably painful.

And then, for the paler enthusiasts, to walk by the diamond on Saturday nights and see the hamlike shoulders of the Requenas and Rodriguezes powering line drives that had spectators diving for cover when your own Friday-league team had a batting order that couldn't scare the Brownie troop was similarly excruciating.

But then two things happened. First, when the townspeople took over the quarry ownership, shifts and hours were adjusted and overtime became rarer. This was fine with the workers because they'd also received a 22 percent jump in salary. That meant that the quarry, on Fridays, blew its last whistle at three-thirty.

Second, Father Gaskin, who wasn't getting any younger, had announced at the end of the previous season that he could not keep doing both nights and, since his presence was vital to keep the peace in the Friday league, had regretfully decided to resign his role in the Saturday league.

Pablo Sanchez was now the assistant manager at the quarry, and so took turns with Royal Deacon attending Chamber of Commerce meetings. The Tuesday after Father Gaskin's announcement, Pablo was approached by several members of the Friday night team, who more or less begged for a merger. In fact, if you had brown skin and were known to hit, throw, or field, you were a popular man that

week. It hadn't taken long. And now, after many years of having either great batting (Clement's bursitis had put an end to his domi-
nation of the league) or great pitching (Lane and Ben Nichols had
formed a formidable bullpen for the last ten years), Eudora now
had both.

This was, by far, the most satisfactory year of softball Eudora
had ever experienced. The look on the faces of the other teams
when they clocked, say, Jesus Requena warming up, the bat looking like a toothpick in his massive hands, was priceless. Margery
Lupin and Zadie Gross, who had been attending games on and off
for some thirty years, just about laughed themselves sick. Margery
once nearly fell off her lawn chair, even though there was nothing
in her cooler but diet root beer and orange soda.

Phil Walker was enjoying himself immensely. At one time Phil
had been the only reliable hitter, and he had played third base for
years. However, now that the team had the speed and agility of
Johnny Sanchez for the base, Phil had retired to left field. It was a
terrific situation from which to view the discomfiture of the visiting
fans and more than made up for the loss of the base. The fact that
no one on the team was really speaking to him didn't seem to matter. Out in left field, suited up, he could pretend that everything
was normal.

But of course, it wasn't.

Nobody had any idea what Pattie Walker was thinking. In a
small town like Eudora, when a couple undergoes marital problems,
there is a useful convention that holiday and family and public occasions are split. As interested as the town is in the problems, they
do not want to actually participate in them. So, it is expected that
the two people involved will, either by communication, indication,
or psychic vibes, work out a way to avoid each other in public, if at
all possible. And it was entirely possible for Pattie not to attend the
softball game that night. Phil, though relegated to the outfield, was
still a useful hitter and so was indispensable. But Pattie was only an

intermittent spectator. It would have done her no harm whatsoever to stay home.

And even now, after everything has settled down and gone back to normal, some townspeople still see her attendance that night as wilfully provocative.

She brought the boys.

Imagine seeing this from left field. A pregnant woman in a striped cotton shirt that once belonged to you walks behind the chain-link fence to the entrance. Three little shadows trail her, decreasing in size, all wearing baseball caps. She passes the point where she used to wave to you, when you were playing third base and sleeping in her bed. But she doesn't stop and wave. She goes directly to the Lion's Club refreshment stand and emerges with three sno-cones, doled out to the shadows, and a tall cup of Coke.

And now you might notice that two of the shadows are pointing at you. These are your children, who you haven't seen for three weeks. Surely, at this point, your attention might wander from the pitch. Especially when the smallest shadow throws down his sno-cone, screams, "Daddy!" and breaks into his lightning sprint across the field of play. The Eudorans present witness this incident in just this way, from Phil's point of view. Because he might be a rat and he might be an outcast, but he's still a father, and you have to feel for the guy.

So Ben Walker runs, the way only he can, tearing down the baseline, past third base, heading for his father's arms. And his father ignores the whack of the bat, the high-popped fly ball, which comes with speed as singular and breathtaking as Ben's own directly down into left field.

Pablo Sanchez, in center field, is scrambling over. Phil finds himself surprised to tears. Everyone on the team is calling his name as he reaches for his son and the ball inevitably surrenders to the law of gravity.

This is not the movies, so the bases are not loaded. But there are two runners. They begin to steal as the batter nears first. The ball actually hits Phil in the back, but he doesn't notice, he is so busy catching the four-year-old who jumps toward him from several feet away. Pablo arrives, breathless, as Phil staggers back from Ben's velocity and Phil accidentally knocks Pablo over. Pablo frantically stabs his glove in the grass and fires to Johnny at third base while still on his knees. But by then, three runs have been scored.

Lane Nichols comes off the mound and complains to Father Gaskin. Phil, at this point, is barely noticing the uproar. Until Pablo pokes him in the ribs and shouts at him, he just cradles Ben to his chest. Players from both teams surround Father, all shouting. The crowd is on their feet and some onlookers are shouting as well.

Father Gaskin holds out his hands and takes off his mask. It gets quieter. He waits until it is relatively quiet and then says, "There was an obstruction to play." He waves the runners back to their bases, saying, "No runs," and picks up the bat and hands it to the batter. "Two balls, one strike."

Lane Nichols nods in satisfaction and goes back to the mound. Phil hands Ben back to Pattie, patting the other boys on their shoulders before trotting purposefully back out to left field.

The other team grumbled and two or three of their fans loudly protested. But for a moment, it looked like it was all going to settle down.

The batter, muttering, knocked the bat against his tennis shoe soles and stepped into the box. He spat and raised the bat onto his shoulder. And then he said, "Cheating wetbacks."

Catcher Don Requena had been having trouble with his knees and sometimes found it difficult to rise out of his catcher's crouch. But this was not one of those times. He sailed to his feet and planted a strong right to the batter's jaw, which dropped him where he stood.

The visitors' bench emptied and Don was buried in a mound of kicking, punching players. Don's brother Jesus tied with Johnny

Sanchez to be the first to arrive at the plate. Johnny pulled the visitors off Don and pushed them to Jesus, who picked them up by their collars and belts and threw them, one by one, a good ten feet away.

Lane Nichols stayed on the pitcher's mound, rubbing his face, and Phil Walker in left and Park Davis in right field just looked at each other and shrugged as Pablo ran in and began dancing enthusiastically but ineffectually around the margins of the scrap.

Father Gaskin raised his mask, held out his hands, and said, "Now, now," and a visiting player rather overenthusiastically punched him in the nose. A woman screamed.

It all could have gone on a lot longer, but Ben Nichols ran to his car and came back with his holster. He shot his .38 police revolver into the air, making a deafening roar that stopped everyone in their tracks.

"The next person who throws a punch gets arrested for assault," he said into the subsequent silence. And then, "Go home. This game is over."

The home players went to their bench to gather their things. "Nice one, Phil," Lane Nichols grumbled.

"I'm sorry," Phil said, and then addressed the whole team, saying it louder. "I'm sorry, all right?"

Don Requena, who had been looking at his battered mask, turned to Lane. "Why is *he* saying sorry?" he asked. "*You* should be saying sorry."

"What?" Lane scowled. "What did I do? *I* didn't start playing with my kids in the middle of a game. *I* didn't lose my temper and start hitting people for no good reason."

"What?" Don shouted. "The *pendejo* calls us all wetbacks and what am I supposed to do, thank him for it? And where were you, *compa,* when I was getting the shit kicked out of me?"

"What?" Phil asked.

Park said, "I didn't know he said that," at the same time.

"Yeah. He said *that*." Don's voice was heavy with sarcasm. "Or do you think I hit people for no reason?"

"I didn't think we should *all* start hitting the other team," Lane said. "I didn't understand what was going on."

"Man," Jesus said. "You don't wait to find out if your friend is right or wrong when he's getting beaten up. You save his ass first and then maybe you have to kick it later." He turned and spat. "This isn't *our* team. This is your team with some hired help."

"What?" Lane said. "Don't be stupid."

"Look, that's just silly," Phil Walker chimed in.

"Oh, this is getting better," Don Requena said. "Now we're not just wetbacks, we're stupid and silly wetbacks."

"What's going on here?" Father Gaskin joined them, taking the ice pack off his nose.

The team looked up to see the bleachers emptied. Ben Nichols was loping back across the street from where he'd seen the visitors safely into their cars.

Lane and Jesus looked at each other. Father looked between the two of them, his chubby face creasing into lines of worry.

Jesus spat again. "Nothing," he said. "There ain't nothing going on."

Father Gaskin looked at Lane. "Nothing," Lane corroborated.

But it wasn't nothing.

Saturday morning can be quiet, in Eudora, or it can be busy. It's busy if there's a high school game or another community event. It's busy if there's a sale on something timely and useful. And it's busy if there's a lot to discuss.

That Saturday was a busy morning.

In knots on street corners, people grouped to discuss the events of the previous evening. At the counter of Gross Home Cooking, people did the same. Outside the library, outside the Eudora Empire Cinema (where Bob and Jim had reinstated the Saturday morning kids' club after investing in one of the new industrial vacuum cleaners), people traded in news.

It was perhaps the worst time Phil Walker could have chosen to walk the six blocks from Chuck's ranch house at the back of the Beer and Bowl to his family home, and he had also chosen the worst route to do it. He passed, on the other side of the street, the library knot and the windows of the diner. He had to walk right through the movie knot, noticing without surprise that the knot grew silent as he approached, that he was not much greeted by the knotees as he went past, and that the volume of the knotting increased on his retreat.

Now, Phil couldn't help but notice this. And he might also have noticed something else. There were two knots to pass through, one white and one brown. For, eager as we are to follow Phil Walker home, it is essential to notice this.

Pattie and the boys were having a late breakfast. They had been making waffles together. Daniel was due at softball practice in an hour and Patrick was going late to the children's club at the movies, but they'd all decided to make the waffles. Pattie's job had been to sit on the kitchen counter and answer questions and warn of possible disasters, and she couldn't remember laughing so much.

It was a noisy table, the boys disputing who was going to load the dishwasher and who was going to clean the countertops and wipe down the waffle iron. Ben was always stuck sweeping the floor, since he couldn't reach much else, but he was always willing to take sides in an argument and put forth his own point of view. The prize job was the dishwasher, since it involved machinery of some sort. Priss had told her mom that they seemed to find any house or yard work that involved a machine or something with wheels more adult and manly than anything that didn't.

We learned all about it from the doctor, and Priss Lane, who had it straight from Phil and Pattie, respectively.

When Phil walked in, the kitchen fell silent. Ben, suddenly re-membering his gaffe of the night before, looked down at his plate with a trembling bottom lip. The older boys just looked at their plates.

Pattie said that she felt immediately angry. She'd wondered how he dared to just walk in like that, and ruin our morning? She felt he should have called first, or at least knocked.

Meanwhile, Phil noticed that they had been laughing before he came in but had chosen, instead of sharing the joke with him, to fall silent. But gamely said, anyway, "I thought I'd take the boys out today."

Still looking at his plate, Daniel said, "I'm going to the movies."

Patrick raised his head and looked his father in the eye. "I've got softball. And after that, me and Darren are going to ride out to Food Barn and get candy. And after that, I've got some yard work to catch up on."

"Yeah," Daniel chimed in. "I'm gonna help."

Phil slowly nodded. "I see," he said. "Well, what about you, Ben? Would you like to come to the lake with Daddy?"

This was a blow. The lake. It meant that Phil had access to Chuck's stunning array of motorized water toys. And now, since they had already told their father that they were unavailable, only Ben would be able to take advantage of the treat.

Daniel shot a questioning look at Patrick, who sternly shook his head. No, he was saying, we can't cave in to temptation. In reply, Daniel hunched his shoulders, clearly indicating that while he agreed with Patrick's moral position, life was hard.

Ben had taken his time to answer. The idea of playing at the lake all day with his father, untroubled by his far more able and knowledgeable siblings, was extremely attractive.

But, "No, Daddy," he finally said. "If I go to the lake with you, Mommy will have to do the grocery shopping all by herself. It's not fair."

"You see, Dad," Patrick said, "if someone has a lot of work to do, and you just take off and play, it's not fair. That's not what families are all about."

"I see," Phil said. He looked at his boots, nodding. "Well," he said slowly, "how about if I help with the yard work, later?"

"I do the mowing," Patrick said quickly.

Again, Phil nodded. "Deal," he said, and held out his hand to be slapped. Patrick and then Daniel slapped it solemnly.

"Wanna come to Food Barn?" Ben asked. "I can't reach the bottom of the cart and Mommy's new baby gets in her way."

Phil looked at Pattie, who shrugged, as if she didn't care, even though she was actually holding her breath.

"Okay," he said. "I'll come and reach the bottom of the cart."

Ben beamed. "We've got a list of stuff we're out of that Priss gives us. But we also just throw stuff in we like the look of. But you gotta read the back of the boxes sometimes to make sure it's not full of crap."

"Ben, that's cussin'," Patrick said sternly.

Ben colored. "Sorry, Mommy."

"It's cool," Pattie said.

Daniel jumped up from the table and took his father's hand. "Why don't you sit down here," he said. "I'm done. Do you want a waffle?"

Phil sat down, inch by inch, as if afraid at any moment Pattie would stop him. "A waffle would be nice."

"Get him a fresh plate," Patrick muttered.

"I was gonna," Daniel muttered back.

He ran up the set of steps and came back with a fresh plate. "I'll just put this in the dishwasher," he said about his own.

"No, you won't." Patrick tried to take it from him.

"Yes, I will." Daniel snatched it back.

"Dishwasher is my job."

"Just one?" Daniel pleaded.

Patrick looked at his father and his eyes narrowed. "Okay," he said reluctantly. "Just one. But I get to do the rest. And I'll get Dad some coffee."

Pattie told Priss that Phil was so amazed she could hardly keep a straight face. He nearly forgot to eat his waffle and bacon, watching the three boys whiz around the kitchen. At ten to ten, they lined up for shirt and face inspection and Pattie pronounced them clean.

Patrick said, "I got my glove and spikes and my candy money."

"Great," Pattie said. "Don't forget to walk Daniel to the movies first and ride safe." They kissed.

Daniel was given five dollars for the movies and told to walk home with the neighbors. After his kiss, they left, not walking safely with Patrick wheeling his bike, but with Patrick riding and Daniel clinging on from the bike rack, which reassured both parents that the boys were still human.

Pattie noticed Phil looking at her with a warmth that had been absent in his eyes for many months. She even thought his hand was perhaps beginning to reach out across the table to touch her.

Then little Ben said, "Well, no good sitting around on our butts doing nothing. Let's hustle out to Food Barn."

While Phil Walker drove his wife and youngest child to the grocery store, an additional flame of news hit Main Street. It was started by Becky Lane, who came running out of the diner, down Main Street, and down Elm. Nobody knew she had it in her, but she put on a remarkable display of speed and agility, running so fast that the Harper aunties, preparing for their weekly trip to the supermarket, looked for the rabid beast chasing her.

She pounded on Mark Ramirez's door. Mark was showing the strain of his relationship woes when, all unshaven, he opened the door wearing shorts and a wrinkled T-shirt.

Becky Lane threw her arms around him anyway. "Janey doesn't have to go to Iraq," she cried joyfully. "She's pregnant!"

Mark's face split into a grin of pure joy. Still holding Becky, he dropped to his knees and clutching her by the leg, recited a Hail Mary.

The Harper aunties stared for a moment and then went back in the house to use the phone.

The wildfire had swept to the outlying areas by lunchtime.

Carla Bustamonte was helping Kylie Requena choose netting when the news roared by Eudora Fashion Fabrics and Carla's Creations. Kylie was attending the local installment of Hector and Kelly's engagement party that evening, and was refurbishing a previously worn frock with some new trimming.

Margery Lupin had come in to see if she could buy a roll of nickels during this transaction and, since she had previously attempted to buy them at the similarly change-afflicted diner, was fully informed. Margery seemed totally elated by the news.

Carla and Kylie, still considering the effect of pale pink netting against tan chiffon, discovered that they were much less than elated.

Kylie herself felt deflated. At first she thought it might just be due to the fact that she was, once again, alone with her worries about Bruce.

Carla and Kylie took their time over the purchase, and discussed the news thoroughly. They agreed that they were happy for Mark and Janey and made all the right noises about hoping the pregnancy went well, as it was early still. Kylie was especially generous about hoping that this news would get the couple back together for good.

But though they couldn't quite put their finger on the cause, neither one of them were as happy as you'd expect.

Others were even less happy. Coming so quick on the heels of the divisive softball match, the news of Janey Lane's escape from mobilization left a sour taste on many tongues. Over in the hall of

St. Anthony of Padua's Catholic Church, where the Mayan Memories staff was preparing the catering for the party, it just about made Linda Bustamonte sick, and she said so to her friend and employer, Maria Lopez.

Maria bristled. "What do you mean?" she said.

"Well, how many people do you know in Iraq? There's Bruce Requena for one, from right here in Eudora, and there's three Bustamonte cousins from the city that I know about and probably more in the Chicago part of the family. And how many of them are white? My cousin's boss was National Guard, just like Janey, and he got sent over and was back in less than a year. *He* was white." Linda lined plates with unnecessary vigor. "My cousin has been there for two."

Maria said, "Hey, this is Mark's baby. What do you want them to do, send her to Tigrit anyway, let her have it in Iraq?"

Linda shrugged. "I'm just saying," she said.

"This is stupid," Maria said. "This is all about that stupid softball game."

Linda shrugged again. "I'm just saying," she repeated, making Maria slam out the back door and visit Our Lady of Guadalupe's grotto on the west wall of the church to try and calm down.

Even on a Saturday afternoon, lit candles flickered below the compassionate countenance of the statue in her beautifully carved recess. A display of silk roses, wired against the wind, was arranged at the Virgin's feet. When her family had first came to the parish, the statue was dirty. Dead leaves had been caught behind it and bugs were living there. Now, everything was clean and pretty.

Maria thought about her son and the danger Linda's attitude posed to his unencumbered future. It wouldn't be only Linda, either, she thought. Lots of people would be thinking that way. Maria felt so helpless that she grew even angrier than she'd been when she left the hall.

So Maria Lopez took some decisive action. She put her hands together and prayed.

Mayan Memories didn't often close its doors for a private function. Usually Maria found a way to either instruct the customer on reheating or use additional staff and managed both the function and their regular restaurant service. But the scale of the engagement party for Hector and Kelly had meant that a decision had to be made and Maria had made it weeks ago, letting all her regulars from both town and city know.

It was supposed to be a joyous occasion, and it .was certainly a large one. Mr. Rodriguez had invited everyone who had spoken to him about Hector in the last month and a half. This included the entire Mexican American population of Eudora, cousins from the city, the owners and employees of all the businesses he frequented in town, and some people he had been in line with at the post office.

Most of the guests dropped off presents and bottles on the way to six o'clock Mass, many coming a bit early to help with crepe paper and balloons and to spread tablecloths. Big Al Lopez and his Conquistadors had also come early, and some of the band, too, had taken advantage of the vigil Mass. Though this might be seen as admirably pious, most of the partygoers attended this service strategically, in the hope of sleeping late the following day. So many of the congregation retired to the hall after communion that the church was nearly empty for the announcements and closing prayer.

So, while Spector and LaDonna Williams (the barber and his wife) feared they were early when they arrived at seven-thirty, the majority of the guests had already been around for two hours. Usually, LaDonna said later, when you get to a party that early, you can chat to the host and hostess and help with any last-minute things and someone gets you a drink and you kind of stand around with them, waiting for everyone to arrive. If there are other people you don't know, you find out their names and maybe make a little small talk and find out if you've got anything in common.

But this hadn't been like that. LaDonna said that Spector waved at Mr. Rodriguez but that Mr. Rodriguez had only waved back briefly and turned back to his circle of friends. The music was already playing and it was pretty loud. There were some empty places at tables, but the way the people sitting there looked at them, LaDonna thought they must be taken already, so they ended up at a long one on their own. Nobody came to tell them where to get a drink or say hello or anything. Nobody even really looked at them.

Park and Stacey Davis did not usually mix with Spector and LaDonna. Indeed, LaDonna had always thought Stacey was a bit snotty. However, when, five minutes later, the Davises arrived, LaDonna jumped up and waved gaily, beckoning them over to the table.

"What's going on?" Park shouted.

"We don't know," Spector shouted back. "It's kinda freaky."

Just then Clement and Nancy McAllister arrived, bearing a small white box. This time, Stacey did the frantic-beckoning thing, wanting to be both bolstered against the general atmosphere of the occasion and the particular gaucheness of the Williamses.

Nancy was smiling brightly. "Well, isn't this nice?" she trilled. "Half the town is here!"

Clement squeezed her arm just above the elbow and said something in her ear. He went to join Mr. Rodriguez's circle, slapping Mr. Rodriguez on the back. Now, at this point, Mr. Rodriguez stepped back a bit and turned his body to one side, so that he could welcome his son's employer. And this, ordinarily, would be the cue for all the other men in the circle to take a half step back and enlarge that circle, so that Clement would have the space to join them. Whatever liquid refreshment was being partaken of would then be offered. Right now it was beer, which looked exotic and desirable, in brown, long-necked bottles.

But none of these things happened. Mr. Rodriguez shook Clement's hand, thanked him for coming, and walked him to the beverage table. He then shook his hand again, appeared to be deaf to Clement's question about the brown, long-necked bottles, and returned to his circle.

Clement brought back to the table three Buds, and some punch for the ladies. "What in the Sam Hell is going on here?" he hollered. "I felt like a goldarn gatecrasher."

Nancy stood up and tugged at the jacket of her neat little pink suit. "I'm going to see Mrs. Rodriguez," she announced.

"Good luck," LaDonna said mournfully. Stacey traded with Park, taking his beer and pushing her punch over to him.

Nancy crossed the floor.

"There's a porcelain horseshoe in that box," Clement shouted genially. "It came from England, where Nancy's brother was stationed, and it's fine china. He sent it over for our engagement party. Nazis got him before the wedding." He took a drink of his beer and scowled. "Let's see if that don't warm things up a little."

Mrs. Rodriguez had stood to welcome Nancy, but nobody at the table had gestured that she should take their chair and join the table while they talked. You could see Nancy handing over the box and bending a bit to shout in Mrs. Rodriguez's ear about its contents. Mrs. Rodriguez looked bewildered, but kept nodding as Nancy talked. Finally Nancy stopped, and straightened up.

"She's getting nowhere," Stacey shouted. "They haven't even asked her to sit down."

"I'll be damned," Clement shouted back.

At this point, LaDonna Williams said, she thought it might be a good idea to just go. But how to leave an engagement party before the happy couple had even arrived was beyond her. She considered attempting to faint, and really, she said she felt so sick and uncomfortable it would have been easy to do it.

But just then, Pattie Walker arrived with Phil, his brother Artie, and the doctor. She was glowing with happiness and wearing a red silk dress that had a twist knot just above her bump that made the most of her pregnant bustline. Phil and Artie swaggered, the way they always did when they entered a party together, and the doctor, who had Pattie on his arm, was saying something to Pattie that made her laugh, her dark glossy head shining and her white teeth showing strong against her red lipstick.

Well.

Every Eudoran in the place was immediately consumed by an intense desire to know what the heck was going on. Why did Pattie have three escorts? And why, rather unfairly, were they three of the most desirable men in town? Where was Lottie? Where was Julie? Given that one of them would have been minding the Walker boys and little May Walker, where was the other one? Were Pattie and Phil back together? Heads bent and what passed for whispering, given the efforts of Big Al and the boys, ensued.

Phil had been seen with Pattie and their youngest out at Food Barn. Phil had been clocked taking grass clippings to the dump with his oldest. And didn't Pattie look happy?

The strained atmosphere the Williamses, Davises, and McAllisters had noted did not seem to affect the new arrivals. They milled confidently around the entrance, the men with their hands in their pockets seemingly concentrating much effort on making Pattie Walker laugh.

Going to a party should be an easy thing. What, after all, is there to worry about? One eats, one drinks, sometimes one dances or plays cards and chats to one's fellows.

And some parties, somewhere, are like that. But this party, as we have seen, was not like that. And the new arrivals just couldn't figure it out.

We can forgive the doctor. He was, after all, still new in town, and he'd had a rough spring, what with the teddy-bear-and-pile-of-blocks wallpaper (which Don Simpson had finally had to hang), and the sympathetic pregnancy and all. Getting dressed up and going out on the town with the Walker brothers would have come as such a relief that a bit of obtuseness about the atmosphere of the occasion was understandable.

But Phil and Artie and Pattie, that was another story. Phil, especially, had actually *been* at the softball game and had been outcast for weeks. There was no reason for him to presume he was so welcome.

Phil went over to Mr. Rodriguez and slapped his back and then took his hand and vigorously pumped it. He leaned over and extracted, from the cooler between Jesus Requena's feet, three long-necked bottles of brown glass and laughed when Jesus caught his arm. He passed two out to his fellow guests and none of them seemed to notice the glares from the circle of men he had just left.

The doctor greeted the mother of the groom, pretending to take her pulse and joking that she was too excited. Later, he said that he put her lack of response to this witty repartee down to shyness.

Pattie had a quick drink of fruit punch and then Artie swept her onto the dance floor, where they began to polka. When the next song, a slow one, came on, Phil tapped Artie on the shoulder and spun his wife into his arms, whirling her gently around the center of the floor, just like, as Kylie Requena said later, he thought he was Patrick Swayze or something. Artie and the doctor waved gaily at the table in the corner to which their paler fellow guests had retreated, causing Clement McAllister to prophesy, "This ain't gonna end happy."

"Oh, I don't know," his wife said, her smile fixed and her tone perky. "Maybe somebody just needs to break the ice."

Clement snorted into his beer bottle.

At the same time Phil and Pattie retired from the dance floor and joined Artie and the doctor (who were still standing around near the entrance, laughing and joking), Hector and Kelly arrived. At a signal from Mr. Rodriguez (for which they'd been waiting), Big Al nodded to the Conquistador in charge of percussion and there was a drum roll. Then, in Spanish, Big Al announced the arrival of the happy couple.

Kelly looked absolutely amazing in a bright blue dress and matching shoes. Hector, in his dinner jacket, looked even more like a movie star than Kelly. Mr. Rodriguez came and kissed Kelly's cheek and shook Hector's hand. Folks applauded. And now it was time for Mrs. Rodriguez to do the same. But she couldn't get through. Because Phil Walker, Pattie Walker, Artie Walker, and the doctor were in the way with their backs turned to her.

And then they were smiling and talking to Hector and Kelly and then, would you believe it? Pattie reached over and kissed Kelly and they all began shaking Hector's hand, before the mother of the groom had even greeted the happy couple, like the family was not even important, like they were some kind of very important people who just didn't care about how things are supposed to be done.

Well.

Big Al and his friends had been playing in a low, background kind of way, to provide the entrance with that little something extra, but when this happened, the music somewhat faltered and then, in a confusion of tangled bass lines, died.

Jesus Requena, who had had at this point, he later recounted, about enough of the Walker family, went over to direct traffic, moving Phil out of Mrs. Rodriguez's way by repeatedly shoving his shoulder and allowing him to stumble back against the edge of the nearest table. The doctor and Artie began to look worried, and then Clement intervened, shooting out of his chair like a tight end shoots out of formation and clearing three tables in an end run in order to take people by their arms and guide them safely to the pale ghetto table in the back.

But Clement only had one pair of hands. Phil and Pattie were left in the middle of the suddenly silent hall. Mrs. Rodriguez came, trembling, to greet Kelly and Hector and Phil turned to Jesus and said, audibly, "Oh, man, I'm really sorry, Jesus. I had no idea we were supposed to . . . "

Jesus shook Phil quiet, saying, "Hssssshhhh," and then hissed, "Don't you think you already made enough trouble?"

At this point, Pattie broke in to defend her man, saying, "Jesus, we didn't know."

As Big Al leafed desperately through his notes for the title of the song the Conquistadors were supposed to play for Hector and Kelly, Jesus Requena narrowed his eyes and an unpleasant smile crossed his face.

"Oh, there's a lot you don't know, Miz Walker," he said nastily. "You might not even know your husband has been growing mo—"

The opening bars of "Wind Beneath My Wings" took the rest of his words away from everyone but Phil and Pattie. The lights dropped, and the area near the top tables and the buffet was only lit in blue, with intermittent blinding flashes from the rented glitter ball. Pattie stared at Phil for three long flashes. And then she turned and ran out the door, ungainly, with the baby displacing her center of gravity and her red dress fluttering behind her.

Maria Lopez, bringing out a tray of rice to go onto the buffet bain-maries, stared after Pattie and saw, but mercifully did not hear, Phil say something to Jesus.

She slid the rice into the bain-marie and walked over to the two men. "What the heck is going o—" she started to say, as Jesus delivered a powerful uppercut to Phil Walker's jaw.

Park Davis and Artie Walker now broke Clement's record for the sprint from the third row of tables. The doctor was not far behind. He raised Phil from the floor while Artie concentrated on shouting in Jesus's face from a distance of about three inches and Park purposefully rolled his sleeves. Now Johnny Sanchez had come over and began shouting at Artie, gesticulating wildly until Park popped him in the nose. Jesus swung at Park but Artie grabbed his arm, ending up nearly hanging from it, shouting wildly at Jesus to "Calm down!" which was the only thing that could be heard above the meaningfully intoned lyric.

"*El viento que impulsaba mis alas,*" Big Al growled throbbingly, and the band soared for a dramatic instrumental.

Stacey arrived with Park's jacket as Johnny Sanchez drove one into Park's breadbasket. Park bent over, winded and gagging, and Stacey pulled him out the door still doubled up. Clement and Nancy weren't far behind. The doctor had gotten Phil to his feet and Clement had the presence of mind to grab Phil Walker's arm and forcibly pull him into the parking lot. Spector and LaDonna did the same for Artie.

When Kelly finished her dance with Hector, she was the only pale person in the building. "Papa Rodriguez?" she asked, as her father-in-law-to-be claimed her hand. "What's the matter with Maria Lopez?"

Maria was standing, looking at the door with dismay written plainly across her features.

Everyone turned to look at Maria for a moment and then turned back to see what Mr. Rodriguez would say. He shrugged.

"It's nothing," he said.

With so many Latino members of the congregation attending the Saturday night Mass, Father Gaskin was not surprised that the Sunday morning Mass was paler than usual. Having already heard something of what had passed the previous evening, he was also not unduly surprised that Pattie Walker was paler than usual.

Eucharist is a telling time for the observant. It takes a powerful distraction for a Catholic to receive the body and blood of Christ on autopilot, and Father Gaskin was aware that this was what Pattie was doing, that for all the attention she was paying the occasion, she could just as well have been sampling a new cracker variety out at Food Barn. Mrs. Walker's mental anguish radiated from her like a sixteenth-century Italian halo. Instead of guiding the boys with hands on shoulders and backs of necks, the boys guided her. And now it was Father Gaskin's turn to be on autopilot through the following five or six recipients as he wondered what he could do to save this family, given how wrong things had gone during his last intervention.

But the next intervention would come from a much different place.

Miss Tiffany Nordelson was twenty-four years old and a native of the county seat. She had recently returned to live there, having failed to establish herself somewhere in the Rockies. She was pleasing to the eye, if you didn't mind the obvious artificiality of several of her attractions, and had a low, sexy voice, which she cultivated with late nights and Jack Daniels.

Tiffany had recently installed broadband, and it had been a pain. Such a pain, indeed, that a senior telephone engineer was required to inspect the work of three previous members of staff and resolve the various issues involved. This is how Tiffany had become acquainted with Phil Walker. Tiffany, making not-so-discreet inquiries, had discovered that Phil was a family man in the midst of marital crisis. For most women, this information would substantially lessen any interest they had developed, but Tiffany was a farsighted young lady who seemed to feel that a mortgage-free family home and a wife with her own business augured well for Phil's future as a divorced and available mate.

Now, though the vast majority of Eudora spends its Sunday mornings scrubbed and clean and in houses of worship, and a clear majority of citizens in the county seat does the same, there are other ways of spending Sunday mornings. A substantial proportion of citizens in the county seat spend Sunday mornings sitting in the sun and wishing they'd remembered to buy beer on Saturday evening, or in front of the television quietly getting stoned, in the blissful realization that they will not be working for another twenty hours.

Tiffany was among the latter group, and she suspected that Phil Walker was also one of life's hedonists, and that in his current domestic sojourn as Chuck Warren's houseguest, he would welcome a visit from a like-minded young lady.

So Tiffany packed up a present, something she'd been saving for just such an occasion. She took a clean white envelope and put in it a bud of the strongest skunk she'd ever smoked, popped the envelope in her purse, and sprayed herself liberally with Thierry Mugler's Angel fragrance. And then she went to call on Chuck and Phil.

Phil had fully intended to go to Mass that morning, but his jaw had ached so badly that he'd taken a codeine acetaminophen in the wee hours of a sleepless night and had then conked out and missed the service. Brushing his teeth had hurt so much that he decided against shaving, and his shower had gone on so long that Chuck needed the bathroom before Phil'd had time to dry his hair. So when Phil, barefoot in his jeans and T-shirt, unshaven and with wet, messy hair and bleary eyes, answered the door to Tiffany, he seemed to reinforce Tiffany's characterization of a fun-loving party animal.

Assuming she was a guest of his host, Phil let Tiffany in, saying that Chuck was in the shower and asking her if she wanted coffee. Chuck had switched on the coffeemaker while he waited for Phil's interminable shower to end, and the machine had just finished wheezing through its cycle. A pleasant aroma emerged from the warming pot. Phil and Tiffany sat and engaged in small talk, except when Phil thought to tap on the bathroom door to warn Chuck they had company. As Tiffany and Chuck were acquainted through Jeb the former marijuana grower, when Chuck (forgoing his usual morning attire of a grungy old terrycloth dressing gown) joined them at the kitchen table, the small talk continued with his additional contributions.

After about half an hour of this, Phil and Chuck began their own, silent conversation. With eye movements and body language when Tiffany's head was turned, Chuck asked Phil why Tiffany was there. With eye movements and body language when Tiffany's head was turned the other way, Phil let it be known that (a) he had no idea, (b) he really thought Chuck should know, and (c) he was outraged to be suspected of encouraging Tiffany's presence in Chuck's home. With eye movements, body language, and some suggestive hand gestures, Chuck, when Tiffany's attention was once more claimed by Phil, indicated that he, Chuck, was by no means averse to Tiffany's presence and that he found her sexually attractive. He also managed to convey that Phil's presence was undesirable.

Phil was just about to excuse himself when Tiffany leaned forward and put her hand on his forearm, saying, "I haven't even thanked you yet. You were just marvelous. It had been so long that I didn't think anyone could make it work for me." She fumbled in her purse for the envelope, allowing Chuck to make it clear (again by sign language) that he no longer believed Phil Walker to be uninvolved in Tiffany's presence and that, indeed, he thought Phil had been pulling a fast one.

Tiffany drew out the envelope with a smile and said, "It's so fast! I get where I want to go so much quicker now, since your help, and I can stay for as long as I want."

This caused Chuck to choke on his coffee, and the accusatory looks he shot at Phil while Tiffany patted him on the back made it clear he'd taken Tiffany's artless speech of gratitude for Phil's help with her broadband completely the wrong way.

"Go ahead," Tiffany said, "open it."

Forty minutes later, Pattie Walker knocked at the door and Tiffany Nordelson answered. It took Pattie, she said later, several seconds to take in Tiffany's presence and ask for Phil. Tiffany then held open the door in such a way that Pattie'd had to squeeze to get by. Pattie found Phil and Chuck in the living room, on the sofa together, watching a fishing program on the huge television.

Phil looked at her blankly, as though he wasn't sure who she was.

She called him by name, "Phil?" But he could only blink at her. "I came by to talk to you," she said.

Phil's eyes rolled imploringly toward his host, and Chuck said, his own head lolling from the effort, "Phil can't really talk right now."

Tiffany sank down into Chuck's chair and chortled with glee.

And once again, Pattie Walker turned and ran.

Sunday dinner in the Lane household was a little later than it was for the majority of the households in Eudora. Becky Lane was a fervent agnostic. At one point, she flirted with the notion of becoming Episcopalian, but it had come to nothing. For this household of hardworking females, Sunday morning was a rare time to stay late in bed.

Dinner preparation, was, therefore, desultory. The Lanes frequently wandered around the house in various stages of dress for most of the day, waiting for inspiration to strike as they wandered through the kitchen, lazily poking into the contents of cupboards and fridge. It was a time when music was shared on the stereo, instead of privately enjoyed on headphones, and if it was sunny and warm, the back deck was often filled with half-naked women, soaking up the sunshine like lizards, while tunes flitted out the sliding doors and an assortment of dishes bubbled on the stovetop and baked in the oven.

Mark Ramirez had, by degrees, become a welcome participant

in this ritual of sloth. Indeed, until his recent relationship woes, he had weekly gone to the house straight from Mass.

Now, late on Saturday night, there had been a great storm. Not enough wind to do damage, and not hard enough rain to flatten anything, but a lot of thunder and lightning. On Sunday morning, the air was fresh and clean and it was fifteen degrees cooler than it had been all week.

Knowing the girls would be on the back deck, legs and arms akimbo in the light breeze, was too much for any mortal man to resist. Even though Becky had sternly warned him not to push things and to let Janey make the first move, Mark had to see his beloved.

And her family. When Mark's parents had died so tragically shortly after his fourteenth birthday, he was left alone. He had a large sum of money from the insurance settlement, and roomed, first with an elderly Bustamonte couple and then on his own in an apartment above Main Street, in relative comfort. But his peers had been unable to deal with his loss and Mark had dealt with terrible loneliness. As Jim Evans once grumbled, shortly after Mark had been hired to become Lottie's assistant at the stationers, "That boy looks like he talks to the mice."

All that had changed when Mark became intregal to the Dougal family finances and intimate with the Lopezes. Shortly afterward things had clicked with Janey and his life had become immeasurably rich. But there was a shadow of this long loneliness on his heart. And that meant he was unable to face another Sunday afternoon alone.

For a while there, it looked like it might work. He went over at eleven, even though he'd actually been to Mass the night before, despite, in the end, not bearing to attend the party stag. He let himself in, calling, "Hi! I'm here," just like he always did.

Linda Lane smiled at him as she walked by with a bottle of sunscreen on her way to the deck. Becky called from the kitchen, "Hello, honey. How does fresh applesauce sound?"

"Sounds good," he said, giving her a kiss on the cheek and proffering a bottle of wine for later.

Priss called from the deck, "'Lo, Mark. Change the music, will you? I can't take any more of this country and restroom Mom's got on." And Mark obediently went to the racks of CDs.

Throughout these exchanges, Janey Lane had been utterly rigid on her sun lounger, exuding outrage. Now, she hastily rose, casting a towel around her bikini-clad body, and marched to where Mark hesitated between Lynyrd Skynyrd and the Allman Brothers (two selections that were universally popular in the Lane household and therefore unlikely to cause dissent). "What do you think you're doing here?" she hissed.

Mark shrugged. "Trying to decide between "Gimme Three Steps" and "Ramblin Man," he said. "What do you think?"

This approach might have worked, but when Janey said, "Mark," and tugged on his shirt, he made the mistake of looking down and fell into the deep well of Janey's rich brown eyes.

He couldn't help himself, he confessed to Becky the following day, as she upbraided him in front of an interested audience at the diner. He looked down and there she was, safe and sound, the woman he loved and *the mother of his child.*

And he said, "Ay, *mi amor,* you've *got* to marry me now, don't you?"

Before everything fun became illegal, the readers of this chronicle might recall setting off their first cherry bomb. Far from the tame reactions of, say, a lady finger or a black cat, this was a firework of some ferocity. Even its fuse seemed to sputter with unrestrained aggression. When the firework finally went off, the subsequent boom could be felt in one's solar plexus as well as one's ringing ears.

This corresponds pretty closely to what Mark Ramirez experienced that morning at the Lane household. He found himself on the front stoop, breathless, some minutes later, not really knowing what had happened. All he knew is that he was winded, and had the beginning of a bad case of tinnitus.

The Lane family residence is three blocks away from the grand Victorian neighborhood just off Main Street. The front door is not a solid piece of oak, but a panel-ply affair, about two inches thick. But it might as well have been two thousand miles thick for all the closer Mark Ramirez could get to Janey Lane.

What with getting up so early and going to bed before nine, Margery Lupin had spent much of her life being just that little bit late with the news and just that little behind with events and the currents of civic concerns. And this is why, on this particular Sunday afternoon of all Sunday afternoons, Margery baked some of Betty Requena's own recipe for empanadas, packaged them up beautifully, and took them over to the Requenas, to have their long deferred talk about the future of the bakery.

No one answered the doorbell, but the yard was not fenced and she found Don in the back with his shirt off, smoking a cigarette and drinking something cold in a tall, frosted glass. The vegetable garden showed evidence of recent weeding and a hoe and rake leaned against the picnic table where Don sat, his feet on the seats, his backside firmly in the center of the table. He threw away his cigarette when he saw Margery approach.

"Hello, Don." They'd had a good relationship over the past three years. From the time Margery had approached the subject of selling the bakery to Betty Requena, she had found Don to be helpful, trustworthy, and respectful. Don had seemed to find her the same, and since Betty's horrible injury, they'd worked hard together to bring her back to work.

But now he squinted at her as he exhaled. "Hello, Miz Lupin," he said. "Would you like an iced tea? I just made it."

And although Margery smiled and accepted, and although she sat down at the picnic table (properly, using the seat as a seat and the table as a table) and waited, she was already uneasy. This was never going to be a comfortable conversation, but it was already more uncomfortable than she'd bargained for.

When Don emerged, he said, "I told Betty you was here, but she's finding it hard to remember much today. She's just sitting on the bed, doing some crocheting." At some point in her recovery, Betty had asked for a crochet needle and some fine yarn. She had begun making lace, at first quite lumpy and twisted but then increasingly fine. Why she was making it, no one knew, but it now stretched to over twenty yards—and sixteen yards of it was gorgeous. On bad days when she found it hard to talk or to recognize people or things, her hook flew.

Margery cleared her throat. "I'm sorry it's one of her bad days, Don, but I felt like we needed to talk. Maybe just you and I can talk and then you can discuss things with Betty later." She opened up the box. "I made some strawberry empanadas."

Don made the right appreciative noises, and took one out of the box. But then he just held it in his big hands, turning the little pastry parcel over and over. "It looks just like one of Betty's," he said.

"Well, it's her recipe." Margery sighed. "She's put a lot into the business. You both have."

"Yeah," Don said. "It wasn't easy."

"No," Margery said. "And when you did all your calculations, you never thought you'd have to pay me to run the bakery for you. You can't be making what you'd planned."

"No," Don said.

"And I don't want to keep working, Don. I'm tired."

"I know." Don bent his head, hunching between his massive shoulders. He nodded for a moment, and Margery waited. She thought he might have questions. Like how long would she stay or who might buy the bakery or something like that. But the question he did have flummoxed her.

"Why today?" he asked.

Margery blinked. "What do you mean?" she asked.

"We been going on like this for months, years even. So why does it have to end today? Why do we gotta have this talk today?" Don sniffed, as if trying not to cry, but his eyes were hard and cold.

"I don't know," Margery said, taken aback. "I just woke up and thought we really ought to . . . I don't know why today. It had to be soon. I guess it should have been months ago, but . . . " She realized she was chattering, and also realized that Don Requena wasn't really listening.

"Was there some town meeting only white people got invited to?"

"*What?*" Margery was horrified at even the mention of race, let alone the meaning of Don's words.

"I mean, did you all decide we was getting above ourselves? Too comfortable? Do you need to slap us down, maybe? Put the beaners back in their places?"

Don stood up then, swinging his legs out from under what now seemed to be an entirely too insubstantial table. Margery, older and less agile, struggled to rise without turning her back on what had become a large and furious stranger. This was not the gentle, respectful Don Requena with whom she'd always dealt. This was somebody altogether different.

"I can understand the softball, because it's just a stupid game. And I wish Mark and Janey all the best with their baby. And maybe the Walkers just don't have any manners. But *you*, who paid Betty nothing for years—"

Here Margery attempted a hot denial, whereupon Don swept the contents off the table with one massive hand and Margery discovered she could stand up a lot quicker than she'd thought. "Nothing!" he thundered. "And *charging us* for keeping the bakery going while Betty got better."

"I did it for free the first year," Margery said, beginning to cry. "But I had to pay Zadie something for rent. Hector had already bought my place!"

"And *stealing* my wife's recipes!"

"That's not true, Don! You know that's not true! I've been making them just like in the bakery book!" Margery, backing away, stumbled into the side of the house.

Don, engorged with righteous anger, loomed above her.

"*Tío! Tío,* stop it!" Kylie Requena had looked unbelievably beautiful to many, many people, but never as beautiful as she looked just then to Margery Lupin. She took her uncle by the hand and led him to the back door, casting frightened looks back at Margery Lupin.

Margery turned and scuttled back to her car and then drove four blocks before stopping because her knees were shaking too badly to allow her to accelerate. When she made it back to Zadie's, she was crying so hard she could hardly see.

Zadie and Margery discussed the argument and the situation at the bakery in general for hours and many phone calls were made, one to Maria Lopez, who came over and wept, setting Margery off again. But in the end, there seemed only one thing to do.

When you arrive in a place with one suitcase, you think that you can leave with one suitcase as well. But humans tend to accumulate things, and Margery Lupin was very human. Zadie went out to Food Barn, sniffing, to get some boxes.

The night holds no terrors for a baker. It did not bother Margery Lupin that it was near sundown when she posted the keys to the bakery through the mail slot.

But it bothered her to be leaving. Several people saw her stand there in front of the bakery, just shaking her head. And then, after patting the door, she climbed into her loaded car and drove slowly away.

An hour later there was a knock on the door. Zadie Gross, feeling that she'd had just about all the excitement she could handle, rose from her recliner in a less than hospitable mood.

"Yeah?" she said as she swung open the door.

Don Requena was on the stoop. "Is Margery still up?" he asked, fumbling with the screen door handle. "I need to talk to her."

Zadie said she gave him Margery's cell number, but nobody knows whether or not he got through.

Pattie and Lottie had connections in the world of law. Perhaps that's why they seemed so comfortable with contracts and settlements. Only ten days before, Pattie had called on her legal adviser to draw up official documents reorganizing the business of the fabric shop, and the long dark sedan had arrived and stayed at the fabric store for some time, Julie Walker presiding over the cutting (trusting angelic May to Priss and her boy cousins for the morning) while Pattie and Carla remained closeted with the visitor in the back room.

But now the visitor was back, and Pattie was once again closeted, this time on her own.

It did not take long for interested parties to determine the nature of Pattie's need for additional legal advice. Spector Williams lived on the cul-de-sac where Chuck Warren's extensive ranch house was located and had seen the comings and goings of Miss Tiffany Nordelson. Mark Ramirez had taken some time for a haircut that same morning, and Mark's connection to the sisters being well known, Spector felt it his duty to provide a full account.

Of course, Mark was not the only customer that morning. Another customer suggested another, totally different motivation for Pattie to consult a lawyer. This was phrased delicately, but had to do with the communal realization regarding Phil Walker's activities at the Evanses' place and considered the legal advantages of not having communal property with anyone who might be involved in such activities. Pattie Walker was an astute businesswoman, and so, the thinking went, she might be safeguarding the family's assets by hurrying to disassociate them from Mr. Philip Andrew Morrison Walker.

On his way back to the stationery shop, Mark Ramirez stopped by Mayan Memories to talk to Maria Lopez.

Maria was gratifyingly horrified regarding the news of Tiffany and the reappearance of the large dark sedan.

"I know she don't *want* a divorce," she said.

"I know," Mark said. "But he's kind of got her in a corner."

"Well," Marie said, "her parents were separated for . . . how many years?" She turned to Linda Bustamonte. "How many years were the Dougals living in two houses?"

Linda, who had been stocking the ice bin, stopped and came around the counter. "I'm sick and tired," she said, "of talking about these *bolillos* as if they're the stars of a telenovela." She shrugged. "I don't know how long Pattie and Lottie's parents lived in two houses, and I don't give a shit."

"Linda!" Maria exclaimed.

"Don't Linda me," Linda said. "I know you think you and Pattie is best friends, but I ain't seen her in here lately except for quesadillas. And she don't ask you to go running over there."

Here, Maria remembered the crucial night when Pattie *had* asked her to come running over there and she had not. She began to explain but, now that the true extent of Pattie's need that night was understood, found it hard. Instead she said, "Oh no, now this is gonna be just like that stupid fight at the party."

Linda nodded vigorously, taking the clean white cloth she always kept on her left shoulder and beginning to polish some salt-and-pepper shakers. "You got that right," she said. "And it's just like the softball game and like every other time when you can clearly see that there's one rule for Latinos and one rule for *bolillos*."

Mark said, "I just don't think that's true, Linda."

But Linda said, "Oh, you don't? Well, it's pretty funny that everybody I know that actually has to go to Iraq has brown skin and everybody I know that sliiiides out of it somehow"—here she made a gesture of one hand skating off the surface of another—"has white skin."

Mark had just begun to ask, hotly, "Are you saying that Janey—" when Manuel Bustamonte burst through the door that led to the *tortilleria*.

He immediately related some news at a breathless pace.

It seemed Park Davis had been eating breakfast with Clement McAllister and Tony Bumgartner, discussing the fine points of the Fourth of July fireworks display, which this year would once again incorporate a musical element, after last year's phenomenal success. Manuel emphasized, using the coffee cups and various cruets on the table as markers, that the party was at an exposed table and that Park had been seated with his back to the door.

Such was the power of Manuel's narrative intensity, that Linda Bustamonte overlooked the fact that all the major players were white and only registered her disapproval by folding her arms. This didn't make her listen any the less, Maria noticed.

Of course, the fireworks display was not the only item on the agenda. The three businessmen, like the entire town, had also been discussing Margery Lupin's abrupt exit, how much it might have to do with events at Hector and Kelly's engagement party and then, when the news had arrived, the reappearance of the lawyer's sedan at the fabric shop.

The closed bakery had so far had little impact on the town. Some people had been inconvenienced, but Monday was not a big donut day. Monday was often, for much of the populace of Eudora, an "I'll start that diet today" day. However, throughout the day little problems to do with the bakery's closure were going to occur.

One of the first of these problems was that when Odie Marsh and Ben Nichols pulled up in their county cruiser, the bakery door was locked. No sign, nobody there. Being men of regular habits, they needed their customary sustenance. As Manuel said, "You always have a little something about nine-thirty and you get hungry for it." And so, "They come in Zadie's place for some coffee and to see what was going on."

Park Davis, Clement McAllister, and Tony Bumgartner had just reached the same conclusion about Pattie's motivation for initiating divorce proceedings as had the other barber customer. And so Park leaned back in his chair a little and said, in a clear and carrying voice, "Well, if Phil Walker really is growing tango tobacco, you can't blame Pattie for trying to keep her hands clean."

Odie and Ben walked in on *Well,* and Manuel said that by the *if,* Clement and Tony were making frantic hand and head signals. But Park, who Stacey often complained was in love with the sound of his own voice, just went ahead and finished his sentence. And after he did, while Ben Nichols winced and closed his eyes and Odie Marsh's forehead wrinkled with the unfamiliar effort of thought, the only sound to be heard was, as Manuel said, "the sound of the egg I was flipping landing on my shoe." This had sounded "like a bomb or something because it was so quiet I swear nobody was even breathing."

For a second, the silence was echoed in Mayan Memories. And then, the fight or flight instinct took over. Mark whipped out his cell phone. "I'm gonna call Miz Dougal." It is a mark of his emotional state that in this crisis he reverted both to using Lottie's last name and to using her maiden one. He stepped outside (reception in Eudora is patchy) and punched numbers.

After a brief conversation he stepped back in. "Janey already told Lottie," he said. "Lottie said she has an idea." Mark looked meaningfully at the rest of the table, who all rolled their eyes to heaven. Maria Lopez actually made the sign of the cross.

"Seems like Phil Walker called in sick this morning," Mark continued.

Linda returned to her plastic bucket and prepared to go back to the ice machine in the alley. "Now we'll see," she said. "If one of us was growing *mota* out in a field somewhere, we'd end up in Leavenworth." She turned to go but then turned back. "I wonder if Lottie would have such a good idea if it was you, Mark," she said.

Manuel, his story told, had dashed back into the *tortilleria* for the cornmeal he'd ostensibly come to borrow.

Mark and Maria looked at each other for a long moment.

"What do you think?" Maria asked.

Mark shook his head and got up, heading for the door. "I don't know what to think," he said.

Out at the quarry, they didn't know what to think, either. Royle Deacon and Pablo Sanchez stared at a piece of paper on Royle's desk as if it were a spitting cobra.

"We got no reason not to," Pablo said, not for the first time. And not for the first time, Royle Deacon sighed.

He supposed it was inevitable.

The quarry was doing well. Just two months ago, he had polled the shareholders (which included all of the employees and half the rest of the town) and they had decided to cautiously expand. They were advancing in two directions—fine stones (mainly used in interior decorating but also in sculpture) and gravel. Two men, Johnny Sanchez and Jesus Requena, were being sent to do training in stone masonry, and additional equipment had been ordered to allow the quarry to expand into dressed stone. That meant taking two men permanently off the gravel operation. There were openings.

One was to be filled, easily enough, by a Requena cousin who lived in the county seat but was happy to commute. He was second generation, had his papers, and all was well. The other position had been a little tougher.

In the bad old days, when the quarry often ran unregulated, ignored by both Immigration and OSHA, somebody would just make a phone call and a few days later a new, Spanish-speaking employee would turn up and begin working on a cash-only basis. But this option was not possible anymore, and Royle was largely grateful. Pablo was largely ungrateful, as this was how he himself had become a quarry employee and he had a cousin back in the suburbs of Jalisco who kept asking him for a job.

But regardless of their attitudes to the current human resources limitations, it had led them to this point, where they had to consider this piece of paper.

On the far side of town, down near the railroad tracks, there is a pocket of cheap housing. You walked past the Lanes' house a good four or five blocks, or came at it from the high school, due north. Becky Lane had, in fact, lived in this area when she was married to the shiftless Barney Lane, which just shows that not all the people who live there are economically deprived because they are lazy good for nothings. There are exceptions.

Royle Deacon and Pablo Sanchez sincerely hoped that the person who had made this application was one of the exceptions. He was going to be the first white quarry worker Eudora had employed since Eisenhower was in office.

We have not been following the recovery of Jim Flory, but it has been, considering the state he was in last time we checked on him, both remarkable and comprehensive. He still couldn't run, but he was taking longer and longer walks. If his management of the cinema showed a trifle less zeal than after he had found sobriety, it also showed a steadiness of purpose that was felt to be of greater importance and permanence than zeal. He had hired help—two high school kids who cleaned and did the popcorn and Cokes, which allowed him to concentrate more on ordering and planning. He was seen both weeding his flowerbeds and mending the crank on an awning—as close to normal as Jim Flory got.

But still, Bob had not gone.

If you went swimming at the high school pool, he was often there, laboriously doing lengths in a smart crawl, or in the changing rooms where it was noted that he (thankfully) did not linger. He shopped. He had breakfast with Jim at Gross Home Cooking and they dined once a week or so at Mayan Memories. He and Jim had dinner a few times with the doctor and Lottie Emery, cooking for each other in their respective homes. From time to time Bob vanished, presumably to look after his own cinemas, and each time much of the town was hopeful that he would stay vanished. But he always returned, and indeed, now that Jim had help at the Eudora Empire Cinema, Jim often now accompanied Bob on these trips.

Jim's face had settled back into its ordinary shape and the dental surgeon in the city had done great things with his teeth. He was no longer young, of course, but he was still a handsome man. And he seemed handsomer than ever these days. A sheen of contentment had replaced Jim's nervousness, as if the beating had transformed him, lifted him somehow onto a higher spiritual plane.

He was kinder now, too, asked about you more, remembered your own troubles in a way he'd never done before.

As the town watched Bob and observed these changes in Jim, the citizens came to what was, for some, an uncomfortable understanding. This was love, or looked very much like it from the outside. And even the staunchest of the Leviticus-readers in the Eudoran population could not help but feel that if Jim Flory could not find it in himself to either remain abstinent or to change his sexual orientation, that this relationship, while clearly still technically a sin, was not a bad solution. Compared to the groups of young men who had visited the Flory house in Jim's youth, Bob was . . . well . . . he was . . . normal. Which made what happened all the more surprising.

We do not know exactly what Lottie Emery said to Chuck and Phil that morning. It was an intense conversation with some shouting (LaDonna Williams was hanging sheets out to dry at the time and reported raised voices). We do know that, at one point, Chuck ran out to his truck to get out of the glove box the articles Jeb had given him about harmful THC levels in modern marijuana, because he dropped one and LaDonna tidied it up for him.

We also know that shortly thereafter, Chuck and Phil piled into this same truck and drove away at top speed. Also, we are aware that Lottie Emery then visited Jim Flory and Bob and that soon the two men, carrying some sort of cardboard signs on short lengths of one by two, got into Bob's light blue metallic Audi and went west on the old highway toward the county seat.

Jim Evans did not own a cell phone, never could see the use of one. He and Mary had the kind of relationship that held few daily surprises and he was a man of regular habits for whom meals could be reliably prepared. He owed no immediate attention to anyone else. They could leave a message on the home phone and wait.

We can only imagine the tension with which Chuck and Phil drove to the Evans place and how they were greeted once there.

Mary would be surprised at their knock. Drying her hands on her apron, she might say doubtfully, "Well, he said he was going to fix something in the machine shed, but . . ." Just to watch them run away on the last of her words.

By the time the sheriff's patrol arrived, they were already backing out a harvester. Ben Nichols tells the story well.

Odie was at his most officious, asking Jim what he was growing and if he could see the crops.

Jim said, "Well, Odie, I've only put in a bit of corn this year, and you can see that from right there."

Ben said that he'd never seen a corn crop striped with such an intense green before, but refused to elaborate on this when questioned. The field lay right in back of the barns, which were not far away from the house. It was on a bit of a rise, which Ben said (again refusing to elaborate) was a good thing. Odie peered at it, blinking. He rubbed his eyes and peered at it again.

He said, "I'd like to have a closer look."

Jim looked at Odie levelly. He said, "Well, I reckon you'll need a warrant for that."

Odie said, "Not if we got probable cause."

And Jim said, "But I don't think you do, Odie. You've just got some silly tittle-tattle you heard in a diner." Ben said Jim was cool and calm and looked at Odie as if he found the whole thing rather funny. Ben said you could see old Odie wilt a little bit, thinking of what would happen and how much everybody would laugh at him if he had it all wrong.

He said, "Well, we'll see."

And Jim said, "I expect we will," with that same expression of detached amusement.

Jim said later, about something quite different, that sometimes you think you've got nothing to lose and do something foolish, only to realize, once you've placed everything in danger, how much you actually do have. Phil said, when hearing this later, that it reminded him of that day on the farm. But Phil also refused to elaborate.

It's not difficult, however, to imagine Jim Evans's feelings, as he watched the county cruiser make the turn and disappear down his driveway. It's not hard to think about him looking at the house with Mary inside making the kind of lunch old country people call dinner, and then him turning to take in all the equipment in the sheds and the acreage rising and falling gently behind. It's not hard to understand the full force of how much he did have to lose hitting him, and hitting him hard.

It turned out to be a hot day.

After moving stock from a pasture adjacent to his cornfield, Jim Evans harvested corn in a strange, irregular pattern, not actually harvesting it, but mowing the whole plant down, and far too early for the corn to have cropped. The Barfords, who said they happened to be birdwatching from their porch in that direction, could clearly see the harvester making what seemed to be random right turns. The results only filled one trailer, but filled it to heaping.

This trailer was then taken to the now-vacant pasture, and the unnaturally bright green corn plants were pitchforked out onto the ground by two men (the Barfords said it was impossible to say if it was Phil Walker and Chuck Warren from that distance). And then from eleven in the morning to four in the afternoon, those men stayed in that hot pasture, with Jim Evans (recognizable even from that distance by his signature John Deere gimme cap) turning the corn plants over and over in the sun. From time to time Dorothy Barford looked to see if the county cruiser was coming back, but it never did.

One of the men then got out what looked like a garden rototiller and went out to the field with it, tilling the corn stumps into a fine tilth, while one of the others used the tractor to make a huge heap of the dried corn plants. The bonfire was quite spectacular, the Barfords say, and smelled rather unusual. George said that the buzzards who flew over it came down and asked for chocolate chip cookies and pizza, but this is not evidence, only a juvenile joke. The evidence, if indeed there ever was any, was ash, which, before night truly fell, was then watered carefully into the earth.

While it was still burning, one man was left to watch over it, while the other two spread straw over the rototilled areas of the cornfield. It was, Dorothy said, the darnedest thing.

Ben Nichols and Odie Marsh had every intention of returning to examine Jim Evans's cornfield more closely. Odie'd had no trouble getting his warrant, and indeed, if he had worked with the other relevant authorities, could have had the state drug enforcement plane flying over in no time to check the crop aerially. But Odie and his superiors had not wanted to involve the various other agencies concerned with marijuana farming.

There were several reasons for this. First, the sheriff was aware of a somewhat low recent arrest record in the department, in spite of a spate of burglaries in the county seat and some vehicle thefts around the county. If there was, indeed, a collar to be had from this situation, he wanted that collar for himself. Second, the sheriff was well aware of the marginal competency of Odie himself, and, just in case this turned out to be another wild goose chase, didn't want to look like an idiot.

So Ben found himself sitting once again in the passenger seat, traveling along the old highway from the county seat to Eudora. In honor of the occasion, Odie was flashing his lights and they were, Ben said, proceeding rapidly. Which is why it took them so long to brake.

Odie's eyesight might not have been great, but even he could hardly miss it. At the top of a prominent rise, Jim Flory and Bob were standing beside Bob's Audi, holding hands. Jim held a large sign that read, MAN LOVE. Bob held another, reading, WE WANT TO BE MARRIED. They were smiling at the county cruiser. And they were both totally, utterly, bare-ass naked.

You can still see the skid marks. They stretch halfway up the rise to halfway down the other side and clearly show a great deal of sideways locomotion. Ben said Odie just about stood up on the brakes and that his eyes were bugging out of his head.

It took several hours to process the couple. Bob had thought-fully packed two sets of sweats and some apples and bottled water in a Neiman Marcus bag, which, after searching carefully, Ben had allowed them to take along. But Odie didn't want to tamper with the evidence, so he made them ride naked back into the county seat, though he spread a blanket in the back of the cruiser for the journey after they were cuffed and their signs put in the trunk. It was remarkable, Ben said, how far away you could stand from somebody and still manage to put the cuffs on. He said he could hardly say a word because he was holding in his laughter so hard that he nearly had an incontinence episode.

They were charged with indecent exposure, causing a hazard to traffic, lewd behavior, protesting without a permit, and illegal parking. But they were home in time for supper.

By the time Odie and Ben arrived at the Evanses' place early the following morning, they found Jim at the kitchen table with Mark Ramirez, commissioning signs and leaflets. He walked them through the corn maze after swearing them to secrecy.

Jim pushed his gimme cap up on his forehead and grinned at Odie, saying, "I'm real sorry about giving you guys the run-around yesterday. But you get a good idea around here and you gotta keep it pretty close to your chest. I wasn't ready to talk about it."

Mark said he and Ben Nichols just couldn't look each other in the eye. He said you could see Odie kind of shrinking as he stood there, looking at the walls of corn.

Odie said, "You got a lot of water running to this field."

Jim scratched his chin. "Well," he said, "you gotta make sure you get real big plants. It's a bit of a gamble, but I hope it pays off."

Mark said that when Jim said that, Ben looked at him real sharp. Ben said, "Would you go through the same process, if you did it again next year?"

Jim didn't have any trouble looking Ben right in the eye. They stared at each other for a minute, Mark said. Then Jim said, "No, sir. I reckon I'd use much different seed if there was a next time."

And Ben said, "Good. Because I'd hate to see you lose big on this."

Jim swallowed. "I made a mistake, there. But you don't need to worry. It's all sorted out now."

And Ben said, "Good," again. And then they looked at each other again, Mark said, and he just couldn't believe that Odie didn't catch on to what they were saying. But Odie was walking around, looking at the corn plants, nudging the straw aside with the toe of his boot, his hand in his pockets, looking sad and small.

"Right," he said to Ben. "Let's get out of here."

For a moment after they left, Jim Evans sat at the kitchen table. Mark said his face drained of color and turned an unappealing gray shade. He swallowed a few times and then said, "I remember when we first started sowing corn broadcast. I didn't like it—I'd always liked the hills and rows of a cornfield. Getting in and out if you needed to was horrible, and you had to spray something awful . . ." He broke off, looking at Mark. Mark said it was obvious that Mr. Evans could tell Mark didn't know what the heck he was talking about.

Jim Evans sighed and took a big drink of coffee, saying, " 'The Lord works in mysterious ways, His wonders to perform.' "

And then, returned to his normal red and brown, he continued the commissioning process for the Grand Opening marketing materials.

Don Requena seldom felt ill. For a long time, the quarry had been a terrible employer, and if you missed a day's work, you also missed that day's pay. Don had seen people drag themselves through the gate, shaking with fever and chills, seen men moving politely to one side to vomit into the bushes or over the scrap during the working day. Like them, he had been motivated to consider any illness that did not actually incapacitate the body a trifling disorder to be ignored.

But he had called in sick Monday because he felt sick. He felt so sick he could hardly move. And so, on Tuesday, he was in the doctor's waiting room. When he was called for his consultation, he was surprised to see both doctors. "I hope you don't mind if I sit in, Don," Lottie said.

"Not if I don't get charged extra," Don answered. He smiled to let them know it was a joke, but he found it hard to make the smile stick on his face.

He said, "I'm just real tired. I never been this tired before. I didn't even do the dishes last night." He looked at the floor. "And," he said, "I guess I'm kind of touchy."

The doctors looked at each other, having heard the story of what had happened with Margery. Jim nodded to Lottie. He said, "It's only natural you should be feeling a bit low, considering everything that's happened to you lately."

Lottie said, "We'll do some tests, but we're pretty sure you've got depression, Don. And it's hardly surprising, after everything you've been through with Betty and the bakery."

Don hadn't thought of the attack on Betty and the subsequent problems at the bakery as something he, personally, had been through. He had thought of the whole interlude as problems that belonged to other people, which he, Don, had been more or less able to solve. It was a considerable revelation to think that they all had an effect on him, as well, that he himself was also allowed to have problems that might be unsolvable.

He felt better already.

Lottie said, "There's lots of ways to help with depression, Don. You can get a prescription from the doctor, here, which can help. You can try an herbal preparation, which can also be useful. Both of these take a few weeks to really start to work. And you can also try talking to someone about everything that's been happening to you and how you feel about it. Sometimes you might want to do two of those together."

Don nodded. Again, this was a revelation. Not only was he allowed to have a problem of his own, but people were actually going to help him with it. But then another potential problem occurred to him. He said, "If I talk to somebody, they aren't going to put down that I'm crazy on some kind of record, are they?"

The doctor said, "Don, with all you've been through, I think counseling is a very good idea right now. Nobody will be surprised or think you're crazy if you talk to somebody about what you've had to deal with in the last few years."

Part of Don really was enjoying this conversation, this concentration on himself for a change, but part of him was still worried about that piece of paper, floating around somewhere, saying he was unable to take care of things himself, that he was damaged or defective in some way.

The doctor said, "The police have trauma counselors for officers who have been in difficult situations. Even soldiers and CIA agents get counseling after they've been through something hard. You've just been through an extremely tough time . . . and your insurance covers it."

So Don signed up for the referral. He went home, did the dishes, vacuumed, made some sandwiches for Betty's lunch and packed some up for his own. And then Don Requena went back to work.

The energetic, fundraising Rotary Club cycled its catering between the three culinary establishments that blessed the town of Eudora. One month, it would enjoy flautas, *tortas,* and chips and dips from Mayan Memories. The next month, it had cups of soup and Dagwood sandwiches from Gross Home Cooking. And then it would be the bakery's turn, and the club would enjoy meat empanadas, cheese puffs, egg and tuna croquettes, as well as various sweet pastries, along with a relish tray.

This was a bakery month and the meeting was on Thursday. And so, on Tuesday, just as Don Requena dragged himself into the doctor's office, Blake Bumgartner called Maria Lopez at Mayan Memories to ask her if she could provide the food that month instead.

Maria thought for a moment and said, "Blake, I'm not really sure about doing this. Have you even talked to Don about it? He might have found a baker to run the place and be able to fill the order. I don't want to take business away from the Requenas if you haven't even asked Don. . . ."

But Blake, calling in a fifteen-minute break from his responsibilities in insurance sales, said, "Look, I'm afraid I haven't got time for this, Maria. I'll talk to you later."

And then Blake called Gross Home Cooking, where Zadie, distracted by a hush puppie crisis (they had all, for some reason, stuck together in the deep fat fryer), promised to take over the catering for that month and wrote it down on the calendar without a second thought.

So when Maria phoned Don and asked him if Blake had got in touch with him, and Don said that he hadn't heard from Blake, Maria did two things. She first told Don that there was a big order due on Thursday at eleven and that if Don wanted to save the bakery and all the money he and Betty had sunk into it, he'd better find another baker. She gave him some numbers of employment agencies in the city specializing in restaurant staff.

The second thing Maria Lopez did was call Zadie Gross and ask her if she'd taken the job away from the bakery.

Zadie, asleep in her recliner in front of *CSI,* said that yes, she'd taken the job, but she hadn't meant to take it away from the bakery, and that she'd be glad to swap months to make it up.

Maria said later that she'd just about bitten her tongue clear through. As if Zadie Gross had never heard nothing about cash flow, she said to Linda Bustamonte early on Wednesday morning. As if Zadie didn't know they was running that bakery on a shoestring.

Maria was doing some food prep, just because she needed to be doing something with her hands. She said she hadn't slept a wink, she'd just laid there and fumed. She said this as she savagely chopped at a big pile of onions.

"And Jim Evans and them *cabrones* from the bowling alley

didn't get arrested for growing *mota,*" Linda said. "The law didn't even look at it for very long, I heard. They just poked around for maybe two minutes. Mark says that Ben Nichols knew all about it. You can bet if it had been us, we'd be in jail right now. But it's different for them, isn't it?"

Linda stomped around with the salt-and-pepper filling tray, while Maria chopped in silence. "What does Bill think about this *bolillo* quarry worker? What's his name? Kevin something? My Carlos says that now the jobs they got are decent, the white folks are naturally gonna want them for themselves."

Now, normally, Maria would have hotly refuted this point of view. But today, in light of Blake's and Zadie's behavior, she only chopped more savagely.

When Linda asked about her tears, she blamed them on the rising fumes.

Since Mark could get no direct information about Janey Lane, he dropped by the diner most mornings to talk to Becky. That morning, as he chatted to her, he noticed two things. One was that the diner seemed unusually empty, especially considering that the bakery was still not open for business. And the other was the total lack of brown faces beside his own.

"Where's Manuel?" he asked, after hearing about Janey's nausea (a good sign, according to Becky) and fatigue.

"He called in sick," Zadie said. "I told him I'd call him if it got busy, but I think we'll be okay without him."

Mark nodded slowly.

"Why," Zadie asked. "What's the matter?"

"Oh," Mark said, "it's nothing."

The reason that your, say, adulterers or pawnshop customers travel to the county seat or the city for their activities is because there is a large chance that such things can go undetected in these localities. If a husband's car were parked outside a motel in Eudora (which, indeed, no longer boasts such an establishment, but let's just say "if"), news would be all over town in a New York minute. If someone who enjoyed good credit were seen taking, say, a stereo to a pawnshop in Eudora (and likewise, there is no pawnshop, but again, let's just say "if"), they would find that their credit facilities had dried up within twenty-four hours of sighting.

But if you go out of town, you might just get away with it. At least for a while . . . because it is distressingly common that one's fellow Eudorans, most of whom would rather remain in town, will find they need to travel to wherever it is you least want them to be, at just the wrong moment. But in this case, except for Ben Nichols, who never said anything about his work unless specifically interrogated, nobody in town seemed aware of Bob and Jim's protest and arrest.

For the next few days, the cinema owners went about their business.

Gardening season was now truly upon us. The drought had not yet arrived, but the temperature climbed steadily, and what rains there were fell briefly and gently. It was the season of vigorous hoeing and watering, of pest control and staking.

It was also the season of challenging child care. Some teenagers who had not managed to find exhausting enough jobs for the summer painted rude body parts and four-letter words in glow-in-the-dark paint all over the post office, causing a three-car pileup on Main Street once night fell. A large picnic out at the state park ended with two tribes of ten-year-olds "hunting" and "holding" their terrified juniors in a competition to see which tribe would make the best cannibals. The pool at the high school became a no-go area for adults from nine A.M. until five P.M. Odie and Ben wrote seven tickets for skateboarding on Main Street in a week.

And then you had the annual turmoil of people leaving and returning from summer vacation, which causes a lot of disruption in a town like Eudora. Committee meetings become impossible, staging any kind of event is tricky, and strange faces tend to pop up where you don't want them, like behind the desk of the pharmacy.

It's a busy time. People don't notice things that they would usually notice.

One hot day, two men arrived in a white county truck with a bucket riser to inspect the tornado warning sirens. That these inspection visits had become largely ceremonial was something the county workmen and officials did not share overmuch with the population at large.

The company who had supplied the extensive (and quite costly) early warning system had gone out of business three years previously and spare parts were quite difficult to find.

It was particularly difficult to find one vulnerable component, which linked the sounder to the signal wire. The design of the horns caused these components (copper-based, like all the wiring in the system) to be exposed to corrosion, especially if the sounders faced the prevailing winds of the area and were, thus, exposed to the vagaries of Midwestern weather, which can include baking heat, intensive rain, hail, sleet, snow and high winds, occasionally all on the same day.

Now, it so happened that the horns on the south side of town, including those that served the neighborhoods of the hospital and golf course, as well as one side of Main Street and half the downtown, all faced the prevailing winds. And it also happened that they all, without exception, failed to sound upon that day's inspection.

The inspectors then duly noted down that the component needed to be ordered and replaced. They noted this even though they knew that the official in charge of such things was reduced to sitting up until late at night and bidding frantically on eBay for these very components. They noted it in the full knowledge that said official was in tough competition with thousands of other county officials in the same boat and that pigs would fly before they'd take delivery of enough of the things to completely renovate Eudora's early warning system. So though the crew jotted down the number of the parts needed with brisk efficiency, they also did it with total mendacity.

However, since the sirens on the other side of town (the side with the high school, the development of ranch-style houses favored by the Mexican American community, and the less salubrious areas to the south of the Lane household) were all working fine, and since Clement had insisted way too many sirens be installed in Eudora, the county inspectors thought that the town would be perfectly safe in the unlikely event of a tornado.

If they'd come just a week before, or a few weeks after (when everyone gets into a routine fighting the various herbal and insect invasions of their vegetables and comes to grips with the astonishing consumption of water and feed), the people in the neighborhoods in which these inspections took place would be out, offering the inspectors iced tea and advice. Mayor Hector Rodriguez would not be manning the tills at the bank (in order that his two female bank clerks could spend a week shopping in New York together) and would have hastened over to look at the inspection notes. Zadie Gross would not have been visiting Margery Lupin (at last settled back into her retirement plans in Chickasaw, Missouri), and Becky Lane would have had time to interrogate the inspectors when they stopped for lunch at Gross Home Cooking.

But none of that happened.

Don Requena had not slept much on Tuesday night. It had been a very busy day, with many revelations, and then Maria's phone call sent his mind spinning. He missed only his fourth day of work in twenty-two years at the quarry, calling in with business troubles this time, and consulted the list of phone numbers.

Don was a competent man. He had surmounted a number of challenges in his life, including providing for his mother and sisters since he was fourteen, successfully immigrating to the United States and eventually becoming a citizen, raising two children, and caring for his injured wife. But this, this hiring a baker, seemed beyond him.

Someone knocked briefly at the front door and then opened. "*Tío!*" Kylie said in a surprised tone. "I saw your truck, but . . . what are you doing home? You don't feel sick again, do you?"

Don explained about the order for the Rotarians, and the employment agencies that specialized in restaurant staff. Kylie looked at the list of numbers herself, chewing on her bottom lip. "I could call them for you, if you want," she said.

Two hours and a pitcher of tea later, the hard facts had to be faced. "It's an awful lot of money," Kylie said. "And you'll have to go into the city to interview them. And there's no way you'll have somebody for tomorrow. Really," she said, "you need somebody today, because some of that stuff needs to rest."

Don looked at her questioningly.

"You know," she said. "Resting. You got to make the dough, but you got to leave it in the refrigerator for a few hours so that you can work with it. If you don't chill it down for enough time, it gets all sticky and you can't roll it out, not even with those big rollers. You feed sticky dough through that thing, you'll be cleaning that machine for a week."

Don looked at her again, this time speculatively.

Kylie said later that she felt it coming. That at first, the idea seemed like something horrible about to descend on her, like a big piece of black cloth about to cover her up. But then she thought about Margery Lupin, who was always done with work by two-thirty in the afternoon, and raising four children and keeping a nice house. And then she thought about the unfortunate truth regarding nursing, that it was very unpleasant to deal with the bodies and bodily fluids of strangers, and that it would be much nicer to deal with, say, strawberry jam. And then she thought about being in charge, about being the boss. And then before she could help herself, she thought about the kinds of things she could wear, all white, cute little white wooden clogs and white T-shirts and jeans with a long apron tied snugly at her trim little waist, and being on display, as it were, in the bakery, so that anybody driving through could see her.

So when Don said, "You know, *m'ija*, you could—"

Her interjection of "No, no, no" was not heartfelt.

"Your mother and Rena could help."

"No," she said softly, thinking of the clogs.

"We could send you to night school for the business stuff, and if you wanted to do some cooking classes."

Here Kylie betrayed herself. "Cooking classes? Growing up female in this family is one long cooking class! If I was going to do this job, I wouldn't need any cooking classes, thank you very much!" And then thought for a moment. "The business classes might be good, though. I don't know anything about taxes or keeping records or stuff like that."

Don kind of pushed her out the door and into the truck while she was still talking. Kylie had only come over to see if Betty and Don needed anything at the store, because her mom was going. She didn't have her phone with her, or lipstick on or anything. She was wearing shorts and flip-flops. But in no time, it seemed, she was standing in the bakery, and Don was putting a large ring of keys into her hands.

He said, "The recipe book is over here. And they put the orders they got on this clip, so all the stuff about the Rotary Club should be on there. Yeah, here it is."

And Kylie said, "But *Tío*, we haven't talked about money or . . ."

He said, "We'll decide that later. You won't be working for me, *m'ija*, you're a partner. You'll get half the profits, after all the rent and the utilities and everything is paid."

Kylie said her eyes filled with tears. She hadn't expected that. Don said, "If I could give it to you, I would. But we've got everything in this place." He looked at her, and it's amazing, Kylie said, how little and helpless he looked just then. He said, "Come on, Kylie," and then he looked at the floor, saying, "I don't trust nobody else."

And really, that was it. Kylie walked over to the clip and looked at the order. She said, "You might as well show me how to light the ovens right now. Then I'll go home and call the hospital and change my clothes." She peered in some of the big bins. "I hope I guess right what's in these things."

Kylie made sure that she dollied the four large white cardboard boxes down to the bank's boardroom at ten forty-five, just as Blake Bumgartner was arranging the chairs and putting out pens and pads. She said the look on his face was worth all the work and the worry.

Blake attempted to remonstrate, saying he'd made other arrangements, but Kylie said, "I'm sorry, Mr. Bumgartner, but our order wasn't canceled," and continued unpacking the goods. Everything had turned out perfect in the end, Kylie said, and it all looked fresh and good on the white doilies. Blake signed the delivery note in a daze.

Manuel Bustamonte had parked his loaded bus cart next to the bakery dolly at the bottom of the stairs and was looking at the dolly balefully. Kylie smiled sweetly, saying, "I sure hope they're hungry."

And Manuel said, "Look, I need this job. I just do what Zadie tells me."

And Kylie said, "The Nazis said that, Manuel. You better be careful," before maneuvering her dolly out of the stairwell and bouncing it out the door.

▪ ▪ ▪

Eudora is tolerant of fundamentalism in all its many forms. Eudorans know how easy it is for a person to get backed into a philosophical corner and they also know that, once there, it is easier to pitch your tent and go ahead and live in the corner than it is to face the shame of publicly repudiating your expressed views.

Take the pervasive model of the man who turns into a cowboy. Turning into a cowboy usually happens to men during puberty, or at other crisis points in their lives, such as fatherhood or the midlife crisis. It begins with the boots, generally, as it is difficult at such points not to be attracted to an instant two-inch boost to one's stature. Some people stop there, but the true cowboy victim will buy some of the shirts with pearl snaps and pointed yokes. A hat may follow. By this time, he has usually traded in his sedan for a pickup truck of some description and begun to listen exclusively to country and western music. In no time, he has a pointed yoke suit and a bolero for formal occasions and he has completed his transformation. He is now a cowboy, and may refuse to recognize that he has not always been a cowboy.

If, for some reason, this man wishes to de-cowboy himself, he either has to have a major health crisis ("I had to wear sneakers for balance," "That truck was just too high for me to get in and out of") or leave town to do it. There is no other known way of reversal.

And it is much the same problem for your other fundamentalists. Once you start speaking in tongues and using the Bible to determine what to have for supper, it's really quite hard to go back.

But just like the shining boots with their instant height boost, the shining certainties of any system of thought can prove irresistible. A wise person leaves the shoe store and the tent meeting when they begin their siren calls and walks briskly in any direction until the urge fades. But Eudorans have reason to know that people are not always capable of being wise.

▪ ▪ ▪

It was inevitable that the news of Jim Flory and his friend Bob's protest would eventually filter its way into town. However, given that Ben Nichols hadn't even told Molly and that Odie Marsh, after Armor All–ing the backseat twenty-four times, had resolved just to try and forget about it, there was a delay.

For Jim and Bob, waiting for the fall-out had not been comfortable, especially considering there was nothing they could do to hurry the process of discovery. They could not say loudly at the diner counter, "Funniest thing happened last week—I got arrested for being naked on the old highway."

They just had to wait.

In fact, the dramatic way the facts were revealed was due to one Judith Hucklestump, a city girl interning at the county newspaper. Judith, a keen graduate with an irreverent sense of humor, had been given the job of "filing up" to the national wire service, and since this was one of the first chances she'd had to actually write some copy, had done a very thorough job, poring over the various press releases and, more relevantly, the police record. She was able to acquire the arrest report and made an extremely funny story from it.

Reuters liked the story. And so Linda Lane (complete with her new and fashionable New York hairstyle) disturbed Hector Rodriguez in his office, telling him that there was a phone call from *USA Today.*

"Tell them to call Kelly's publicist."

"It's not about the wedding. It's something here."

Now, Clement McAllister had frequently bellowed from his office. Indeed it was not unknown for him to charge out on the banking floor behind the tellers, red-faced, waving some mistake in the air and yelling his head off about it. But Hector was much less volatile and had a calm manner and a smooth, unruffled managerial style.

So when Hector slammed down the antique telephone and began shouting in Spanglish, charging out of the bank in his shirt-sleeves, one of the more senior employees turned to another and said, "This is just like old times."

It would have been better if Hector had not found Jim and Bob quickly. It would have been even better if he had not found them at all. It was extremely unfortunate that he should have found them in front of the Eudora Empire Cinema, just down the block.

As Jim and Bob surveyed the coming attractions signs, they were accosted by the handsome mayor, a horrible scowl marring his perfect features. "What on earth were you thinking about?" Hector yelled, beginning the conversation. "Are you both *son tontos*?"

Jim Flory and his friend Bob grinned, just like the Walker boys when discovered in some heinous misdeed. This enraged Hector further. "You think it's *funny*?" he shouted. "Don't you got any idea? This town is just holding together by a f—"—he broke off and swallowed, but continued at the same volume—"by a thread, and you *jotitos* choose right *now* to start some silly protest campaign?"

He shook his head in disgust. Bob and Jim had stopped smiling. "What do you mean, it's hanging by a thread?" Jim asked.

"Typical *gabachos*," Hector said. "Never see anything happening right under your noses, unless it's to you."

Bob said, "Now, wait just a minute—"

But Hector ignored him. "If I were you, I'd take a long vacation," he said. "I just had *USA Today* on the phone, and when it hits the paper and the Holy Rollers hear about this, they are going to *kill* you." He spun on the heel of his shiny black oxford and strode back toward the bank.

"*USA Today*?" Bob said weakly, the color draining from his face.

But Jim wasn't listening. "What was he talking about, hanging by a thread?" he asked.

"I don't know," Bob said. And then he said, "Listen. I think I have a little problem, here. Let's get some coffee at the diner."

The seventh month of pregnancy is a sobering time. It is then that a woman discovers that undoing the buttons of her overalls will no longer make them fit, that continuing to work until the week of birth is very ambitious, that the various maladies and discomforts mentioned in the prenatal books do not just happen to other people.

Janey Lane, watching Pattie Walker's stately progress down the street, turned to Pattie's sister and said, "Lottie? It's been an awful long time since Pattie actually made it to one of her appointments."

Lottie spun around from the filing cabinet to confront Janey and Janey found herself covering her mouth with her hand, suddenly nauseous.

It was the maternity smock. Lottie had inherited her mother's extensive wardrobe and had worn it, more or less, all of her life, just filling in gaps with bits of things she had found on her travels. She had turned to this vast resource when her waistline expanded so dramatically and had fixated on what seemed to be an endless collection of prints from the seventies. These had a strobe effect when she moved quickly, which turned Janey's stomach.

The current smock was a kind of mustard swirl with bits of burgundy and dark green, all outlined in black on a cream linen background. It clashed horribly with Lottie's henna-enhanced hair.

Lottie came around and peered over Janey's shoulder at the computer screen. "Well, I know she's been a bit erratic," she said. "What with one thing and another, I haven't really nailed her down."

"She keeps making excuses. The hospital called us, said she's missed two ultrasounds."

Lottie whistled and then straightened up and stretched her

back. "I better waddle on down there and see what's happening," she said.

There are sisters, we know, who are best friends and who share each other's worries and joys in an open, trusting relationship strengthened, not threatened, by ties of blood. But they weren't Pattie and Lottie.

With every waddling step, Lottie grew more angry. Here she was, working to try and save Pattie's marriage by every means at her disposal, and also attempting to ensure that Pattie's pregnancy was safe and successful, and Pattie seemed determined to ignore both—to actually be undermining both—as if they were not the most important things in the world to her.

It was insanely irresponsible. As Lottie reached the fabric shop and opened the door, those very words were in her mouth. Insanely irresponsible. She rehearsed them, rolling them around on her tongue.

But when she opened the door, she found Pattie already embroiled in a heated argument.

"You have got to be joking," Carla was shouting. "I took fifty-one orders at the bridal show. I'm going to be sewing until Christmas! There is *no way.*" Carla seemed rumpled and unkempt.

"Oh," Pattie retorted. Her face was red and she looked hot. "Oh. You've got fifty-one orders. Well, then. I'll just tell the baby it has to wait. I just won't *get* eight months pregnant. Is that the idea?"

"Pattie," Lottie interjected. "Your blood pressure."

They turned to her as one. "Shut up," Carla said. "This has got nothing to do with you."

"Well, actually"—Lottie gave a small cough—"I do own a quarter of the business."

Carla's jaw dropped open. "A quarter of what business?"

Lottie shut the door behind her, and hung the BACK IN FIVE MINUTES sign before answering. "A quarter of *this* business, Carla."

Carla went over and sat on the steps. "Dougal Enterprises," she said in a bitter tone. "I thought that was just you." She spat the word *you* in Pattie's direction.

"I told you we needed to talk more about the contracts," Pattie said peevishly. "But you were just too busy."

Carla's bravura suddenly collapsed. She took off her wrist pincushion and threw it across the room and then buried her face in her hands. "You mean I'm working this hard, and the money is—"

"Half the money," Pattie said.

"Yeah," Carla continued bitterly, "half *my* money is going to *your* bolillo families."

"Hey," Lottie said sharply. "Less of the race talk."

"Oh yeah," Carla said. "Let's not talk about racism. You ladies have me and Mark working like sharecroppers. But that's not racist, is it? That's just business. And the white people have the business and the brown people make the white people money."

"Hey," Pattie said, "Becky and I ran this place for years."

"Not like this," Carla said. "I *did* remember to look at the income projections. I'm already twenty units over, just with these bridal fair orders. Not to mention the one Kelly bought, that we had written off as display." She laughed, but it was really a snort. She wiped her eyes with the back of her hand.

"Okay," she said. "Okay. You go put your feet up in two weeks and have another nice white baby. You got your immigrant worker here to keep the money rolling in."

Carla started to walk up the stairs. Lottie looked at the pincushion. She said, "Carla, I'd pick that up for you, but I can't get down very well right now."

"I'll get it later." Carla sounded exhausted.

"Don't go like this," Pattie said. "Let me make you some coffee. I'll go get those bear claws you like from Kylie."

But Carla kept walking.

"We can work something out," Pattie called up the stairs.

But Carla shut the door.

Pattie sat down on the steps. "Well," she said, with false cheer. "That went well, didn't it?"

As Jim and Bob turned to go to the diner, Lottie Emery came storming down the sidewalk. Usually Lottie walked a hundred miles an hour, and even now, she moved surprisingly quickly for one so encumbered. She was looking at the ground, or what she could see of it, and muttering to herself. She nearly ran right into Bob.

"Sorry," she said, preparing to go around the pair.

But Jim Flory retained her with a hand on her arm. "Lottie," he said, "Hector said there's something going on, something serious." As Lottie's creased face raised to his, he continued, "It seemed to be something about . . ." Jim paused, frowning. "He used a lot of Spanish."

Lottie sighed. She raised her eyes to the sky and dashed two tears away with the back of her hands, one hand for each tear, one tear for each eye. "Yeah," she said sadly, "Carla just used a bit of Spanish, too."

Bob, chewing his lip, tugged gently at Jim's arm, but Jim ignored him. Lottie said, "She just didn't listen to anything we were saying. It was like she couldn't hear us."

Jim nodded slowly. "Yeah," he said. "Hector, too. Like he could only"—he tilted his head to one side and narrowed his eyes—"see us?" he said, in a speculative tone.

Now Lottie nodded slowly as well. "This *is* a problem," she said.

Bob, with worries of his own on his mind, asked, "What? What?" impatiently. "What's a problem?"

Jim patted Lottie's arm. "It might be nothing," he said.

As interested as Zadie Gross was in what Jim and Bob were discussing in their booth, she was distracted by her own conversation with Manuel Bustamonte. She only heard snatches of the long monologue Bob was delivering to an increasingly worried-looking Jim. Bob evidently had a son, and this son, whose name appeared to be Tony, didn't know something.

Manuel also didn't know something. He didn't know that he was about to get fired. Zadie was hopping mad. She'd been in the diner since five A.M. It was now nearly closing time and she wanted to get home to shower before the softball game, but Manuel was asking her to clean and close for him so that he could go and visit his cousin. He said she was very upset and needed to talk. Zadie thought they could just as well talk *after* Manuel bricked the grill and changed the oil in the deep fryer and mopped the floor.

Finally, grudgingly, she agreed that Manuel could come back later that evening to finish cleaning up and could go talk to Carla now. But she'd been this close to telling him not to come back at all.

Somewhere in this discussion, Jim and Bob had left their money on the table and gone. It wasn't until Zadie turned around from locking up and saw Bob walking from the Flory place to the light blue Audi with his suitcases that she understood the significance.

Father Gaskin was not an excitable man, which was just as well, considering his vocation and his various roles in the community. And yet, as the opposing team waited balefully and the minutes ticked by, he began to sweat, even though the heat of the day was fading.

"Anybody got Jesus's cell number?" Ben Nichols asked.

Phil Walker raised his head from contemplating his tennis shoes and gave Ben a look. "If we were on cell phone terms," he said, "we wouldn't be in this mess."

This seemed to hit Ben hard. He punched his fist into his glove.

But Phil wasn't done. "Take a good look at the crowd," he said.

Ben scanned the bleachers. "Hell, there's nobody here."

There were, of course, spectators, including, interestingly, Pattie and the Walker boys, sitting with the Lane family. But none of them were likely to have Jesus's cell number and none of them were brown.

It wasn't just Jesus who was missing. It was also Don, and Pablo and Johnny Sanchez. First, third, shortstop, and right field.

"You've got five minutes and then you'll have to forfeit," Father Gaskin put in.

Ben uttered an expletive and spat on the ground.

Phil ran out to the bleachers and came back with his son Daniel, who was grinning from ear to ear. "Here's our shortstop," he said. Daniel thumped his fist into his glove in what he hoped was a convincing manner. "I'll play third and Patrick can field." Patrick waved from left field, where he was hurriedly finishing a purple bomb pop.

The rest of the team perked up. "Okay," Lane said. "Ben, you'll have to pitch the whole game, so take her easy. I'll play first."

Of course they lost, but it was close. Patrick missed an easy pop fly in left field but later made an amazing catch of a burning line drive in center, the impact of which on his little hand made tears roll down his cheeks, even through his triumphant smile. Lane was slow and heavy at first, but indefatigable. And Phil felt old and creaky at third, failing to stop an important double play just because he couldn't bend as quick as he used to. Daniel was a complete star and there was talk, afterward, of his ability to go all the way to the pros if he kept it up.

But though it had been an exciting game, and though the team lingered by the bench and finished their cooler contents in the warm summer night, there was a sourness at the back of Phil's throat that no amount of Bud Light could cure. Later, instead of driving back to Chuck's, he ended up cruising in his truck around the back of the high school and down to the development where most of the Mexican population had bought their homes. He pulled up outside Jesus's house and turned off the truck. After a while, the curtains parted in the living room and an eye regarded him. But nobody came out of the house, and he found, to his shame, that he simply lacked the courage to go up and knock on the door.

He felt that he had done something terribly wrong, but he didn't know what it was. Guilt, never far away from your Catholic man, descended on him with the weight of centuries. He was the conquistador. He was the border patrol. He was La Migra. He was responsible for everything that had made this situation, but although he accepted this responsibility, he didn't know what to do about it. As he pulled up to the crossroad, he saw Ben Nichols's Chrysler. Ben rolled down the window and waved Phil to a stop.

"What were you doing over there?" he asked sharply.

Phil ran his hand through his hair. "I don't know," he said. "I guess I wanted to talk to Jesus . . . apologize or something."

"It might not be a good idea, just showing up, this late," Ben said. He looked at Phil in an appraising manner.

"I'm not drunk," Phil said. "And I wasn't there to pick a fight. It's just—" He broke off, chewing the air with a few trial syllables, but at last, grew silent. Ben's PT Cruiser purred patiently.

"I don't know," Phil said. "Stupid idea."

"Go home," Ben said. "And while I'm telling you what to do . . ."

Phil looked down from the cab of his truck and grinned. "You're off duty, you know. You ain't the boss of me."

"Well," Ben said, unimpressed, "since I'm telling you anyway, isn't it about time you *did* go home and took care of your wife?"

Phil said, "Well, you know, Ben, that's another place I drive by a lot."

Ben shook his head.

"I'll see ya, Ben."

The white truck pulled away, leaving just two small taillights in Ben's rear view. Because he was Ben, he waited to make sure he also saw two brake lights at the stop sign before going home to Molly.

Often, Ben took the long way home, and drove through the less salubrious area of town. Odie called it "maintaining a presence," and Ben had often noticed that heated arguments in the circles of lawn chairs became instantly less heated when his car was recognized, and that people loitering on corners or vacant lots suddenly found direction and purpose resulting in dispersal.

But tonight Ben was tired and drove the short way home.

So Ben Nichols missed the four men, with the extension ladder, removing the copper wiring from the early warning sirens on the north side of town. They continued their systematic work in a brisk and efficient manner, carefully coiling a significant amount of the wire in the rusted bed of an old Ford pickup. The wire showed up for resale at the county seat the following day.

It is obvious, to the most casual observer, that if these men put as much thought and care into their paid employment as they did into their criminal activities, they'd be much richer and happier. But it does not seem obvious to the men themselves. It is thought to be something about resistance to authority.

At one point in the evening's activities, one of the thieves turned to the others and asked, "What if there really *is* a tornado?"

But another said, "There's plenty of [expletive deleted] sirens on the south side of town. The [expletive deleted] inspectors just [expletive deleted] checked on the [expletive deleted] bastards last [expletive deleted] week."

Which just shows how odd their relationship with authority had become. At the same time that they ignored the law, they also felt protected by the county inspectors. Like a toddler, who both refuses to go to bed and insists on being cuddled, they wanted the protection of authority without its limitations.

But this, while interesting, obscures the main fact. Eudora now had no siren system whatsoever.

That was the night the heat hit hard. Instead of the usual twenty-degree drop in temperature as evening fell, Eudora only dropped five and those who had not watched the weather forecast and lowered the thermostat, or those who had inefficient air conditioning, tossed and turned. Saturday morning the heat went ahead and climbed twenty degrees as though it actually had dropped the night before. Needless to say, there were no large congregations of shoppers on Saturday morning. In fact, the downtown sidewalks seemed nearly postapocalyptic. People who stopped by the bakery (and plenty did, not wanting to start their own ovens) left their cars running and dashed in and out. Ham slices and potato salads were big sellers out at Food Barn.

The drought had begun.

If you have never spent a summer in the area, you may not understand the misery that late July brings to the populace. Eudora, situated as it is between two waterways, habitually registers humidity of over 90 percent and, in common with the rest of the mid-continent, temperatures of over 110 degrees Fahrenheit. In this weather, waving goodbye too vigorously can mean you need another shower.

It is now that gardeners with timed irrigation systems allow themselves to feel smug and those without are waking up early to give their charges a thorough drenching. In the cool of the evening, they will inspect anxiously to see what has fried, but for the remainder of the day they merely worry.

The lakes shrink a few feet, leaving a ring of moistened mud in which the mosquito population thrives. The plague thus commences. There are horseflies, too, that bite hard enough to make an eleven-year-old boy cry in front of his friends. Cicadas tune up and some years are so loud they drown out the TV with the windows shut.

Even such indefatigable porch sitters as Pattie Walker withdraw from public view during the drought. News, perforce, slows down. However, when anything does happen, it takes Eudorans about twice as long to get around the supermarket.

That said, there are exceptions. There are pieces of news that cause people to go running around like Wile E. Coyote in the desert. Saturday morning Clement McAllister, the semiretired banker, was sitting in his booth at the diner, sedately examining a newspaper and enjoying his forbidden steak and eggs in the secure knowledge that Nancy was ninety minutes away at the big mall in the city, when suddenly he hopped up and tore into the barbershop as if his shoes were on fire. Pattie Walker, who was having a touching breakfast in bed (though the toast was somewhat overdone and the orange juice had spilled, meaning she'd have to change the sheets later), threw down her paper, jumped up, and got into the shower with all the speed she could muster in her advanced stage of pregnancy. Becky Lane, wondering idly what had made Clement run out without paying and only halfway through his illicit steak, read a paragraph in the paper and ran outside to call home on her cell phone, taking the coffee pot with her. Father Gaskin, just gearing up for confessions, found his telephone ringing off the hook.

The news hit the round booth full of old farmers shortly thereafter (as they tended to wait for an abandoned paper rather than rush out to purchase their own). First came the ejaculatory remarks, "I'll be goldurned!" and "Lord!" being favorites. Then came the shaking of heads and a few angry, hurt remarks about what would have happened if the assembled had seen the news item in action. Another round of coffee (Becky had, at this point, returned and renewed the pot) was then poured and the theological and philosophical elements of the case were opened.

Jim Evans, however, took his time and examined the article thoroughly, noting the date and the time of Jim Flory and Bob Magnusson's protest and arrest. While heated remarks flew around the table, mainly concerning various interpretations of the letters of the apostle Paul, Jim remained sunk in the shadow of his gimme cap, one hand ruminatively scratching the bristles of his chin.

Rosemary Walker, in a large sunhat and with a preposterously large sunshade over May's stroller, was just turning off Main Street when Pattie came lumbering past at high speed.

"Pattie!" she said. "I was just coming to talk to you."

"Can't stop," Pattie panted.

"But it's about the fabric shop!" Rosemary cried to Pattie's retreating bulk.

"Ask Carla," Pattie threw over her shoulder.

"Great." Rosemary looked down at May. "Can you go a bit farther?" she asked.

May looked up at her mother with wide eyes. She didn't answer.

Dr. Jim Emery took one look at his sister-in-law's face and went to get his bag out of the closet. "Lottie!" he bellowed, pushing Pattie down onto the settee.

"I'm elevating my feet," she called in a tinkling tone from the living room.

"Well, stop elevating your feet and come here," he bellowed again, with his head in the closet, but it was too late. When he turned around, Pattie was already halfway down the hall.

"Sit down," he said in the living room, again pushing Pattie into a chair.

"I know this was you," Pattie said, waving the *USA Today* at her sister. "It smells like you. It reeks of you."

The doctor took out his blood pressure cuff and quickly strapped it around Pattie's waving arm.

Lottie smiled in an infuriatingly kind manner. "Stop that," the doctor said to her.

"I'm afraid I don't know what you mean," she said. "Either of you." Her calm, dulcet tones caused both her husband and her sister to glare at her.

"You do so," Pattie said. "Jim means to stop being so horrible. And I mean that you put Flory and his boyfriend up to doing that protest, so that Ben and Odie didn't make it back to Jim Evans's farm in time. And you know very well exactly what both of us meant, so just stop—"

"Shut up," the doctor said. "Both of you. I need to take this pressure." For a moment, Pattie fumed as Jim pumped the small rubber ball. "Just what I thought," he said, shaking his head.

Then he approached Lottie. "Now you," he said.

"Don't be ridiculous." Lottie shrank into the cotton cardigan around her shoulders.

"Give me your arm," the doctor said.

Lottie said, "I'm fine," and didn't move. She said, "If that's all the thanks I get, Pattie, for saving your husband and, incidentally, your marriage and your financial security, then . . . "—shrugging. But the doctor simply took one of her shapely wrists and tugged it, slapping on the cuff.

Pattie fumed. "Did anybody ask you?" she said. "Did anybody want you to be the savior, yet again? How do you think you're going to save Jim Flory? What about *his* marriage . . . I mean, his relationship? Have you thought about *that*? No you haven't, any more than you've thought about how Janey Lane is going to cope as a single parent."

Lottie raised her eyebrows and Pattie said, "Don't look at *me* like butter wouldn't melt in your mouth," she said. "Everybody in our family knows what rosemary does for barren women. And in honey. And at the full moon. The poor child."

Lottie sighed and looked down her feet, pushing a stray curl behind her ear. "I'm sorry you feel that way, Pattie," she said, again in the calm tones that made her nearest and dearest yearn to give her a good slap.

"It's not about how I *feel*," Pattie said. "It's about what's actually happened. It's about what you've *done*, meddling *again*."

The doctor finished his reading and, nodding, went to the telephone in the corner and dialed a number.

"I hate to interrupt," he said. "But I'm admitting you both to the hospital."

"What?" Lottie flashed. "I'm not going into a hospital. Neither of us are. Branch women never go to the hospital."

"You've both had high blood pressure all pregnancy," the doctor said. "Now you're both off the scale. I am not going to risk preeclampsia with either of you." He turned away and gave an extension number.

"My blood pressure is not high," Lottie said indignantly.

"Tell it to the Marines," the doctor said, unimpressed. "The dial doesn't lie, Lottie. You were higher than Pattie." Now he asked for a name and then another name.

For a moment, Pattie smirked at her sister. "I always knew that cool act was fake." But then her face registered horror. "The boys! I just ran out and left them."

The doctor said, "I'll go over there and then get ahold of Phil. It's about time you two stopped acting so ridiculous, anyway."

Pattie began to struggle to her feet. "I haven't packed a bag," she said. The doctor said something into the telephone and laid it down on the table.

Once again, the doctor pushed Pattie down onto her chair. He handed her the pad and pen they kept by the phone. "Make a list and tell me where everything is," he said. "I'll bring it later." He turned back to the telephone.

Pattie and Lottie looked at each other for a moment, shocked. Pattie was the first to recover. "Don't you think you're off the hook," she said. "I don't know how I'll ever look Jim Flory in the face again."

"Good news," the doctor said, as far away an ambulance began to whine. "They can put you into a double room. So you can continue your argument at your leisure." The siren seemed to be coming closer. "There's your limo now," he said, smiling tightly.

Lottie reached for his hand and looked at him imploringly, but while he stooped to kiss her, he also patted her back briskly. "I'll get your bag," he said. "I'll see you both there after I find someone to watch the boys."

Pattie scribbled a few things on the pad. "This will get me through for the day," she said. "I might want other stuff for tonight."

"That's okay, I'm not busy," the doctor said. "You two need to stop worrying and start relaxing."

The siren became deafening and suddenly stopped. Pattie sighed and turned to Lottie. "This is all your fault," she said to her sister.

Rosemary Walker and young May were wilting by the time they got to the Fabric Shop. Carla took one look at them and disappeared into the back room, returning with iced tea for Rosemary and a glass of water for little May, which she had to be restrained from sucking down immediately.

"No, no," Carla said. "You'll get a bellyache." She gave May another little sip and turned to Rosemary. "What are you, crazy loco?" she asked. "It's like a million degrees out there."

Rosemary said, "Artie has the car. I was only going to go see Pattie but she told me to come to you and I thought it might be early enough in the day . . . "

May said, "I'm hot. I want to get down."

Carla said, "Sure, honey," and bent down to undo the straps on the stroller. May sat down on the steps that led to Carla's apartment.

"Whew," May said, drawing her little hand across her flushed forehead. "It's a scorcher."

Carla and Rosemary laughed. Then suddenly Rosemary became self-conscious. "Thanks for this," she said, raising the tea.

Carla asked, "What did you want to talk about?"

Rosemary blew out her cheeks. "Well," she said, "it seems silly now. I mean, I probably look a mess and I haven't shown such great judgment today."

Carla folded her arms. "So?" she asked.

Rosemary blushed. "I, um," she said, "I wondered if you have any openings."

Carla leaned forward. "Meaning?" she asked.

"It's just that I don't really know if I'm going to have another baby right away and May had such a good time over at her cousins' place the other day and I think she might like being with other kids some more and"—she took a deep breath and continued in the same manner—"and I really enjoyed it the other day, you know I like to sew and it was good being . . . you know, knowledgeable and helpful and kind of useful for something except wiping bottoms and making Kool-Aid and . . . "

"You want a job?"

Rosemary gulped and nodded.

"You want to work here?"

Again, Rosemary nodded.

"With me?"

"Yeah," Rosemary finally said. "If you want."

"If I want?" Carla said. "*Ay Dios!* You're saving my life! When can you start? What hours can you do?"

Rosemary smiled. "Really? Well, I talked to Priss and for the summer, anyway, I can come . . . I thought four days a week?"

"Four whole days? And you don't mind being alone in the shop?"

"Oh, heck no," Rosemary said. "I'm used to doing about twenty things at once."

Carla looked up to the ceiling. "I'm going to Mass tonight," she said. "This is like an angel coming through the door."

Rosemary blushed again. A soft sound made them turn to see that May had fallen asleep on the steps. "She can't get to sleep at night because of the sun," Rosemary explained. "And then she wakes up so early."

"*Pobrecita.*"

The telephone rang and Carla went to get it while Rosemary settled May back into the stroller, unzipping the back so that the seat reclined. She put May's feet, floppy in their white sandals, onto the rest.

Carla said something into the phone that sounded like Spanish swearing. "No way," she said. "No, just forget about it." She slammed down the phone. "*Cabrón,*" she said at it. Rosemary knew that *was* swearing.

Carla came back to the door and looked down at the sleeping two-year-old. "You sure you want to leave her that much?" she said.

Rosemary smiled. "I think I'm smothering her a bit," she said. "Artie thinks we're doing a great job, but I think she's a little too good. Some time with her cousins should fix that." She adjusted the sunshade again. "Is there"—she nodded toward the phone—"anything I should know about, if I have to answer it?"

Carla said, "We got two rings, one for the shop and one for Carla's Creations." She looked appraisingly at Rosemary for a moment and then changed her tone. "To tell you the truth, it's the magazines. They want me to tell them all about Kelly's dress, what it looks like, give them drawings. That . . . "—she pursed her lips—"that *person* just offered me five thousand dollars."

Rosemary's mouth fell open. "That's horrible," she said. "It would spoil their wedding." She thought for a moment. "And good for you, saying no," she added.

Carla shrugged. "Now, if they'd said six . . . ," she said. She looked closely at Rosemary, but Rosemary only smiled.

"Or even five and a half," Rosemary said. "But now that I'm your employee, I get half, of course."

"Clearly." Carla found herself smiling back at Rosemary. "I think this is gonna work out," she said. She put the BACK IN FIVE MINUTES sign on the door and spun the lock. "Come out the back way," she said. "I'll run you guys home."

Lane Nichols hadn't been himself for weeks. As strong men are apt to do, he fretted, hugging his worries to his chest and making life a misery for those closest to him. Lane is an unlikely hero, but if he had not done what he did, when he did, Eudora might be a very different place today, if indeed it existed at all.

And the thing was, Lane, wrapped up in his guilt and pain, didn't even know what he was doing was difficult. He just knew he had to do something.

The Mexican American community largely resided behind the high school. There was a development of ranch houses that had gone up just about the time the recent immigrant population was in a position to afford a down payment and get a mortgage and once three or four of the houses went to the immigrants, many of the more established Irish, Scottish, Polish, Swedish, and German immigrant families felt uncomfortable moving in.

Here, the gatherings of people so absent on Main Street were still present in driveways. The men who worked the quarry were hardened to the vagaries of the weather. Deep snow or a tornado warning (not just a tornado watch) would keep them from their duties, but a little bit of hot sun was nothing. If you were a wimp, you might have to wear a bandana, but otherwise you just put on an old long-sleeved shirt with the cuffs torn off and got on with it. Lately they had been laughing a great deal at the new recruit, who had to sit down and rest an inordinate amount of time when it got hot. And although he was getting quite an education in Mexicano swear words, he didn't seem at all grateful about it.

When Lane Nichols pulled up outside Jesus Requena's house, a knot of men was outdoors, surrounding Jesus's truck, making helpful comments and handing tools as Jesus attempted to replace a speaker. Most of them were drinking coffee out of thermoslike cups that had been a Mayan Memories' promotional item the year before.

"No," he could hear Jesus saying. "I mean one of those little bitty Phillips ones. Like for glasses."

Now, though much of the subsequent muttering as three other men poked about in various tool chests was in Spanish, Lane was only too familiar with the sound of someone not finding the tool they sought. So he turned and went back to his truck, which had a large metal locker in back of the cab that held a variety of automotive and other implements. For a different man, this might be a formidable array but for Lane, it was only a skimpy travel kit compared to what he kept at the garage and at home.

He then walked directly to the truck with a small black plastic case. "How little is it?" he asked. "I've got the number o-o, the number o, and the number one."

The gathering fell silent and Jesus Requena's head appeared from the bottom of the double cab door. Lane walked over and proffered the case.

For a moment, things were tense. Then Jesus took the biggest one and disappeared again. "I got you now, you . . . " But we will gloss over the remainder of his speech. Suffice it to say that by the time five minutes had elapsed, Lane was upside down in the back of the cab with Jesus, a valuable assistant in a successful operation. And that after half an hour had elapsed, he was sitting in a lawn chair on the driveway with a cup of coffee of his own, listening to some *narcocorrido* from the truck's repaired sound system and being gently teased by the men he had replaced.

Pablo Sanchez said, "I thought you two were getting a little too friendly for a minute, when you were rotating the collar. I thought maybe you wanted to be alone."

Don Requena snorted.

Pablo took this as encouragement. "Yeah, I was afraid maybe you guys would be out protesting with Jim Flory next week."

At this point, while everybody else was laughing, Lane asked, "What do you mean, protesting?" and had to be filled in on the news item in *USA Today* and the subsequent communal outrage.

Jesus said, "I don't know why all the *bolillos* are so upset. The *maricones* have been playing house all summer. Just because they did something that made them notice, now it's all a problem."

Lane said, "I didn't read the paper today. I was in such a hurry to get over here."

Jesus turned to face him. "Yeah," he said. "Why *did* you come over here? Did you get some psychic vibe that a beaner needed an o-o screwdriver or something?"

There was a moment of silence while Lane thought, chewing on his bottom lip. "I been . . . ," he started, and then got another run up at it. "I been worried about Bruce," he said. "He was writing me, but he stopped. I came to see how he was . . . and . . . "

Again, the assembled courteously waited while Lane thought and chewed. "I guess I was wanting to . . . I mean"—he scooted up onto the edge of his chair, as if he might have to get up in a hurry—"the army was my idea," he said. He looked at the driveway and chewed his lip furiously.

Jesus nodded slowly. He said, "Well, the army was everybody's idea. Even Rena's papi told him to do it. And me."

Lane closed his eyes briefly and sighed. Then he nodded.

"Bruce isn't saying much these days to anybody. The women are worried." Jesus pursed his lips and spat. Don grunted his agreement.

Lane said, "It's a mess over there. I would have never . . ."

Again the small group fell silent.

Pablo broke the silence. *"Oye, cabrónes,"* he said. "Why so sad? He's a Requena. You can't kill a Requena. Did anybody ever tell you about when Don got run over by his own truck?"

Lane smiled and shook his head. "No," he said. "Nobody ever did."

"Well," Pablo began, "he was trying to change the brake pads on the rear . . ."

We will leave Pablo's story for another time. Let's look at the scene from above, the hot sun on the white gravel driveway, and the scant shade by the garage and under the acacia tree, where five men sit, talking and laughing.

When we think of how to ease racial tension in our communities, the plans usually involve a great deal of expenditure and are complex in their execution, requiring highly educated specialists. A o-o Phillips screwdriver and a cup of coffee might not be thought of as useful initiatives during the planning stages and a garage mechanic might not have his résumé put in the interview pile. But in Eudora, where municipal money is tight and people have habits of making do and mending, they tend to use whatever's available.

Now, it just so happened that the meat distributor for Mayan Memories had sent Maria Lopez a little present to say sorry for their mangling of the previous month's bill. They sent a whole picnic shoulder of pork.

Pork moved a bit slow at Mayan Memories. People usually ate chicken or beef when they ate out. So for a few days, Maria had thought about making a pork special but then, aware of local attitudes toward hot weather and hygiene and how they related to the restaurant consumption of pork, thought it would just be wasted. Maybe two or three people would eat it and then the rest would end up in the dumpster.

Talking about this on Saturday, Bill Lopez mentioned that he wouldn't be averse to doing a bit of barbecuing that evening. Well, one thing led to another and before anyone really knew it, a spontaneous street party had kicked off with Maria's cochinita pibil roast as the main attraction.

The bakery was closed on Sunday, so Kylie brought home everything that hadn't sold. Someone went to Mayan Memories and got a stack of tortillas before the *tortilleria* shut for the weekend. There was talk of a keg, but instead four young men drove into the county seat and came back with several cases of Negro Modelo beer distributed among various coolers, while their mothers got busy in their gardens and kitchens making various salads. By the time Maria abandoned the Saturday service to Linda Bustamonte and Gabe Burgos, the Sanchezes had run their stereo speakers out the windows on wires and the party was in full swing.

Maria got Mark Ramirez on the phone and he walked across town in time to get the last two tortillas. As he stood with his overloaded paper plate in the circle of men by the coolers, the dancing started. Pablo and Consuelo Sanchez took to the asphalt of their driveway as if it were a ballroom. In no time, five or six couples of all ages strolled and rotated to the corridor. Somebody would get some *banda* out soon, Mark knew, and then somebody would for sure turn their ankle or fall. It happened every time.

Suddenly Mark had no appetite. That should have been him and Janey out there. They had just been learning to dance together, as Janey's previous experience was with freestyle, more suited to a disco than couples dancing for public celebrations. At first she'd been rather clumsy. But that hadn't mattered. Mark was sure Pablo and Consuelo had been clumsy together at first, too. But after thirty years or so of dancing together, you got good at it. Looking at the couples circling the driveway in their perfectly matched two-steps, Mark felt an emptiness in the bottom of his stomach that could not be filled, not even by Maria's cochinita pibil.

Luckily, he was among friends. So when, after gazing at the dancing couples, Mark threw his half-full plate into a black plastic sack thoughtfully provided by Rena Requena, his buddies were there for him.

"Look at Mark, here," Johnny said. "He's missing his woman." This last word was elongated ridiculously.

Everyone laughed. "Hey, Mark," Jesus Requena said. "You got her pregnant, man. You got the bird in the cage. Now all you gotta do is shut the door."

Again, general laughter. Someone removed Mark's beer bottle from his hand and pressed a colder, fuller one into it instead.

Diego Rodriguez put his arm around Mark's shoulder. "Unless," he said, "you ain't the daddy, ya, *cabrón*?"

Mark's face burned and he shrugged Diego's arm from his shoulder.

"Ooooh," Jesus said. "Diego, that's low."

"Yeah, don't listen to him, Mark," Johnny said. "He's just jealous. The *güeras* never look at him, only at his sexy brother."

Mark, who had been about to leave, relaxed at Johnny's words. Diego thought for a minute and shrugged. "Well, I don't understand it," he said. "If the baby is yours, why's she being so hard to get?"

"Women," Jesus said and spat. "They get your heart and then they play with it, like a cat plays with a mouse."

Here there was general agreement. Mark found himself nodding. It was a relief to be here, among old friends, and among people who did not tiptoe around your difficulties as if they were shameful, but who came right out and asked about them. He took a long drink of Negro Modelo and felt an affection for his community spread through him. He put his arm around Diego's neck and choked him lightly before letting him go again and Diego patted him on his bottom.

"Oye, watch that," Jesus said. "Bob's out of town and if Jim Flory finds out how much you like touching men's butts . . . " He made a rude gesture.

The men were laughing when Kylie Requena walked by in a sundress and flip-flops, her hair piled loosely on top of her head. The laughter came to an abrupt halt as they reverently watched.

"Oh, man," said Johnny Sanchez. "Sometimes I think I'm going to die if I don't get a piece of Kylie Requena." He turned his face to the sky. "Just once, God," he pleaded. "Just one hour."

This chronicle will not indulge in stereotypes of macho behavior among Mexican American males. However, there was something in Mark that yearned to prove something to Diego, Johnny, Jesus, and whoever else was watching. And so he pressed his beer into Diego's hand, wiped his mouth on the back of his hand, and went after Kylie Requena.

Less than a minute later, they were dancing together in the Sanchezes' driveway, their steps perfectly matched.

"*Ay Dios,*" Johnny Sanchez said, wonderingly. "What's he got that I don't got?"

"Half his own business, a place of his own, nice clothes," Jesus said. "Women kind of like stuff like that."

"Hey," Johnny said, "I got nice clothes." He looked down. "This is a genuine Tweety Bird T-shirt," he said. "It's got the little *c* in the circle and everything."

"You go tell Kylie," Diego said. "I'm sure that's gonna make all the difference."

Over by the food table, some of the neighborhood women sat on folding lawn chairs, drinking iced tea. Two big white bakery boxes were open at their feet and twelve pairs of brown eyes were fixed on the sight of Mark Ramirez dancing with Kylie Requena.

"I don't get it," young Donna Bustamonte finally said. "What does Janey Lane think she's doing?"

Eleven heads were shaken. "I don't know," said Juanita Requena, her birdlike head cocked to one side. "But if it was me, and I had a bun in the oven, and *mi novio* had an old girlfriend who looked like Kylie . . . "

Rena grunted as she reached for a slice of chocolate-and-peanut-butter cake. She said, "I like Mark," she said. "But I'll kill Kylie if she gets back with him now."

"Girls break your heart," Esperanza Bustamonte intoned heavily. "They're so sweet when they're babies but they're like snakes when they get grown."

"Thanks a lot," her daughter said, while Donna, her granddaughter, laughed.

"You wait," Esperanza said to her daughter-in-law. "This one is turning now." She pointed to Donna, who abruptly stopped laughing, looking self-conscious.

Kylie's hair had fallen down with her exertions. She'd stepped to one side to put it up again, but had had trouble with the barrette. Mark was helping. They made quite a picture, Kylie standing in front of him, her lovely neck exposed, holding up her hair, while Mark concentrated on working the barrette, his hands buried in her curls.

"Maybe it would be better," Juanita said. "Maybe he needs to marry into the community, not get any further out of it."

Esperanza sighed. "There's a lot of truth in that," she said.

Maria Lopez stiffened. "What truth?" she asked.

And Donna Bustamonte said, "I think that's racist. Like we're so weird that nobody else can understand us?"

"Don't call names," her mother said. "And maybe we are weird."

"Anyway," Esperanza said, "there's a child, now. It's too late for Mark to start thinking about these things. What's done is done." She rattled the ice in her empty aluminum beaker at Donna, who immediately got up to replenish it. "The poor *niño* will never fit in anywhere."

Maria asked, "What if the baby fits in everywhere?" She said, "I'll have a refill, too, *por favor,* Donna," and continued, "I mean, what if Janey and Mark are only the beginning and people stop thinking about being ethnic so much and all the children get mixed up. It's already happening in the city."

"*Mio Dio,* I hope not," Rena said. "I was there two weeks ago for a family wedding and my cousins are having half black and half Korean kids. The bride was Irish, with this red hair." She shuddered. "It was weird, like we was disappearing."

"A-ssim-i-la-tion," Donna said. "Look it up in the dictionary. It's what happens to immigrant populations. If you don't like it, sell your house and go back to the rancho."

"Watch your smart mouth," her mother said. "Unless you want a slap."

Esperanza sighed. "Like snakes they get," she said. "Without exception."

Long after the last of the beer and brandy was consumed, after the stray paper plates were bagged up and the lawn chairs returned to garages . . . after that part of town grew quiet and the rest of the community slumbered, one door opened.

Chuck Warren had not been sleeping well since Phil had moved home. It was ridiculous to think that he actually missed Phil. He just missed somebody, or even perhaps something, coming into the careful construction he called his life.

Suddenly Chuck could see the endless future of his regular existence. It left him cold. Quite literally, cold. Even under his zebra-striped comforter, staring up at the ceiling in the dark, Chuck shivered.

He pulled on a T-shirt and shorts and went out into the heat of the night to get warm. He felt he had to move, to get away from the bed. The house itself seemed to be closing in on him. Out of habit, he stuffed his keys and his cell phone into his pockets on the way out and they pulled at the aging elastic of the shorts, slipping them down to his hips. He had lost weight.

It was quiet, at first, but not as hot as Chuck had expected. There was a wind, an almighty wind, blowing dust into his eyes. This was warm, but strange, and brought an almost metallic taste to the back of his mouth. He squinted and spat and rubbed his eyes.

Then he looked up and rubbed them again.

It was far away, but even in the night, which was growing increasingly dark, he could see a funnel shape in the sky. And then it came.

He said one minute he was standing there in a warm wind and the next minute he was doused in freezing rain with bits of sleet peppering his bare skin like birdshot. The sound was incredible, a roaring noise, more like a fleet of trucks than a train. It sounded like it was going to hit him.

Chuck shielded his eyes and peered up at the tornado as it whirred closer and closer, the long end of the funnel jinking left and right and up and nearly down and then back right again. It was smack over Main Street. If it touched down . . .

Chuck found himself backed against his truck, as if he were pasted there. He fumbled in his shorts for his cell phone and flipped it up. But who should he call? 911? They'd take forever to get there. Phil? Why worry him . . . he'll either be okay or he won't. Chuck would have loved to pass on the responsibility of the moment to Hector, but he didn't have Hector's home number.

The moment seemed to last forever.

And then, quite suddenly, the funnel cloud rose into the sky and disappeared. The rain stopped, the wind pushed the clouds away and the stars were revealed. And then, while Chuck shook the sleet out of his hair and rubbed his eyes again, even the wind faded.

Chuck sat on the stoop of his house. Warm air seemed to seep out of the ground. He looked around, dazed, at the other houses. As it grew still, it got warmer and warmer. The cicadas started again.

Chuck went into his home and the a.c. seemed frigid. He went back out into a hot summer night, now hot like he had expected it to be when he'd come out the first time. He walked around his yard, looking for damage from the wind, but could see nothing.

The sirens hadn't gone off.

Had he dreamed it? Dreamed the whole thing? Had he just now gotten out of bed and just dreamed a tornado above Main Street?

Again he opened his cell phone. He was relieved to find it slightly damp. It was three-thirty in the morning. He sat down again on his stoop, looked at the sky, and called Tiffany Nordelson, apologizing for waking her.

She said she hadn't been sleeping all that well, anyway.

They talked until the sun came up.

When Maria stopped by the hospital and told Pattie and Lottie all about the ladies' conversation at the street party, they laughed so hard the nurse made Maria leave. Lottie tried to remonstrate but the nursing staff had already had enough of Lottie and told her that if she didn't rest, they'd take away the salt-free chips and salsa Maria had brought. Pattie shot her sister a venomous look.

"Whooo," Pattie said, after they were alone together, wiping her eyes. "I think the old dragon is right. I can feel my heart going boom-boom-boom."

Lottie plucked at the thermal blanket. "I guess," she said, thoughtfully.

"What?" her sister demanded. "What are you thinking?"

"You know, Pattie," Lottie said, "that's probably the most unattractive habit you have, asking people what they're thinking. Isn't it enough we're trapped in here together? Do you really want to climb right into my head with me?"

Pattie looked hurt. "I just wondered," she said. She looked past Lottie out the window at the sunny day. "I'm a little bored," she admitted.

Lottie relented. "I was doing some wondering myself," she said. "About that party. I mean, it was funny and everything but don't you think that it's a little like when Barney Lane was running for mayor? Only in reverse? I mean, that now it's *them* who think *we* are taking over?"

Pattie rolled her eyes. "Don't get all upset," she said. "It's nothing."

"No," Lottie said. "I don't think it is nothing. Look at what Carla said to us."

"Carla gets hysterical when she's tired. Take no notice." Pattie fished next to her bed and hooked the Travel section of the Sunday paper.

"Evidently Hector was saying something similar to Jim and Bob," Lottie said. "I don't think it's nothing."

"But Hector is marrying a white girl," Pattie pointed out.

"I think we should do something," Lottie said. "I've actually already got an idea."

"No," her sister said sternly. "No, Lottie. If I may draw your attention to your abdominal area, you've got enough work to do right now."

Lottie shifted her baby monitor. "This is all nonsense," she said. "This baby's heartbeat is steady as a metronome." She, too, looked out the window. "I can't just sit still," she said, "and watch our town pull itself in two."

Pattie threw the Travel section at her sister, catching her on the forehead. "Shut up!" she shouted. "Concentrate on your own life for a change. Leave people alone."

"Hey!" Lottie said, rubbing her temple. "I'm only trying to help."

"People don't want your help, Lottie," Pattie said. "And you've got a family of your own now."

The nurse appeared in the doorway with the blood pressure machines. "You girls must like it here," she said. "Because if you keep on fussing and fighting like you are doing, you are going nowhere."

Phil Walker had often suspected Father Gaskin of tampering with the liturgical calendar. Surely, he thought, Gospel passages could not fit the town's needs so neatly. So, while the boys loaded the dishwasher after Sunday lunch (a Food Barn roasted chicken with his own mashed potatoes, gravy, and fresh-picked vegetables), he got on Pattie's laptop and typed in "Catholic Gospel" and the date.

Sure enough, The Good Samaritan popped up. He had wronged Father.

But who would have thought it possible? The impromptu street party in the Mexican American neighborhood had meant that most people present had missed the Saturday night Vigil Mass and also had, while drinking plenty of coffee and cursing whoever had brought out the three bottles of black Jamaican rum when the brandy ran out, missed the eight o'clock. That meant they all went to the ten o'clock family Mass, with the rest of the town's Catholic population. For the first time in weeks, the congregation was mixed.

The Gospel had been a powerful thing, but the homily really knocked the assembled's socks off. Father asked them all who they wanted to be. It was a choice, he said. You could choose to look at someone's nationality, or race, or lifestyle and decide to walk by them like the pharisee or the lawyer, he said, or you could choose not to notice those things and help them like the Samaritan. Because, he said, we are all in need. Life batters and bleeds us all. At some point, we are all left by the roadside, hurting, while others pass us by.

Phil Walker, after the events of the summer, knew that he himself was seriously bleeding by the roadside. The entire Mexican American community, with the exception of a few strong-willed individuals who had resisted the rum and coke the night before, felt with the moroseness that a terrible hangover induces that they, too, were hurting and had been neglected, really, all their lives. The doctor, thinking of Lottie and Pattie and how much they needed each other and how little they knew it, thought of how wounded they both had been by their parents' problems and their mother's early death, and felt proud of himself for keeping them prisoner in Eudora General.

By communion, as often happens in small communities like Eudora, a virtue had become fashionable. Forgiveness was the order of the day and pettiness and small-mindedness were to be heroically concealed in, if not completely eradicated from, one's bosom.

There was always a bit of chatting after service on the lawn of St. Anthony of Padua, and Phil Walker went over to Don Requena and put out his hand. It was shaken and the two looked each other briefly in the eye.

Phil said, "I'm real sorry about . . . "

But Don said magnanimously, "It was nothing. I had stuff on my mind." They stood awkwardly for a moment, Ben clutching Phil's leg while the other two Walker boys played a violent version of tag with the braver of the parish's youth.

"Moved back into the house?" Don asked, and Phil nodded. "Well," Don said, heading for his vehicle, "you stay there."

Jesus came up and slapped Phil on the back. "Dude," he said. "How's it hanging?"

Phil patted Jesus's arm. "Not bad," he said. "How about you?"

Jesus winced behind his sunglasses. "Don't ask," he said. "We had a bit of a party last night. You should have been there."

An awkward few seconds descended, as they remembered the last party they'd both attended. Then Jesus shrugged. "You can see I ain't changed," he said. "I still got lots of tact."

Phil grinned. "Oh," he said. "Me too. I got loads of it myself."

Rena signaled from the truck. "See you," Jesus said.

Phil picked up Ben as Jesus walked away. "On Friday night?" he called, but he couldn't be sure if Jesus had heard him.

In the study that afternoon, the liturgical calendar still open in Firefox, Phil sipped his iced tea and wondered.

"Okay," Daniel interrupted. "We're almost done. We better move our butts out to the hospital if we're gonna go see Mom. We gotta get back in time for the ice cream social tonight. Don't want to be late for that."

"All right," Phil said, shutting down.

"And anyway, what are you sitting around for? We need some help with the thing in the sink that chews stuff up. We think we might have got a fork down there and we're not allowed to put our hands down it."

Phil jumped up like he'd been scalded, nearly spilling the iced tea onto the keyboard. "No!" he said. "I'll do that!" His reflections were at an end.

Bible texts were left more to the discretion of the ministers at the Baptist church at the end of Main Street. Both St. Paul and Leviticus featured highly in that service. Hymns this week were more about walking the straight and narrow than about salvation through grace. Virtues of tolerance and forgiveness were not preached there that Sunday. Instead the preacher (a young visiting minister, as Brother Carter was appearing in several neighboring hamlets that morning, drumming up business for the ice cream social) concentrated on the evils of fornication and the duration and probable temperature of hellfire that would be faced by those who did not desist from practicing abominations.

The young preacher seemed to suggest that tolerance for anyone participating in perverse sexual acts was a moral weakness. Finally carried away with his own discourse, he came right out and said that Eudorans, by not giving firm guidance to any who had so strayed, had not only failed to save their straying brother but had allowed the poison of such perversion to spread. No, had willfully *aided* the spreading of such perversion. He waved a copy of the previous day's *USA Today.*

"Where were you when your brother needed you?" he asked.

Mary Evans shook her head shamefully. "Umm-hmmm," she said, regretfully.

"Did you take him by the hand?"

"Umm-hmmm."

"Did you point out the error of his ways?"

"Umm-hmmm."

Mary was enjoying an orgy of culpability.

"Brothers and sisters, you cannot help him once he enters the gates of hell. You will not be able to give him a single drop of water. Will you?"

"No!" Mary answered.

"So if you want to help him, you got to help him now." The organist played a rising chord. "When are you going to help this man?"

"Now!" the congregation chorused and the choir, all six of them, stood up in their rose-colored robes to sing as the organ wheezed its way into a melody.

The young preacher mopped his brow with a folded white handkerchief and smiled at the congregation. He seemed pretty pleased with himself, until he found two piercing blue eyes looking at him steadily with an expression of extreme distaste. The eyes were set in a weathered farmer's face. A tan line ended abruptly halfway up his forehead where it was obvious a cap habitually rested. Above this was iron gray hair with such a severe part that it looked burned into the scalp. A vintage black suit and a blinding white shirt were set off by a clumsily tied tie, largely hidden by the man's tightly folded arms.

Not many people had seen Jim Evans look at them in just that way. Rattlesnakes had, and a few hen-eating foxes had. But nothing much that had lived long enough to talk about it afterward had seen that look.

The young preacher's brilliant white smile faltered a little bit. He didn't meet Jim Evans's eyes again.

It would be nice to report that Phil and Pattie Walker had a dramatic end to their marital hostilities. It would be wonderful to write of Pattie's tears upon knowing, finally, that she was valued by Phil just as she was. It would be lovely to include in this chronicle Phil's touching and manly realization that his yearning for adventure would, in fact, be filled by his role as a father, husband, and telephone engineer.

It would be so nice, indeed, that one is tempted to begin writing fiction. But this chronicle deals only with the known facts. And none of that actually happened.

What did happen was that Pattie and Phil discovered that they were about to have a baby girl and that the girl appeared to be healthy. They spent their visits together discussing the logistics of child care, various financial matters, telephone calls that had to be made, and some issues to do with the management of the fabric shop and stationery store (this last with contributions from Lottie). Phil took Pattie's hand when he sat on the bed next to her, and he kissed her goodbye on her cheek. Lottie noticed that Pattie no longer closed her eyes and leaned into the kiss (as she had done every time in the past twenty years since Phil's first game of spin-the-bottle at Pattie's tenth birthday party) but that she did not pull away, either.

And that seemed to be that. They had been apart. The depth of Pattie's feelings for Phil had been revealed. And now they were together, and that depth was once again concealed, if it even still existed. Lottie confided her worries on this point to the doctor later as she lay against him in the narrow hospital bed after Pattie was asleep. "Her feelings for him could be completely dead. And they won't really even know until about six months after the birth."

"It'll be okay," the doctor said.

"But she used to adore him," Lottie said. "I don't think she adores him anymore."

The doctor extricated himself from the bed and stretched his back. Then he sat down and took Lottie's hand. "I don't think it does people all that much good to be adored," he said. "You were insufferable when I adored you."

Lottie sighed. "I suppose," she said. "You were a complete pain while you were adoring me, too." She rolled onto her side and curled up to sleep. "But Phil's kind of used to it."

"He'll get unused to it," the doctor said. "He's a bright guy. He knows what he's nearly lost."

"Mmm." Lottie was unconvinced. Sleepily she said, "He had his freedom. And he's handsome. There'll be other women after him. There always are."

The doctor laughed. "You haven't met Tiffany Nordelson," he said.

Lottie was suddenly less sleepy. "You mean that tart who was hanging around the Beer and Bowl?" she asked. "How did you meet her?"

"I went over for a beer," the doctor said. "She was there."

"Hmmm," Lottie snorted. "Watch it. You know what you're like with women." But even on the *like* her eyes were dipping shut. The doctor waited until she started to snore. And then he stood, looking at the fetal monitor readings for a long time before he left the room.

Jim Flory had not been seen since Bob left town. Oh, he was spotted filling up with gas, and he'd been around the movie theater to give his staff instructions, and people had seen him carrying in shopping bags from the big grocery store in the county seat (where he sometimes went to stock up on olives and dried mango and other outré comestibles), but nobody had been able to actually talk to him.

He kept wearing his Panama hat and his face was always shaded. No one could tell if he was upset or not. He did not respond to greetings called from the sidewalk when he sat on the porch, but the Flory place sat well back from the road, and those who called out couldn't be sure if he was ignoring them or just not hearing them.

Phil Walker and the boys had arrived early for the annual Baptist Ice Cream Social. Phil, indeed, meant to have words with the doctor for giving young Patrick a watch for his birthday present, since Phil's own free time was now completely ruled by Patrick's watch's tick. However, Patrick's excellent timekeeping meant that they got the first batch of Mary Evans's ice cream and good seats under the largest maple tree. Ben and Daniel went for the reliable strawberry cone. Patrick was more adventurous, trying a scoop of the peanut-butter-and-jelly flavor on the top of his, while Phil's first bowl (for he intended to get outside of at least three) had a scoop of chocolate chip, a scoop of lemon, and a scoop of lime with coriander and chile.

Phil had already discovered that he needed to eat the chocolate chip scoop fairly rapidly, since it would not enhance the other two if it melted, when he was joined by Park Davis and Stacey Harper, the pharmacist and his wife. Shortly thereafter, Phil's brother, Artie

Walker, arrived on his own (letting Rosemary deal with young May's crippling indecision at the tubs); and not long afterward, the little band of happy eaters was joined by Zadie Gross, who was starting out with vanilla, she said, and working her way up.

For a while, in the shade of the maple tree, there was a hush only broken by the squeaking of the folding chairs and the soft sounds of spoons tinkling against bowls; a hush only highlighted by the distant wail of May Walker's frustration.

Then Zadie nodded toward the Flory place. "Do you reckon he'll come?" she asked.

"Doubt it," Park said. There were murmurs of agreement.

Stacey Harper leaned forward. "I saw an ad in the city paper," she said. "It was for a historic movie theater in a stable, village-type rural community."

This was so shocking that even Phil's and Artie's spoons were momentarily stilled. "Never," Phil said, though his voice held some doubt. "The Florys were founders."

Zadie sighed. "It's always been hard for Jim, around here," she said. "Not that I'm saying it's right, or anything." By which she meant that though she did not condone his gay lifestyle, she sympathized with Jim as a person.

Artie Walker said, "It might not be a choice, you know." And, though he had received absolutely no encouragement to continue, continued, "There's plenty of studies that show sexual preference is innate."

"Never played ball," Park said. "Never played war. Cried during gym."

"Well." Zadie leaned forward and lowered her voice. "You might not want to advance that theory real loud, considering where we are. I heard that the preacher here this morning was just one step away from advocating intervention."

At this point Phil Walker discreetly belched and went to get in line for his second bowl. Mary Evans was still scooping, though she usually retired early from the fray and supervised younger arms from a lawn chair already in place and waiting. She said, "What are you going to try next, Phil?"

"Whatever you reckon is good," Phil said. "After that lime, chile, and coriander, I'm about ready for anything as long as it's cold."

Mary smiled. "I didn't have the guts to even taste that one myself. I made Jim do it. Only you and Clement would even try it." She began scooping. "What about some of this orange chocolate and then some peaches-and-cream and then the very vanilla?"

Phil said, "It's a pity I can't take some to Pattie and Lottie, but they're on that high blood pressure diet." He then braced himself and added, "Jim Flory would love that chile one. It's a shame he didn't feel up to coming."

Mary continued to scoop steadily. "Jim Flory is very welcome at this church," she said sweetly.

"Do you think he knows that?" Phil said. "I heard he was thinking about selling up."

Mary smiled, again with a determinedly sweet expression. "That'll be five American dollars," she said.

Phil went back to his seat under the tree, defeated. Spector Williams and Rosemary and young May Walker had joined the party, May delightedly sampling six different flavors in the two bowls she and her mother shared.

Spector said, "Well, I've thought about doing the same. It's bad enough smelling of Three Flowers brilliantine half the day, but I can't stand it when my customers act like I'm going to cheat them."

"I travel to Mexico all the time," Stacey Harper said (and with this utterance it was understood by all assembled she was attempting to establish cast-iron evidence of her own racial tolerance). "But maybe it's time we moved into the city. The kids could go to the academy and Park could get someone to run the pharmacy for him."

From Park's expression, this vision of the future was new to him and not at all welcome. He nearly choked on his ice cream.

"Yeah," Spector said. "I gotta say, you just have to know when to leave them to it. You want the town? It's yours."

Rosemary was looking alarmed, shooting pleading glances at her husband. But it was Phil who spoke up.

"Hang on a moment," he said. "Why are we all selling up and running away? What the heck did I miss?"

There was an uncomfortable silence. Then Spector said, "Like tonight. Why don't any of the Mexicans come support the social?"

Artie Walker said, "Ummmm?" and pretended to think. "Because they're all Catholics?" he suggested.

"You and Phil are Catholic. You come."

At last Rosemary could contain herself no more. "Carla Busta-monte just hired me," she said.

And now it was Artie's turn to look surprised. "Did she?" he asked.

Rosemary swallowed. "Just for a few hours a week, while May plays with Ben," she explained hastily and not altogether truthfully. "I don't think Carla expects all the white people in town to go away and leave the town to them. Or she wouldn't have been so grateful."

"Hunh," Artie said, nodding. "Rosemary's got a point."

Park was still looking at Stacey as if she'd suddenly turned to salt. "We wouldn't get diddly-squat for our house," he said. "We'd dang near have to live in a shed for that price in the city."

Stacey sighed. "We'd get a mortgage," she said. "You have heard of them, haven't you?"

They had heard of them, but only Spector had ever actually had to pay one. The rest of the assembled had inherited their houses, Rosemary from a childless uncle, Phil from his parents, Park from his. The idea of all that money going out every month was frighten-ing to them in a way that would have been more understandable to the generation that had seen the introduction of the railroad than to most of their contemporaries in the Western world.

"You gotta be joking," Park said flatly.

To which his wife replied, "This is good, but I wish they'd make some low fat. I'm so full," and left her bowl nearly untouched on the ground to go and search for her children, Damien and Frieda.

Phil Walker looked into his bowl of ice cream for a moment. And then he said, "You know, I think Rosemary's right. That whole racial tension business is over."

To which Park replied shortly, "Nobody cares what you think, Phil." And left to search for his wife.

"This town's gonna be the death of me," Zadie Gross remarked, after licking the back of her spoon. "It's just one damn thing after another."

Just then Maria Lopez, looking cool in a flowery rayon dress, walked onto the church lawn. With her was her brother, Oscar Burgos, her husband, Bill, and her little son, William, who immediately ran to the front of the ice cream line and began staring hungrily at the many varieties.

"Not that anybody cares what I think," Phil Walker said, once again belching gently and preparing to rise. "But if you were wanting some Mexicans, Spector, you just got a bunch of them." He grinned. "I'm going over to say hello to the Mexicans. Anybody else want to talk to a real, live Mexican at an ice cream social? You can come along if you want."

And whistling, Phil left the shade of the maple tree.

Rosemary sighed happily and leaned against her husband's knee. "Sometimes," she said quietly, "you can understand what Pattie sees in him."

Jim Evans had been on his annual duty of replenishing dry ice and helping to haul tubs. They were just about out of Mary's ice cream. She'd been working all year on it, and in just an hour, it was all gone. Now the other ladies all put together only made about half as much, and then for latecomers there was the Food Barn stuff. You snooze, you lose at the annual Baptist Ice Cream social, Jim reflected.

He looked down the street to the Flory place. The shades had been down on the elegant veranda all day and they were still down, even though the sun had worked around the other way. That wasn't like Jim Flory, Jim Evans thought. He thought about last year, how Jim Flory had worn his linen suit and a straw boater to the social with a red bowtie. How he'd attempted to try every one of Mary's creations until his stomach couldn't take any more.

And now he was probably sitting on his veranda and watching through the shades.

Jim Evans could have blamed the visiting preacher for this problem. He could have blamed the absent Bob for deserting Jim Flory. He could have blamed Lottie Dougal, who had probably come up with the whole idea of the naked protest.

But Jim Evans was not in the habit of blaming others for his own shortcomings. And so, he walked over to Mary and asked, "How's that chile stuff selling?"

Mary, who had retired to her lawn chair, said, "Oh, we can't hardly get anybody to try it," while fanning herself briskly with a Maple Hill Funeral Home advertisement.

Jim Evans then went over to the back of the table, removed a ten dollar bill from its compartment in his capacious wallet, and put it in the strongbox. Then he took the whole remainder of the lime, chile, and coriander ice cream tub and began walking with it down Main Street.

"Now, what the heck is *he* doing?" Zadie Gross asked those assembled under the maple tree.

Phil Walker took one look and jumped to his feet. "Watch the boys, will you, Artie?" he said. And put on a surprising burst of speed to catch up with the old farmer.

■ ■ ■

Jim Flory was sitting on the porch swing with a glass of iced tea and a bored expression, which both Jim Evans and Phil Walker knew was assumed.

That he had been considering risking the social was obvious from his clothing—seersucker board shorts with a matching short-sleeved blue velour hoody, worn with white espadrilles. Only his severest critics would have said he was too young for it. Both Jim Evans and Phil Walker could tell (though neither was fashion-conscious, they both had been married for a considerable amount of time) that the outfit was new and had been bought especially for the occasion.

Jim Evans sat down beside him with the tub of ice cream. "I knowed you'd be here," he said. "But I plumb forgot the spoons."

"I'll get them," Phil volunteered.

Jim Flory sighed. "Don't bother with bowls," he said. "Just bring some paper towels."

They talked, as men do, about everything else. About how Pattie and Lottie had been holding up in the heat. About the Grand Opening of the Corn Maze the following weekend. About how busy the social was.

Finally Jim Evans said, "I'm real grateful for what you boys done."

And Jim Flory said, smiling sadly, "Don't worry about it. It was fun."

Jim Evans nodded up the street. "That ain't fun," he said. "You sitting here, while we're all there." He cleared his throat. "And where's your young man?" he asked.

Phil grinned. He couldn't imagine anyone else calling Bob a young man. But he also couldn't imagine Jim saying the word *boyfriend* or *partner*. And the mere idea of hearing Jim Evans say the word *lover* almost made him laugh out loud. It cost him some chile ice cream up his nose just holding that laugh in.

But what Flory said next wiped the smile off his face pretty fast. "I'm thinking about selling up," he said. "I'm thinking about leaving."

"Jeez Louise," Phil said crossly. "Every damn person I talk to is thinking about selling up. It's like the Dust Bowl or something."

Jim said, "Bob's not happy where he is, either. Nobody in his town knew . . . before the paper . . . "

But Phil said, "You can't seriously think about leaving this house. You've put your whole life into it, Jim."

Jim Flory turned his patrician profile to look back out the crack of the porch shades. He said, "You might notice that there's quite a few rocks in the yard," he said. "None of them have actually hit the windows yet, but pretty soon they'll recruit some pitching star and I'll be paying out a fortune in glass." He shrugged. "I had my car egged. I was teepeed a couple of nights ago." He shrugged again. "Took me four hours to get the toilet paper out of the trees. It's nothing now, but I remember when Betty got hurt . . . "

He shivered. He said, "Since I got that last beating, I'm just not so brave anymore. I did the protest and it was okay because there were two of us. But now I'm here alone and . . . "

"Do you want to come over to our house?" Phil offered. "We've got a nice spare room."

Jim Flory shook his head no. He said, "Look, you guys should be at the social. Thanks for the delivery, Jim."

And Jim Evans and Phil Walker found themselves walking down to the sidewalk again. "He's right," Phil said. "There's an awful lot of rocks."

But Jim Evans was sunk in thought.

Janey Lane also did not attend the Annual Baptist Ice Cream Social. It was the first one in her twenty-three years that she had missed. When the rest of her family returned, they found her sitting on the front stoop.

"What are you doing, honey?" Becky Lane sat down beside her.

"It's stupid," Janey said. "I want to go running, but I'm afraid it will hurt the baby." She covered her face with her hands. "Don't look at me," she said to Priss and Linda. "I feel so stupid."

"Of course you can go running," Linda said. "You can do anything you're used to doing. All your books say that."

"But what if I get tired and then have to keep going? What if I get so hot that it's dangerous? What if I strain something inside me?" Janey sighed. "It's like I can't do anything right these days. And I just want to run away from it all, but that's not right, either."

"Come on," Linda said, pulling her to her feet. "I'll change into my running clothes. Priss will follow us with the car. We'll go the dirt road to the lake and Priss can put the flashers on. It'll be like we're in a marathon or something. Then if you get tired, you can get in with Priss."

Janey smiled weakly. "Okay," she said. "If you guys don't mind."

Priss said, "Well, I—" But Linda pinched her arm from behind, hard. "Ow! . . . I've got nothing special to do," she amended quickly.

So just before sundown, the Lane family cavalcade left the town limits, going around four miles an hour. Becky had come along for the ride and had brought her Glen Campbell's greatest hits CD. Priss was muttering bitterly under her breath as Becky mentioned how well the sunflowers were doing this year and how the grass was still pretty green, in spite of the heat. Campbell sang Jimmy Webb's gentle antiwar ballad, "Galveston," as Janey Lane picked up the pace, making her sister sweat to keep up. Linda said something that made Janey laugh and Janey put on a sudden sprint, tearing down the dirt road, leaving both Linda and Priss's Ford Mondeo in her dust.

Just then, another figure was seen running toward them.

"Look," Priss cried, with the joy of one who is greatly bored upon spotting a distraction, "it's Mark!"

"Oh no," her mother moaned. "That's all we need."

"Why?" Priss asked.

But by the time "By the Time I Get to Phoenix" was playing, Priss knew. Even from that distance and over Campbell's crooning, she could hear the odd word. *Irresponsible* and *stupid* were two of the main ones. Janey was having trouble getting a word in edgeways.

Mark grabbed Janey by her upper arm and hustled her back to the car, opening the back driver's side door and thrusting her in. Linda, normally so feisty, just hung back and panted, watching.

"And you," Mark said bitterly into Becky's window. "If you want to get rid of this baby, if it's inconvenient to you, you should come right out and say it."

"Mark, you've got this all wrong," Becky said. "A little running won't hurt the baby."

"A little running? Did you see how fast she was going? Are you crazy? It's over a hundred degrees out here!" His face was stern and he wiped the sweat from his brow crossly. He opened the rear passenger door and said, "Get in," to Linda, who, amazingly, got in.

He slammed the door behind her, and shot another venomous look at Janey. "That's my baby, too," he said. "And don't you forget it again." Then he patted the roof twice and Priss drove away.

"They're all like that," Becky said. "Even your father used to get all upset if I tried to do anything. Didn't mind me working up until the day of the birth, but woe betide if I tried to go for a walk, or take out the trash."

Still Janey sat, her beautiful eyes filling and spilling, over and over, as if she'd turned into a fountain.

"If you want, we can go on up to the lake where you can run in peace," Becky offered.

"No," Janey sniffed. "It's not that."

But still the tears flowed.

■ ■ ■

Lottie Emery was not a good patient. She argued. She didn't listen. She questioned everything, even the processes behind the generation of her lab results. She called the fetal monitor "useless" and argued that a heartbeat could not generate the kinds of data implied by the monitor report. She resisted frequent ultrasounds, saying that all that sound bouncing around was intrusive. At one point, she burned smudge sticks and they set off the fire alarms on her floor. After that, she used essential oils on her pillowcase and the laundry couldn't get them out.

Most tellingly, she argued that her high blood pressure was not a sign of preeclampsia, that she had none of the other indicators, like her sister did, and that she was a perfect candidate for a home birth.

To be honest, the obstetricians were, by that point, happy to agree with her. They really just wanted her out of there.

So on Monday afternoon, Lottie was packing. This process was protracted, as she'd brought with her some rugs, some sheepskins, some pillows, a small herbal kit (which had included the smudge sticks and the essential oils), four rather fetching vintage nighties with matching vintage bed jackets, a velour maternity track suit in moss green and some marabou-trimmed slippers.

Pattie pouted, leafing through a magazine as if she couldn't care less that her sister was being released.

At last, Lottie came over and sat on her sister's bed. "I just got a text from Jim," she said. "He's had a patient who needed my calendar time. Clement and Nancy are going to run me home."

"Hmmm," Pattie said absently, while savagely turning the page, "that's great."

"You're going to be fine," Lottie said. "But your blood pressure's been high all pregnancy."

Pattie looked at her sister. "I can't believe you're going to leave me here, all alone," she said. And then, "It's all my fault. I didn't really concentrate on this baby like I did with the boys. I wanted each of them so much that I watched every little thing . . . " She stroked her bump around the monitor. "And now," she said, "I just want her to be okay so bad."

Lottie said, "That wasn't really your fault, Pattie. Phil's been a complete idiot this summer. Anybody's blood pressure would go up. Anybody would be distracted."

Pattie nodded. "I know," she said.

For a moment, they looked at each other measuringly. Lottie was dying to ask if Pattie still loved Phil. Pattie was dying to tell her how she felt. And yet their whole history lay in the way.

Pattie opened her mouth to speak, but just then Lottie's phone tinkled with a text message.

Lottie muttered as she dug in her bag, but when she saw the message envelope, she smiled. "Clement's getting really handy with these," she said. "They're at the front door. Nancy says she can come get you tomorrow, if you need a ride home, too."

Pattie raised her eyebrows ironically. "Tell her not to keep her day free," she said. "I don't think I'm going anywhere fast."

A few hours later, as *he* sat on Pattie's bed, Phil Walker's cell phone also tinkled with a text message. He said, "Chuck wants me to call him right away," and went outside to do so.

When he came back to his loving wife with news, she interrupted him with, "Hey, who's putting the boys to bed?"

"Doc," Phil said. "He said he could help more now that Lottie's home, so I could spend more time here with you."

"Oh." It was clear that Pattie had no objections to this agenda. "Practice will do him good," she said.

"If it doesn't kill him," Phil added, and they both laughed.

Pattie said, "I'm sorry, you were going to tell me something."

Phil sighed and shook his head. "I just can't believe it," he said. "Chuck was offering me first refusal on his boat. He's leaving town."

"What?" Pattie screeched. "No *way*!"

But, "Way," Phil insisted. "He and Tiffany went to go find his folks in Lawrence the other week. His dad's dead, but his mom is still alive and his sisters were real glad to see him. Chuck's buying a bait shop, says he's already got a buyer for the Beer and Bowl."

"I don't believe it," Pattie said, in wondering tones. "After all this time! And what about this Tiffany? Are they serious?"

"Well." Phil shrugged. "I don't know. You know how it goes with Chuck. She seems to be hanging in there so far." He said, "Chuck's gonna offer Mark Ramirez first refusal on the house."

Pattie nodded. "This first refusal stuff is kind of cool," she said. "It's like making your will without dying."

"It's a good price on the boat," Phil said. "And you know how well Chuck took care of it. If I'm ever gonna buy one, it seems like this is the time."

Pattie nodded. "Boys are at the right age," she said. "They'll be wanting to water ski pretty soon, spend time at the lake looking at the girls in bikinis."

Phil winced. "I don't want to think about what happens when Patrick and Daniel hit puberty," he said. "We better start an IRA for the paternity suits."

There followed a tender passage, which was witnessed by the night nurse, who shopped at the bakery and who had come in for a pressure reading just at that moment. But we do not know what was said or how tender it indeed was, as she only mentioned in passing, when Kylie asked her how Pattie was, that she seemed healthy enough to canoodle with Phil. Since the nurse was an early customer, Kylie disbursed this reassuring news with her baked goods for the whole of the morning.

We are able to reconstruct this entire conversation to our satisfaction only because Phil later told the doctor much of what had passed between himself and his wife that evening. Of course the doctor could not keep from discussing such interesting developments with Janey Lane, especially as the doctor, in common with the whole of the town, had hopes that if Mark Ramirez did indeed buy Chuck's split-level, he would be sharing it with Janey and their child. And Janey mentioned what she had heard over the dinner table, and so it became common knowledge.

But Phil did not tell the doctor everything.

You would think, given that reporters were trying to get a glimpse of Kelly Brookes's wedding gown, that somebody at some point would have asked the happy couple where they intended to reside.

But no one had.

All of Kelly's world assumed that Hector would move to the West Coast. All of Hector's world assumed that Kelly would soon be a permanent resident of Eudora.

Kelly had been quite busy working on a film in which she'd had a meatier part than was usually accorded her, but had been paid correspondingly less. It was set in Alaska, though the mosquitos were so bad that year that the production team had moved to Vancouver for some of the shooting, having found a small island nearby with the requisite cabin that looked more like Alaska than, indeed, many scouted locations in Alaska had.

It was a tense, psychological drama and left Kelly feeling rather tense and psychological herself.

She had arrived in town on Wednesday and was upstairs at Carla's Creations Thursday morning, having what would either be her last fitting or her next to last fitting, depending on how it went.

Carla told her about the journalists and Kelly was gratifyingly horrified and appreciative. She herself had developed a habit of disposing of personal correspondence at the airport after someone had gone through her trash in order to read her credit card bill. The resultant story, "She Might Be Pretty But She Can't Cook!" detailed her dining habits based on the evidence of the statement.

Carla said she couldn't stand living like that.

Kelly said she didn't like it, either.

So then Carla, who, as we have seen, has even less tact than Jesus Requena, asked, "So where are you gonna live after you get married?"

And Kelly said, "I don't know. We haven't really talked about it."

Carla laughed. "Well," she said, "you got six whole weeks to work it out. Why rush?"

Kelly turned to the side, and examined her reflection. "This," she said, "is a really amazing dress."

Carla said, "It's even more amazing on you." She thought for a moment as she pinned. "This place is gonna be crazy," she said. "It's gonna be ten times worse than the Maple Leaf Festival."

"I know," Kelly said. "Clement's talking to somebody he knows in the air force to try and stop helicopters flying over." She sighed. "I know it's my job and everything, but . . ."

"It's nobody's job to be hassled that much," Carla said firmly. "Look what happened to Princess Diana."

Kelly turned the other way. "Yeah," she said, stroking the gorgeous dress. "Yeah," she said again.

Mark Ramirez was still cranky when he went to bed on Sunday night. On Monday, he was cranky all day. On Tuesday, he was so aggressive in negotiations with the Ford Isuzu dealer that he came away with a margin of 80 percent on their annual Christmas calendars and had to go back and blame it on his calculator. This made him even crankier.

Wednesday, Maria Lopez was worried enough to go and warn Becky Lane to keep well out of his way. She had Bill take him bowling, but it didn't help. Bill said Mark threw the ball down the lane like he was trying to go through the back wall. He said they went through four frames so quick that when he got home his recliner was still warm.

Jim Evans saw him walking down the street early Thursday

morning while he and Mary were passing in the truck. Jim said something to Mary, and it might have been one of his trenchant and apposite remarks. But we will never know, because Mary wasn't talking much to anyone. When asked, she said that Jim had told her something and that it was troubling her mind. She had been dropping into church to pray quite a lot and was found there most days for an hour or so in the afternoon, reading and rereading her well-thumbed Bible in a quiet corner.

This chronicle will therefore have to say that Mark Ramirez was madder than a wet hen by Thursday. Hopping mad. Furious.

Anybody more interested in his fellow man than Chuck Warren would not have entered the stationery store that morning, when Mark was behind the counter, but would have waited for Mark's assistant, who was, in fact, changing her shoes in the tiny room that served as warehouse and office to the rear of the shop. It is, indeed, due to this assistant that we have the entire script of the conversation.

Chuck was casual and, to the assistant's mind, odiously happy and self-satisfied. Smugness was leaking from his every pore, she said.

Mark greeted him curtly. He was greeting everybody curtly.

Chuck said, "It's about the house. I'm wondering if you could let me know tomorrow."

At first, the assistant thought a mouse had gotten into the storeroom (it wouldn't have been the first) but then realized that the squeaking sound was coming from Mark. She peeked through the crack in the door and saw Mark's face turning an alarming shade of deep red.

At last he choked out one word, "Sure."

"After all," Chuck said, hitching up his shorts and beaming out at the world from the display window, "a man's got to make up his mind sometime. A man's got to decide just how he's gonna live his life." He turned to Mark. "Your time is now, Mark," he said, and there was the small tinkle of the bell to let the assistant know he had let himself out.

Mark breathed deeply for a few moments and the assistant took him a solicitous glass of water, which he downed so quickly he got some drops on his crisp lilac shirt.

Then he handed her the glass, like, the assistant said, a bull-fighter tossing off his cloak.

"Chuck's right," Mark said. "It's time to make up my mind."

Once again, it is beyond the laws of nature that as many people who claim they witnessed the following events were actual eyewitnesses. As often happens in small towns, the key occasions quickly become enshrined in legend and are told so often and by so many people, that the entire town buys into the event, invests in it personally, so that each citizen actually believes it happened to them.

But just for the record, let us note the following:

1. Ben Nichols and Odie Marsh were enjoying their rather late midmorning break, and taking turns admiring Odie's new glasses both on and off Odie's old face.
2. Manuel Bustamonte was at the back door, picking up Zadie's dinner roll order for the chicken fried steak special.
3. Kelly Brookes was looking in the window at the donuts, trying to remember the last time she had let herself eat a cinnamon twist.

and

4. Linda Bustamonte was rolling down the awning at Mayan Memories.

That is all. There were no more witnesses, unless you count Mark's assistant, who could only see him walk across the street.

Actually he didn't walk across the street. He strode. He seemed much taller and broader than he had ever seemed before, and that had little to do with the exercise regime necessary for his role in the National Guard and everything to do with his mood and resolve.

He didn't say a word. All the eyewitnesses agree.

He just flung up the portion of the counter that divides the baker's workspace from the retail environment of the customer, plucked Kylie from where she searched for the clipboard of orders that she needed Manuel to sign for Gross Home Cooking, turned her to face him, his hands on her slender waist, brown and strong against her slim white aproned form, and kissed her ruthlessly.

Ben Nichols says that Kylie hesitated for a moment and then returned the kiss with some fervor, whereupon Mark tightened his hold on her waist and kissed her again. Then he put her down and looked at her, and she looked at him and everyone else goggled at the both of them. Manuel said Odie spit coffee all down the front of his uniform and that Ben choked on his churro.

And then Mark said, "No," seemingly to nobody in particular, and, "Sorry," to Kylie Requena and strode out of the bakery, even more purposefully than he had strode in.

Kylie gave a small cough and brushed flour from her highly desired chest. "Well," she said, and looked for the clipboard once again while Odie, Ben, and Linda Bustamonte peered down Main Street at Mark's retreating back.

Again, eyewitness accounts can be unreliable, but Kelly Brookes is certain that Mark did not hesitate in his trajectory. He went directly to the health clinic.

In the waiting room were:

1. Don and Betty Requena (who needed some interpretation of a specialist's report);
2. Jim Flory (depressed);
3. Priss Lane with the three Walker boys (Daniel and Ben had terrible poison ivy);

and

4. Nancy McAllister (who suffered from her usual malady of living with Clement).

Mark threw open the door and did not close it, letting the cool air escape and the baking heat enter. Young Daniel Walker immediately, and somewhat piously, got up to shut it for him.

But Mark had already made it to Janey's desk, where he seized her and kissed her ruthlessly. He said, "Oh yes," and then, "You're going to marry me next week, *mujer*," and kissed her again.

"But . . . " she said weakly, caught between him and her desk. On her face dawned a beatific smile.

"And," he said, "I want you to write Chuck a check for five thousand dollars. It's half the deposit on his house. It's perfect for us."

Her smile dropped away. "Oh!" she said, and it was obvious, Jim and Nancy agreed, that she was vexed and hurt. "You only want to marry me to get that house."

"Janey!" Priss wailed in despair. "Please don't be so stupid!"

But both Janey and Mark ignored her. Mark simply seized her again and, bending her backward over her desk, gave her the kind of kiss most people never even see, except in the movies, and certainly never experience in real life. Nancy said later it reminded her of the young Ricardo Montalban. Jim said he would never be able to look at Mark the same again.

"Don't be stupid," Mark finally said, releasing his fiancée. Janey, dazed, sank down into her chair. "Now get out your checkbook." He buzzed the doctor's phone while Janey began to write a check, seemingly on autopilot. "Doctor Emery," he said. "Janey will need the next two weeks off. She's getting married and then she's going on her honeymoon."

The entire waiting room erupted in spontaneous applause. Janey blushed and tore off the check, handing it to Mark with her big eyes shining.

"That's fine," the doctor said down the speaker. "That's just fine."

Lottie came running down the stairs to see what was going on. She was about halfway down when her foot slipped on the step. Suddenly, horribly, she began to fall.

"And she's okay?" Phil Walker nodded to the other hospital bed, where his sister-in-law slept. He had arrived late to visit Pattie, but had brought her a personal DVD player he'd picked up during his lunch hour, and a stack of movies.

Pattie had been touched and grateful. She said, "Yeah, she's all right. She's going home again tomorrow."

Phil sighed and rubbed his eyes. "This single-parent business will wear you out," he said. "I don't know how you managed it, with the baby and all."

Pattie yawned. "It wasn't easy," she said.

"You told me to stop saying sorry, so I won't," Phil said. "But you gotta believe me. It was like I went crazy for a while."

Pattie yawned again, bigger. "I know," she said.

Phil said, "I'll let you get to sleep. But . . . "

Something about the tone of his voice warned Pattie that there was something going on. "But what?" she asked, suddenly more alert.

"It's nothing," Phil said. "But I've got to go to Jim Evans's Grand Opening tomorrow afternoon." He took off his baseball cap and rubbed his head. "And then I got softball . . . if I make it."

Again, the "if I make it" sounded ominous to Pattie Walker. "What do you mean, if you make it?" she asked tartly.

Phil said, "Well . . . me and Jim Evans and Chuck . . . we kind of owe Jim Flory something." He said, "Now, this is all Evans's idea . . ."

■ ■ ■

Down at the nurse's station, one nurse turned to the other. "Do you think I should make him leave?" she asked.

"Not if he keeps making her laugh like that," the other advised. "It's the best medicine, just like the *Reader's Digest* says."

Chuck Warren and Hector Rodriguez had been closeted for some twenty minutes. It was going to be surprisingly easy to extricate Chuck's financial ties from the community. Hector thought, as they discussed the sale of the house and filled out forms to change his bank, that Chuck's forty years in town had been more like four. Margery Lupin still had two accounts in the Eudora State Bank, after two years of working on her retirement, but in just moments, Chuck Warren was virtually already gone.

They rose to shake hands, and Hector prepared to show Chuck out. But then Chuck stopped and sat back down again. "I've got to tell you something," he said. And he told the young mayor the story of the tornado.

Hector gradually grew less and less engaged as the monologue continued. His body language became stiff and he pushed back against his chair and away from Chuck just as far as he could go.

Chuck, observing these signs, said, "And I wasn't on drugs. At all. I'd had two beers at eleven o'clock and that was it."

Hector pursed his lips. "Ummm," he said, uncommitted.

"And look at this." Chuck slid a small section of the county newspaper onto Hector's desk. "Same night a twister hit near Leacompton. Took out two barns and a baler."

"But there weren't any sirens," Hector said.

"C'mere," Chuck said. He led the way out of Hector's office, across the trading floor of the bank and out the door. Hector, unrolling his sleeves, followed.

At the corner, they turned left and walked five blocks north to the nearest tornado siren. Chuck pointed. "There's not a damn wire left in the thing. Those stupid rednecks stripped them out for the copper."

"What?" Hector said. "All of them?"

Chuck shook his head. "Near as I can tell, only the north side sirens. I don't know why the ones on the south side didn't go off."

Hector thanked Chuck profusely and then marched right back into the bank and his office, where he rummaged through the files until he found the inspection report.

Once again, bank employees heard Hector shouting.

There hadn't yet been a maize maze in the county, so there was quite a crowd at the Grand Opening celebrations. The co-op had a Diversity and Enterprise fund and they had subsidized the refreshments and decorations and the head office had done the public relations. There was a radio crew from the county seat, a television van from the city, and several members of the print fraternity, including a young man interning for *Successful Farming Weekly*. He was writing an article entitled "New Tricks for Old Dogs."

Chuck and Phil had been out at the farm since lunch, helping to hang bunting and getting in Mary's way while decorating the picnic tables. Mary had made twelve tubs of vanilla ice cream and would be selling cones, along with punch and barbecued cobs on sticks (elote recipe courtesy of Maria Lopez in exchange for liberal distribution of Mayan Memories' marketing materials around the site).

Hector Rodriguez, accompanied by his beauty queen/movie star fiancée, was due to cut the ribbon at four. At about three-thirty he arrived, met the co-op president who was to give the opening speech, and made sure the scissors were handy and sharp. The red ribbon was already in place, hung over the entrance by means of two nails driven into two wooden stakes.

Children, already high on sugar, ran around the area of the farm yard that had been clearly roped off for such activity, clambering over the hay bales and generally whooping it up. What with them, the bunting, the balloons, and a couple of Jim's vintage tractors in the background, the photographers thought it might make the front page.

One of them said as much to Jim Evans, but Jim only ran his finger around the inside of his collar, as if it were too tight, and didn't say a word.

Clement and Lucy McAllister were there with Nancy. The doctor, looking just as nervous as Jim Evans, was present. Oscar Burgos was there, with his nephew William, Donna Bustamonte, and three or four of the youngest Requena cousins. Oscar, with his afternoons free, frequently collected a truck full of children to go to the lake, or to the state park, just to give their mamas a break. This week it was the Grand Opening.

Jim Flory was absent, of course. He had eventually had two windows smashed and his car keyed. Even if he had wanted to attend, his morning had been spent filling out forms with Ben and Odie, and the afternoon would be taken up with insurance claims. There was talk, at the county seat, of putting one of their two mobile CCTV cameras at the Flory house.

What business Jim Flory did scuttle out to do around town was not pleasant. He'd had to go to the pharmacy the day before and a sullen Park Davis had barely spoken to him. That this was nothing to do with his protest or his lifestyle was something Jim Flory would not know for some time. It just seemed all of a piece to him. He was not, in his current state of mind, drawn to participate in any civic affairs.

We will rely on Dorothy Barford's testimony in the main to describe the events that followed. The Barfords, as neighbors and fellow farmers, were well placed to understand and comment on the proceedings. Also, Dorothy is a calm, unflappable woman (as so many farming partners either are or, from necessity, become), and her account lacks the hysteria and hyperbole of many other versions.

The mayor and the president of the co-op were just about to line up, when Jim Evans excused himself. Mary Evans then turned white as a sheet and ran into the house, dropping her ice cream scoop onto the yard gravel as she went. Dorothy said that she knew something was up right then, and she went and picked up the scoop, fully intending to follow and help. However, just at that moment, Dorothy also noticed that the doctor, Phil Walker, and Chuck Warren followed Jim into the small door on the side of the machine shed and something about the way they walked made her hesitate.

Hector, Kelly, and the president, waiting for their host, looked at the small side door, but it had been closed. There were voices raised in the shed, sounds of activity and even stifled laughter. But then the sound of the door opener began and the big front door began to shudder and then rise slowly.

Dorothy says that the first thing you could see was a bunch of bare feet. And then you saw a bunch of bare ankles. When it got to the bare knees, mothers and fathers began to gather their children close and hide their eyes. But still the doors rose.

When all was revealed, Jim Evans, Chuck Warren, Phil Walker, and Dr. Emery were standing there and not one of them had a stitch of clothing on. Decency, Dorothy said, was preserved by their hand-lettered sandwich boards, which covered them front and back and were duct-taped together at the side and top.

You could tell, Dorothy said, that men had made these signs. They were a bit crooked and some of the writing you could barely read, especially the doctor's. It made quite a picture, the light flooding into the shed shining brightly on the four faces. Three of them are grinning widely, while one seems drawn and tight. The doctor's sign read, JUDGE NOT LEST YE BE JUDGED. Chuck's read,

LOVE THY NEIGHBOR AS THYSELF. Phil had, BUT THE GREATEST OF THESE IS LOVE, while Jim Evans, ever an iconoclast, had eschewed Bible verse and simply written, QUEERS ARE PEOPLE TOO (only, as Dorothy pointed out, he hadn't remembered the comma before *too*).

They are, as a group, unusually handsome men. Jim's shocking white torso, upper arms, and legs were an amusing contrast to the mahogany tone of the rest of his body, and Chuck's hair, as usual, needed a trim. But that said, it's not an unpleasant photograph to view. The short video footage that made the ten o'clock news and was shown repeatedly over the weekend was even better, because they were smiling and laughing among themselves.

For the past two years Kelly Brookes had never been completely ignored by photographers. But now she was.

However, as the doctor hit the button, and the door began to close once again, they swung around to get a shot of Hector, open-mouthed, his scissors drooping in his hand, and the co-op president covering his own mouth with his hand, his eyebrows in his hairline. You can just see Kelly in the corner, doubled up with laughter.

Back at home, in her blowsy floral bedroom, Lottie Emery picked up her cell phone and read the doctor's text message. "We're going for it. Wish us luck." And she smiled. She forwarded it to her sister's cell with the message, "Would you really want not to be married to these idiots? What would we do for fun?"

But in the middle of her laughter, she suddenly frowned, passing her hand over her baby's bump.

But it was not, currently, fun. As the door to the shed went down, so did Jim Evans. The doctor, still only wearing his sign, immediately knelt down next to him.

Jim Evans raised a trembling hand to his head. "My head," he complained. "It hurts like a som'bitch."

"Call an ambulance," the doctor said to Phil Walker. "Now!"

From Dorothy's line of view, Phil Walker suddenly came stumbling out the side door, wearing only his T-shirt and boxers, his jeans tangled around his ankles, already dialing his telephone, into which he talked urgently, shouting over the crowd and the questions. When Dorothy heard Phil giving directions, she remembered the ice cream scoop in her hand and her duty to Mary and began hurrying into the house to get her.

Meanwhile, in the shed, the doctor was raising Jim Evans's head with his own and his co-conspirators' clothing. When Phil came back in, the doctor asked for pillows and a blanket, and Phil ran back out again, and into the house, where he saw Mary, nearly as white as her husband, coming out. "I need pillows and a blanket," he said.

"On the sofa," she answered. She hesitated, as if afraid to see what lay in the machine shed.

"He's okay," Phil said. "The doctor's with him."

Dorothy said she had to half-carry Mary to the shed, but that once she was there, she suddenly snapped to life, helping to raise Jim and cover him. She said to Phil Walker, "He's got some sweats in the bottom of his drawer. Top of the stairs, turn right, smallest chest." And Phil trotted away again.

Dorothy left at this point to tell her nearest and dearest what had happened. By then, Jim had also complained of not being able to move his left arm (he had wanted to see what time it was). So, even if the doctor was hesitant to diagnose a stroke, Dorothy was not. She told them, she says, she told them straightaway, and she was right.

By then, she said, everything was getting in a mess. The ice cream was melting on the table and kids were running riot. So George told Hector to cut the ribbon, which he did without the benefit of the co-op president's speech, and the kids flooded into the maze. Dorothy then went over to the ice cream and barbequed corn stand, swapped the melting tubs for some fresh ones, and began serving, while her son and his wife mounted the maze observation platform and wiped down the picnic tables.

People, Dorothy says, don't really care about the big things, it's the little things that seem to matter. So once the tables were clean and the stock refreshed, people lined up and bought ice cream, drank punch, ate corn on the cob, and took turns going up to the platform to make sure their children were still lost, even though their host was lying on the machine shed floor.

Nobody knows who rang Ben and Odie, but they showed up just about the same time as the ambulance and helped the crew and the doctor load Jim and Mary into the back. Although Vivien Merton complained that the protesters should be arrested, Ben explained that nothing lewd or obscene had been actually on view and that it was private property. He then asked if she'd stand to one side so that he could get the doctor to the hospital, please.

Dorothy said that Vivien looked like she was disappointed something terrible.

Now you might think, after events like that, that the last thing Phil Walker would want to do is go play a game of ball.

But you'd think wrong.

For some men, there is something about the baseball diamond that is restful, even when play is at its most gripping and stressful. Some argue, indeed, that it is precisely when play is at its most gripping and stressful that the restfulness occurs. Five forty-five saw Phil Walker trotting down the street, pulling on his glove as he ran.

Don Requena, already in his pads, nodded at Phil as he approached the bench. "How's Mr. Evans?" he asked.

Phil shrugged. "Doc says we won't know for sure for a few days, but it looks like the kind of stroke you get better from. I can't re-member what he called it, but he said it was the one where parts of your brain don't really die."

The team gathered around, nodding at the information. "I'll light a candle for him tomorrow," Don said. "He's always been real nice to me and Betty."

Again, the men nodded. Lane Nichols, Johnny Sanchez, Ben Nichols, Pablo Sanchez, Don and Jesus Requena, and Phil Walker. Just then, a boy skidded up on a bike and Daniel Walker came trot-ting in. "You got nobody in center," he said. "Want another glove?"

Phil nodded at Lane. "You're the captain," he said. "What do you say?"

"Can you hit? These boys don't throw easy."

Daniel spat. It landed on his shoe, but it was in the correct spirit of the thing. "Sure, I can hit," he said. "And you got a helmet, don't you?"

Lane smiled. "Hell," he said. "We nearly got a whole team. Let's nail these wusses."

He lost the toss, and as they trotted out to take the field, Jesus called over to Phil, "Hey, Felipe," he said. "You want to try and keep your clothes on? I got a weak stomach."

Phil punched his glove while everyone else tittered.

"*Oye,* batter," Johnny Sanchez called. "Watch it, man. Don't go near third base. My man here likes to get naked."

The Eudora team laughed so hard they had to be cautioned by Father Gaskin to keep the play underway.

Doc Emery was lucky. The helicopter crew that had flown Jim Evans to the city hospital had dropped the doctor off back at the Eudora hospital on their way to another run, a stable spinal frac-ture that wouldn't travel well by road. He was walking wearily to his SUV when he saw Artie Walker crossing the parking lot.

Artie looked upset. "Lottie's in there," he said. "I drove her in.

She says there's something wrong with the baby, but they keep telling her—"

The doctor was gone; he'd found an extra bit of energy and sprinted to the entrance.

It didn't take long for Dr. Emery to find Lottie. She was shouting at the top of her voice.

"No, no, no!" she cried. "I don't give a rat's ass what that stupid monitor says. I need an ultrasound. *Now!* If you have to wake up somebody smart enough to work the scanner, wake them up!"

The X-ray department was not far from the entrance. One of the obstetricians was in it, confronting Lottie. A resident cowered in the corner.

"Look, Mrs. Emery," the obstetrician, Dr. Frank Haley, said calmly, "there is no reason for you to be concerned about the fetus. The monitor clearly shows—"

She looked, Jim thought, like she was about to hit him. He cleared his throat. "What's going on?" he asked, and Lottie threw herself into his arms.

"There's something wrong with the baby," she said. "It's not right. It's not moving the same way." She said this in a scared, piteous tone. But then she turned to the obstetrician and growled, "And if you *dare* try to tell me again about increased size and the perineal drop I'll scream," before turning back to her husband. "They just won't listen to me," she said, again in a shaky, frightened voice. "I want an ultrasound right now. I'm really scared."

"Look," the obstetrican said, in a rather smug tone. "You were the one who convinced me that repeated sonar—"

"Get the machine," Dr. Emery said in a tone that brooked no back-chat.

The obstetrician risked some anyway. "The monitor—" he began, but got no further.

"My wife," the doctor said, "is an experienced health care professional. She has delivered over fifty babies. She also has a highly developed ability to recognize changes in patient pathology. If she thinks there's something wrong, I'd get pretty worried, if I were you." He took a moment and then gulped. He said, "I'm pretty worried right now."

They held each other's eyes for a long moment. Then the obstetrician said to the resident, "Fire up the ultrasound machine."

"I already did," the resident admitted.

Lottie flung herself into the chair and bared her belly, with no care whatsoever for modesty. "It's serious," she said. "I think it's something to do with my fall."

"But we looked so carefully after the accident," the obstetrician said. "I really don't see . . . " His voice trailed off as the baby's profile filled the monitor. He hit a few buttons and scanned a bit further up on the head, zooming in. "My God," he said. "We've got a subdural hematoma." Again he turned to the resident. "Call the helicopter."

"Ah!" Oddly Lottie smiled, leaning back against the chair. Then she turned to her husband. "Don't worry," she said. "Don't worry, Jim. It's going to be okay."

The doctor wavered on his feet, pale. His slim fingers clutched her hand tightly.

The obstetrician was writing notes furiously. "You're going to need a caesarean," he said. "Neurology will probably want to drain the hematoma as soon as possible." He looked at both Lottie and the doctor. "A fetal hematoma usually results in some damage," he said.

"It won't this time," Lottie said firmly. She sounded so relieved that she very nearly sounded exhilarated.

"As long as you're okay," the doctor said. "As long as *you're* okay, Lottie."

"We're both going to be fine," Lottie said. "I knew Frank here would find out what it was, if I could only get him to look."

The resident came running breathless back into the room. "They're turning back," he said. "They said the spinal fracture can travel tomorrow. Surgery isn't due until end of the week, anyway. They said they're going to make you join their frequent flyer program."

The doctor didn't smile at the joke. Not long ago, he had lost his first wife and his unborn child on a helicopter ride to the city hospital. That had been horrible. But losing Lottie or their baby would be beyond horrible. It would be unbearable.

The obstetrician had gone out and run back with a wheelchair. He scribbled furiously on the chart as the resident pushed Lottie. The doctor, dazed, held on to her hand. "Here," he shouted, against the copter's roar, as they went out the big double doors to the pad and he pushed the file into the doctor's hand. And Jim Emery, for the second time in his life, got into a helicopter with a pregnant wife, racing against time.

Pattie Walker had heard her sister's voice echoing up the stairwell in the near-empty hospital. She immediately buzzed the nurse. "What's going on?" she asked.

"Nothing," the nurse lied. "Why don't you try and get some sleep?"

"Why don't you try and tell me the truth?" Pattie said sharply.

The nurse shrugged. "I don't know," she said. "You want me to get the resident on duty?"

Pattie shook her head no, and waited. Lottie would never come to the hospital and not come see her. If all was well, Lottie would be walking through that door any minute.

She waited. And, just for a moment, she did drop into sleep a little. And then she heard the helicopter. Pattie's room was at the back of the building. She disconnected the monitor and leapt out of bed to see Lottie and the doctor climbing in.

"What the hell?" she shouted, and waddled down to the nurses' station. "What the hell's going on with my sister?" she asked. "She's just gone off in the Medi-Lift."

The nurse asked, "Would you like to talk to the resident on duty?"

But Pattie said, "I saw Frank down there. Page his ass."

The nurse tried but then said, "I'm afraid he's going home."

"Do you want me to run out into the parking lot?" Pattie demanded. "Do you want me running up and down the stairs, trying to find out what's happening?" Her face turned an alarming shade of puce.

The nurse said, "Calm down, Mrs. Walker," and, "I'm paging the resident now."

Pattie stormed away as if she couldn't bear to be still. She pounded down the hall to her room and watched the red, flashing dot of light until it disappeared in the eastern sky.

The resident said, "I'm sorry, Dr. Haley has had to go home. I understand you're concerned about your sister?"

Pattie turned from the window and the resident's face slipped from "young man trying to please" into "worried health care professional." "Sit down, Mrs. Walker," he asked, reaching for the blood pressure machine. While he attached the cuff, he asked, "Could you please put your fetal monitor back where it was?"

Something in his voice made Pattie comply instantly. She looked anxiously at the needle that again began to scratch on the paper.

The resident listened intently for a moment and released the pressure in the cuff. He then stood up and looked at the monitor readings.

"Your sister, Mrs. Walker," he said briskly, "has just gone to the city to have a caesarean section. Her baby has had a small injury as a result of her fall, but it's nothing to worry about." This last was a lie, but said with the same brisk certainty as the rest. He was learning well. He then said, "Now I am going to call Dr. Haley and ask him to return so that you can have your own caesarean section. I think it's time we got this little girl out and got you stabilized."

"Is she okay?"

The resident's smile was confident and clinical. "Both your baby and your sister are fine," he said reassuringly. "But I have to go now."

Pattie fumbled in her bedside table for her cell phone and speed-dialed Phil.

Noise blared out of the phone as he answered. "Hey, Pats," he said. "We creamed Mannitaw Springs. Fourteen to two."

"Where are you?" she asked, although she knew.

"The Beer and Bowl," he answered, as if she'd been stupid to ask.

"Well, could you come here, please?" she said, trying not to cry.

"What?"

"Come here. I'm having a caesarean," she shouted.

"Now?" he asked. She could hear people asking what was wrong.

"Now!" she shouted, and then the ridiculousness hit her, and she didn't want to cry anymore. She laughed as she clicked off the phone. "What a doofus," she said to herself, and then, "What a doofus you've got for a daddy," she said to her tummy.

Then there was nothing to do but wait and try to make sense of the little lines that went up and down, up and down, up and down and meant something. And to pray that whatever they meant wasn't something awful.

While Lottie and the doctor were in the Medi-Lift, and Phil Walker was trying to find someone sober to drive him to the hospital where Pattie waited for the obstetrician and the anesthesiologist as well as her loving husband, Maria Lopez and Linda Bustamonte were trying to close Mayan Memories. Gabe had taken the night off to go into the city for a cousin's wedding, and the two ladies were tired at the end of a long week, but Kelly and Hector were locked in a serious conversation and they still had cleaning to do, so Maria and Linda left the couple sitting and talking until it was time to mop the floor.

It had been a strange conversation, but they had monitored it closely. Kelly had done most of the talking. Hector's part seemed to be mainly saying no and then giving a reason. Then Kelly would talk a long time, while Hector looked skeptical. Then he would say no again and give another reason.

Linda said to Maria that Kelly must be some kind of saint or something because she would have conked him over the head during the sopa de limon, let alone last all the way past the Isla de Holbox pumpkin squares to the coffee.

"It's important," Maria said. "I think it's something about where they're going to live. I heard a bit when I brought out the salads."

Linda thought about this as she scrubbed the big black quesadilla pan. "What," she asked, as she drained the dirty water and shook it dry, "does she want him to go to Hollywood? That's what's been bothering me. Hector's a good mayor, and Clement McAllister is too old to come back to work."

"Well, Linda Lane could do the banking," Maria said. "But—"

"Excuse me, but no she couldn't. It's not just about numbers. That woman's got no people skills. And I don't want no lady banker. It's not right."

Maria frowned. "What do you mean . . . ," she began, but then decided to let it go. "Never mind," she said, continuing, "Hector doesn't want her to move here. Not full-time. I think she wants to give up the movies."

"No!" Shocked, Linda went for the mop bucket. "Still, that last one all she did was run from the alien with hardly any clothes on. And the one before that all she did was cry with hardly any clothes on. And hold that baby at the end, like anybody would have a stomach like that after having a baby."

"Well," Maria said, "she's still almost a star. And do you really think she'd be happy doing Hector's cleaning and shopping out at Food Barn?"

There was nothing left to do, and Hector seemed to have agreed to whatever it was, because Kelly suddenly leaned over and threw her arms around his neck, giving him a big kiss. Maria and Linda had to quickly pretend not to be watching.

"Sorry," Hector called from the door. "Didn't realize it was getting so late."

"It's no problem," Maria called back. "We had to clean the kitchen, anyway."

As the door swung shut, Hector put his arm around his beautiful fiancée's shoulders and walked her toward the lovely home he'd made and that they soon would share.

"I wonder what that was all about," Maria said, clearing the table as Linda began to mop.

"We'll find out soon enough," Linda said, quite correctly. But then she said, "And it's nothing to do with us, after all." But here she was, as she later realized, completely and totally wrong.

In the city, the staff at the city hospital ran out with a gurney for Lottie, and though she felt silly, she didn't argue, but got on it and lay down. The team met them by the elevator on the third floor. Lottie sat up as the surgical team talked her and Dr. Emery through the procedures involved.

The team were going to deliver and stabilize the baby and then almost immediately drain the hematoma by inserting a fine needle through the baby's soft skull. The neurosurgeon and the obstetrician felt that the quicker they relieved the pressure on the baby's brain, the more of a chance the brain would have to react to the pressure as it would have to the compression of the head by a vaginal delivery.

Which was why they were going to use a general anesthetic for

the caesarean, the anesthesiologist said, as they pushed Lottie toward the operating rooms. He was going to prep her straight away
and do it immediately. An epidural would, the anesthesiologist explained, take too long.

Very unusually for them, neither the doctor nor Lottie asked
many questions. The doctor would ordinarily have gone extensively
into the curriculum vitae of the attending, but he had already
worked with them both. Indeed, when the obstetrician left to
scrub up, he patted Jim's back and told him not to worry, that Lottie would be fine.

Lottie was being very brave, Jim thought. Nearly too brave. But,
as the nursing team came in and began to invade her body with IVs
and catheters, she reached for his hand through the tubes and people and held it tightly. "You won't leave me," she begged. "I know
you're used to surgery, but for me this is . . . really, really horrible."

"I'm not going anywhere," Jim promised. He could do that
much, he thought. He could stand there and hold her hand. He
could watch the surgery. He could watch both of them. He just
couldn't do a damn thing to help.

Lottie said, "I'm going to do something now that I think will
make the baby stronger. So don't worry, okay? If I don't talk much
from now on? I'm concentrating."

She closed her eyes and began mumbling something under her
breath.

The doctor looked at her fondly. Lottie was the one in an alien
environment, the one with her body being invaded. So why did
Lottie look as if she were in charge of it all?

Forty-five miles away, Pattie Walker's anesthesiologist said, "No,
Mrs. Walker, I'm not going to give you an epidural. Not with that
blood pressure."

"But doesn't it lower blood pressure sometimes?" Pattie argued.
"Wouldn't that be good for me?"

Frank Haley had finally arrived back at the hospital and was his usual irritating self. "You need general," he said. "It's quicker, too." He looked at the monitor. "I really think we need to be quick right now."

"Just do it, Pats," Phil said. He still had his softball shirt on and smelled of beer. A large stain from a seventh-inning slide graced his knees and stomach. "Come on. You've got to do it."

"Oh, all right," Pattie said crossly, taking the clipboard. "But if my sister was here . . . "

"Give me directions," the anesthesiologist said a few minutes later. "Tell me how to get to the hardware store from Food Barn."

"Well, you have to go out the old highway," Pattie said. "You go straight west about five miiiiiiiiiiii . . . " *Whoosh, whoosh, whoosh, whoosh,* she heard as the light and voices faded. It's my heart, was her last thought.

For a while, she drifted in a white sea. And then she heard Lottie's voice. Lottie sounded scared. Why won't she ever let me help her? Pattie wondered bitterly. She's still pissed off from when we were kids. All big sisters hate their little sisters. It was nothing personal. Nothing to hold against me now.

The thoughts pulled her up to a bright place where she hesitated fearfully. There was pain on the other side of the white door. Pattie pushed herself back down.

"I need more," Lottie said. She sounded so sad.

"I have some," Pattie called. "Whatever it is, I'll get it for you."

For a moment, Pattie could nearly see Lottie's face. She could smell her sister's perfume, that amber mixture she cooked up on the stove. "Are you sure?" Lottie asked, and all the suspicion was gone from her voice. She sounded like a little girl again, the small and needy little girl Pattie had despised. Pattie didn't despise her anymore, hadn't ever, really. Not really.

"Are you sure?" Lottie asked again.

"Take it," Pattie said. "Take it, Lottie." Pattie summoned up all the love she had for her sister in her heart and pushed it in Lottie's direction. She felt something pulling, pulling, in her diaphragm. It was too much. Lottie was taking too much.

But Pattie didn't mind.

Phil heard, not a cry, but a kind of a gurgling bleat and then silence. He leaned his head against the wall. He had never prayed so hard in his life. Not the night his mother had died. Not the night Artie had been in that car wreck.

But then the nurse appeared out of the swinging doors with a small bundle. "She's perfect," the nurse said.

Phil hadn't thought about what it would be like to hold his daughter. He had fallen in love immediately with all of his sons, and, through the various challenges of raising Walker boys, had always felt a strong and unshakable bond with each of them. But this was something different. The baby arched her back a little and opened blue eyes.

"Hello," Phil said, giving her his finger to clutch. "Aren't you a little rosy posy?"

That's when he noticed all the people running in and out of the operating room.

"What's wrong?" he asked the nurse. She gave a small, wincing shrug. "Mrs. Walker is bleeding a little more than we'd expect," she said. Another nurse ran past them with bags of blood. "It happens sometimes."

"I can hold Rosy here," he said, "if you need to go and help."

"It's all right," the nurse said. "I need to take her down to the obstetrics."

"Don't take her," Phil begged, watching someone else run out of the operating room. "Don't take her right now."

"I won't," the nurse promised.

For a moment, they waited, watching the door. Rosy turned her head to snuggle it against Phil's shirt. "I'm all dirty," he said.

"It doesn't matter," the nurse said. "They're resilient little things."

Another long moment passed. "What are they doing in there?" he asked.

Again the wincing shrug. "They'll be trying all sorts of things," she said. "They'll be giving her some medication, doing some light massaging of the uterus to simulate post-partum contractions . . ."

"God," Phil said. He looked down at Rosy. The idea of losing Pattie was absolutely unthinkable. But for this little tiny girl to never know her wonderful momma . . . Phil had thought he had been praying hard before. Now he knew better.

"It's extraordinary," the neurosurgeon said. "I've done over forty newborn procedures, but I've never seen such a lively newborn. He's so alert."

"When can I see him?" Jim Emery asked.

"As soon as we get him settled in the high-risk neonatal ward. We'll run a scan on Monday. But, honestly, Dr. Emery, the moment we drained off the fluid, he seemed to revive. The ultrasound was still scanning . . . we hadn't even withdrawn the needle . . . and you could see the brain already expanding. It was almost as if he was impatient for us to be finished so that he could start healing." He shook his head. "Extraordinary."

Jim grinned and shook the neurosurgeon's hand. "I owe you a case of wine," he said. "Thanks for giving up your evening. . . . I'll go let Lottie know."

Lottie looked small and weak in the recovery suite. She had hemorrhaged, just a little, in the operating room and now she looked pale. She would hate waking up, Jim suspected, would hate the hangover of the anesthetic, the discomfort of the catheter. She would hate her incision, since she frequently complained that surgery was barbaric. She would be pushing for the early removal of the IV.

She would be a complete pain to everyone around her.

Jim couldn't wait.

Phil still clutched Rosy to his chest. "What do you mean, you can't?" he asked. "Why can't you?"

"We've tried everything else," the resident said. "We can't risk clotting with any more medication. She's already had three units of blood."

"But a hysterectomy?" Phil said. "Pats has always told me about how horrible they are, how doctors can't wait to take a woman's womb." The nurse reached out for Rosy and Phil gave her up and turned to rest his fists on the wall. "I just can't do it to her," he said. "I can't butcher my wife."

The resident said, "Mr. Walker, we don't know of anything else to do. And while you think about it, your wife is still bleeding."

"Oh God." Phil Walker closed his eyes, burying his hands in his hair. "Do it," he choked. "Just do it."

Lottie Emery opened her eyes and blinked. She tried to talk but her throat hurt.

"He's fine," Jim said. "The surgeon just couldn't believe it. Said he'd never seen a newborn so strong. Said he'd be really surprised if he doesn't make a full recovery."

Lottie looked neither surprised nor relieved. "Pattie?" she croaked.

"What?" Jim asked. "Your sister?"

"Pattie," Lottie insisted. "Go find out about Pattie."

"Honey," the doctor said, "you're confused."

Lottie shook her vibrant head crossly on the pillow. She seemed to be having trouble keeping her eyes open. "I took too much," she said. "But she told me to. And I needed it."

Something about this speech caused Jim to begin fumbling in his pockets for his phone. "Lottie," he said. "What have you done?"

"She loves me," Lottie said. "She really does. And I love her, too."

"I'm going to go outside and call now," Jim said. "I'll tell you right away."

Of course, this series of events did not become general knowledge until Jim's mother came into town for the baptisms of Patrick Emery and Rosamund Walker and ended up sitting late in the Walkers' kitchen with Maria Lopez, after they'd done all the dishes from the party and the new parents had collapsed into beds in their respective houses. And still, some members of the community feel that such talk is nonsense, that human beings simply do not have these kinds of powers.

As evidence, the believers point to the new understanding between the sisters. Previously, they had held each other at arm's length, but Pattie Walker and Lottie Emery seemed to be spending most waking moments of their maternity leave together. Every time you saw them they were chattering away, pushing their baby buggies down the sidewalk. Lottie, who had never been that touchy-feely, now frequently stroked her sister's arm or clutched her in a hug.

But the nonbelievers also use this as evidence. How could one sister who had been used so blatantly by the other sister indulge in such intimacy?

This chronicle, which heard all this straight from Linda Bustamonte, is inclined to believe that strange things happened around Lottie Emery, and to leave it at that. There are some parts of the human experience into which it is best not to pry.

...

The wedding of Mark Ramirez and Janey Lane happened on a Saturday morning. The bride wore a simple white suit, hastily altered to fit Janey's growing figure, embellished with a flower pattern of crystal beads over one breast by Carla Bustamonte. Her hair was up in a French twist with a comb ornament of feathers forming a small hat. Dr. Emery gave the bride away and her sisters, in lovely floral dresses, were her bridesmaids. Mark's cousin Vince drove in from the city to be his best man and Johnny Sanchez was his groomsman. Becky Lane sat in front with a large box of tissues.

Father Gaskin presided, even though they had not managed to complete their prenuptial course of instruction. It was not, of course, a Mass, because Janey was not Catholic. But considering how moved she appeared during the service, many were hopeful that she would consider conversion.

For such a simple affair, it was remarkable how many people turned up and how many people afterward came to the bring-a-plate lunch reception with huge bowls of food (and if there was a preponderance of tomatoes and zucchinis in the ingredients, no one minded, it was just that time of year).

It was not the elegant occasion that Mark had wanted, but it was a wonderful time, a party that flowed naturally, with children from all over the community running around the edges. Kylie Requena had brought an absolutely stunning cake with small green linked *M*'s and *J*'s all over it, functioning as leaves for the deep golden roses that matched Janey's bouquet. When it was cut, it was discovered to be marbled white and chocolate inside.

It tasted very sweet.

When the doctor got back to the city hospital that afternoon, he dropped in on Jim Evans. The old farmer had, with typical resilience, already recovered much of his powers of speech and was making great strides with his physical therapist, indefatigably working on his exercises. Even while the doctor talked to him, Jim Evans incessantly clutched at and released a rubber ball with his left hand.

Mr. Evans seemed oddly happy, the doctor thought. Out in the hall, Mary confided why. She said, "I been wanting to move to town for thirty years. When Jim told me we had to sell the place, he thought I'd be disappointed in him, but I just looked him in the eye and said, 'Good.'" Here she chuckled. "Course at first he thought I was lying, but when he saw I was telling the truth a weight just lifted from his shoulders."

Mary's bright eyes snapped with new energy and purpose. She said, "I went through all the paper and I've been to see Clement down at the bank. There's just no way on earth Jim could have carried on. It's not his fault with the way prices are and that weather we had last year. Lots of good farmers are going broke. We're auctioning off the machinery next weekend and the farm's for sale, too." Here she frowned. "I wish the Barfords could buy it, but it might go to a corporation."

The doctor had been in town long enough to know to say, "I'm sorry about that, Mary. But you can't always fight these things."

She nodded sadly at the floor like a little bird pecking at the ground. Then she tilted her head up to look at him again. "Clement and me are trying to do it all before Jim gets out of the rehab unit. The Williamses are ready to move and their place don't need much doing to it. It'll be a nice, easy walk for Jim to get around town and it's close to church for me. That Ramirez boy and Janey Lane are moving in next door, so that'll be fine." (Mary Evans and Chuck Warren had never seen eye to eye.)

The doctor said, "It's a good idea to send him to the rehab unit while you're moving, if you don't mind doing all the work. I think the stress of having to move is what led to . . ."

Mary said, "I don't mind. He's been taking care of me for fifty years. I guess it's more than my turn." She took some time to think again, looking at the floor and nodding. The doctor, who wanted to go and see his wife and child, had trained himself into a patience he did not truly possess. He had learned that healing in this community consisted as much of moments like this as it did of the physical assistance he had learned in med school.

The moment seemed to stretch a long time. The brightly lit hospital corridor, the man in a crumpled suit with icing on his tie, his eyes weary but kind, stoops slightly over a smaller, rounder figure. The small figure stares at the floor. The man shifts his weight from one foot to another. People pass, carrying boxes, pushing other people, carrying flowers, but still the man waits.

At last, Mary peered back into the doctor's face. She asked, "How is young Mr. Flory doing?"

"Jim?" the doctor asked. "He's okay."

"Is he still having the trouble? With the windows and all?" Mary screwed up her lips. "I never held with that kind of thing," she said.

The doctor scratched his head. "No," he said. "I talked to him a couple of days ago, when he called to congratulate us. He said since the Grand Opening, the vandalism has pretty much died off."

"I'm glad about that," Mary said, straightening her little back. "I'm real glad about that. You tell him we said hey."

"I will," the doctor said. "He asked about you and Jim as well."

"He's a good boy," Mary said, her eyes blinking brightly. "He's a good boy, really."

And so the summer came to an end. There was the usual panic over school supplies and the tearful partings from offspring beginning a course of higher education. Eudora then cleaned its houses with a vengeance, going ruthlessly through the rooms and rationalizing every object, throwing away broken toys, stubby candles, holey sweaters, and books it never wanted to read again. Thirty-four copies of *The Vortex* went into the book recycling program the first week.

Also during this week, the county siren inspectors arrived with five components and a great deal of copper wiring. Hector Rodriguez interrupted his duties at the bank to provide them with his views on their previous work. There was extensive testing that week. It seemed like every time you opened your mouth to say something important the accelerating drone of the sirens would drown it out. But nobody complained.

Everyone had forgotten that Kelly Brookes's father was a big man in clothing manufacturing in the city. But he and her mother came for a visit the day of Mark and Janey's wedding. That night, Hector Rodriguez and the Brookeses talked long into the night with Carla Bustamonte, at first at Mayan Memories and then upstairs in Carla's apartment, where passersby (and the restaurant staff) could clearly see Carla at her desk by the window, getting bits of paper and files and then carrying them back to the rest of the group.

The second week after Pattie was home from the hospital, her lawyer's long dark car once again appeared in front of the fabric shop, and Pattie was closeted a long time with Carla, Kelly, and the lawyer. When he left, the sign got turned around to BACK IN FIVE MINUTES and the women disappeared from view. However, Rena Requena, who still liked to walk down the alleys when she did her downtown shopping, saw them sitting by the back door, looking out at the Japanese knotweed while they passed around a bottle of champagne and giggled.

The Walkers kept Priss Lane. Ben and May went to Candy Cane Day Care, which was also going to accept Trick Emery and Rosy Walker in a few months' time, but Priss was taking care of the older boys after school and picking up the little ones. There was a bit of worry when the art classes at the junior college at the county seat looked like they would clash with her work the following year, but this had been resolved.

The Walker families had discovered that Priss had actually been accepted to, but couldn't afford, the prestigious arts conservatory in the city, where the studio time and instruction was more flexible. They paid the difference in the registration, pledged the fees, and got Priss a more reliable car so that she could drive back and forth. Her sister, Janey Ramirez, had always found the city commute too tiring, but no one expected Priss to feel the same.

The Walker boys did not continue their model citizenship after their parents' reconciliation (by the second week of school they were in detention for resetting the bells to ring every ten minutes) but Priss's influence was still felt to be beneficial.

Chuck Warren left town about the time the crate of *The Vortex* was hauled to the recycling center. He took his truck and one U-Haul trailer. Chuck's Beer and Bowl closed, and for a week there were concerns that it would not reopen. But then a crew of men had come, taken down the sign and then come back the following day and rehung it without the word *Chuck's* in its neon curves. It now read, THE BEER AND BOWL. The entire town breathed a sigh of relief. Not only were the citizens pleased to know the establishment would remain a bowling alley (there was some loose talk about a shoe warehouse) but they also realized that they had grown fond of the winking, looping glow of the sign itself.

Stacey Harper also left town, taking Damien and Frieda with her and very little else. What with Stacey's job there in the gallery, it wasn't much of a change for anyone but the old Harper aunties and Park Davis.

Park suffered as many men do. He grew morose and inflexible. His grooming slipped in small but noticeable ways. But he did not turn to drink and the pharmacy continued to be as clean and welcoming as ever. It was, however, noticed that when Park welcomed you with his customary smile, it now never reached his eyes.

■ ■ ■

Specialist Bruce Requena had been successfully involved in a volunteer initiative with the local populations around his base of operations in Tigrit. While on a routine supply run, Requena halted to give aid to a stranded motorist, who Requena appeared to recognize. The "motorist" was actually a suicide bomber, who then deployed his explosive. In the last moments of his life Specialist Requena drove his vehicle out of range of subsequent sniper fire, saving the lives of his companions and ensuring the safe escape of the remainder of the convoy. He was posthumously awarded the Bronze Star with the Valor device for this action.

Specialist Requena's remains were flown to his hometown of Eudora, where he was buried with military honors. Eudora public schools and businesses were closed for the event, and the entire town attended the ceremony.

A few weeks later, on a Tuesday afternoon, Kylie Requena served Odie Marsh and Ben Nichols, then returned behind the bakery counter. The new young barber, who lived in the county seat but drove in five days a week from another establishment to see to the tonsorial needs of Eudora and the surrounding area, had finally gotten up the nerve to ask Kylie Requena out on a date. Odie settled his new glasses more firmly on his nose and crossed his arms, frankly enjoying the display, while Ben Nichols more circumspectly chuckled behind his paper.

The barber, who, it had been noted, did not sweep his floor as often as he should and spent a great deal of time sitting on his butt reading the magazines when he could have been cleaning the windows and mirrors, was getting nowhere with Kylie Requena.

"What about Saturday night?" he asked.

"I'm sorry," Kylie said. She had grown, it must be said, even more beautiful since her recent loss. She smiled at the barber briefly as she bagged up sliced white loaves for the diner. "I'm busy."

"What, another party?" he asked.

Kylie nodded, shaking in another loaf and twisting the bag shut. "Uh-huh," she said, "my cousin's birthday."

The boy pushed back his bleached blond locks. "Don't you want to get out of here?" he asked. "Do something else? I mean, nothing ever happens in Eudora."

Kylie's eyes snapped. "That's just not true," she said. "Lots of things happen here."

"Like what?"

Ben stopped pretending he wasn't listening and put down his newspaper.

"Well, just a little while ago we had that protest at the Grand Opening for the maize maze," Kylie said. "That made the front page of your paper."

"Yeah, and then we never heard about it again," said the cosmopolite from the county seat, with a sneer.

"We've had two people leave town and somebody got married."

The boy rolled his eyes as Kylie continued, "And an old farmer had a stroke and . . . for a while it looked like the softball team was going to break up . . . and a white guy came to work at the quarry, but he didn't last . . . and . . . these sisters were having babies and . . . " She trailed off, uncomfortably aware of the young barber's unspoken derision.

"I could pick you up late," he said. "You could go to your cousin's party and then just leave a little early. The band won't start until almost ten."

But Kylie was staring off into space somewhere over his left ear. "I'll think about it," she said absently, and the young barber, growing tired of being the object of Ben and Odie's amusement, expressed barely concealed impatience and went back to his duties at the barbershop.

For a moment, Kylie continued to lean on the counter and

think. And then she snapped out of it and came around to collect Ben's and Odie's plates and to offer coffee refills.

"I guess he's right," she said, looking out the window at the Harper aunties taking a foil-wrapped tray of some foodstuff into the pharmacy. "I guess nothing ever does happen in Eudora."

Ben stood up and brushed crumbs from his lap. "That's just the way we like it," he said.

But Odie said, "I don't know about that. We've got Hector and Kelly's wedding coming up. And then the Maple Leaf Festival. It's gonna be a zoo around here." He added, "I wouldn't go out with that boy if I was you, Kylie. Jim Evans said he did a good job but that he didn't have any follow through. A pretty girl like you don't want to bother with a man with no follow through."

Ben frowned. "I know the wedding is gonna be kind of a big deal," he said. "But it's just a wedding, after all. There's nothing all that unusual about it." He opened the door for Odie.

As Odie went out he said, "Nothing all that unusual? Then why are we having four planning meetings to coordinate law enforcement for the big day? Did you have that when you married Molly?"

"No," said Ben, his voice loaded with sarcasm. "But it's still just a wedding."

The door cut off Odie's exasperated reply. As the car pulled out, Kylie could see the disagreement had become heated. She smiled, wiped the table, turned the sign around to CLOSED, and then clicked her white wooden clogs back around the counter.

Evening settles slowly on the prairie. The huge dome of light above fades gently as the sun rests on, then slips below the visible horizon. Two figures, walking from the state park down the side of the old highway, stop and the larger figure takes a sweater from the smaller figure's waist and helps her pull it over her head. They continue walking hand in hand.

A light blue metallic Audi drives past them, nosing into the parking lot of the Beer and Bowl. A man gets out and fumbles with keys, finally finding the one that opens the front door. He turns on the lights inside and the sign outside and walks around a little bit, looking at this and that. And then he shuts it all down again and re-locks the door.

The Audi drives down Main Street and pulls into the long drive-way of the Flory house.

Dusk is leaving the sky navy blue. As the man pulls his suitcase out of the back, another man runs out of the house toward him. But it is too dark to see what happens when they meet.

The streetlights come on, and the Audi's shiny roof forms a ref-erence point as we zoom back toward the farming insurance satel-lite once again. Out on the prairie, small shapes bound and coyotes prowl after them. Already, foxes trot down side roads and on the outskirts of town, deer come to browse on what they can reach of garden produce. By this time of year, the exhausted gardeners are pretty much glad to let them.

As we pull back, one more farmhouse lies empty and dark. The Barfords' place seems to shine ever more bravely in its isolation, as the North Star will on a cloudy night. Eudora is the Pleiades, a misty cluster of pinprick beams. But in the center of this constella-tion, a single yellow traffic light beams and blinks, beams and blinks, urging caution at all times.

Acknowledgments

A book always looks like it's been written by one person, but really it's a team effort. I have had a wonderful team on this book. I need to thank Anika Streitfeld, my talented editor, who has supported me all the way through the writing and given me invaluable help with the next-to-last draft. I also need to acknowledge my sources: Rick Schneider and Jim "Daddy Cool" Schwada, who helped with botany and the stories in *The Vortex;* Helen Harrell, who gave me the inside skinny on the life of a wheat farmer; my wonderful cousins and cousins by marriage (Barbara and Bryan, Margie and Pat, Christine and Ed, Teresa and Walt, Dan and Jan, Shon and Jackie, Connie, Kim, Heather and Mike, etc., etc., etc.), who keep me in touch with home; the Kaw Valley Hemp Pickers; Mona Tipton and Kelly Howell, for being my best friends every ten years or so; Carol, Jane, and all the rest of the old *Sangha,* who taught me so much about community; and the two communities I live in now, the parish of St.

Dunstans in Keynsham, and The School of English and Creative Studies at Bath Spa University. I also need to thank early readers and listeners: Andy Wadsworth, Richard Kerridge, Carrie Etter. And then, as usual, I need to thank my friends and family, for letting me totally ignore them when I'm in the throes of composition. Your generosity is very valued. Last of all, but not least of all, I want to thank Mom, Katy Beard, for giving me the love of books and the even greater love of her own warm heart.

THE CORNER BOOTH CHRONICLES

Mimi Thebo

A READER'S GUIDE

A Conversation with Mimi Thebo

Richard Kerridge is an eminent ecocritic who is very interested in the relationship between literature and place. Richard taught Mimi Thebo for seven years, first as an MA lecturer and then as her PhD supervisor. Today they are colleagues at Bath Spa University. Although they have the highest respect for each other, they frequently disagree.

Bath Spa's Newton Park campus is an old manor farm owned by the Duchy of Cornwall. Richard and Mimi's offices overlook a paddock used for pasturing beef cattle and a small fourteenth-century castle. It's here they have some of their best arguments.

Richard Kerridge: Eudora is presented as a rural town of a certain size. Your writing includes details of many different kinds of work and play, typical of such a town. How did you research this?

Mimi Thebo: When I was finishing my BA in the early eighties, gas was cheap and global warming was something I could shove to the back of my mind. One of my favorite pastimes was driving to small rural communities, often with friends. We'd go to diners and honky-tonks and just talk to people before driving home again. For years, my husband and I worked as waiters in national parks, and we would travel across America sometimes four times a year. We always took the state highways because of our interests in out-of-the-way places and other people's lives. I like talking to people, and that's how I started to understand the concerns of small rural communities.

Later, some of my cousins and friends lived in small rural communities, and keeping in touch with them also kept me in touch with the kinds of issues people there faced. It has just been harder and harder for some of them to survive. I know of a wheat farmer whose farm used to provide all the income his mother and father and siblings needed. Now that he's inherited the farm, it's just his hobby. Both he and my cousin Christine have to work in town to pay the bills. When they get a good crop, that's a bonus. Ed never really stops working, and yet he won't let that land go without a fight. The wheat crop is still planted right up to the edge of the back garden, and even though he leases some of his land, he still thinks of himself as a farmer first. I knew I'd got Eudora more or less right when Christine and her neighbors said it was just like their hometown.

RK: Some writers immerse themselves in a locality for a long period, reading local newspapers and talking to people. Annie Proulx, I believe, begins to put together a portrait of a place through collecting local stories, local characters, and mythology, folklore and kinds of knowledge and vocabulary to do with the types of work that are most important in that place. In this novel, you've written about an imaginary place, in some ways a very generalized place. Nevertheless, you have managed to conjure the illusion of this density of local culture.

MT: I've stolen some of my favorite things from many small towns and rather rolled them together. The people are all amalgamations of very real people, and I've only put them into my imaginary town.

In another country, this might be difficult, but Americans tend to move around quite a bit, and I think this makes for a degree of homogeny, especially regionally. And perhaps we haven't had time to establish the kind of unavoidable particularity of, say, an English village. After all, even the "long-time" residents are third- or fourth-generation descendants of immigrants. And when I say "long-time" . . . the town would probably have been founded in the 1860s.

We're discussing this question here at Newton Park. It's been cultivated for thousands of years. It was in the control of one family for nearly six hundred years. The culture of the village here has had a thousand more years than Eudora to achieve a clear and particular character.

And still, there are some local characteristics in my imaginary town. The citizens are, nearly without exception, formidably nosy. And they are also passionate and competitive gardeners.

At first Eudora seemed fuzzy to me. Now I know street names and could probably draw a quite credible map. I also have a clear idea of it geographically. I know it's on limestone, that there are two rivers, that there is a state park boundary just northeast of town. I know that there are a few hills around the river bluffs but that the area is largely flat prairie. I know a great deal about the animal and plant species that live in the more woody park/ravine environments and on the higher prairie. But these elements can be found in pretty near the whole of the Midwest.

Basically, if buffalo used to roam there, you're in Eudora.

RK: In order to achieve a typical Midwestern location, did you make a decision not to provide any specific regional identity?

MT: Yes, although some reviewers say that Eudora is in Kansas, I never do. Readers from Illinois, Ohio, Nebraska, and even Eastern Washington have all decided that Eudora is their hometown. I think they're right.

This goes back to the famous *New Yorker* magazine map of the United States. There were details for the west coast and the east coast and in the middle, one tiny little dot labeled Chicago. It made me feel very cross when I saw it as a child, and I still think it's indicative of a certain attitude. . . . Those non-people from nowhere grow much of the world's food and though they may not be numerous, or even particularly vocal, that doesn't mean they aren't very important.

RK: The narrative voice is a sort of collective Eudora voice, with the intonations of local gossip. Was this difficult to write?

MT: Yes. It's tricky in terms of crafting the voice. It's easy to slip out of consistency when handling the traveling point of view. It's also tricky in terms of feeling able, ethically, to travel everywhere, to everybody. Some of the people in the narrative are so far removed from my own background; I start feeling a bit panicky about using their voices and seeing through their eyes. And yet, if I don't, I'm making them outsiders in the narrative and the town. In *The Corner Booth Chronicles* I'm greatly in debt to my old school friend Michele, who helped me with my Spanish idioms.

RK: Also implicit in this voice is an ability to see everyone's point of view, and speak for everyone. Are there any limit cases, people you can't or won't speak for?

MT: There's a section of Eudora where the poor white people live. I rather imply that there's plenty of work and that these people just don't have the get-up-and-go necessary to thrive. The first time I wrote about Eudora I did write a character from this part of town, but in *The Corner Booth Chronicles,* they are a rather shadowy minority. I have story lines in my head that would allow me to write from this point of view, but those stories haven't seemed important enough . . . yet!

So, I suppose, yes. The "undeserving poor" of Eudora haven't yet got a voice. I need to pull up a lawn chair with sagging webbing, grab a lukewarm Buckhorn beer, and have a chat with them soon.

RK: In *Welcome to Eudora,* you write about the emergence from invisibility, as you put it, of the Mexican American community. You do this by making them gradually more obvious in the narrative, until a tipping point in consciousness has occurred. Do you think that the reason you haven't done this for certain elements of the population of Eudora is that you need a part of the community that remains in the shadows and never becomes visible? You need people whose point of view you cannot adopt with optimism, such as Jim Flory's assailants or the people who throw rocks at his windows. In a way, they are doing the novel's dirty work for you.

MT: I suppose that might be true. I think part of what defines a community is the boundaries. Some of these are physical, but some are social. A community is partly described by those who are excluded from it.

It's not just the rednecks who are excluded. The senior hospital staff is also excluded from the community because they live out by the golf course and don't mix. In a way, both parts of the town have opted out of community life.

But that's not really what you're talking about. The narrative voice is judgmental and discriminatory. It continually condemns or praises someone, usually as a result of town consensus. If the plots require bad guys, the voice also needs to fail to understand everyone, to judge some people as unacceptable.

RK: I would call that quality of the narrative voice a social know-ingness. In some cases, it becomes bitterly ironical. I am thinking especially of the passage narrating the violent assault on Jim Flory. Your narrator discusses the techniques of violent assault on gay people in almost the same tone used elsewhere for cooking or soft-ball or dressmaking. Why did you use that tone?

MT: A few years ago, I was shocked when an important member of my hometown literary community was beaten up because of his homosexuality. When he talked to me about the incident, he kept saying that "they knew what they were doing." It also came from a memory of the late seventies in my hometown. One night my friends and I saw a bunch of fraternity boys jump out of a pickup truck and beat up a punk on a moped. By the time we could run across the street, they'd hurt him quite badly.

The assailants were wearing cowboy boots. Later, when I dated a frat boy, I learned that he and his brothers always called such boots (which I also often wear) "shit kickers." Useful when kicking the shit out of someone, I assumed. It struck me then that for some people beating others up is a pastime.

I gave this thought to Jim Flory during the attack. I've been the victim of violence myself and have attempted to think myself else-where while being hurt, so I thought Jim might dispassionately consider these issues while he's being beaten. I hate hurting my characters.

RK: We hear a lot about how the U.S. is a divided society, driven by "culture wars," split into "red states" and "blue states." Perhaps the recent election shows how this is changing, making your novel particularly timely. Eudora, I would guess, is in a red state. The two Eudora novels offer many examples of reconciliation. There is comedy of manners arising from the clash of cultures, but agree-ment and alliances, sometimes surprising ones, nearly always follow. Does this mean that you are fundamentally optimistic about those culture wars?

MT: My hometown is Lawrence, in Douglas County, Kansas. Douglas County is a tiny blue dot in a big sea of red, always by a tiny margin. Both sides are vocal, passionate, and convinced that they are in the right. You'd think visiting the area would be a tense experience, with frequent confrontations. But it's not like that. We get hot under the collar about politics, but we all wait in line to eat breakfast at Milton's or First Watch. We all go to the County Fair and we all go to Art in the Park. And on the last day of the year that the municipal pool is open, we all take our dogs swimming.

The good thing about being in the middle of nowhere is that we tend to know what's important. And what's really important is keeping these things going. Who is mayor is important, but not as important as keeping authentic Mexican food downtown. When rents started getting too high for local businesses and it looked like all the big chains were moving in, a cross-party task force worked together to sort the problem out.

I think the problem with America goes back, again, to the attitudes so humorously expressed in that *New Yorker* map. Because we have large spaces and isolated populations, we can start thinking that "our" kind of people are "real" and "other" kinds of people aren't real. That lets us think that our issues are important and theirs aren't, our health care is an issue but theirs isn't, etc.

I think that global warming and the financial crisis may be the "threatened authentic Mexican restaurant" issues on a nationwide basis. They may help us figure out what is really important to us all.

So yes, I am optimistic. The people of America are largely reasonable, sincere human beings, with a great capacity for community service. If our government can help to harness this, there's nothing we can't do.

RK: Your plots often move by building up tension very powerfully until there is a carnivalesque moment of release, such as the demonstration held by Jim Evans, Phil Walker, and Chuck Warren at the Grand Opening. This takes place at an actual carnival, a public event, as do many of your most dramatic scenes. You move between domestic spaces, and shared, intermediate spaces, such as the diner, to these grand public occasions.

MT: Yes, I'm interested in the community and how private concerns become public concerns. I suppose these large set pieces are chances for that to play out.

RK: That's what makes this narrative innovative. There's a great American tradition of modernist novels that depart from the deep immersion in individual experience that characterizes the realist tradition, and seek instead to represent communal viewpoints. John Dos Passos, for example, did this by using collage and cut-up, with excerpts from news reports interspersed with short snatches of viewpoint from socially diverse characters. These modernist techniques emphasize discontinuity, fissure, and atomization. Your communal viewpoint is very different: a continuous tide, a confluence of diverse viewpoints, in an organic community that experiences wounds and divisions but consistently proves capable of healing itself. Individuals may be temporarily alienated, but not irretrievably.

MT: Some are. Some leave: Stacey Harper leaves and so do Spector and LaDonna Williams.

RK: Yes, but the narrative doesn't follow them, any more than it follows the rednecks who steal the wires from the tornado sirens. The narrative stays with the majority of the community.

MT: I suppose that's what I'm interested in. I'm not interested in the alienated individual. I feel like I've read enough about that . . . I know what that's all about! I like the idea of a community that is a living organism, capable of healing itself.

RK: You use what is almost a Dickensian plotting technique. New jobs, new benefactors, and new alliances are always popping up in the nick of time. It's as if your job is to provide your characters with timely opportunities to discover their better selves and do the right thing. Isn't there a danger that you make solutions seem too easy? If those opportunities fail to appear on cue, what then?

MT: Then Eudora becomes like the other dead towns surrounding it. There's only one way for it to survive and so many ways for it to die. I do mention how many ghost towns surround Eudora, but perhaps for the reader they don't stay in the mind. For me, they are always looming.

Do you remember when I spoke of the many small towns I used to drive to to visit as an undergraduate? Nearly a quarter of them are now dead towns. I think for me, and for anyone who knows towns like Eudora, they are present in the shadows.

RK: But perhaps for people who don't know these towns, the shadows aren't present. And without something like the ghost towns, it can all seem a bit too easy.

MT: Well, it *is* easy. All it takes to maintain a successfully organic community is constant vigilance and total commitment. I suppose I want *The Corner Booth Chronicles* to make that sound easy.

RK: Even at the risk of making it all a bit too cozy?

MT: There's nothing wrong with cozy. In this world, we can all use a bit of cozy. We've fallen into this terrible assumption that intelligent writing should be painful and upsetting. I don't believe that any more than I believe students will learn better if they're sitting on beds of nails. Monet asked us to question perception but painted very pretty flowers for us to do it with. I'm all for being comfortable when we can.

Questions and Topics for Discussion

1. How would you describe Eudora? Do you have any experience with a town similar to it?

2. Mimi Thebo says, "Although some reviewers say that Eudora is in Kansas, I never do. Readers from Illinois, Ohio, Nebraska, and even Eastern Washington have all decided that Eudora is their hometown. I think they're right." Why do you think she is vague about Eudora's exact location?

3. Who is your favorite character, and why?

4. Which character surprised you the most?

5. The seasons and what they bring are central to the town's traditions, from harvesting to the Maple Leaf Festival and the competitive gardening that so many of the townspeople engage in. Why do you think this is?

6. If you've read *Welcome to Eudora,* how would you describe the changes that the town has undergone?

7. In what ways do the characters in Eudora subscribe to traditional gender roles? In what ways do they challenge these roles?

8. Do you think Lottie and Pattie have a typical sisterly relationship? How does it change over the course of the novel?

9. The businesses downtown (the restaurants and bakery, the stationery shop and the fabric shop) are often stages for the scenes in the novel, and the entire town is often interested in the events in those scenes. Does this happen in real life?

10. The novel has a nostalgic, even cozy, feel. What do you think are the drawbacks to such warmth in the narrative? What do you like about this tone?

11. Kylie Requena is an extraordinarily beautiful young woman. Do you think that affects how the other characters feel about her? Does it affect the way you feel about the character as a reader?

12. Kelly Brookes comes home to Eudora from her glamorous Hollywood lifestyle. What do you think are the pluses and minuses of living in a town like Eudora? Would you choose it over Hollywood?

13. The Mexican American community seems to have integrated well into Eudora at the beginning of the book, but then racial tensions erupt again. Do you think these tensions are resolved at the end of the novel?

14. Eudora has quite a few churches and only one bar—the Beer and Bowl. How does religion affect the events in *The Corner Booth Chronicles*?

15. Comedies traditionally end with a marriage. What new beginnings come at the end of *The Corner Booth Chronicles*?